WHERE THE BODIES LIE

DI ROB MARSHALL
BOOK TWO

ED JAMES

GREY DOG BOOKS

PART ONE
OUT OF THE SHADOWS

CHAPTER ONE
THE SHADOW MAN

Ten Years Ago

Getting dark. Cold, too. The day's been bitter, but mercifully still. On any other evening, the bright sun and cool air would've made him rejoice in being alive. The smell of the freshly cut grass on the banks of the path. The distant lapping of the lake, slower and heavier than usual.

Now, though, his focus was on what he couldn't see. What he couldn't hear.

He'd fucked this right up.

Got overconfident. Arrogant.

Useless prick. Useless.

No.

Distant footsteps. Regular and fast. Left, right, left, right. A runner.

The hazy darting of a head torch, scanning the path through the woods.

Was it *him*, though?

He crouched low and grabbed the cord in his hands, twisting it around as he waited.

Watching.

Listening.

Smelling.

'Come on, you can do it.' Gasps, deep and strained. 'Not long now.'

Half a mile until the car park – this was the home straight of a twenty-mile run. To some that would be impossible to conceive of; to others it'd be a trivial warm-up.

He waited.

Waited.

Waited.

Nobody else around, just one car in the car park, his own two miles down the road, hidden behind some trees. Nobody would know he was here.

The runner was speeding up now, using those final few calories stored away to power through the last gasp of the run.

And the head torch's glow was enough to show the face.

It *was* him.

Definitely.

Now!

He pulled the end of the cord and hauled the line up to neck height. Snapping tight, then shaking, then tight again.

Invisible in the darkness.

'Come on, you've—' The runner caught the thick cord in the throat and flipped over, landing on his back. His head cracked against the hardcore path.

He let go of his end of the cord and picked up the heavy rock, then walked over. Calm, cool, analysing.

The runner was lying on his back, moaning. Struggling for breath. The torch now lay over to the side, shining at him, lighting up his face. His throat looked like something out of a butcher's window.

He hefted the rock up above his head and crashed it down onto the runner's skull.

Blood smeared the side of it. He chucked it away and it rolled off into the woods.

The runner just lay there. Eyes wide open. Dead.

Sometimes it was like that – too easy.

He reached into his pocket for his pouch and unzipped it. The compartments flapped open and he grabbed a roll of duct tape. Took a few seconds to find the end, but he soon gagged the runner. Might have snuffed it, but he didn't want the dead man telling any tales.

One cable tie secured his wrists behind his back, nice and tight. The other snapped around his ankles. A nasty looking gouge on his left. Maybe that explained why the runner was so slow, why he'd arrived here a lot later than scheduled – let doubt creep in, that the plan was a mistake.

He put the bag back then grabbed the runner's shoes and dragged him off the path and up the embankment's thick clods of grass, then through the gap in the dying nettles towards the trees.

He didn't know how long he was dragging him, because all he could think about was what was in his pocket. What he was going to do.

He almost missed it, but the tang of freshly dug earth hit his nostrils and snapped him to the present.

The shallow grave was deep enough to fit a human being.

He pushed the corpse in and stood back, admiring his work. Even let out a sigh.

It felt good.

The body moved.

What the fuck?

'Mmf! Mmmmf! Mmf! Mmmmmmmmmf!'

Still alive.

Well, that wasn't such a disappointing outcome.

He stepped into the freshly dug grave and flipped the runner over.

Wild eyes stared up at him. Blood from his head wound trickled down his face to the mess that used to be a throat. 'MMMMMMF!'

He reached into his pocket and pulled out a knife, the blade catching in the last light of the day. He grabbed the hilt with the tip pointing downwards – somehow he was much stronger that way.

He lifted his arm and smashed the knife down, stabbing the runner in the chest.

The eyes went even wider.

He stabbed again. And again and again and again.

For the second time in a few minutes, he lost track of what he was doing.

Until he stopped. Panting, unable to get his breath back under control.

He couldn't look at the ground anymore. Couldn't look into the grave. He stepped out of it and grabbed the shovel, then started tipping the mud in. Covered the body in seconds.

He reached into his pocket for the stake and wedged it into the soil. When they eventually find it, they'll know who did this.

WE LIVE IN THE SHADOWS

CHAPTER TWO
MARSHALL

Monday
Two days later

R ob Marshall sat in the passenger seat of a car the driver considered classic, but to anyone else was just a rust bucket. No power steering, so every turn meant freewheeling arms elbowing Marshall. No satnav either, so Marshall had a five-year-old map book open on his lap.

Professor Jacob Goldberg steered them around another bend, his bony elbow digging into Marshall's arm again. 'You *will* clean up once you get out, won't you?'

'Of course. My car should pass its MOT today, so I can only apologise for—'

'You're from near here, aren't you?'

The convenience of the map light pointing right at the book meant Marshall didn't have to look at Goldberg taking his eyes from the road for way too long so he could peer at Marshall; it was just a blur of movement in his peripheral vision.

The map showed the big blue expanse marked Kielder Water. Rural Northumbria – up the hill was Carter Bar, marking the Scottish border. Down here it was all evergreen trees around the misty lake – not a loch – and pissing rain.

'That's correct, sir. Melrose.'

'A lovely wee town.' The words jarred against Goldberg's Home Counties accent as much as when he used words from the north-east – barry, bonny, canny. 'You don't talk about it much.'

'A few good reasons for that.'

'You go home much?'

'Not really, no. Not in the last ten years.'

'Ten years?' Goldberg was scowling at him. 'That concerns me, Robert. I need my protégé to have a clear head, not to be clouded by self-doubt and personal tragedies.'

'Next left, sir.'

'Okay, okay.'

At least this time the outbound elbow was flailing on the other side.

The square car park was almost full, lots of dark saloons sitting in the rain. A scenes of crime van still had its engine on, pluming in the late morning gloom.

Goldberg gave him another couple of inadvertent elbow jabs as he steered his jalopy between two half logs. 'There we are.' The engine died in a way that sounded like it would take necromancy to bring it back to life.

Marshall opened his door and got out.

'Robert!' Goldberg was holding out his drum of wet wipes. 'Tidy up, please!'

Marshall swallowed his sigh and tore out a tissue, then rubbed it all over the cracked leather of the seat. And the battered glove box. And the map book. 'That do you?'

'There's a reason I don't like anyone else in here, Robert, so please stop being facetious.' Goldberg might be a germophobic neat freak, but he could walk very quickly.

Marshall slammed the door and had to jog after him to catch up.

Goldberg was already signing them in. 'You know, being the UK's leading criminal profiler should mean I can delegate matters at times. I'd appreciate it if your boss, DI Bruce, would bear that in mind. Mm?'

The bored uniformed officer snorted and shivered, his neck a mess of spots and shave burns. Barely eighteen, but he'd been entrusted with guarding the crime scene's outer locus. Kid was going somewhere. 'I'll pass that on to him, sir.'

'See that you do.' Goldberg stabbed the pen onto the page, then handed it all back. 'Come on, Robert.' He squelched along the forestry road, bare hardcore tipped out years ago when the trees were planted, only to be used by walkers, runners, cyclists and horse riders until the inevitable forestry operation would turn the mature trees into timber. Some years to go before that.

Goldberg squirted hand sanitiser into his palm and rubbed it all in, giving off the fumes of a seasoned alcoholic. 'What dimwits like Bruce don't understand is that I'm an academic, Robert. Being dragged out into the field by policing is—'

'You'd rather sit theorising in your office at the university and giving lectures to the next generation.' Marshall might have close to thirty years on him, but he was a lot less fit than Goldberg. 'I get it, sir.'

'Do you?'

'Of course I do.' Marshall wasn't that experienced, but most profilers he'd met in his training, in the day job or at conferences were eggheads and bookworms. Seemed a lot like a complete disdain for the real world with no interest in solving crimes was what got you ahead in the game. Just present your theories, bask in the praise from colleagues, challenge rivals and debate them. Ignore the fact these were dead bodies, lives ended in the worst ways.

'Need I remind you, Robert, that the victims are not people.' Goldberg's mantra. 'They cease to be people when they are killed. There's a hard line between academia and policing and we need to work to maintain that. Our expertise is in our emotional distance. Our rationality. Our logic. Our experience. More than two victims to the same suspected killer and they become crucial data points. And data is everywhere.'

'Which is why I think it's important we visit crime scenes, sir. Data could otherwise get missed. Seeing it with our own eyes can only make the profile stronger.'

'Yes, yes, which is why I've got you and— Ah, there she is.' Somehow Goldberg managed to accelerate.

How could someone walk that fast?

Marshall was out of breath by the time he caught up with them.

'Jake.' DI Jonathan 'call me Jon' Bruce of Northumbria Police held out a hand to Goldberg. 'Good to see you again, mate.' His accent was deepest, darkest Newcastle.

Goldberg looked at the hand like it was going to eat him or infect him with bugs. 'It's been a while, Inspector.'

Marshall took the hand and shook it. 'Hi, Jon. You okay?'

'Nope.' Bruce was partially suited up, with the blue Smurf suit dangling and catching the light breeze.

Another figure floated next to him in a mask and goggles. Dr Liana Curtis pulled them clear of her face. A tousle of red hair tumbled out of the hood. 'Took your time getting here, Dr Jones.' Her smile was as infectious as Goldberg's germs. Her accent still had traces of the Mancunian in it. She looked at Marshall. 'Take it he was driving, Indy?'

Indy...

That nickname...

Made everything that little bit more familiar than it should be.

Marshall didn't want to get into that again, so he nodded.

Bruce was frowning. 'Dr Jones? Indy?'

'My nicknames for these two.' Liana gestured at them, her finger moving precisely. 'You know that Indiana Jones film? He's Sean Connery, he's Harrison Ford. Goldberg's grooming Marshall to take over. His *protégé*.'

'Ah, right.' But Bruce didn't seem to want to get involved in another office's banter. More than enough of that in a police station.

Besides, Liana wanted Goldberg's job way more than Marshall did, which wasn't much at all. He just wanted to get on with stopping monsters killing people.

'Suit up, lads.' Bruce tossed them a crime scene suit each. 'Sadly, there's been another victim of the Shadow Man.'

Goldberg hauled his suit up to the waist then dug around for his left arm. 'I'll be the judge of that.'

'Sure you will.' Bruce chuckled. 'DS Williamson couldn't get hold of you two, so I managed to get Liana out here first. And she agrees with my assessment.'

'Again, *she*'s not the arbiter of whether this is the Shadow Man. I am.' Goldberg finally caught the left arm hole. 'Can you buy these things for home use?'

'You do what you want in your own time, sunshine.' Bruce was smirking. 'Gather you were summoned to the scene, Jake?'

'Chief Constable to University Chancellor.' Goldberg managed to get the other arm through the hole. 'Believe me, the last thing I want is to be out in the field. I have students who can take photographs and write reports of their findings. I have these two to assess and direct. *I* shouldn't be here.'

One thing Marshall was quicker at than him was suiting

up. Felt like he'd seen more crime scenes than he'd given seminars to Goldberg's classes. 'I want to see it for myself, even if he doesn't.'

'Come on, then.' Bruce led them in silence along a path wide enough for a lorry. Both sides were mowed.

A CSI was cataloguing a patch over to the left, but Bruce took off through a wood, over uneven grass that'd been flattened by countless feet.

A crime scene tent stood between two larch trees, their needles already carpeting the forest floor.

Bruce pointed for Marshall to go first.

He took a deep breath and stepped inside the tent.

A group of CSIs worked away, lights flashing and voices muttering into recorders.

In a shallow grave, the corpse of a man was being excavated carefully, like a mummy at Pompeii.

'Oh heavens!' Goldberg coughed behind him. 'Just, just, just think of the millions of bacteria floating around this cadaver. It's *disgusting*. How can I be expected to concentrate here?'

Marshall saw the stake and the sign:

WE LIVE IN THE SHADOWS

He shifted his gaze back to the victim. It matched the others. Young man, fit and athletic. And savagely attacked, just like the others.

Total overkill – slashed with a knife, maybe sixty times in the chest. His throat was slit wide open with a deeper gouge.

Just one difference.

'The only thing I'm noticing is the wound on his head.'

Liana was next to him, arms folded. 'Blunt force trauma. Implies our killer waited to strike. Same as the others, he caught him in the throat but he hit him with something. This lad here is a big guy like you, Rob, so my theory that he's a smaller male or female is starting to bear fruit.'

'Could be he just didn't want them struggling anymore.'

'Could be.' Liana glanced around the others, but nobody was looking at her apart from Marshall. 'And the shallow graves... He's a planner, preparing it all in advance. We know that. He's getting them in isolated places, but why does he not dig a deeper grave?'

'He wants to show off his work, burying them just enough to make an exit and confound early discovery... but not for long.' Marshall was trying to spot anything else. 'Cable ties on the victim's arms and legs show he doesn't get off on the thrill of the chase, just the act of killing. It's a release for him. I suspect he's disgusted with himself afterwards, or just spent.'

'Good point.' Liana gestured at the stake. 'Every grave has that same message. "We live in the shadows". Why we call him the Shadow Man. But...'

'But we have no idea what it means.' Goldberg was as far away from everyone as he could get. His goggles were all misted up. 'What do you know about the victim, Inspector?'

Bruce sighed. 'Found a BMW one-series in the car park. Been there a few days. Got a hit from the plates – left Newcastle on Saturday lunchtime. Found a wallet in the glove box. Photo matches his ID. Name is Toby Wilder. Twenty-three. From Witney in Oxfordshire. Postgraduate student at Northumbria University.' He left a gap, but nobody filled it. 'Fits the profile of the Shadow Man's victims – young and healthy adults. Also, a brand-new Beemer for a student, shows his parents have a quid or two.'

Goldberg shot him a glare through smoky goggles, raising a gloved index finger. 'Inspector, I and I alone will decide what fits and what does not. You are not qualified.'

'If you say so.' Bruce laughed, but his eyes betrayed a slight nervousness. 'So, is he another one or not?'

Goldberg just stared into the grave, seeming baffled by this whole situation.

A man of inaction. Of theories, lectures, empty pontification. Talking himself up, but what did he deliver? He'd delegated the four other crime scenes to Marshall and Liana. Now he was finally forced to be here, it was down to him. And Goldberg clearly hated having to provide expertise in the moment.

Marshall clapped his hands together. 'Okay, here's what I think. The prior victims have all been white-collar workers – two accountants, an HR manager, and a social media entrepreneur. Two women and two men. Now this Toby Wilder guy is a postgraduate student. If he's on his way to being an academic, that's a slight difference in salary.' He focused on Bruce. 'Spoken to anyone at the university?'

CHAPTER THREE

Northumbria University was pretty much slap bang in the centre of Newcastle, like a knife in the heart. Liana's tiny Daihatsu was much comfier than Goldberg's Jag – it had satnav and, like any car built after 1992, power steering so her elbows barely moved as she navigated the one-way system at lunchtime. The footwell was all dirty from being out in the wilds of rural Northumbria and the back seat was a morass of discarded magazines, newspapers and a gym bag. Marshall doubted there was space there to fit even a small child.

Out of the crime scene get up, Liana's dark-grey trouser suit was more banker than criminal profiler. Sterile, but the perfect foundation for her red hair. 'Why did Goldberg go back to base?'

'Why do you think?'

'I think he's already in a disinfecting shower, moaning like he's been exposed to anthrax or Ebola.' She looked over, her lip curled up at the side. 'Too harsh?'

'Nah, fair enough. We know why he's gone back. He hates the real world. Books and papers, that's where he exists.'

'Too bloody right.' She pulled up outside a building that looked like a spaceship, a sister landing craft to the Gateshead Sage over the banks of the Tyne under the famous bridge.

Marshall was first out, but at least he didn't have to contend with Goldberg's walking speed now – Liana might be a runner, but at least she kept to a human pace.

Bruce was already out of his car, tapping away at his phone.

'Apologies for Goldberg back there.'

Bruce looked up and grinned. 'Oh, there's nothing to apologise for. This case is fucking shit, mate, but at least his eccentricities give us something to laugh about, eh?' He smiled at Liana. 'Shall we?' He led them into the building. Didn't even have to go up to reception, just a flash of his warrant card was enough. 'Dr MacGillivray's expecting us.' He pushed through a door and trotted up the stairs. 'Need his formal sign-off to let my boffin get access to all of this lad's internet accounts.'

Liana kept two-step pace with him as they climbed. 'You know Goldberg is thinking bricks and mortar on this, right?'

'I do.' Bruce smiled at her. 'What about you pair, though?'

'I tend to agree with you. The virtual world is full of possibilities.'

'Lass after my own heart, pet.'

Marshall took it slower, one step at a time. Taking deep breaths. Grabbing the handrail. Couldn't speak. Christ, it was one flight of steps. A very long one. The door rattled shut and he pushed through into a corridor. No sign of them.

Shite – he really needed to get fit.

He heard a braying laugh coming from a room on the right and followed the sound.

Bruce and Liana were sitting by a desk.

A little goblin man was standing behind it. Navy trousers hauled almost up to his armpits. Lime shirt, dark green tie. Completely bald, with cold eyes. 'Ah, you must be Dr Marshall?' He waved a hand. 'Dr Aestor MacGillivray, at your service.' He tucked the hand back in his trouser pocket. 'Just saying to DI Bruce here that his IT boffin is getting *full* access to Toby's account.'

'That's good to hear.' Marshall stayed standing, giving enough space between him and the others. The days of people using their university accounts for everything virtual were long gone – most had their own laptops, so the uni side would just be coursework and emails to mates. But he wasn't going to say anything. 'Listen, we're all sorry about—'

'Toby was a good student, doing solid work. Ask me, he was on his way to the top in business studies in this university. But there's a hard ceiling there.'

Bruce scribbled in his notebook. 'So he was on track to be an academic?'

'Know what they say – those that can't do, teach.' MacGillivray's braying laughter erupted, high and keening. Not infectious in the slightest. 'I mean, I imagine yourselves know all about that?' Another giggle. His joke didn't land.

Liana folded her arms. 'What's that supposed to mean, sir?'

'You two are Professor Goldberg's protégés, aren't you?' MacGillivray's grin widened. 'I know Jacob and I know his reputation. Impressive work, but it's not *real* work, is it?'

'Professor Goldberg is—'

'—trying to turn this profiling malarkey into a business. Make his department a profit centre in the university. I get it. Consulted on it, even.'

'Okay.' Marshall looked at Liana and her frown suggested she was thinking the same as him. The guy was, like so many in this line of work, a boring twat. 'Would Mr Wilder have expected to earn much once he'd finished?'

'I myself have made a decent career out of teaching. It's rewarding work. I gather you two earn a decent salary.' His gaze switched between them. 'Why do you ask?'

'The other victims all had six-figure salaries, which is a lot for this area.'

'In this day and age, an academic isn't at the top of society. That's long since been given over to lawyers, bankers, entrepreneurs. Not even captains of industry. And Toby wouldn't have been earning even half of that by the time he was my age.' MacGillivray collapsed into a chair. 'Way things are going, you do academia for the love of it.'

'Did he love it?'

'I don't really know. Never got that close to him. A few sessions a month to discuss progress, but that's it. Kept himself to himself.'

Liana tilted her head to the side. 'But?'

'Not a popular guy by any stretch. And... he had an issue with a couple of students.'

'What kind of issues?'

'A complaint.'

'From other students?'

MacGillivray nodded.

'Female students?'

MacGillivray folded his arms. 'I'm unable to divulge that. We investigated it. That was all that needed to happen.'

'Come on, man.' Bruce thumped the desk. 'The lad's been killed, like. We need the truth.'

'Right, well, yes. The allegations were of a sexual nature.'

Which didn't fit the profile.

The other victims were all squeaky clean. Unless there was something they had all hidden – which was difficult in the modern age, but not impossible – then Toby Wilder was giving off the flavour of being an outlier.

'Like I said, he was under investigation but he was cleared. The women involved even apologised to him.'

Sounded weird to Marshall. Or like a future legal case brewing.

'Was it a drinking-related incident?'

'God no, Toby was teetotal. It was stalking. He thought the women were sexually attracted to him and he'd seen a few too many Hollywood films and movies and listened to a few too many love songs. Upshot was he didn't know when to back off.' Another braying laugh. 'We cleared it up and no harm was done. Just a misunderstanding.'

'All the same.' Bruce slapped his notebook on the desk. 'We'd like the names of both alleged victims. And a copy of the report.'

'I'll have to—'

'This fella's dead. That means they're suspects. How about I give the dean a ring? Sure that'll go down well.'

'Of course. I'll see what I can do.'

Marshall was already thinking ahead. 'You said he was teetotal?'

'Correct. As far as I know, Toby's only real passion in life was exercise – he was a runner.'

Liana craned her neck around to Marshall. 'That's maybe something. Two of the previous four ran. The other two were cyclists.'

Bruce's mobile rang. He checked the display and shot to his feet. 'Back in a sec.' He stormed out of the room, phone to his ear.

MacGillivray shifted his gaze between them – the braying laugh hid a calculating mind. 'This is a serial killer case?'

Liana nibbled a nail, staring at the floor.

Marshall fixed him with a hard stare. 'We're not at liberty to divulge that.'

'Oh, come, come. I know Jake Goldberg. I was at Durham before this and sat in on many interdepartmental meetings with him. Like I say, I consulted on how to turn that galaxy brain of his into a business the university could profit from. Shared a few bottles of wine in the process. Jake always brought his own glass.' That braying laugh again. 'I left there to take up a senior position here. Head of department, you know. Upward trajectory. But I know what he does. So I know precisely what you two do. Was Toby killed by this Shadow Man in the papers?'

Liana nodded. 'The police are investigating that possibility, sir. Robert and I are merely consulting.'

'Like Sherlock Holmes.'

She smiled. 'More like Indiana Jones.'

'Sorry, I don't see how. Ah, because he's an academic?' Mischief twinkled in MacGillivray's eyes. 'And that must make you Lara Croft?'

'Guys.' Bruce was in the doorway, clutching his mobile. 'Need a word.'

MacGillivray followed them over.

'Just Rob and Liana, thanks.'

MacGillivray stuck out his lip like a disappointed toddler. 'I hope you catch Toby's killer.'

'Thanks for your help, sir. Remember to look up the names of those lasses, aye?'

'Of course.'

'Good man.' Bruce scurried off down the corridor. 'My IT guy has access to Wilder's uni account.' He raised a hand. 'I know what you're going to say about IT, Rob, but first thing Alex has done is go through Toby's web history. Usual sites: BBC, Guardian, Telegraph, Schoolbook, Twitter. But he was a heavy user of Xtreme Nutters. It's a message board for runners. The kind of person who thinks a marathon is a light park run.'

Liana opened the door for the stairs. 'Any other activities?'

'Cycling. Rock climbing. Hiking. You name it. They post their routes and times, then their plans for the next ones so others can help with feedback and pointers.'

'Is this a small group?'

'Ish. Couple of hundred, maybes. Not sure if they know each other. Some of them are talking of turning it into an app.'

'If they're posting planned routes...' Marshall set off down the stairs at the same pace as them, determined to maintain it – going down was easier, right? 'That gives anyone the opportunity to know where they're going to be and when. Extreme athletes go to extreme places. Like Kielder Water.'

Bruce stopped at the bottom and held out his mobile. 'Look at this.'

The screen was filled with messages from different people. All with thumbnail photos.

Liana tapped one. A bearded man out somewhere wild and green. 'That's Josh Kidd.' And another. A thin woman, bibbed and mid-marathon. 'That's Sam Harrington-Coates.' She looked at Marshall. 'This is it, Rob. This is how he's targeting them.'

Marshall had that flutter in his chest. She was right. This was it.

'Jon, can your IT guy track down the hosting for this? Maybe we can see if it's an inside job.'

Bruce snatched the phone back off them. 'You're in luck. It's hosted in Newcastle.'

CHAPTER FOUR

The hosting office was just around the corner. Like a lot of cities, Newcastle had its own nascent tech hub near a university. So close, in fact, that Marshall could see Bruce and his team enter the office's front door as they got in Liana's car.

'No reply from Dr Jones.' Liana slid her key into the ignition but didn't turn it. She was looking at the squat block Bruce was in too. 'Just sitting on his mountain top, waiting for people to climb up and seek his sage advice.' She sat back. 'This might be the clincher, Rob. Goldberg's theory that the solution to these crimes lies solely in the real world seemed good, but if he's targeting people virtually... God save us.'

'Think even He will struggle with the internet, Liana.'

'Can't be this simple, can it?'

'Sometimes it just is.' Marshall looked around at her, at those huge eyes that were almost all pupil, such was the darkness of her irises. 'If Bruce can identify the other victims using that site, then that is the link. It just comes down to whether it's someone in the group or someone on the hosting side.'

Liana shut her eyes. She let out a deep breath and reopened them. 'How are you feeling about it?'

'Not great, to be honest. Profiling feels so passive, even if it can help get *them* to the end result.' Marshall waved over to the building Bruce was in. 'Goldberg told us our role is to focus the police on their target, not to do the job for them. "We are scholars, they are not. They can't possibly know what we know and we are far too educated to run around playing Sherlock Holmes for them." Blah blah blah.' He let out a sigh at least as big as hers. 'I'm tired of the inaction.'

'Okay.' She was biting her lip. 'I wasn't asking about that.'

'Oh.'

Her lips, pressing against his.

Her arms around him, hand on his arse.

His hands on her—

'Oh, indeed.' She was looking at him. 'You don't want to talk about Friday night, do you?'

He looked away from her. 'Sorry, I just...'

'Rob. Here's the deal. We were both drunk. We kissed. Like, really kissed. And I'm ... interested in you. Romantically.' She laughed. 'Christ, I'm not very good at this, am I? But you ran off, Rob. Why?'

Why indeed?

'Long story, Liana.'

'I've got time, Rob. We could grab some lunch. Talk it all through. After all, we've kind of done everything we can here. Bruce's got his Superman moment. How about you give me some Clark Kent?'

'Clark Kent?' Marshall's head felt like a pavlova, one he'd made and had collapsed in on itself. 'It was unprofessional, Liana. We work together and I'm in a senior position to you.'

That sounded as weak as his mum's tea.

'I'll explain it to you one day.' For the first time in ten years, since he'd left home with all that baggage, he was thinking of giving up part of himself to someone else. To show that he was an apple with worms and maggots crawling around in the core. 'Liana, there's—'

A back door smashed, the shards exploding in a wave across the slabs. A man burst through, running off and clutching his arm.

Military fatigues, shaved head. Big. Muscular. Looking behind him. Looking everywhere. Dropping his mobile over the wall. Running towards them.

Marshall waved out of the car. 'Do you see—'

The man clocked them, eyes wide, then ran in the opposite direction.

'Shite.' Marshall got out of the car and shot off after him. The guy was almost as big as he was but much faster, gaining with each stride. On territory he knew, or least knew better than Marshall.

Aching shins, burning lungs – this was action. He tasted blood at the back of his throat. But he was following the guy.

Down a back alley, into old Newcastle. Brick buildings at the rear of Georgian edifices. A main road at the end – if the man got there, he'd lose him.

Wait – a grey Daihatsu sat there.

Liana.

She'd driven off, while Marshall had run. She was always smarter than him – one step ahead all the time. Why the hell Goldberg favoured him was probably more to do with what was between his legs than his ears.

The guy stopped. He had spotted Liana. He dived over a chest-height brick wall, into a yard.

Marshall was even worse at gymnastics than running. Still, he flung himself at the wall, trying to get over. He caught his stomach on the top and winded himself, then toppled over, his back landing hard on concrete.

The man was standing over him, threatening him with a Rambo knife, big enough to slice half a cow, let alone all of a man.

'Please.' Marshall was struggling to even raise his hands. Everything burnt with pain. He couldn't breathe. Seeing stars – he must've cracked his skull. 'We just... want to... talk.'

'I haven't done anything!' Local accent, harsh and full of rage.

'It's okay.' Marshall sucked in a long, deep breath. 'We'll... have a chat... and you'll be... You'll be fine.'

'Fine? You lot come into my office, looking for a serial killer! And you think it's me!'

Marshall was on his knees now. 'Nobody said—' He was going to be sick. 'We just want to— I'm not a cop, okay?'

'So why are you following us?'

'I'm working with them. Helping them.'

'It's not me!'

Marshall sat back down again. 'What's your name?'

'Michael. It's Michael.'

'Okay, Michael, let's just—' Marshall caught a flash of motion and shut his eyes, raised his arms.

Waited for the stab of pain from the knife slicing his hands.

It didn't come.

Marshall reopened his eyes.

Bruce stood over him, brandishing a baton. 'You okay there, mate?'

Two of Bruce's guys were helping Michael up.

'I'm fine, aye.'

Bruce held out a hand for Marshall and hauled him up to standing. 'You just saved the day. We started speaking to this guy, he went to the toilet and ran off. Good work spotting that and catching him.'

'I didn't do much. Just saw someone smashing through a glass window.'

'You'd make a great cop.'

Marshall rolled his eyes. 'I've seen how bad the rest of your team are, so maybe.'

CHAPTER FIVE

'How are you doing, Rob?'

Marshall looked around the poky wee room. He didn't want to sit anywhere. Aside from the chairs looking about as comfortable as iron maidens, his legs were stinging from his brief run. If he sat, they'd seize up and he'd never get up.

And his back... His back was like he was actually trapped inside an iron maiden, with the spikes drilling into his flesh.

Still, the coffee in the Northumbria Police headquarters was better than back at the university. An Ethiopian blend, if Marshall had to guess. Filter, but clean and with that buttery taste on his lips. Not what he expected – then again, Bruce's team drank a lot of coffee.

Liana was brave enough to sit. 'I asked how you were doing?'

'Sorry.' Marshall let out a sigh, still tasting that burning blood at the back of his throat. He needed to get fit and soon. 'I'm fine. Thanks for asking.'

She curled her hair around her fingers. 'That was really brave running after him like that...'

'Can we just watch this, please?'

On the cracked TV screen, Bruce sat next to DS Chris Williamson, a squat wee lad from County Durham who looked more at home down a mine than in a police station. 'You mind if I ask you a question?'

Opposite, Michael Shaw was sitting at attention, if that was possible, like his spine had been replaced by a rod of titanium. 'No, sir.'

Williamson was acting all casual, his limbs loose. 'What does "We Live In The Shadows" mean?'

Shaw frowned. 'No idea, sir.'

'It's from an Oasis song, isn't it?'

'Sorry, sir. I don't know, sir.'

'What's with this "sir" stuff?' Liana scowled at Marshall. 'Is he taking the piss?'

'Military.'

'Ah. "Yes, sir. No, sir. Three bags full, sir." Got it.' Her frown deepened. 'Does Williamson know that?'

'Our role is to focus the police on their target, not to do the job for them.'

She laughed. 'Come on, Rob...'

'I'm sure he'll guess. Or Bruce will. They might be cops, but they're not daft.'

Williamson leaned forward and made eye contact with Shaw. 'We recovered the knife you threatened a member of the public with. Looks like there's some flesh in the serrations. If it's human, we'll be able to run the DNA against the database and see if it matches any of the victims.'

'It's not, sir.'

'It's not what?'

'Human, sir.'

'Okay. Thanks for clearing that up.' Williamson stuffed his hands into his pockets. 'Brilliant to just get the truth like that. Don't even need to check, do we? Just take your word for it. Magic.'

Shaw was unmoved. 'It's rabbit, sir.'

'Rabbit. Okay.'

'Yes, sir.'

'You killed a rabbit?'

'Yes, sir.'

'A friend's pet?'

'No, sir.'

'You just found a rabbit in your office?'

'No, sir. I was trained to survive off the land. This weekend I was camping in the Highlands. Caught a rabbit, sir. Gutted it. Cooked it.'

'You were in the army?'

'Coldstream Guards, sir.'

Liana looked around at Marshall and clicked her fingers. 'Well, well. Brownie points to you.'

'And they trained you in how to kill rabbits?'

'Not just rabbits, sir. They trained me in field IT. Hacking into the other lot's equipment in the dust of Kandahar was the difference between life and death.'

'And that's what you're doing as a civvy now?'

'Yes, sir. Database administrator. I learnt a trade in the army. I'm grateful to my country, sir.'

Marshall looked around at Liana again. 'He's not all there, is he?'

'Think a lot of him was left in the dust of Kandahar, sir.'

He smiled back at her. 'Think he's our guy?'

'No red flags against him. Yet.'

'—went in the front door and asked at reception, they told us you run that website.'

'That's correct, sir.'

'And you spoke to us.'

'That's correct, sir.'

'Briefly. You said you needed to go to the toilet.'

'That's correct, sir.'

'And you ran out the back.'

'That's correct, sir.'

'Why?'

Shaw sat there, bolt upright, staring ahead. Didn't say anything.

'Michael, why did you run away?'

'Going for lunch, sir.'

'Lunch. Right. You smashed a window to get out and left your phone on a wall outside, but you were just going for lunch.'

'That's correct, sir.'

'Come on, Michael. That's not true, is it? You were fleeing us. Why?'

'You need to speak to my therapist, sir. I've got PTSD from my service, sir. Sometimes I get triggered by things. I wake up a lot thinking I'm being chased by enemy combatants. When you came in and started asking questions, it was like I was back there.'

'Is that what you thought we were, Michael?'

'Yes, sir.'

'Is that what you thought these people were?'

'What people?'

'Toby Wilder. Josh Kidd. Sam Harrington-Coates.'

'I don't recognise those names, sir.'

'There are more.'

'I don't know them, sir.'

'Thing is, we found these people on Xtreme Nutters.

They're all members of the board. Frequent posters. Do you know what Xtreme Nutters is, Michael?'

'Yes, sir.'

'Go on?'

'It's a website we manage.'

'You're an IT bod, Michael. I get it. But our own IT bods are currently in the process of extracting all the data from your server.' Williamson let that sink in, but it just seemed to bounce off Shaw. 'There's a pattern emerging. Whoever killed these people could tell from the posts they'd made where they'd be at a particular time. He could wait, then trap them like a rabbit and kill them. Now, we wondered if it might be another member of the group. Or it could be someone on the inside. Someone behind the scenes.'

Shaw stared at him.

'Are you a member?'

'No, sir.'

'All five victims were. Someone hunted them down like a wild rabbit. Are you planning on killing all twenty-five members of the group?'

'Not me, sir.'

'Okay, Michael, here's the part where you get to say more than "yes, sir" or "no, sir". Toby Wilder went missing on Saturday. Drove off in his car from Newcastle. Went for a run around Kielder Water. Not seen again until a dog walker found him in a shallow grave. Where were you on Saturday?'

'I don't know, sir.'

'Come on, Michael.'

'I said I don't know, sir.'

'Toby's got family back home in Oxfordshire. They want to know who's killed their son. Their brother. Their cousin. Where were you on Saturday?'

'I don't know, sir.'

'Michael. Don't give me that. Where were you?'

'I don't know, sir!'

'Stop lying to—'

'I was near Aviemore, sir.'

'In the Scottish Highlands?'

'That's right, sir. I told you that.'

'Right, where you hunted the rabbit. Anyone vouch for you?'

'No, sir. I was on my own. I got off the train and just walked. Eventually I made camp.'

'Okay, Michael. I've got a list of names and dates here. Need you to tell me where you were for each of them. Okay?'

'Yes, sir.'

'You're going to tell me the truth, okay?'

'Yes, sir.'

'How do I know you're not lying to me?'

'Because I don't lie, sir.'

'Did you kill these people?'

'No, sir.'

'Okay.' Bruce scraped his chair back and got up. He whispered into Williamson's ear, then left the room.

Onscreen, a female detective took his place and started leading the questioning.

Liana turned the TV's volume down.

The door opened and Bruce came into the observation suite. 'That was quite something.' He took the seat Marshall still hadn't. 'What's your thinking, Lady Liana?'

'Lady Liana?'

'What do you think of him?'

'Three cans short of a four-pack.' Liana rested back against the wall. 'But he fits the potential profile of our killer. He's ex-army. From what I saw, he's clearly trained. Also, a loner. Clearly damaged by his experiences in the army. Maybe he does see these people as enemy combatants, in which case you need to get a PTSD specialist in here.'

'On it.' Bruce tapped something into his phone. 'You agree with her, Rob?'

'Not really. His size is jarring. Guy's huge. Liana already hypothesised that the subject was a smaller male or female. Shaw's a big guy. Trained, built. Why would he need the rock?'

Liana pursed her lips. 'Doesn't necessitate a smaller man. Big guys like you are just as capable of using a rock as little ones.'

Marshall could press the point but keeping his powder dry was a lesson hard learnt.

'She makes a good point.' Bruce looked up from his mobile. 'How about the motive?'

'Hard to say, Jon.' Marshall sighed. 'The Shadow Man is targeting young athletes. We can see how he'd do it. Posting planned solo runs on a forum gives anyone the opportunity. It's not a public forum – you have to be a member to read the information. Which means we've gone from an infinite list to something more manageable. That list contains all the members, but also anyone at the hosting firm who can access it.'

'We've got people going through that list trying to find anyone who's posted in the last week. See if there's not an undiscovered victim.'

'Good work.'

Bruce held Marshall's gaze. 'Nothing on the motive side, though? Why *he* – Michael Shaw – would kill them? Why *they* live in the shadows?'

'Lots of potential reasons.'

Bruce smirked. 'Bottom line?'

Marshall shrugged, then took a few seconds to clarify his thoughts. 'I still don't see a clear motive for the murders.

Opportunity? Sure. Means? Sure. Motive? No. All a profile does is point you towards the right realm, Jon, and gives you things to consider. Once you have arrested someone, that's up to you lot in law enforcement to build a case based on evidence.'

'So, either he does or doesn't fit the profile. Which is it? It's fifty-fifty.'

'It's not fifty-bloody-fifty.' But Marshall wasn't going to argue the toss further. 'The most honest answer I can give is that aspects of his character fit the profile, but others definitely do not. And he's also clearly troubled.'

Bruce shifted his focus to Liana. 'What's your take?'

'The profile we have is for a male loner who endured a difficult childhood or early adulthood. Someone who works a menial job.'

Marshall looked over at her. 'A DBA isn't that menial.'

'Okay, it can be. Before you ask how I know, my brother's one – it's mostly boring. It might be a professional IT job, but he's not working at a bank or an insurer. Where he's working, most of the work is automated. It'll be exciting when something goes wrong, but how often is that? Not very. At a hosting firm, it'll be badly paid, the work will be boring and he could get called out at all hours, which could lead to sleep deprivation.'

'Thanks, guys.' Bruce clapped his hands together. 'I'm convinced we've got our killer.' He narrowed his eyes. 'It's a classic case. The army trained him to kill and he's used that training to murder these men and women, confusing them with people on the battlefield.'

Liana was nodding. 'I agree with that assessment.'

Marshall's legs started to throb from the pain. 'I could go along with that too, but I just can't square him with being our killer.' He tried to straighten his legs and it *hurt*. 'The main reason is... because he denied it.'

Liana frowned. Then laughed. 'That's it?'

'One of the key aspects of the profile is that the killer wants to be caught. The sign, the message, the shallow graves. Michael Shaw didn't want to be caught. He ran, then he threatened me with a knife. And he's still denying it in the interview. He's telling us stuff, but not admitting to the murders. Our guy would be screaming from the rooftops, "It was me!" over and over again.'

Bruce bit his cheek. 'Liana?'

'I see Rob's point, but...' She stood up and started pacing the room. 'Your theory's sound, but it falls apart on one aspect. You've *assumed* he *consciously* wants to be caught.'

Marshall tried to wind his way through her logic. 'You think it's a subconscious need?'

'Right.' Liana unbuttoned her suit jacket and rested her hands on her hips. 'He's in denial about the murders, but he wants to come clean.'

'You're suggesting a sexual component to the killings?'

'Correct. It's maybe not that he goes there to hunt them, or not explicitly. It could be that he's a voyeur and an exhibitionist, that he masturbates while watching athletes. Men and women. And maybe he cruises fit, young people for sexual encounters. And I think the overkill is a result of the self-disgust at this act. Especially with the male victims, where it's much worse. Toby had twice as many cuts as Sam, for example. And maybe the sexual act is after he's caught them. They can't say no when they've been tied up and duct taped, can they? But they can watch.'

'How do you explain the rock to Toby Wilder's skull?'

'Maybe Shaw didn't like the guy looking at him. Or there was an adverse reaction, such as Toby laughing at him.'

Marshall played it all through his brain, still fizzing from the strong coffee. But it just didn't feel right. 'Jon. Any case

depends on the magic glue that holds a prosecution together...
Now you have a suspect, what does the evidence say?'

Liana was frowning again. 'We've got five data points now,
Rob. We've got a suspect. That's a lot to go on.' She looked at
Bruce with raised eyebrows. 'Besides, I'm sure this sexual
theory will provoke a response in him.'

Bruce barked out a laugh. 'I like it.' He shot to his feet and
left the room.

Liana turned the volume back up, just as Bruce reappeared.

The female detective made to leave the room, but Bruce
shook his head. 'Need you to stay, Gina.' He stayed standing,
between Shaw and the door. 'Here's the thing, Michael. This
behaviour of yours is a lot like what we'd call cruising. People
hanging out in an area looking for sexual partners.'

'No, sir.'

'A lot of gay men do it. Lot of straight men too. Nothing
wrong with it, really, so long as it's not in a public place and it's
between consenting adults.' Bruce left a long pause. 'But that's
where you fall down, eh? You do it in public and you don't ask.
You know where these sexy, young, fit people are going to be
and you wait for them. Then you pounce. Attack them. Almost
garrotte them. Then you stand there, masturbating as they die.
And you bury them like you bury your shame.'

Shaw slumped forward. Head on the table. His sides were
moving.

Liana was standing up now. 'Is he laughing?'

Shaw lurched back in the chair and roared. Not laughter
but crying. A deep wail of anguish. 'Please, I just want it to
stop.'

Bruce walked over and put a hand on his wrist. 'Michael
Shaw, I'm arresting you for the murder of Toby Wilder.' He
gestured at Gina. 'Can you read him his rights, please?'

'You do not have to say anything, but it may—'

Liana turned the volume down on the TV.

Bruce barrelled in, grinning from ear to ear. 'Did you see that?' The room was tiny, but he was moving around it like it was Wembley and he'd just won the FA Cup. 'I asked him and... He said, "Please, I just want it to stop". If that's not guilt, then I don't know what is.'

'Jon, that can be interpreted in a bunch of different ways: the interview; the accusations; the PTSD; the rain outside; *Neighbours* on TV.'

'Or the murders he's committing.' Bruce clapped them both on the arms. 'You pair can relax. You've been a massive help with this.'

Liana's grin was at least as wide. 'I'm pleased you've caught the Shadow Man.'

CHAPTER SIX
THE SHADOW MAN

Friday

Four days later

The light had long since died.

Just him alone in the pitch-black emptiness. The sea was lapping down below – he could almost make out the bank of cliffs in the garish moonlight.

Just him. On his own.

No sign of her.

This was almost too good to be true. They'd caught that guy. It was all over the news. He'd got away with it. He was in the clear.

But he couldn't stop.

Had to keep doing it.

Had to—

Wait.

What was that?

The buzzing *fwip* of bike tyres on the cycle path.

A cone of light swept through the darkness.

Someone was coming towards him. Her yellow top glowed. The one he'd watched her leave wearing.

Caroline Blackford.

He held the cord in his hands.

Waiting.

Waiting.

Waiting.

Fwip.

Now.

He hauled it back.

And he missed. Shit. The cord went over her head.

Plan B.

He lurched into action, grabbing the air rifle and training it at the bike. Even in the darkness, he could see her through the scope. His finger squeezed the trigger and she fell forward.

Perfect.

He dumped the gun and raced along the path, clutching a hammer. He didn't look at her as he smashed her in the head. He picked up her racer. The rear tyre was a torn mess. He threw it into the sea with no effort – had to pay a lot to get a bike that light. And Caroline Blackford had a lot of money.

Then he picked her up – she barely weighed anything – and carried her off the path, through the bracken and long grass towards the grave.

Footsteps.

Heavy breathing.

Shit.

Someone else was coming.

He crouched, pressing her to the ground.

She was looking at him, eyes moving.

He covered her mouth with his hand.

She bit his fingers.

He bashed her head with the hammer again.

She stopped moving.

The footsteps jogged past with the long moan of a lost runner. A man in his forties, whippet thin.

He waited for the jogger to pass into the distance, waited until he couldn't even hear him.

Then he picked her up and carried her towards the grave again. Further from the path than the others had been. He dropped her in and inspected the damage. She was all scratched from the crash, a long bright gash up her arms. Her forehead was red like a chip wrapper smeared in tomato ketchup.

He got out his knife and cut her throat. Then he slashed away at her chest.

It could so easily have gone wrong.

He'd been careless. Stupid. So fucking stupid.

He stopped and stepped back, then started shovelling in soil.

The rope didn't work on a cyclist like with a runner, for some reason. He needed to try it lower. Chest height. Yes, that would work. Under the arms.

He had to fix that by tomorrow.

Three more.

His most adventurous attempt yet.

CHAPTER SEVEN

MARSHALL

Monday
Three days later

The Wear swept around the bend down below. Strong flow today, not even a duck or a swan in sight, with only one brave pair of rowers out. A couple walked hand in hand on the far bank.

A couple.

A river.

Dragged Marshall back into the past. A past he didn't want to confront.

The door clattered open and Liana charged in, eyes narrow, clutching two coffee cups with lids on. She slammed one on the desk and dots of coffee spat out of the hole in the lid, spreading across Marshall's notebook. 'Crap, sorry.'

'It's okay.' Marshall brushed it away, but it smudged the ink of his precise handwriting that little bit worse than the trailing fingers of his hand. The joys of being a leftie. He opened the lid and sucked in the smoky aroma. 'Thank you for going to my favourite. You really didn't have to.'

'Hey, it's your birthday. Least you deserve.' She swung her bag around and pulled out a small cake box. 'Et voila.'

'Thank you.' He opened it. A fondant pink pair of cupcakes. 'Thank you, Liana. This is great. You didn't have to.'

'I know.. I did it because I wanted to.'

Marshall could barely look at her. He took one of the cakes out and slid the box over his desk towards her. 'Here you go.'

'God no. I can't eat gluten. Remember?'

'Ah. Okay.' So he was stuck with two cakes. Him, a fat bastard who couldn't say no. He bit into it and got a lovely taste of lemon. 'Thank you. This is magnificent.'

Liana perched against the edge of her desk. 'I like doing stuff for people, Rob.' She slurped coffee through the lid. And stood there, lips twisted. Like she wanted to say something but couldn't bring herself to.

He finished chewing. 'Whatever it is, you can say it. Okay?'

She hid behind the coffee cup. 'I know you, pardon the phrase, don't wish to dip your pen in company ink but...' She took a drink of coffee, her forehead creased. 'But I know how it felt to kiss you last Friday, Rob. How you responded. We get on well. We sit in this office together every day. And... How about we go on a date and see what happens?'

Marshall took his time chewing the cake, then swallowed it down. And took a glug of coffee. 'Their Colombian blend is to die for.'

'That's it? You're just ignoring what I said?'

'Sorry, no. I... I don't know what to say, Liana. What I haven't already said. What I didn't say.'

'I know what you're thinking, Rob. You don't think you're worth it.'

Marshall cradled the coffee cup in both hands. He still

couldn't look at her. 'The difficulty of us being psychologists is we think too much. About childhood traumas and how they impact later life. But I'm not a criminal whose behaviour can be explained by what happened to me at a formative age.'

'All the same, you don't let people get close to you. Over the time we've worked together, though, you've let me get close. What happened wasn't just a drunken fumble. It was an inevitable consequence of us getting closer and closer.'

'Liana, I...'

'Rob, but you deserve to be happy. You're a good man. Kind, smart, funny. Look, just think about it. Okay?'

Some people would think she was arrogant to think all of that, but Marshall knew Liana and how her own childhood traumas made her want to heal everyone and give up too much of herself to others.

'Liana, I need to—'

Her phone rang.

She checked the display. 'Oh, sodomy. It's Bruce.' She snatched up her coffee cup, answered it and left the room.

That was... something.

Marshall felt the cake curdling in his stomach like milk turning into cheese.

She was persistent, that was for sure.

He was attracted to her. No question about it. She was cute, smart, funny. All of it.

But he needed to resolve the noise inside his head.

Fuck it.

It had to be a no.

The door clattered open and he steeled himself for a resumption of the interrogation about his love life.

But it was Goldberg, eyes glazed, fists clenched, looking like he'd been shaken up in a blender. 'What are you doing, Robert?'

Marshall closed his personal notebook and waved a hand at his laptop. 'Working through some changes to the profile.'

Goldberg grabbed a seat and crashed it into the carpet, then plonked his bony frame down in it. 'Why?'

'The police might have their suspect, but he hasn't confessed.'

'So?'

'So...' Marshall took a drink of coffee. Getting to the tepid point, so he needed to finish it. 'I'm just concerned that Michael Shaw isn't a good fit.'

'Of course he matches our profile!'

'But not in a very detailed way.' Marshall finished his coffee. 'You're shouting, Jacob. What's up?'

Goldberg got up from his chair with an almighty sigh. 'Jon Bruce called me a few minutes ago.' He pinched his nose. 'Michael Shaw killed himself on remand.'

Marshall stared up at the ceiling. The cornices were covered in cobwebs. A spider was prowling the area but she didn't have any flies to feast on. He looked back at Goldberg. 'That's...'

'Don't say unfortunate, Robert, because it's much worse than that. Someone probably leaked the small matter of us believing there to be a sexual component to the crimes. Of course, the fine folk in jail take a dim view of sexual offenders in general and sexual murderers in particular.' Goldberg scratched at his hair hard enough to dislodge a tuft. 'They beat him with soap bars stuffed into socks. They defecated into shampoo bottles and filled them with water, so they could spray a brown mess at him. The ringleader said to him, "This is your life from now on. Welcome to every day." He was raped and tortured. Then, this morning, with suspected encouragement from his cellmate, he tied ripped-up blanket strips into a rope, looped it around his neck and tightened it until he died. The cellmate told Jonathan's team under interview.'

Marshall eased up to standing. The caffeine mixed with a jolt of pure adrenaline. 'If my doubts had been listened to, Michael Shaw would still be alive.'

'You think this is our fault?'

'Oh no, Jacob. "Our role is to focus the police on their target, not to do the job for them." Well, we focused them on the wrong target!'

'This is on the police, Robert. Not us.'

Marshall could swing for him. 'That academic distance you insist on turns victims into data points and perpetrators into algorithms we can analyse and predict. Problem is, algorithms don't kill themselves on remand.'

Goldberg collapsed back into the chair.

'Jacob, I told you the killer was seeking attention. The killer wants to be caught. We caught Shaw, but he wasn't blasé about it. He was resigned to his fate. Sat in the interview, answering all the questions. Except those about the murders. Whoever killed those people did it for a reason. And the bullshit Bruce and Liana concocted... that's not the reason. Shaw was scared, Jacob. He denied it. I told Bruce not to go for it, Jacob. But he prosecuted Shaw.'

'DI Bruce contacted me for the definitive answer. He relayed your concerns and I sided with Liana. I believe his exact words were "two eggheads against one". Robert, you can't win them all.'

'This isn't a game! This was someone's life!'

'Robert, you and I have been through hundreds and hundreds of hours of police interviews with serial killers. Forty-three percent of them confess. The others are in complete denial. We had no reason to doubt that Michael Shaw was in the majority.'

'You thought he'd compartmentalised his psyche so he couldn't acknowledge those crimes as his. The reality is he fought for his country and he was damaged by what he was made to do. He's traumatised by it. He's a trained killer, sure, but he's not our killer.'

'No.' Goldberg ran his hand down his face, like a drunk who'd had too much before a family meal.

Out of control.

Out of order.

Wrong.

And he wasn't the one who paid the price.

Liana walked back into the room, clutching her coffee with both hands. Her gaze shot between them. 'You've heard, then?'

Marshall nodded. 'The suicide is on our heads, Liana.'

She frowned. '*Suicide*?'

Goldberg winced. 'Michael Shaw killed himself.'

'Shit.' She looked over at Marshall for confirmation.

He couldn't look at her. 'We were wrong, Liana.'

'*Robert*.' Goldberg glared at Marshall. 'The police arrested him and put him in jail, not us. And DI Bruce basically railroaded me into accepting that Shaw fit the profile. Who am I to argue with the evidence they must have had. Oh, and Liana, who was present, certainly didn't disagree.'

Marshall couldn't believe what he was hearing. 'You're going to stick to that line?'

'Robert. You and I both know that profiling is not an immediate science. We... You, Liana and I, we all needed more time to reflect and process the interview. Never mind the time to recover from such ghastly sights in person.'

'Can't you just admit you were wrong?'

'*I* know we were and I'll take that to my death.' Liana shut her eyes. 'But the reason Bruce called me is they've just discovered another grave. The Shadow Man has struck again.'

CHAPTER EIGHT

W hat a way to spend your birthday...
Marshall snapped his goggles into place and they started misting up straight away.

Down below them, the North Sea bubbled and fizzed, smashing against the cliffs, spraying up like steam from a boiling pan. A giant tanker lay a few miles out. Berwick-upon-Tweed was a faint blur to the south of them.

Across the narrow cycling path was a small wooded area, the only trees for miles on this battered stretch of coastline. The CSI tent hung like a hammock between two of them, preserving what precious little evidence remained and hiding another grisly discovery from view.

'Right, let's go.' Bruce was in no mood to chat, so he just stormed over to it.

Marshall followed behind Liana and Goldberg, his shoulders slumped. Reality, the one thing he wanted to avoid. Especially when the latest data point had exploded in his face.

Marshall stepped into the tent. Empty, save for the four of them and a corpse.

Bruce crouched in front of the shallow grave. 'Same depth as the others.' He waved a hand over the body. 'Amy Croft. Twenty-eight. Worked as an estate agent in Jesmond. And it's the same MO as the others. Well, her throat was slit by a knife rather than by a rope. Just luck we found her. Dog slipped the lead and ran for ages into the woods. Owner followed, the dog was in the grave.'

Liana was crouching alongside him. 'Is he being interviewed?'

'Being hauled over the coals down at HQ. Name is Rufus.'

'I mean the owner.'

'Aye, Rufus Wilson. Dog is called Alun. Wouldn't be the first time a killer just so happened to find a body, would it?'

Marshall was still standing. Something wasn't quite right about this. 'Newcastle to Berwick is a bit of a distance to cycle.'

'Is it?' Bruce looked up at him. 'Seventy miles. Done it myself a few times. Nice run up on a bright day, get the train back to the toon.'

'But this is north of Berwick, though.'

'Aye. Amy told her flatmates she was cycling from Newcastle to Dunbar. Same deal – hundred-mile cycle, LNER train back to Newcastle.' Bruce looked in the direction of the train line a few metres away. The A1 rumbled further over, not far from the Scottish-English border.

Bruce winced. 'Thing is, time of death is wide open. Ten-hour range. But we found a head torch just off the path. Battery's drained, so I'd suggest the attack was late on and it shone all night.'

'Makes sense.' Marshall scanned the vicinity outside. 'If she's a cyclist, where's the bike?'

Bruce pointed out of the tent. 'Sent a diver down. Found it at the bottom. Vitus ZX-1 and then a load of letters I can't remember. Matches the description her flatmates gave. Killer must've hoyed it off the cliff.'

Liana was staring deep into the grave. 'When was she killed?'

'Told you, time of death is wide open.'

'Yes, but you must know which day.'

'Ah, right.' Bruce stood up tall. 'Friday.'

Liana let out a sigh. 'The elephant in the room is that she wasn't killed by Michael Shaw, as Friday was two days after his arrest. He was in remand at HMP Frankland.'

'The Monster Mansion.' Bruce looked away from her. 'This is on me, okay? It was my decision to go to the Chief Crown Prosecutor with the recommendation we charge him. Not you. Either of you. Okay?'

Goldberg couldn't keep still. At least he'd stopped shaking his head, though. But now he was walking around the tiny space, making Marshall feel crowded in. 'You've held back so much detail from the public that nobody could know enough of his MO to copy him. Correct?'

'Course.' Bruce nodded. 'DS Williamson's at the jail, supervising an investigation with the prison service. From what he's told me, I don't think Shaw said anything to anyone in there. Heard a lot, of course, but mostly abuse. But didn't even pass the time of day, let alone minutiae of his alleged MO.'

Goldberg stopped. 'But he could've done?'

'Jacob...' Bruce rested a hand on his shoulder. 'I can see you're in a bad way. Try to deny it all you like, but we've charged an innocent man who killed himself on remand, and now someone else has been murdered. There's no evidence Michael Shaw passed anything on to anyone. I suggest you stop clutching at straws and help us—'

'I'm not clutching at straws!'

'Jacob, it's fine. I get it. You feel guilty for—'

'This isn't on us.' Goldberg jabbed a gloved finger in the air. 'You pressured Liana into—'

'*I* pressured her?'

'You did! You forced her to change my profile to suit the offender!'

Now Bruce was shaking his head. 'Okay, so you're reconciling your doubts by blaming the police. Great.'

'*I* never said Shaw was a match, Jonathan. You always jump to your own conclusions because you lack the ability to reason on your own.'

'Jacob. Mate. There will be some form of inquiry into what happened. Both of us will be good little boys and hold up our hands when the time comes. Okay? But right now, I need your help in finding this killer. Are you up to that?'

Goldberg held his gaze. 'No.'

'What?'

'I can't do this anymore.' Goldberg shifted his focus between the three of them, then let it settle on the dead body lying in the grave. 'I'm putting in a request for retirement.'

CHAPTER NINE

Marshall ended the call and yawned into his fist. He stared out of the window into the darkness. Below, the lights of Durham blurred. Half past four and it was like midnight. He caught a brush of perfume and turned around.

Liana was standing in the doorway, watching him. He'd no idea how long she'd been there. 'You okay there, Rob?'

He walked over to his desk and sat down. 'I'm getting on with the job, Liana. Trying to track down the Shadow Man.' Felt like a task he'd never complete and one he was massively out of his depth in taking on too.

'Rob. It's okay to talk through what's happened. Your mentor – and mine – has left us in the lurch.'

'That's a bit harsh.'

'No, it's not. We're two post-docs who look to him for guidance. He's worked this for thirty-plus years. He's got the experience, while we've just got some second-hand techniques. And he's let us down.'

'Him.'

'Right, him.'

'So, you don't feel at all responsible for what Michael Shaw did to himself?'

'I do, Rob. It's all on me. All of it.' She brushed a tear out of her eye. 'What Bruce said, I made the profile fit the suspect, not the other way around. I was wrong and a man killed himself because of that. A troubled man, who lost his soul serving his country. I'll carry that forever. But all I can focus on is finding the Shadow Man. I see that Goldberg was wrong. We've been approaching this in entirely the wrong way. You're right – we can't do this dispassionately. We need to see the crime scenes. We need to speak to all the people ourselves. We need to work *with* the police, not just guide them.'

Marshall could see a few years of her working out her grief with a therapist. Unpicking all the ways she let the decision to prosecute become confused by Bruce's need to arrest and charge someone.

He should've stood up to her, to them both. Even when he'd been outvoted.

'Rob, is he really going to retire?'

Marshall looked her in the eye. 'The dean just called me. She's going to recommend approving his request.'

'Wow. It'll be quite a difference.'

'We can't focus on him right now, Liana. We need to get on top of this case. An old colleague of Jacob's is coming up from Southwark University. Graham Thorburn. They worked together in the past. He's much more into a deeper collaboration with the police. Embedding us into the investigation.'

'I've met him a few times, Rob.'

'Good. Just for clarity, he was my sort-of stepfather for a few years. He's what got me into this gig in the first place.'

'I wasn't aware.'

Marshall tossed his phone onto the desk. 'Graham's recommending a geographic profile.'

'That goes against what Goldberg would recommend.'

'I know. But I'm in charge until a long-term successor is appointed.'

Those large eyes got a little bit bigger. 'The protégé becomes the master.'

'Liana, I recommended you. Goldberg insisted it was me. Besides, the way we work together, I think we'll have a more collaborative approach. Right?'

'I hope so.' She sat behind her desk. 'I don't know if this is a help or not, but I've been digging into the work the police have done to see if the victim was one of the members of the message board. Their IT guru is still digging into the site's back-ups to get their access logs. The number of IP addresses that access the pages and profiles is finite but they reckon there'll be a few thousand. Minimum.'

'Which is a lot of work.'

'Indeed. A lot can be grouped, but still. Anyone who is hardcore into IT will have workarounds, like a VPN to mask their location... but still, it's manageable, but it'll take time.'

'And Goldberg says the IT side is a fool's errand.'

'It's an errand we'd be fools not to do. Bruce is going to run it all, but it'll take time.' She unlocked her computer. 'Meanwhile, I said we'd test the assumption that the killer is a member of the group.'

'We would? Isn't that a policing activity?'

'Rob, I'm trying to put my feelings about Michael Shaw's death to one side, okay? I just want to lose myself in something constructive for a few hours. Bruce found twenty-five active posters in the group. Four dead before this week. Then Toby Wilder. Now Amy Croft. So there are nineteen alive.'

Marshall walked over and stood behind her. Her screen

was filled with profile pages. He recognised Toby Wilder and Amy Croft in the first six. The others were all potential victims. One of them might be the killer. Might be. 'Have the cops located them?'

'IP numbers are tracked on the board for each post. They've got a warrant to get the names and addresses from the service providers. Bruce's team have interviewed nine since he arrested Michael Shaw. They were trying to track down undiscovered victims.' She swallowed hard. 'He couldn't find Amy Croft.'

'Have you got that data to hand?'

'Nope. He's sending it over.' She went into her email but there was nothing from Bruce. 'Sorry.'

'Not your fault.' Marshall walked over to the wall, where a giant map of the north of England hung. From Lincoln up to the Scottish Borders. 'Give me the death locations. Where they were found and where they were abducted from.'

'It's less than a mile from the running or cycling route in all cases.'

Marshall stuck in a pin in Kielder Water and one north of Berwick. 'Just the locations of the first four then.'

'Morpeth, Wooler, Alnwick and Rothbury.'

Marshall stuck pins in for each one, but it took him a few passes to find Rothbury. 'They're radiating out from Newcastle, away from the city.'

'Getting further each time, right? Berwick and Kielder Water are the furthest two.'

'That could just be coincidence.'

'Explain?'

'He wasn't picking where he was going to abduct them from. He was gleaning that information from their online posts. Just so happened that the last two were furthest away from Newcastle.'

'Okay. What's that given us?'

'Nothing much. But I'd wager he's based in the city or nearby. Have you got victim addresses?'

'Not yet, Rob. Told you Bruce is sending it over.'

'Right, right. Do we have *any* indicators?'

'Their profiles have loose locations. Towns, cities. That level.'

'Read them out.'

'Okay. Ten of them are across Newcastle. Five in Durham, six in Sunderland, one in Alnwick. One in or near Consett and one in Berwick.'

Marshall stuck the last blue pin into Berwick-upon-Tweed. 'That doesn't give us much.' He stared at the map, trying to puzzle it all out. There was something in this, he just knew it.

Then it hit him.

The data source they could access was the same one the Shadow Man had used himself.

'Read out the routes they've done, both cyclists and runners.'

'When they were killed?'

'No. Just ones they've posted. All we've got are six successful kills. There must be failed attempts. Where he bottled it.'

'Okay, but I don't think we can tell that, can we?'

'All the same. Maybe there are locations he's avoiding.'

She unhooked her laptop from the monitor, picked it up and joined him by the board. 'Easier if I do it myself.' She took a purple set of pins and eased them into locations throughout the northeast, including a couple of cross-border ones like Amy Croft's cycle to Dunbar.

Marshall stared at the emerging shape. 'There are a lot of runs down in County Durham but no kills.'

'And Newcastle is the centre of it all.'

Marshall stared at the map as she stuck yet more pins into the board, hoping it'd resolve into something actionable.

A whole lot of nothing.

She stopped, holding a pin in the air. 'Huh.'

'What's up?'

'This.' She rested her laptop down on the bookshelf. Looked like it might topple off at any time. She stuck a pin into the coast just to the east of Newcastle. 'There's one guy who's based in Tynemouth, who's commented on others' routes. Fairly common, but he's never posted his own runs.'

Marshall felt that spike of adrenalin again, stirring in the pit of his stomach. 'We're looking for someone who takes without giving.'

'Correct.'

'What do we know about this guy?'

'Martin Keane. He was interviewed by Bruce's lot on Thursday. Lives alone. Works in a supermarket.'

CHAPTER TEN

Bruce was waiting by the interview room door. The overhead lights were out, leaving the corridor in almost complete darkness, the glow from the obs suite's open door the only light.

Marshall walked up to him. 'Is he here?'

Bruce smiled at Liana. 'Just wanted to wait for the dynamic duo to arrive before we went in. So you can see the fruits of your labour for yourselves.'

'Thanks.' Marshall smiled at him. 'I know Jacob's only just gone, but we want to do this very differently. Not so much active participation in the case, of course, but less passive.'

'That's what I like to hear.' Bruce folded his arms. 'I don't want to belabour the point, but Michael Shaw's death is on both of us, Liana.'

'I know.' She narrowed her eyes. 'I want to help identify who the Shadow Man actually is.'

Bruce thumbed at the interview room door. 'You think it's this guy?'

'I want to find out.'

'I'd offer you to sit in on the interview, but that can't happen, even with your new proactive MO.'

'We're happy to watch.'

'Be my guest.' Bruce slipped into the interview room.

Marshall followed Liana into the obs suite.

By the time they'd turned the volume up, Bruce was deep into questioning Martin Keane.

A thin man in his mid-twenties. Dark hair almost black. Five six, maybe seven. Nine stone, max. Acne scars that gave his face the texture of a golf ball. Thin beard covering his face, patchy like a fourteen-year-old trying to buy beer for a party he's never going to be invited to in the first place. His face was etched with sorrow – the fun was all over and a new game was about to begin.

'Toby Wilder.' Bruce slid a page across the table. 'Josh Kidd.' Another page. 'Amy Croft.' Another. 'Sam Harrington-Coates.' Another. 'Kate Mazzola.' Another. 'Derek Carver.'

Keane took each one, staring at it, then setting it down on the table. Didn't make eye contact. He blew the greasy fringe out of his eyes and looked at them with his soulless eyes. 'What about the others?'

Bruce's forehead twitched. 'What?'

'The, um, the rest of them.'

'Martin, you murdered them. All of them.'

'Yeah, I know. We, um, we all live in the shadows.' Keane paused, squinted at Bruce, wiped his nose and then slowly started to smile. 'But you don't know, do you?'

Bruce got up. 'Martin Keane, I'm arresting you for the—'

Marshall walked over to the door.

'Rob, where are you going?'

'He's playing us.' Marshall pushed out into the corridor, then walked into the interview room without knocking.

'—murder of Amy Croft and the murder of—' Bruce turned

around to Marshall. 'What the hell do you think you're playing at?'

Marshall ignored him, instead focusing on Keane. 'What did you mean by "the others"?'

He wouldn't look at Marshall.

'Come on, Martin. You've just admitted to six murders. Are you saying there are more?'

Keane shrugged.

'I want to help you be understood, Martin. Talk to me. I'll listen. Get it all off your chest.'

Keane looked him up and down, then deep into his eyes. Felt like he was clawing out Marshall's soul. He licked his lips. 'Um, yeah, there are more.' He held up three fingers. The nails were chewed down to the quick. 'Another three victims.'

It hit Marshall like a punch in the gut. 'Where are they?'

Keane sat there, mumbling inaudibly just under his breath. 'Nope... Um, I'm not telling you that. I'm just... not. No thank you.'

'They'll have posted their routes, Martin. We will investigate them. We will find them.'

'Maybe. Or, um, like, maybe not. I don't know. I just think I want to keep them to myself so like, um, people will want to keep me, you know, like, in the light.'

'Why?'

'Why not?'

'Martin, please. You're not getting out of this, okay? You've been arrested for these murders. You've confessed to them. Why these three? Why make their families suffer?'

'No one cared about my suffering.'

'How have you suffered, Martin?'

'You don't get it. You never could.'

'I'm afraid I don't. Come on, Martin. Help me here.'

'Who helped *me*? We all live in the shadows of the one

percent. Billionaires run the whole world. They don't help the other ninety-nine so...'

'You haven't been killing billionaires, Martin. You've been—'

'I've been in everyone's shadow my whole life. I didn't matter to anyone. Until I did. I think that's the part I liked the best.' Keane chewed at his fingernails. 'I was in control and... I just, I *mattered*. It didn't matter if they were richer, smarter, stronger or better looking – I got to win.' He brushed dandruff off his shoulders.

'Please, Martin. Tell us.'

'No. Not today. Ask me another day.'

'Why? You wanted us to know what you'd done. We know now. We know we'll all live in their shadows. But you'll live in infamy.'

'Nope... Maybe a week or two. People forget. I'm forget-table. But if I don't tell, well, then maybe people have to remember.'

CHAPTER ELEVEN

Friday
Four days later

Marshall lifted his hand back, ready to knock, but stopped himself. Force of habit – Goldberg wouldn't be in his old office. Sod it. He still rapped on the scarred wood before walking into the ice-cold room. Just how Goldberg liked it.

'The colder the air, Robert, the quicker the brain.'

Someone was standing by the window.

Bruce turned and lifted his chin, then went back to his staring. 'Never tire of that view, eh?'

'Sometimes you don't notice it. Like when someone's death weighs heavy on you.'

'Cold as hell in here, mind.' Bruce walked over and perched on the edge of Goldberg's desk. No computer but stuffed with books and papers. So many pens and ornate notebooks.

Marshall remembered him trying to inflict some crazy horizontal filing scheme on them – even wrote a paper on it.

He cleared his throat. 'Liana's off sick today. She's been out at the prison for the last three days solid, trying to interview Martin Keane. Trying to get to the bottom of it all. She's not slept. Taking it too hard.'

'Not just her who's not sleeping. I had a long chat with Mr Jameson last night.'

'Mr Jameson?'

'The whiskey.'

'Ah.' Marshall let out a breath into the cold air. 'Self-medicating isn't a great idea.'

'Nope. But it's how I cope.' Bruce glared at him. 'You're not taking this as hard as Liana or I.'

'I try not to. Got to rise above it. Focus on the fact I've done my part in this. Found Martin Keane for you.'

'But you're okay about what happened?'

'No. Of course not, Jon. I'm fucking livid about what you subjected him to. Michael Shaw killed himself because of that. I tried to get you and Liana to see reason. Goldberg overruled me.'

Bruce stared out of the window. Dark sky, thick with clouds. A flock of geese flew south, a plane headed north. 'I'm mortified, Rob. Lost. Embarrassed. Shocked. I don't know how I can ever repay the debt I've incurred.'

'All you can do is try to find these three victims.'

Bruce looked through Marshall, then shut his eyes. 'My guys have tracked down all but three of the regulars on that message board. Alexander Quiller. Stan Di Melo. Caitlyn Westerberg. All live alone. All reported missing at the weekend. All lawyers, junior partners in a firm in the city. Haddaway and Sheidtmann, or something.' He ran a hand down his face. 'Sorry, I shouldn't joke about three murder victims. They all went missing on Saturday. Last sighting was on the A1 heading north from the centre of Newcastle. And we've no idea where they went.'

'How is that possible? *Keane* knew where they were going.'

'Only one had a mobile. Caitlyn. Left it at her flat. According to one of her work colleagues, it was ringing all weekend with work shit, so she turned it off. Could be anywhere.'

'Did any of them post a route?'

'Several in the last six months. We've had dog teams out scouring them all. No dice.'

'Huh.'

'Aye, man.' Bruce slapped a hand to his forehead. 'Only thing we've got from Xtreme Nutters is they were talking about going on a special route. Now, we've been through all of their posts with a view to what could be possible and there's just nothing. Whatever they discussed, it was in private. Maybe face-to-face.'

'But Keane knew.'

'Or he's lying to screw with us.'

'No. He's not a liar. Somehow he knew where they were going. Might be in their emails.'

'But it might be offline.'

'That'd mean he knew them.'

'True. Why is he keeping this information back?'

'You were in the room, Jon. He's doing it for infamy. Thing to remember is he gets off on control. Now, today, tomorrow, always. Preserving the last vestige of control is a powerful motivator, even if he isn't the deepest thinker.'

'So why didn't he speak to us?'

'Because we screwed it up. I screwed up. This is psychological profiling, Jon. If you know the type, you know the motivation, you can develop the interview strategies. Normally, we would've prepared before we went in. Let him talk and tell his tale. Start at the beginning and don't stop until you are done, get it all out. Always be open to other victims, other acts, other circumstances. And let him lead you there. That was the moment he's been waiting for, after all... Maintain control and identify those three. Whereas we lost it. You made assumptions and gave away information. I was rash.'

Bruce nibbled at his bottom lip. 'I'm going to speak to Keane again. I've tried twice now... Once with Liana. Once without. He's just not talking. Like he's not all there or just doesn't understand. Can I ask you to come with me and—'

'I'll think about it.'

Bruce gave him a smile. 'I'll be on my way. Tell Jacob I was asking for him.'

'If I see him, I will.' Marshall stared out of the window, listening to the door close. Down on the Wear, even on a day like this, it was much busier. So many rowers it looked like a motorway from this height. Such a bizarre place, Durham. Right in the middle of the post-industrial northeast and yet it had that tinge of Oxbridge.

The door opened again.

'Forget something?' Marshall swung around.

Not Bruce.

Goldberg. Same suit as he'd worn the last time. Puffy bags under his wild eyes. Even at this distance, he reeked of booze – Bruce wasn't the only one self-medicating. 'Robert.' He didn't say anything else, just went over to a shelf heaving with old textbooks and sifted through them, one by one.

'We caught him.'

'Did you.' Not a question. Still focused on his books.

'We did a geographic profile, which helped narrow it all down. Helped us catch Martin Keane. The data was all there.'

'Well done.'

'If you'd let us do this earlier, Michael Shaw wouldn't have killed himself.'

Goldberg picked up a book and hurled it through the air towards Marshall.

He managed to duck just in time and it battered off the window.

'What the fuck is wrong with you?'

'What's wrong with *me*?' Goldberg was in his face, his whisky breath hissing over Marshall. 'Data is what's wrong.'

'Data?'

'We talk about data. "More than two victims to the same suspected killer and they become crucial data points." All that talk is classic compartmentalisation. I needed to do it to keep my mind free from the guilt of the reality. But when they became real people, I realised I'd lost myself.' He prodded his own sternum. 'I blame myself for his death, Robert. Michael Shaw was a real person.' His head dipped. 'Bruce told me about these other deaths. If we'd caught him earlier, we'd have saved Michael Shaw's life, sure. But also those of three others. Three others they'll never find.'

Marshall didn't know what to say. These were all thoughts he'd had himself. Even though he'd objected to it at the time, Michael Shaw's death still hung heavy on his soul.

Alexander Quiller.

Stan Di Melo.

Caitlyn Westerberg.

Three others who'd torment his sleep for years.

Goldberg picked up the thrown book. 'I built this operation from nothing. Maybe you can make it a force for good.'

'Me?'

'Robert, you can relax. It's all yours. You've won. You're in charge now. You can do it however you like.'

Marshall swallowed and it tasted salty and bitter. 'Jacob, I've quit.'

'What?'

'I followed your lead. When the going got tough, I went to the dean and told her I wanted out. I'm way too young to retire and I'm not on a final salary scheme like you.'

'Robert, that's madness! We built this together!'

'Realised I was Watson to your Holmes. I need to walk a different path. I'm joining the Met.'

'The *police*?' He spat out the words.

Marshall nodded. 'Spoke to our friendly DCI down there and he's approved me as a direct-entry DI. There's a fast-track programme for people with different experiences.'

'Some PC nonsense, no doubt.'

'No, Jacob. Different backgrounds. People like me, who haven't worked their way up from the street, but have an insight others won't.'

'Why are you doing this to me? You were supposed to carry on my legacy, Robert! You're talking absolute codswallop. I know what's best for you. Listen to me – you are capable of doing so much more as an academic!'

'I'm fed up with the passivity. What we do is always one step removed and ten steps behind. This will give me the chance to do the job the right way. Stopping people like Michael Shaw from killing themselves. Catching people like Keane before they've murdered more.'

'Robert, *please*. This is insane! You're my protégé! Your destiny is to take over this department and turn this business into—'

'I never wanted that, Jacob. I don't care about power or control. I just want to do the right thing.'

Goldberg was shaking his head again. 'This won't bring her back.'

'I'll pretend you didn't say that.' Marshall walked towards the door.

Goldberg grabbed at his sleeve. 'Robert, come on! You failed Anna and you keep trying to—'

'I failed her?' Marshall brushed him off. 'Fuck you. I thought you were trying to help me but you're just a small-minded, petty wee bigot with narcissistic tendencies. There's nothing you or anyone can say that'll make me change my mind.' He stepped through the door and strode off down the corridor.

Away from Jacob Goldberg's world.

His ego trip.

His power.

His control.

He was free now.

PART TWO
OUT OF THE GROUND

CHAPTER TWELVE
TEN YEARS LATER

Marshall weaved out of traffic on the A72 towards Peebles, shifting gears and crunching the accelerator like an F1 driver. Or his idea of one.

The Tweed was low, despite the overnight rain, but still had a monster of a current. The river was Scotland's Nile, so many wee settlements on its banks, old mill towns the Borders rail now enabled to be Edinburgh commuter towns.

The old train line wound its way along the banks towards Peebles. Nobody talked about reopening it, but it would certainly be a lifesaver to some. Like his sister. Or Marshall that morning.

This section was an open expanse, a few miles across, wedged between big hills like brackets around a complex equation.

'Uncle Rob!' Thea grabbed the handle over the door. The interior smelled of her rose perfume. She wore her Peebles High uniform like a badge of honour. 'Maybe take it a wee bit—'

Despite the bend, the bus just past it, the rock face on the right and the Tweed on the left, Marshall blasted past a Ford, hitting seventy, then sped up for the straight towards Cardrona. A Hyundai shot towards them, flashing its lights. Marshall slalomed back onto their side of the road. 'I have done advanced driver training.'

'I haven't done advanced passenger training, though.'

Marshall laughed. 'How are you doing, Thea?'

'Me? I'm fine. Why? Has Mum said I'm not?'

'No, it's just... What happened to you in the summer. You don't talk about it.'

'Nope.'

'Is that a no to your uncle Rob or—'

'No to anyone.' She brushed her hand through her hair, fanning it out.

'Thea, that's a big concern to me. If you're struggling to—'

'I'm not.'

'Thea, it's okay to admit weakness. Me, your mum, your granny, we all suffered in the same—'

'I said I'm fine. God! Can't I actually just be fine? Would that be a tragedy? I confronted him, turned the tables. That's it. What is it with your generation and overthinking things?'

'My generation?' Marshall had to slow behind a towed horse box, stuck in his lane by traffic hammering in from the Peebles direction. Thumbs dancing on the wheel. Past her, out of the window, two fishermen stood waist-high in the river at this early hour.

Maybe she was right. His generation hid stuff, judged themselves against a set of metrics nobody could measure up to. Kids nowadays, it was all text and nothing was subtext. Everything was shown. And besides, she'd had therapy for it.

'Are you enjoying being back at your old school?'

She nodded.

'It'll be easier for your mum when you move house, right?'

'Wish I was moving back here.' She waved at the sign up ahead.

Marshall took the left for Cardrona, past the hulking hotel that looked like a prison, just without the barbed wire and the watchtowers. 'You're not feeling Clovenfords, are you?'

'Nothing against the place, but my pals are here. Peebles and Innerleithen. Being over at Granny's in Melrose has been a nightmare. Two buses just to get to my pals' houses.'

'I know the pain of just one bus.'

She laughed.

They passed the old train station, now a café surrounded by new flats that had sprung up recently. 'Still, your sucker of an uncle giving you a lift before his shift starts saves a lot of time.'

'Aye, but it's just to Dad's.' She scowled at him. 'Least I can get the bus in from here.'

Marshall pulled up outside a fancy new-build house. Looked expensive, doubly so given it wasn't jammed in next to the neighbours. A big garden, marked off by a six-foot fence. 'Here you go. Back in civilisation.'

'Hardly.' She shrugged. Didn't seem to want to get out of the car.

'You okay there?'

A frown danced across her forehead. 'I hate being here.'

'It's not that bad.' Marshall swept his gaze around the steep hills surrounding the valley. 'Lots of activities. Mountain biking. Running.'

She looked down into the footwell. 'Aye.'

'Look, if it's about your father, I can drop you in Peebles.'

She looked around at him, fire burning in her eyes. 'I came back from school early one day. Skipped the last class, which was a study period. And I caught Da— my *father* cheating on Mum with some floozy from work. In *our* hot tub.'

Jesus.

It was way messier than Marshall imagined. And his sister hadn't told him. His twin sister. Aye, there was a lot of water under that bridge and not much of it had been discussed. 'That's tough, Thea. Sorry. I didn't know.'

'Pre-pandemic. In our hot tub!'

'I'm sorry you saw that, Thea.'

'Right.' She let out a deep sigh. 'He's still seeing this floozy – that's what Mum calls her. Mum's having a get together in Taylor's tonight. She'll get drunk like a teenager. You saw what she was like at your joint birthday.' Three bottles of wine for the table and only two people drinking. 'They're both acting like kids.'

'They maybe need to blow off some steam.'

'I don't get it. But, like, I don't drink. Do you?'

'It's been known to happen, aye.'

'Are *you* going to Mum's thing?'

'I've been invited. To be honest, I'm nervous about it. First big social event in years in the town. I could blow it off, saying I've got work.'

'I can accompany you.'

Marshall smiled. 'Sounds good. How about I pick you up tonight after work? Take you to the party?'

'Sounds good.' She smiled at him and got out. 'Have a great day, Uncle Rob.'

'Rob's fine.' Marshall joined her on the street, just to watch her go. One of those developments where they didn't let you mark out your front garden with a fence, just wanted them all to blend together. Loud music blasted out of speakers – early Coldplay. Smoke and charring meat.

Thea was already charging up the path towards the front door.

God, in some ways she felt like his own kid. And he felt

guilty for his own personal bullshit getting in the way of spending time with his only niece.

She stormed over to the side gate and tore it open. 'Dad!'

Through the slats, Marshall could see Paul Armstrong standing at an Australian barbecue big enough to feed the whole county. Not exactly dressed for the weather – black shorts and a lemon-yellow shirt under a grey hoodie. Chin covered in a thick goatee, smart hair trimmed to perfection, but that widow's peak was straight out of casting for a vampire. He set off Marshall's creep radar again, just like he did all those years ago, which had put a schism between him and his sister when he warned her.

He'd learnt never to warn her.

And *definitely* never to say I told you so.

Paul looked at his daughter, squinting with the glassy look of the severely hungover. 'Oh, hey.' He sipped from his coffee mug.

Thea stopped far enough away from him that he couldn't kiss her or ruffle her hair like she was a snotty toddler. Couldn't even hug her. 'You were supposed to collect me last night, Dad, but you just wanted to get drunk with your mates. Didn't you?'

'Thea. Listen. I called your mother and told her I couldn't do it.' Paul rolled his eyes, then got out his phone. 'Lunchtime yesterday. My darling ex-wife texted me a volley of abuse back.' He dropped his phone on the grass and took three goes to pick up.

Forget about being hungover – he was still pissed.

'Charming.' Thea looked over at Marshall, then at Paul. Her fierce exterior had given way to the vulnerable side.

Marshall didn't know why he was still here, but Thea needed someone on her side. And as her parents were playing games – and her gran was lost to her own personal grief – he was happy it was him for once.

And she looked like she needed someone to drive her to school.

Great.

Paul flipped over something on the grill. 'Barbecuing some bacon for you, love.'

'I'm vegan, Dad.'

'Oh. Shite, yeah.' He chuckled. 'It's lovely stuff, though.'

'If it came from a pig...' Thea snorted. 'Dad, I need to get to school.'

'Keep your hair on. It's vegan bacon. And I'll take you to school after this.'

'Are you sober enough to take me?'

'Got a cab coming.'

'A taxi?'

'Aye. Bloke owes me a favour. I mean, I own the company, so...'

Marshall's mobile rang. He checked the display.

DI Jon Bruce calling...

Bloody hell.

Marshall stepped away and got in his car. 'It's been a while, Jonathan.'

'Morning, Rob. Call me Jon.' A deep sigh. 'Thanks for taking my call. Heard you're in the Met as a cop.'

'I told you that ten years ago.'

'You did, but I didn't think you'd actually stick it.'

'Charming.'

'When I said you'd make a good cop, I didn't mean it.'

'Oh, I'm not a good one. But I'm a different one.'

'Right, right. Your old boss says you're based up in Scotland?'

'That's right. Been a while. Must get some lunch together sometime.'

'Mm. Sounds good.' Bruce paused.

Through the slats, Thea was eating something, hands covering her mouth.

Bruce cleared his throat. 'No easy way to say this, Rob, but the Shadow Man has requested to speak to you.'

'To me?'

'That's right.'

Marshall felt like he'd been slugged in the stomach. 'Are those bodies still—'

'Still unaccounted for. Probably more like three piles of bones after ten years, mind.'

Marshall paused this time. He wasn't going to offer any help. He got in the car and nudged the door shut.

'Rob, his silk called me up, out of the blue. Asked me to see him, so I sat with him for a few minutes in the prison. He insists whatever he's got to say, it's for your ears only.'

'I want nothing to do with him.'

Another deep sigh. 'I knew that would be the case, Rob.'

Marshall leaned back and stared up at the car's roof. A silvery hair was stuck to the fabric. He tore it off. It was dark at both ends, but silver in the middle. 'I mean it. Absolutely no way.'

'Come on, man. This might be—'

'That bastard isn't going to confess. He's a control freak. This is just him toying with us. With you. With me. The answer's no, Jon. And it'll stay that way.'

CHAPTER THIRTEEN

S elkirk was like Edinburgh's Old Town in miniature. Perched on a hill overlooking a few miles of surrounding countryside until other hills blocked it. The Southern Uplands, as imposing as the Highlands hundreds of miles north.

DS Rakesh Siyal was behind the wheel. The big sod looked as nervous as ever – the last few months under Marshall's wing hadn't done him enough good.

The A7 was a steady climb up to the centre of Selkirk but their target was in the narrow plain by the Ettrick, where Victorian mills had sprung up to take advantage of the Tweed tributary and send wool outwards to the country and the empire. The first couple of mills they passed were all converted into office buildings. One was a distillery.

Idiot.

It was a weaver – still doing the ancient trade, selling tartans and fabrics worldwide.

The last one was two lower buildings joined in a T. Three storeys, unlike the seven and eight of the bigger ones. Looked to be twentieth century as well. Smashed windows and graffiti showed it hadn't been converted into anything since the trade shifted elsewhere.

Still, there were lights on in parts of it.

And sounds.

Siyal pulled up, indicating to the right, and swivelled around. 'Why are you in such a bad mood, boss?'

'No reason.'

'Sure?'

'Sure.'

'Fair enough.' Siyal pulled up driver-to-driver with another car and wound down his window.

Marshall heard the din of a local band making a mess of 'Panic' by The Smiths. Must be renting the rooms out to kids or adults who should know better. Eight o'clock was way too early for that kind of noise. Not that there were any houses nearby to complain about the racket. He looked across Siyal and smiled. 'How's it going?'

Acting DS Jolene Archer was behind the wheel, her blonde hair catching in the early light. Wouldn't even glance over at them. 'Just another manic Monday...'

'Wish it was bloody Sunday.' DI Andrea Elliot was in the passenger seat, jabbing a finger off her phone screen. She was like a craft vodka made from potato and hatred. Her fringe hung a bit lower than Marshall remembered, but then he hadn't seen her in a while. The one time Marshall had tried to see her after she'd been released from hospital, she'd refused. 'Last time we were here, Shunty thought the place down the road was a distillery.'

'I thought the same, Rakesh.' Marshall grinned but Siyal didn't notice. 'No distilleries down this way.'

'Bollocks.' Elliot shifted herself around and winced. 'My bloody stitches.'

'You okay there?'

'What do you think? Some twat slotted me in the guts. Worse than my last caesarean. First day back and it feels like it's just happened again.' Elliot shut her eyes and took a breath. 'And you're talking rubbish. There's a distillery down in Hawick. Very good it is too. And there's Dunpender up by North Berwick, though a colleague investigated a murder there a few years back.' She winced again. 'Still, Shunty's clueless when it comes to what's most likely to be around here. Wool! Shitloads of it!'

Siyal dipped his head. 'You don't need to keep going on about it.'

'Aye, I do.' Elliot sat back. 'Only way you'll learn.'

'First day back, though.' Marshall smiled at her. 'How's it feel?'

'Shite. Just finding out how desperately you've been trying to take my job.' The sort of smile that let that kind of barb seem like a joke even though they both knew it wasn't. Now Marshall was permanently based in the Borders, Elliot saw him as a threat to her goal of taking their boss's job. 'Don't get too comfortable, Marshall.'

'Oh, I'm not. Relieved I can hand this case back to you.'

'Not that you've made much progress in three months.' She faced the front, arms folded. 'When I was forced off on the sick, we were staking out this place morning, noon and night. Now I'm back and we're staking it out two hours a day. Have you got anything to show for it?'

'Not much, no.'

'We do, actually.' Siyal pointed at the building. 'The old mill is getting done up as offices. Local bands currently use it as rehearsal space. The craft brewery are moving into some of those new units by the dump.' He looked around at Elliot. 'And that's where your old pals in the Edinburgh drugs squad have been helpful. The brewery gets cocaine and heroin in the shipment of cascade and galaxy hops from North America.'

'Shame they're bad lads.' Elliot laughed. 'My husband's big into their IPA. It's magnificent.'

Marshall laughed. 'Probably tinged with a bit of coke.'

She scowled at him. 'That's not funny.'

He couldn't help himself – the laugh became louder. 'Why are we here, Andrea?'

'Wanted to see this for myself.'

'We could've done this at the station.'

She nibbled at her fingernail. 'Trying to avoid Melrose.'

There it was – the place where she'd been attacked. Her belly sliced open and left for dead.

Marshall clapped his hands together. 'Given I'm here for no apparent reason, I'll get back to base and on with my—'

'Not so fast, Marshall. You're another skull on the dunt.'

He frowned. 'You're going in?'

'Somebody's got to. Pringle gave me approval to raid once the delivery turns up.'

'Just you two?'

'No, you clown. Us four and the twenty officers waiting around the corner.'

Marshall hadn't seen anyone on the way in. 'Look, I'm not sure that's—'

'Not your choice, Marshall. I'm back, back, back.'

'Andrea. I don't agree with this.'

'Listen to me, Professor Plums. You've been sitting on your arse, scratching those bollocks of yours while that lot have been shifting smack and coke. We're going in today and we're stopping this. Right now.'

Marshall held her gaze. 'DS Siyal's my resource. Same with his team.'

'Taking your ball away, aye?' Elliot laughed. 'Order from

Pringle in an email last night. Su casa, mi casa.' *Your house is my house.* 'You've got Jolene, I've got Shunty. We should swap over now.'

'Andrea, this hasn't come to—'

'I don't care.' Elliot leaned forward, sucking in a deep breath. 'Bastard stitches!' She turned away from Marshall.

'It's been four months?'

'Aye, still bloody hurts.'

'Should you be back?'

She was focusing on a delivery truck pulling into the brewery's car park.

Skinner Rapid
Door2Door, Fixed!

A big lump slid out of the driver's side, carrying a clipboard while TalkSport blared out of the cab.

Oh no – it was Gavin Fraser.

Marshall looked over at Elliot. 'Andrea, he's wanted for—'

Fraser clocked Marshall. That slow narrowing of the eyes. The slowing of his gait. 'Son of a sow.' His clipboard went flying and he tore across the car park.

'Get him!' Marshall got out of the car and chased after him, his heavy feet digging into the pavement and using all that experience in running he'd picked up over the years. Breathing, driving forward, roll your feet from the back to the front.

Despite all that, Fraser was getting away.

Siyal gunned his engine and shot past Marshall.

And past Fraser.

A wing mirror rolled along the ground past Marshall's feet.

Siyal skidded to a halt and blocked the road.

Fraser managed to stop just before he crashed into the hood. He turned and rushed back, heading towards Marshall.

Behind him, Siyal reversed back.

Into a Volvo. A crunch and a smash. Then forward, into a Vauxhall.

Shite.

Fraser feigned left, then burst to his right.

Marshall lurched to his own left, but all he caught was a shoulder to his shoulder. He spun around and went down. In time to see Fraser run into Elliot's baton.

And hit the cobbles.

Marshall stood up and dusted himself off. Surprised his trousers weren't ripped.

Elliot was folding her baton away. 'Want to tell me who I've just brained?'

Marshall walked over to them. 'Gavin Fraser, I'm arresting you for the sexual assault of Shona McAllister.'

CHAPTER FOURTEEN

Marshall was driving – no way was he going to let Siyal do any more to this car. 'You're making it very difficult for the "Shunty" nickname to fade away.'

Siyal was in the passenger seat, watching the countryside whizz past, that stretch between Borders General Hospital and the roundabout on the road between Galashiels and Selkirk. Most other places, this would be heavily built up, but here it was still fields. Some horses frolicking in a pasture. 'First day on the job, I lost control of a car on the ice. Bloody nightmare. Ever since we met, I've tried to listen to your advice and I've tried to own the name so they'll stop using it.'

'There's owning it and there's trashing another car.'

'Come on, I only took out three wing mirrors there.'

'One of them was DI Elliot's. And you crunched into two cars.'

'I inspected the damage myself. Three wing mirrors. That's it.'

'Rakesh, I've been a cop almost ten years and you know how many wing mirrors I've taken out?'

Siyal didn't say anything.

Marshall drove on towards Melrose, cutting down the back of Tweedbank, then he took the scenic route in silence, passing a house on the left that might've been two old wrecks when he was growing up. Now it was all shiny and new with a perfect pebble garden. All order, no chaos.

A council worker on a ride-on whizzed across the rugby pitch over the road, standing up like he was on a motorbike heading across the plains of North America.

'Rakesh, I'll speak to DCI Pringle about this reallocation, okay? You go and do your advanced driver training... Actually, how do they square that with what you've done today?'

'I'll mention it to them.'

'Make sure you do.' Marshall eased through the town, the hulking masses of two of the Eildons peaks visible through the thin woods, then past the turning for Darnick and around the bend for the long entrance into the town.

The church on the corner was gone, demolished in two days a month ago. Where Elliot sustained her injury. Marshall was relieved he didn't have to see it every time he drove in this way, especially with what happened inside.

He pulled up outside the rugby stadium, then took the right and parked in what passed for a station car park, just a row of spaces on the edge of the road near the park. 'Good luck with the training.'

'Thanks, Rob.' Siyal got out and grabbed his rucksack out of the footwell. No idea what he kept in there but it looked bloody heavy. He wrapped it over both arms and scuttled off inside like a snail carrying its house on its back.

Marshall spotted DCI Jim Pringle eyeing him and took his time getting out. 'Morning, sir.'

'Mr Marshall.' Pringle charged over, hand thrust out. 'Congratulations on the arrest of our wee friend there. One less statistic on my,' he whistled, 'whiteboard. Not to mention DI Elliot being able to serve that warrant on the brewery. Sooner we get all twenty supporting officers back on the street, though, the better.' He twisted his lips. 'But you did manage to make a complete dog's bollocks of that obbo.'

'That wasn't my fault, sir.'

'Aye, sure. I believe you. Thousands wouldn't. The only reason we were there was to catch them in the act of delivering a ton of Class A drugs. DI Elliot wanted to wait until we knew we had a handover of the naughty stuff, but you—'

'I spooked him, sir. He saw me and he ran. But the important thing is we've got him for the—'

'Big deal. One rape set against a strategic drug operation.'

'Believe me, I'd rather be taking down strategic drug operations as well as arresting rapists, but Shona McAllister will get justice for what happened to her.'

'Tell that to all the people overdosing in Glasgow and Edinburgh tonight. Just hope the drugs were actually there.' Pringle held his gaze for a few long seconds. 'You haven't replied to my email, so let me refresh your non-existent. Now Andrea's back, I'm splitting the team up. You're going to be working with Jolene Archer and her three. DI Elliot will work with DS Siyal again.'

'I'm not sure that's a great idea, sir.'

Pringle was smirking. 'Talk to the hand, Marshall.'

'This isn't the way to do things.'

'It's the way I do things down here. Besides, there's someone to see you. In the canteen.'

'Okay. Well, if you don't mind, I'll speak to you afterwards. This isn't over.'

'No, it very much is. Adios.' Pringle crossed the road to his old BMW and got in. It disappeared in a belch of exhaust.

Marshall locked his car and entered the building. He'd figure out how to get his way.

The front desk was empty, which let him get into the station proper without much hassle from Elliot's husband.

Calling it a canteen was glorifying it. A kettle and a coffee filter next to a broken tap and a petrol-station beer fridge containing many pots of curdling milk.

A woman was scowling at the coffee maker like it was going to explode. Liana Curtis. She looked around at Marshall, those manga eyes even bigger in her chunky-framed glasses. Her tasteful bobbed hair framed her face and plumped up her cheeks. She had a lightness to her, a wide smile and a knowing look in those eyes. 'Hey, Rob.'

Jesus. She... She was stunning.

Marshall's heart was thudding just from seeing her. 'Oh. Hey.' When they'd worked together, he'd been in deep freeze, but now he'd thawed... He grinned at her. 'Listen. The coffee here isn't quite the Delly Grind.'

'I doubt it's even Northumbria HQ.'

'No, well quite.' Marshall stood there, unsure what to do. Unable to even think. 'Is this anything to do with Jon Bruce calling me out of the blue?'

'Heard you were a cop now. I mean, I know you told me that's what you were going to do, but nobody thought you'd get in or be able to stick the course.'

'Charming.'

'Sorry.' She wrapped him in a hug. He tasted her clean perfume, like it was from some tropical beach. 'But you just upped and left, Rob. Went to London. I've missed you.'

'Missed you too, but I did what I had to. After what happened, I couldn't bear to be around that part of England anymore. London was...' Marshall looked away. 'Different. Like another country in so many ways.'

'I get it. Been down myself for a few cases.' She curled up her lips. 'I spoke to your old boss. Tina Rickards. She told me about that case you were working, but she said you had someone else for the profiling. Wasn't you, was it?'

'Me? God no. Well. A bit. I helped. Did some stuff.' Marshall couldn't help but smile. 'Some geographic profiling helped. I still don't know why Jacob had such a downer on it.'

'Oh, I do. It's to do with technology. Long story, as you'd say.' She reached into the cupboard and pulled out a mug, then clattered it onto the worktop. 'Anyway, the reason I'm here is I'm still Professor of Criminology at Durham. Managed to turn Goldberg's side line into a decent-sized business. Consulted for eight police forces across England.'

'Congratulations. Knew you would.'

She shrugged. 'Listen, Bruce said he called you and—'

'The answer's no. I told him that.'

'Come on, Rob. Please. Speak to the Shadow Man.'

'I've moved on, Liana.'

'Okay, but I'm sure you can still dip your toes back into the old water.'

That stark difference between his old world and the new one.

Criminal profiling versus a sexual assault in Galashiels.

Complex, multi-victim, multi-location crimes with opaque MOs.

Simple domestic situations.

'Liana, I'm sure he wants to speak with today's organ grinder, not yesterday's monkey.'

'Rob, please.'

'Come on. You're the one grinding the barrel these days. I'm sure he'd much rather speak to you.'

'I've been in there with him. Every year over the last ten. On Friday, he talked for the first time. Insisted on speaking to you. And only you.'

'Bruce only called me this morning.'

'I know. We took a while tracking you down. Bruce joked you'd changed your mobile number to avoid this exact situation.'

'Why not get Goldberg to do it?'

'Because... Goldberg's... He *will not* talk to the Shadow Man.'

'I can imagine that.'

'It has to be you, Rob. I tried over the weekend but he is resolute. You're the only one he'll speak to. The one whose work led the police to him.'

Marshall reached into the cupboard and picked out his favourite mug, the chipped, over-sized black one with Deadpool on the front. He filled it with burnt filter coffee and didn't even want to see what kind of yoghurt passed for milk in that fridge, so just took it black. 'Like I told Bruce, no.'

'Come on, Rob. This could be our chance to get closure over what happened. You owe it to—'

He slammed the mug down on the counter. 'That wasn't on me, Liana. I tried to get you to listen to me, but I failed. You said your piece and Bruce charged him. Not me. Nothing to do with me.'

'Rob...' Liana pleaded at him with those big eyes. 'If not for that, then do it for the family of those three victims. Alexander Quiller. Stan Di Melo. Caitlyn Westerberg. Help them achieve closure.'

'If you think he'll give up the locations of those bodies, then—'

'I do. Rob, I do.'

'Why?'

'Because he's said he would. He's not a liar, Rob. Now is the time – he wants to confess. But only to you.'

'But why now, after so many years?'

'Who knows, but he's never offered before.'

'You believe him?'

'I do.'

Marshall took a drink of the lukewarm coffee that tasted like tar. 'Still at the Monster Mansion?'

She nodded. 'HMP Frankland.'

Marshall tipped his coffee down the sink. 'I really don't want to do this.'

'I guessed as much. That's why I spoke to your boss. If you don't come with me, he'll order you to.'

CHAPTER FIFTEEN

His Majesty's Prison.

It was going to take Marshall a while to get used to that. At least he didn't have to deal with King's Counsels up in rural Scotland.

HMP Frankland was in the liminal space between Newcastle and Durham, nestled in the countryside just north of the smaller city. Opposite, a blue tractor ploughed a great open field, at odds with the massive car park and the high walls of the prison.

The last place he wanted to be but everyone wanted him in there.

Marshall followed the road around and spotted Liana's car at the raised gate. Her hand appeared out of her open window and waved him in. He set off through the gate, expecting it to crash down on the roof, but no – he got through. He parked alongside her and got out.

The air was on fire with the stink of fertiliser – any poor souls on courtyard exercise behind those walls would have to endure that on top of everything else. Not that there were many inside the Monster Mansion.

Liana was on a call inside her car. She clocked Marshall staring at her, then ended the call and got out. Gloves, coat, hat. She was tiny compared to him and he just had a shirt and suit jacket on – he'd sweat in a walk-in freezer. Only a defence against the harsh weather around here if you were from even further north. And she was looking him up and down. 'You're looking well.'

'I reckon I look like I died a few years ago only for someone to resurrect me as a zombie but thank you. You haven't aged a day.'

'Bollocks.' She tugged at her hair. 'This is all dyed. Should see my roots.' She set off towards the prison. 'Our old stomping ground, Rob.'

'I interviewed a lot of people in there, with and without Goldberg. With you a few times. Even once as a Met cop.'

She glanced over at him. 'You didn't let me know you were in the area.'

'No.' Marshall stopped in the cold. 'Sorry. I...'

She placed a hand on his arm. 'I get it, Rob. It was a tough time for all of us.'

'Reason I'm a cop now, Liana. From what I hear, you've gone from strength to strength. You always were much better than me.'

'Charmer.'

'I'm a fair judge, Liana.'

'Bruce's already inside, so shall we...?' She started walking over, shivering. 'Bit of a surprise when I heard you're up in Scotland. Back home, right?'

'Right. Some stuff happened down in London.'

'What kind of stuff?'

'People died. I blamed myself. You know how it is.'

'I do.' She tilted her head to look up at the bright blue autumn sky. 'Heard you'd quit the police, though.'

'I had. I'd put my papers in, aye. Had no idea what I was going to do with myself. Count penguins in Antarctica or something. But a case came up back home. Ended up...' Marshall looked at Liana, at those giant eyes. 'Let's just say I'm in a much better place now. Reconnecting with my family. Boss is a bit of an oddball, but I even do a bit of profiling for them, as well as leading a team of detectives.' He held the front door for her but didn't enter. 'I've thought about it all the way here.'

'It?'

'Keane.' He let the door swing shut again. 'How you've been in once a year to speak to him but he just stonewalls you. I still don't get why he wants to speak to me. It just seems bizarre.'

'Rob, we deal with serial offenders. Or you used to. And you've done so in the police too. Bizarre is bread and butter to someone like the Shadow Man.'

'Please, can we just call him by his name?'

'Fine.'

'I've been replaying my profile of Keane. All the times I watched him being interviewed while I served out my notice. All the help I gave Bruce and his team. The Keane I saw would've insisted on tormenting Goldberg or yourself. Even Bruce. Why does he want me?'

'Rob. Don't you think that maybe it's because you were the one he opened up to? You listened to him. Someone like Martin Keane has a very tight logical circuit in his head. Immaculate. It processes everything efficiently, perfectly. But it's dependent on the input being sound. He shoves some absolute bullshit in and... You know that phrase – garbage in, garbage out. He thinks he's doing the right thing here. Everything makes perfect sense to him because his worldview is so skewed.'

'See your point.'

'Good.' She pulled her glasses away from her face and rubbed at her eyes. 'Every time I sat there with him, he tormented me about what happened to Michael Shaw. Despite all the therapy I've undertaken over the years, despite the inquest clearing us, despite being ten years older and having met people even worse than him... It still got to me. The reason I do this job – why I keep on doing it – is to make it up to Michael Shaw and others like him. I'm just trying to be the best criminal profiler I can be. Solve all the serial murder cases before they get to that stage. Probably a similar reason as you being a cop now.'

'More or less.'

She was staring hard at him. 'But I'm wise enough now to recognise I've got all this professional jealousy about him insisting on you. All those hours I put in over the years trying to build rapport with someone who murdered nine people... and he won't give me the time of day, other than to torment me.'

'The long drive down here let me develop some interview strategies to draw the information out of Keane. Unlike the past where Goldberg was there independent of the police, and Bruce neither wanted nor needed any interference from us, I know now that the profiling role extends well beyond catching the perpetrator. Keane is all about power reassurance. The only way he feels potent is when he is in control and making others suffer. Keane can't have a lick of control over me. I have to walk in there totally indifferent to him and be prepared to walk out at any point. You need to be okay with that.'

'Wish I had your confidence.' She pushed the glasses back up her nose then gripped his forearms with her gloved hands. 'Just play the game. See what he says. If he gives up the locations of those victims, then all of our debts will start to be repaid.'

He stared deep into her eyes. 'I'll play a game, but I'm playing mine, not his. Not yours. Not Jacob Goldberg's. Mine.'

'That's all I ask, Rob. Just get him talking.'

CHAPTER SIXTEEN

The interview room in Frankland was a tiny space, smaller than you'd find in any police station.

A table that must've touched hands belonging to the murderers of hundreds of people. Somehow the surface was mostly intact, just a few scars near the edges. Most people Marshall had interviewed had just sat there, stock still.

Three cameras in there. Two guards would be watching outside and Liana would be in the observation suite, swearing and sweating over it.

DI Jon Bruce was next to Marshall. Older, greyer but maybe not wiser. His fighting suit was a better quality than he used to wear – Markies machine wash rather than Asda or Tesco.

Martin Keane hadn't aged a day in the past decade, at least not in his face. Those same vicious eyes, soulless and lacking any spark, as if the pilot light went out in them many years before and no one thought to ignite it. Hard to picture him lost to the throes of his overkill, but that was probably the cost of his current serenity. He'd relive those moments of savage abandon at will. Those brutal memories seemed to be enough.

Or was it the torment he'd put the families of the undiscovered corpses through? Was that more satisfying than the murders themselves? Physical torture was less than the mental anguish of devouring someone's soul while they were still alive.

The institutional food and access to weights had added some pounds of muscle, but he had to look the part to gain respect as a killer.

His lawyer was familiar from much more recent times. Mark Davidson was so goblin-like he belonged down a mine, trying to steal gold from a dwarven king.

Marshall focused on him first. 'You work for an Edinburgh-based firm, correct?'

'Headquartered on Charlotte Square, correct.' Davidson smiled, showing the rotten teeth of an original Seventies punk. 'My firm also has offices in Newcastle and Carlisle. Not many work cross-border these days, but I'm a specialist in both Scots and English law. Spend two days a week on average in the northeast. A day a month in Carlisle.' He tilted his head back. 'And I know what you're thinking. We did meet. Back in July. In Scotland.'

'That clears that up.' Marshall focused on Keane, eager to get on with the main event here now he'd shown him he wasn't the most important person in the room. 'Here I am, Martin.'

Always call him by his first name to assert dominance.

Keane picked something from between his teeth, then inspected it and put it back in his mouth. 'I thought you'd look older.'

'Older?'

'Like in my mind. Haven't aged much.'

'Been thinking about me then. Why?'

Keane dug a pinkie in his ear, regarded the yellow gunk

then wiped it on his trousers. He shrugged without looking at Marshall. 'There's a lot of stuff in my mind.'

'Hell of a build-up, eh?' Bruce was sitting there, arms folded. 'Like in that film, *Heat*. Al Pacino and Robert de Niro spent their whole careers not being on screen together. They were both in *The Godfather Part II*, but Pacino played Brando's character as a young man.'

Marshall frowned at him. 'De Niro did.'

'Eh?'

'De Niro played a young Vito Corleone in those flashbacks. Pacino played Michael, his son, in all three films.'

'Well, well, well. Don't really consider the third to be a proper entry in the series. Nor does Coppola. He re-released it under a new title. Something like *Godfather Coda. The Death of Michael Corleone.*'

'Quite the film buff, eh?'

Bruce nodded. 'My dad was.'

Marshall twisted around, waiting until Bruce turned to flash a wink with the eye facing away from Davidson and Keane. 'Get out of here.'

'Eh?'

'I told you outside about not taking this seriously. I'm not having this in my interview, especially with all the incompetence you've demonstrated so far.' Marshall pointed at the door. 'Go.'

'I'm not leav—'

'Go!' Marshall sat there, listening to his shout echoing around the room. Then to Bruce getting up and leaving. He waited for the door to click, then finally turned back to face Keane. 'Okay, Martin. Let's take this seriously.'

Keane laughed. 'Right.'

The ploy seemed to work and Keane now knew Marshall was boss.

If a killer was going to give something up, it would be one-on-one. Marshall didn't want Bruce interrupting any of the themes or ploys he was working, though he didn't know how he could remove the lawyer from the equation.

The unblinking eye – or three – of the video camera was enough for corroboration, so why have someone like Jon Bruce muck it up?

'Okay, Martin. I've driven for two hours just to sit here with you. So, what's so important you're only going to speak to me?'

Davidson cleared his throat. 'As you know, my client is trying to be good.'

'Mr Davidson, your client's inside for six life sentences. Unless he's immortal or just very long-lived, he's not getting out of here. No way in hell, no matter what he says. No matter what he tells us. There's no deal on the table.'

'I don't need a deal.' Keane picked his teeth, dislodged something unidentified and flicked it into the corner. He cast his eyes around the room, then stared up at the camera mounted above the door. 'I like it here. Food's good and I've got time to work out and to read. If I got out, I'm back to being a nobody again. Or I'm dead.' He brushed his fringe out of his eyes and stared directly at Marshall. 'In here, I matter.'

Marshall knew that truth too. On the outside, Keane was a shelf-stacker, but in prison, murderers were at the top of the food chain. Serial murderers were the top of the top, the apex predators. Martin Keane had nine kills to his name – the only people with more in England were dead. He was the top dog in any prison in the nation.

'Fascinating, Martin, but you're wasting my time here.' Marshall scraped his chair back and stood up. 'You're nothing to me.'

'Wait.' Keane pointed at the empty chair.

Marshall stayed standing. Keane was used to being the top

dog. He wouldn't see many people on a daily basis – guards, other prisoners – but they'd all do his bidding. Well, he'd just met someone who wasn't going to bend so easily. 'Say please, or I walk.'

Keane glared at him, fire burning in his eyes. Marshall saw the rage in there and, for the first time, the face of the monster nine people met in their last hour on earth.

Marshall wondered if he'd overplayed his hand. But he needed to restore the power imbalance Bruce gave Keane when he let him keep three victims.

Keane bit off a big chunk of thumbnail and spat it onto the floor. A trickle of blood slid down his thumb. 'Please. Sit.'

Marshall hated the fact he was the only hope those three families had of getting closure. 'You've got ten minutes to tell me where the bodies lie or I leave.'

Keane inspected his bloody thumb. Lips twitching like he was digesting that last line. 'I read how you were the one who figured me out.'

Marshall thumbed towards the door. 'My job was to help the police. After you were safely away under lock and key, then people in my profession could sit down with you to work out why you did what you did so we can stop others doing it again. But not me.'

'There's nobody else like me.'

Marshall smiled. 'Sure. Keep telling yourself that. The world's full of small men like you who think they're important.'

'Small men. Right. Like Goldberg. I read how I made him quit.' Keane leaned his elbows on the desk, like he was a bored man in a travel agent looking for a cheap flight to Magaluf. 'They offered to let me speak to him. Your old boss. Goldberg. But I'm not having any of that. How is he?'

'Goldberg?' Marshall shrugged. 'Haven't heard from him in years.'

'Read about him. Do a lot of reading. Heard how he helped catch five other serial killers. Goldberg thought someone called Michael Shaw was the Shadow Man. Cost them both, eh? I deserve credit for that one too.' He gave Marshall another death stare.

Marshall gave a polite smile like he was talking to a boring neighbour about their holiday to Bognor Regis. 'You could've got anyone in here to talk at about your prowess as a serial killer. Why me?'

Keane sat back and sighed. 'I read about you three months ago. You're a cop now.'

Marshall felt a trickle of sweat. The news getting to Keane, locked away as he was, made his stomach clench. He got up again. 'Waste of time.'

'Want me to tell you where the bodies lie?'

Marshall nodded at him. 'See you around.'

'Don't go. Please.'

'Martin, you'll know yourself how bad the traffic around Newcastle is. It's not got any better since you were caught, believe me. Brutal roadworks on the A1(M) just now around the Metro Centre. So I'd quite like to get off soon and be home at a reasonable hour.' Marshall walked towards the door and pushed it open.

'Lovely town, Melrose. Know a few places around there you could hide a body.'

Marshall stopped dead. His blood was ice cold.

'They're buried so close to your hometown. Weird, eh?'

Marshall felt his head bow.

Shite.

Shite, shite, shite.

'I read about your past. You had it bad too. But you took a

different path to me.'

Marshall stayed in the doorway. Twitching hands in his trouser pockets, balled into fists. 'We all live in someone else's shadows, Martin. I know about your past. But you wanted to be caught, Martin. You marked the shallow graves. We knew it was you who did them.'

'Those stakes... We live in the shadows...'

'You killed because of your childhood. You grew up with a mum and dad who gave you no control over your life. No power. You lived in their shadows. They're both dead now. Dad about twelve years ago. Mum a year after. Undiagnosed heart defect, but she'd not been looking after herself in the wake of your dad's death. Of course, her heart was literally broken after realising her son was a serial killer.'

Marshall knew precisely how to manage an interview. Being aggressive like that seemed to work – Keane's wide eyes stared at him. 'It's possible you are bright but just socially inept. Or it is equally possible you're average or a bit below. Doesn't take a mastermind to plot the murders of unsuspecting people. So I think you're just playing with me. You've run out of people to torment. DI Bruce. Liana Curtis. Goldberg won't see you. When you saw an article about me, it reminded you of when I worked your case. When I sat in a room and got you to confess. But I just see someone who's playing games. Sorry, but this is over.'

'I said I'd tell you where they are and I will.'

'Bullshit.' Marshall worried he was pushing Keane too hard. But... Fuck people like Martin Keane, murdering liars who manipulate people. 'Psychopaths like you never come clean, Martin. You live with no regrets and with no conscience to bother you. But you wanted to be found, didn't you? The shallow graves, the message. You wanted the world to know your name. To go down in history. You held back the other three victims because you needed to keep something to gain true notoriety. You needed to be as renowned as Harold Shipman or Fred West or Dennis Nilsen. But why now?'

'I've been talking to a podcaster. And you're missing the first victim. I killed a friend I was out running with. He started lagging behind. *Kept* lagging behind. He got angry and he hit me. I hit him back. He fell over and hit his head and... I'd killed him. Total accident. But I got away with it.'

'Funny, we don't have that one on record. Another body you're keeping back from us.'

'I liked killing. That power over life and death. I feel guilty about that one, Robert, but not the other three.'

Marshall roared with laughter. 'No way in hell. Martin, you'd *never* feel guilt. It's impossible. You're a diagnosed sociopath. Everything in your life comes down to transactional arrangements, so there has to be something in this for you. What are you after from me?'

'A game. I'll give up one. Keep two. See if you lot can figure out the rest.'

'What else?'

Davidson cleared his throat. Marshall had forgotten he was there. 'Deal is no further prosecution for these three. My client knows he's not getting out of here, but he doesn't want to face court again. And I know you'll want to do it for the victims' families.'

'The podcaster gets to broadcast his interview.' Keane smiled, his teeth yellowed and crooked. 'And I show you the grave in person.'

Marshall didn't feel like he had a choice. He didn't want to do this. Didn't want to give in.

But those families...

Keane pointed up at the clock. 'Ten minutes to decide, Robert.'

CHAPTER SEVENTEEN

Marshall stood in the observation suite, his hands shaking as he tried to get his phone to dial. Then waiting for Pringle to answer. 'Jesus fucking Christ.'

Liana was outside, talking on another call. He could see her through the security glass, her hands windmilling in the air as she spoke.

Bruce's eyebrows touched his hairline. 'Ten minutes. Ten fucking minutes.'

'I know...' Marshall wanted to smash his phone against the wall. 'I hate being played by someone like him. This is how he gets his kicks. Manipulating us. Tormenting us. Controlling us. Making us believe this bullshit.' He got out his phone again and dialled. Bounced again.

Bruce got up and blocked his path. 'What happened in there?'

'What do you mean?'

'Kicking me out...'

'I needed to assert dominance over the man who put him away. Sending you out achieved that.'

'You could've warned me.'

'Needed your reaction to be genuine, Jon.' Marshall hit dial yet again and Pringle bounced the call yet again. Straight to voicemail. 'Sir, this is super urgent.' He tried Elliot but she didn't pick up either. He sifted through his contacts looking for Siyal or Jolene. Not Kirsten, though.

Bloody hell – they'd still be in that brewery in Selkirk.

'Listen, I don't mean to sound cross, but what are we going to—'

Marshall's phone rang.

Pringle calling...

Marshall put the phone to his ear. 'Sir, it's Rob. Did you—'

'A lot of voicemails on my moby, all saying the same—' Whistle. '—thing. Please, please, Mr Postman – just textify your love in future. Okay? I can read a text in a meeting. Can't very well whip out my phone and answer a call, can I?'

Marshall's pulse thudded in his throat. 'How do you want to play this, then?'

Pringle did a trilling whistle, the thin sound oscillating rapidly down the line. 'How do you, Inspector?'

Pringle had no idea what to do but needed someone to blame.

Marshall should've known he'd palm it back. He checked his watch. Seven minutes left, give or take. 'Honestly, I'm worried he's playing us.'

'Of course you're being played, Marshall. The nature of the timorous wee beastie, isn't it? But it's your job to play back, and to be a goddamn winner, you feel me?' Quite why he'd decided to talk like a rapper was anyone's guess. 'Like you were trying to tell me this morning, Sir Robert, you can only investigate minor crimes in Gala for so long. This kind of malarkey is why I employ you. If I want average I can get plenty of that from Elliott.'

'I'm sitting right here.' Her voice was distant, but her anger was in the foreground.

'You know what I mean. Andrea's a good, solid cop and you're... Well, you're special, Sir Robert. One in a million. And this is why *you* joined the police. Not finding those bodies was painful. Upsetting.'

'I know that, but... Now Keane's offering them on a plate... It's hard to trust him.'

'There's another but there, am I right?'

'Right. He's offering it on the plate. The chance to give the families closure.'

'Well, Marshall, I'll let you decide.'

'I was looking for guidance.'

'This ain't on me, pal.' Pringle was trying a Glaswegian accent on for size now, one of those stabby ones. 'I mean, I'll no doubt have to carry my share of the case, won't I? I've already spoken to Northumbria Police and, if we find any bodies up here, we'll both run it. But whatever you decide to do, I'll back you.'

'Thank you—'

Click and he was gone.

Great.

Just fucking marvellous.

Marshall looked around.

Liana was back in the room, jabbing her finger in the air at Bruce. 'No fucking way!'

'Of course it is!' Bruce was backed into the corner, hands in front of his face like she was going to hit him. Or already had. 'At least half!'

Liana could be a little terrier at times. Or worse. 'What happened to Michael Shaw is on you and the Crown Prosecution Service.'

'Bullshit! He died because you—'

'ENOUGH!' One thing Marshall liked about being this big was he was also that loud. Gave him authority too – people know he probably wouldn't tear them apart, but he could.

Liana and Bruce turned to face him, then bowed their heads like two naughty school kids caught snapping a fresh box of crayons.

'We haven't got time to go over all that stuff.' Marshall tapped his watch. 'We need to be back in that room in less than two minutes. So no bullshit. We're making a unanimous decision here, okay? First, let's see where we are.' He held out his hand, clenched. 'On a count of three, thumbs up for yes. Tight fist for no.' He waited for them to touch theirs to his. 'One, two, three.'

Liana and Bruce were thumbs up.

Marshall held his steady.

'Fuck sake.' Bruce stared up at the ceiling, then at Marshall. 'What? Why?'

'Because I knew you'd both go for it. I want to discuss it.'

'Discuss what?'

Marshall sniffed. He didn't have much. 'In a lot of policing matters, instinct kicks in. Our feet are in the air before you even ask, "how high?". I normally like hours or days to consider things. We've got seconds now.'

'What are you worried about? That Keane could try and run? Not possible. We've had contingency plans drawn up for years covering this eventuality. Signed off by the Home Secretary.' Bruce held up his thumb. 'One, he's not allowed to the site.' Then his forefinger. 'Two, if he insists and we let him, then he goes but he'll be in cuffs and ankle restraints and we'll have dogs and squads of cops and prison guards, one of whom will be cuffed to him. No chance he'll get away.'

Marshall was still shaking his head. 'I think it's too big a risk to take. Wherever it is, he'll know the land better than us. After all, he buried the body there.'

'Local cops will—'

'Still think it's too much of a risk.'

Liana was staring at him. 'Rob, I know you're against it but the parents of the three undiscovered bodies need closure. This is the first time in ten years they've even had a *whisper* of hope.'

'For one of them.'

'Maybe we can all put our heads together and extrapolate from there and find the other two.'

Marshall stared at the floor for a few seconds. Sweat pooled on his back. His concerns were buzzing around his brain but they didn't settle on anything concrete, certainly nothing that outweighed hope. 'Thirty seconds left.' He looked at Bruce then at Liana. 'Fuck it, we've got to do this.'

They both nodded.

'Okay, leave this with me.' Marshall charged out into the corridor and went back into the interview room.

Davidson laughed at something Keane said. Took a particular kind of creep to even sit in a room with a serial killer, even if he did have two massive prison guards to protect him – it was something else to humour him to that extent.

Keane stared up at Marshall. 'Well?'

'Okay.'

'You're sure?'

'I'm sure.'

'Good move, Robert. I'll show you where the body is.'

Marshall felt a little of the tension slacken off. Like he could breathe a little bit easier. 'That's fine.'

'One more thing.'

'Go on.'

'I want Jacob Goldberg there.'

'Why?'

'Because I want to see him suffer, or there's no deal.'

CHAPTER EIGHTEEN

Chirnside was one of those villages you usually found closer to Edinburgh or Newcastle where a nice row of old cottages had been swallowed up by housing developments over the last fifty years. It seemed to have escaped unscathed until the last ten maybe and was all the better for it – the development was full of big houses that at least looked in keeping with the older homes. And they had more than two inches between them. Gardens too.

If it wasn't for a Borders winter making the commute over to Melrose an absolute nightmare, Marshall himself would consider one – it'd get him out of living with his mother.

Liana was outside an old farm cottage on the Kirkgate – what would be called the old town in a Mediterranean resort. Not the designer chaos of the new estates, but a random arrangement built up over centuries. Opposite the church that gave the street its name, which itself hid behind a war memorial to the parish, the road had to bend around the cottage and the house peered back the way like it was judging anyone who approached.

Talk about the perfect place for Jacob Goldberg to retire to.

Liana pressed the doorbell and looked inside. 'I shouldn't have put my thumb up.'

'You don't think we should be doing this?'

She shook her head. A gust of wind blew down the lane, stealing whatever words she had to say. '—be played by Martin Keane.'

'No. You were right to insist on this. Letting him show us the body. As much as I hate letting Keane control the situation, I think the families need to grieve. It's what I've learned to do myself.'

She stared into his eyes but didn't say anything. Didn't ask. Just pressed the bell again.

'He won't be in, darling.' A red-faced man strode past them. Red trousers, green Barbour. Walking three black labs, all off the lead. 'This time, Jake will be sinking his second of the day.'

Liana smiled at him. 'In the pub?'

'That's what I said, wasn't it?' He pointed back to where they'd both parked. 'Waterloo.'

'Thanks.' Liana set off at a pace Goldberg himself would be proud of.

Marshall was no slouch these days and managed to keep up with her, more or less, as she charged back the way, kitten heels clicking on the road.

'Rob, can I ask you a question?'

'Just ask it.'

'Why haven't you spoken to Goldberg in ten years?'

'Because...' A gust of wind pushed some grit into Marshall's mouth. 'Look, this case broke him ten years ago. It's why he retired. Why I quit this role.'

'And why I've ended up with Goldberg's position?'

'I didn't say that. I told you, you're way better than I was at this. If you've been doing that job for ten years, you deserve it.'

'So why not speak to him?'

'I didn't want to trigger him.'

'Bullshit. You didn't want to trigger yourself.'

'No. Okay. It's something he said to me the day I told him I was quitting to join the Met. He cut me to the bone, you know? I hated him for it. And that's something I've worked on, Liana. I'm not proud of it. I... I ran away from danger. I didn't fight it. I learnt that as a coping mechanism. Now, at least I stop myself from making an automatic decision.'

'Why have you ghosted me?'

'Come on, that's not true.'

'Sure about that?'

'It was complicated between us, Liana.'

'I kissed you once, then I asked you on a date and you quit the job to avoid it.'

'That's a pretty fair assessment, aye.'

'I'm still single.'

Marshall kept walking.

'And you're still not interested.'

'Liana, I—'

He had to grab her coat and haul her back – she clearly hadn't seen or heard the removal van barrelling towards them. 'Steady!'

'Christ!' She waited for it to pass then checked both ways and jogged across the road.

If you came up the main road at the top of the village, you'd think Chirnside only had one pub, but the Waterloo Arms was an old coaching inn lurking at the bottom. Judging by the smell, it was focusing on food rather than drink these days. Which was a bit of a relief – it meant Goldberg wasn't just drowning his sorrows.

Liana slipped in first.

Marshall stayed outside to catch his breath. God, she was always so full on. Nothing was kept back, at least not for long. Still, you always knew what was going on behind those eyes.

He entered the pub.

Liana was standing by the fireplace, hands on hips.

Goldberg was sitting down next to her, tucking into steak and chips. A large glass of wine and a pint of beer in front of him, both half-full. He'd aged twenty years in ten and put on a lot of weight. His face had the redness of someone who was drinking every day. And hard.

Marshall joined them. 'Jacob, it's been a while.'

Goldberg dropped his cutlery onto the plate. 'What's he doing here?' Not even one o'clock and he was slurring. He wouldn't look at Marshall. 'My Judas.'

'That's a bit harsh.'

Liana shot Marshall a glare. 'Jacob, Rob spoke with Keane.'

'Well, well, well.' Goldberg picked up his cutlery again and sliced into his steak – if there was something rarer than blue, he was eating it. Blood dripped from his chin, making him look like a sated vampire. 'How contemptuous of our profession can you get?!'

The two other diners at another table were staring at him with wide eyes.

'Jacob, Keane is going to show us where one of the bodies is buried.'

'One of them?' Goldberg dropped his cutlery again and sighed. 'I'm going to the little boy's room.' He stood up and knocked his wine glass against the beer. Unlike with the lorry outside, Liana was sharp enough to catch it before it spilled everywhere.

Goldberg staggered off towards the toilet, lurching from side to side like he was at a conference at two in the morning.

Marshall sat down in the empty place setting opposite. 'We can't take him to see Keane like that.'

'You're right. Keane'll break him in seconds.' She picked up a chip and ate it. 'Starving.' Then another, held in front of her mouth. 'We could take him but keep him silent and away from Keane.'

'Doubt that'll work. Keane's doing this to torment him as well. He'll want him to talk.'

'So what's our plan B?'

'Blag it. Say no dice on Goldberg. He'll choose the column inches over torment.'

'You think?'

'I hope.' Marshall looked through the place. Maybe living near here would be nice. Somewhere he could walk and have a nice meal. Drink with friends. Game of pool. Live the life. Live *a* life. 'He's been a while in the toilet.' He got up and walked over to the gents and went in. Both stalls were empty and the urinals were clear.

Christ, he'd run off!

Marshall raced back out. He hadn't slipped past Liana.

A door led out the back towards a beer garden.

Marshall charged over and stopped dead.

Goldberg was at the bar, throwing back a whisky. He slammed the glass down then pointed at the glass and clicked his finger.

The barman winced, then poured out another shot free hand.

Marshall grabbed Goldberg by the arm and hauled him away from the drink.

Goldberg was reaching for it like a smackhead would his stash. Eyes rolling around his head, absolutely blitzed. 'Judas. You betrayed me! You were my protégé and you quit on me!'

'I'm nobody's protégé.' Marshall shook him. 'Jacob, we

need your help. Get yourself sober because you're coming out of retirement.'

'I'm a washed-up failure. People die because of me. You should speak to my replacement in Durham.'

Marshall pointed through the bar. 'Who do you think's eating your chips, Jacob?'

Goldberg squinted then closed one eye, then the other.

Liana joined them. 'Come on, Jacob. Let's get you a very strong coffee and—'

'I'm done with this charade!' Goldberg pushed Marshall away and lurched towards his whisky.

Marshall grabbed his arm again and stopped him necking the shot. 'You owe us, Jacob. You let us down. It's your fault Michael Shaw died.'

'My fault?' Goldberg was swaying. '*My* fault?'

'You were in charge! It's on you. And this is how you repay the debt. Okay? You're coming with us and we're going to find that body.'

Goldberg looked down at his shoes. A grey patch appeared on his crotch then started spreading. Then he jerked. Once, twice, then threw up over his shoes. About two bottles worth of red wine sprayed across the bar floor.

'Shite and stovies.' The barman raced out and grabbed Goldberg's arm. 'Come on, Jacob. Let's get you home, eh?' He led him out like Goldberg was in his nineties and had gone missing during the night.

The manageress rolled into action, pulling out a bucket and mop, then going to work on the urine, vomit and second-hand booze. 'Hope you're pleased with yourself.'

Marshall winced. 'Sorry, I didn't know he was this bad. We should've—'

'Happens fairly often, just not usually at lunchtime.' She squeezed the mop into the bucket. 'He's a regular. In here every day. Can't bar him, otherwise we'd have to shut down. If it wasn't for him and a few others, we'd have gone to the wall years ago.'

Liana was shaking her head at the retreating figures staggering through the bar. 'Rob, it looks like we're blagging it.'

CHAPTER NINETEEN

Marshall knew the single-track road along the south bank of the Tweed well, but mainly from his youth. Him and pals hurtling between Galashiels and Peebles. Not a care in the world – until it all fell apart for him.

Very different from this morning's blast out to Cardrona with Thea – every time he got up to thirty there was another tight bend. Also, he was sure it used to be a lot more heavily wooded, but Storm Arwen last winter must've decimated the local area, turning fifty-year-old trees into matchsticks overnight.

Not that he'd been here. Instead, he'd been investigating a crash in northwest London that seemed very fraud-y. Driving home that night felt like a giant grabbed his car and kept shaking it.

Liana was behind him, following a bit too closely for his liking. While there were no leaves from this kind of tree, the surface was slippery.

Marshall turned yet another bend and headed downhill.

The Tweed splayed out wide. Over the valley was another plantation where he used to go mountain biking. Birling up to the top of the hill, then shooting off down shonky paths like they were on landspeeders in that *Star Wars* film.

So many memories – maybe coming back here to live wasn't the best idea.

No, he'd lanced that boil. No way was he ending up like Goldberg. Lost to self-medication. Angry at history constantly dredging itself up.

Trouble with running from your problems was, no matter where you ran to, there you were.

Up ahead was the first sign of any action. At the bottom, before the road started climbing again, a row of parked cars squeezed the single lane like a clogged artery. He recognised most of them as pool cars – the knackered pair of Audis, three Volvos. He pulled in behind Pringle's BMW and got out into the fresh air.

Cool. Getting dark, or at least thinking of it. Then again, the sun always set early behind the massive hills. Nothing like mountains – munros or corbetts – but the great elevation of the Borders made them feel that much taller than they were.

He set off along the lane, passing a few familiar faces, then Liana's heels clicked towards him.

'Not the right footwear for this, is it?' She clapped her gloves together. 'Didn't expect to be doing this when I left the house this morning. Perfect place to dump a body.'

'Or three.'

She frowned at him. 'You think they're all here?'

'They all left Newcastle in the same car. Assuming Keane didn't break his MO of burying within a mile of where he killed them, they're here.' Marshall waved a hand at a green Forestry Commission sign marking out Elibank and Traquair Forest. 'You can cycle or run for about twenty miles up there without even seeing the road. Can bury them miles apart from each other.'

'That's a lot of ground to cover. And Keane would struggle to carry them.'

The prison van was parked around a sharp left turn back the way. Engine still running. Marshall counted four guards in there, plus a driver who looked like he knew what he was doing. Birdlike movements of his head, scanning the vicinity for any threats. None around, unless you counted a squad of uniform scratching their arses.

Two uniforms manned a gate blocking vehicles from accessing a path climbing up the hill, though walkers and cyclists had gouged away at the grass then got around the posts on either side. A steep cliff blocked access to the south, brave trees blanketing it all the way up.

Pringle and Elliot were standing right in the middle, looking like they were waiting for a rock concert to start. And one neither was particularly keen on.

Marshall led Liana over to them. 'Sir, Andrea, this is Professor Liana Curtis. She's the head of Durham's Centre for Criminal Profiling. DCI Jim Pringle. DI Andrea Elliot.'

'We met earlier, sir.' Liana smiled at Pringle, then shook Elliot's hand. 'I'd say it's a pleasure to meet you, but I'd rather we didn't have to do this.'

'Indeed.' Pringle stood there, smiling. Not saying anything else. Maybe he could stop himself making all the whistles and weird phrases, but only by not speaking.

Elliot smacked Marshall's arm. Hard enough to hurt a bit. 'We got Fraser to confess to the drugs shite.'

'What about the rape?'

'No chance.'

'What, he denied it?'

'No commented it.'

'We've got a bucketload of DNA. He's not getting off with it.'

'Good. But the back of that van contained a few tons of dried hops from North America and several kilos of dried coca from South America. He's working with our chums in Edinburgh to turn over the whole operation.'

'Sounds like a decent result. Congrats.' Marshall smiled at her, but she didn't react. 'How's it looking here?'

'We've secured the area.' Elliot stuffed her hands into her pockets. 'Got a big squad here from Edinburgh and Newcastle. Police dogs, forensics. DI Bruce is riding the happy bus with this Keane chap.'

A Ford Ranger burst around the corner, going faster than necessary. One of those pickups where the cab roof was extended to cover the flatbed. White, labelled in green with 'Forestry and Land Scotland'. The driver's door opened and a big man hopped out. Flannel shirt, green walking trousers and big boots. He wrapped Marshall's hand in a tight grip. 'Alastair Bett-Leighton, pleasure to meet you.' He worked around Pringle, Elliot and then Liana, squeezing tight. 'I'm the deputy area co-ordinator for the Tweed Valley Forest. Apologies you've got me to contend with. Boss is on holiday. Can't get hold of him, but he's probably three sheets to the wind on his last day.'

'DCI Jim Pringle. I'm the big cheese on the policing side here. When did it stop being the Forestry Commission?'

'April 2019, mate.' Bett-Leighton leaned back against his truck. 'We're in charge of all the plantations in the south of Scotland, basically. But the Tweed Valley has eight of the buggers. Massive area. Good news is my lads have secured all entrances from here to Traquair and flushed out the cyclists. Which got a fair amount of invective, but we've given them free parking season passes to Glentress, which seemed to placate them. Bloody motorcyclists been in the last few days on dirt bikes too. Chews up the ground like nobody's business.'

'Dirty buggers, eh?' Elliot barked out a laugh. 'Anyway, what's the plan here?'

'Like I said to your boss here on the phone—' Bett-Leighton nodded at Pringle. '—I'm at your beck and call. Same with my lads and lasses. I can take your murderer up in the truck along with at least two guards.'

'Shotgun.' Elliot laughed, then barged Marshall over to the side. 'I feel I should be leading this.'

Marshall shrugged. 'Fill your boots.' He walked over and peered into the back of the truck. 'Happy to sit in here, if that's okay?'

'Sure, but if it rains...'

'I can handle the rain.'

Raised voices rattled around.

The prison van door opened and Bruce stepped out, followed by a burly guard toting a baton.

And then the star of the show.

Martin Keane hopped down onto the carpet of pine needles with the swagger of an American wrestler, just a very short one. Surveying the assembled police officers and prison guards like they were his audience. Not often a wrestler would be shackled at the ankles and cuffed at the wrists, with another pair going to each of the guards.

Keane scanned the faces, then narrowed his eyes. 'Where's Goldberg?'

Marshall looked at Liana, but she didn't seem to want to step up, so he stared at Keane with all the ice he could muster. 'Jacob's not coming.'

Keane frowned. 'He's dead?'

'No.'

'Dying?' Keane smiled wide. 'Is it cancer?'

'No. He's an alcoholic.'

'Oh.' Keane looked up into the sky. 'That's even better.'

'Why?'

'He thought he was better than me. Better than everyone.'

A car pulled up at the entrance and was immediately surrounded by a gang of uniformed officers.

A man got out, tall and balding. He was pushed back by the wave of cops. 'I am in on this!'

'Hey, let him go!' Keane tried to raise his arms but his two guards stopped any movement. He was looking at Marshall with puppy dog eyes. 'That's the podcaster. Alexander Vickers.'

Marshall scooted off towards the car, splashing through the boggy ground. 'There are rules here.'

Vickers was appealing to Acting DS Jolene Archer's better nature – good luck, there wasn't one. 'I don't play by any rules.' Refined Newcastle accent.

Jolene pursed her lips. 'Bad boy, aye?'

'Kind of.' Vickers thumbed behind him. 'I've got four people with me. Parents of the three victims.'

Marshall stopped dead.

Shite.

Was that what Mark Davidson had been laughing about with Keane? Sick, sick bastard.

He looked at Liana. 'What do you think?'

'Fuck knows, Rob. You?'

The podcaster was one thing, but him showing up with surviving family members...

This many people at a crime scene was a complete nightmare.

And the power balance had shifted.

Marshall charged back towards Keane. 'Absolutely no way. *You* shouldn't even be here. I okayed him, but *them*? No. We should be getting you to write down where you put the bodies, then checking it out.'

'He's in.' Keane was smirking. 'Deal breaker. Lot of land out here. Could be anywhere.'

Marshall looked over at Pringle. 'They're not coming with us.'

'Then take me back to Frankland because that's the deal.'

'You do that.' Marshall shrugged. 'I don't care.' He held Keane's steely gaze until he wanted to look away himself. Like staring down the barrel of a loaded shotgun. 'This is your chance to get some more spotlight, Martin, but you're refusing it over this trivial matter.'

'It's important.'

'Nope. Not going to happen, Martin. This is over.'

'I'm in charge here!'

'No, I am.' Pringle was standing next to them, clicking his tongue. 'And here's the deal. You show us the bodies. You and only you. Otherwise, you're going back to Frankland.'

Keane adjusted his wrists, then stared at the ground. 'Fine.'

Marshall turned around and looked at Liana. 'Can you...?'

She nodded back. 'I'll talk to them. All of them.'

'Thank you.' Marshall walked right up to him without looking at either guard. 'How about you just show us where this body is, eh?'

'We're going to a part of the trail that's only accessible by a four-by-four. Otherwise it's a 10k walk.'

CHAPTER TWENTY

Marshall was in the back of the Ford Ranger, bumping and rolling as Bett-Leighton took it too fast up the hill. The cold air hit Marshall's face as hard as the smell of fresh pine. Something flashed by – might've been a red squirrel. They were in the grey exclusion area after all.

When they cleared the tree line, the forest continued to the right, but the left side was wide open. Looked like it'd been cleared sometime in the last few years, just a few native species left standing in amongst the stumps of evergreens from Scandinavia. The field in the shade of the hill was staffed by cows who were very interested in what was happening over here.

A squad car was up ahead, taking it slowly, with another behind.

Bett-Leighton had to slow, but then he wasn't a trained officer and he had a multiple murderer in the back seat.

Bruce was sitting opposite Marshall in the back, staring at him. 'You were brave back there.'

'What, refusing him?'

'Yeah. Why do that?'

'Why not? Keane feels like he's in complete control here, but it's important he understands who is the boss. And sure, we want to find the remains to help the families, but Keane wants to prolong his infamy. No body, no story.'

Bruce shook his head. 'What a guy.'

'He's insane.'

'I meant you.'

Marshall sat back and watched a patch of evergreens pass. 'Martin Keane is someone who's killed nine times and tormented another six people by denying them closure on their children's deaths.'

'Two of the parents died in that time.' Bruce swallowed hard. 'Met every one of them every six months to listen to their stories. Got to know them. It's fucking sick what he's done to them. You just see this blankness and emptiness in their eyes.' He looked right into Marshall's. 'You know what that feels like.'

'I do.'

The truck stopped and Bett-Leighton got out.

Another area, wooded on all sides. The road twisted on into the forest, with another one heading up the barren hill range back towards Gala. The steep hill directly above them was thick with pine trees.

'Guess where we're heading.' Bett-Leighton pointed at the little path leading in, worn down by cyclists and walkers.

The occupants of the car in front were two handlers with two good boys and two good girls. An Alsatian and a spaniel each.

The car behind emptied of five vanilla uniforms.

Elliot was out of theirs, opening the back door. 'Come on, sunshine, time to show us your moves.'

The first guard took a few seconds getting out, such was his sheer size.

Keane was out in a flash, shackled to a prison officer. He sucked in a deep breath and swung around, taking in the view. Then he tilted his head towards the wood. 'Up that way.'

'Come on, then.' Marshall led, walking slower than even he'd like. The path was steep and worn through the undergrowth by cyclists bombing down it like he had as a kid. Several world-class mountain biking courses around here. Folks travelled down from the Central Belt every weekend to cycle anywhere on the Tweed Valley. Also come up from the northeast, like Keane's last three victims.

Surprisingly alive under the canopy of trees – the bracken or ferns were turning brown, but the grasses were still thriving. A few tree trunks were studded with mushrooms.

Keane was walking like he still ran twenty kilometres a day. 'I like it here in the woods. It's peaceful.'

Elliot laughed. 'Aye, until you start murdering folk.'

Keane looked around at her and grunted. 'Put them out of their misery.'

'How do you get that?'

'Everyone living in the shadows of the rich. All on their phones, doing selfies and bragging about their perfect lives.'

'Seem to know a lot about that for someone who's been in prison for ten years.'

'Seen people in the waiting area. What are they looking at? Absolutely nothing.'

The path kinked around to the right, then sharply to the left. Marshall knew it was called a berm from his cycling days – a much better way to climb a hill rather than face first. But walking was a lot more steps. All that fitness work he'd done and he was still out of breath.

'I knew which route they'd be taking. Came out first thing.

Set up wires across the trees. Waited from dawn. Up the top of the hill, can see them coming with a pair of binocs. I knew they'd arrived and got myself in place.'

Another berm. Must be halfway up and Marshall was struggling for breath now.

Keane was fine, despite ten years inside. 'They cycled up the path a few miles to the west. Then came along the logging path at the top of the hill. They bombed it down here. Just had to pull my wire. Took them all out, one by one. Three seconds. All down. Didn't kill them, though. They were injured, bleeding from the neck. I slit the throat of the least injured, then did the same with the middle one. The most injured guy, I took my time killing him.'

'Was it different doing more than one?'

Keane looked around at Marshall. 'It wasn't three times the fun.'

The ground angled up the way, rough with exposed roots breaking through the soil. 'Whose body are you taking us to?'

'Alexander's.'

Marshall turned around. 'How'd you know they'd be here?'

'Heard them.'

'In a chat group?'

'In a pub by their office. They never even saw me.' Keane stopped and checked a gap through the trees. A small monument sat there, the grave of a fallen forestry worker. Marshall had been here, after all. Keane tried to raise his hands but they wouldn't extend far. 'I think it's about forty metres through the bracken here. Between two trees. One has an X marked near the ground.'

'Okay, guys, you heard the man!' Bruce led the team into the woods.

The dogs were in the lead, going wild.

Three CSIs were following and some uniforms.

'Start digging here.' Bruce was by a tree, pointing between them.

The X was there but stretched out and deformed.

Marshall couldn't look at Keane, so he walked away, fidgeting with his phone. Keane was right – these things controlled us now. Just like Keane was controlling him. The sickness inside his head, at not divulging the locations of the others, just so his message could persist.

Message. What message? Some words from an Oasis song. The first track on their second album. Ripped off a Gary Glitter song, of all things. Hardly a manifesto.

'Are you okay?'

Marshall swung around.

Kirsten Weir was almost fully suited up. Her hood was flapping in the stiff breeze, wafting that sweet perfume towards him, but her hair stayed perfectly still – he'd seen it blue and green before but now it was silver. And the shaved side was growing back.

Cast in the fading light, she looked beautiful.

Holy shit, the way his heart fluttered when he saw her. The way his gut churned. He felt like he was sixteen years old again.

And he'd been such a twat to her. Yet another victim of the curse of Rob Marshall.

She looked up at him – even when she was standing uphill of him, that foot height difference still counted. 'Rob, I asked if you were okay.'

'Aye, fine, just taking it all in. Haven't thought about this case much since I joined the police and now here it is.' He looked over and saw a chaos of dogs and digging. No matter how well trained the beasts were, they'd still revert to their nature.

'Think we'll find anything?'

'I'm not sure. I hope we do.' Marshall stared into space for a few seconds. Could have been minutes, even.

'Got something!' Bruce was waving his arms at them.

Marshall stormed across the rough terrain towards him.

Bruce pointed into a patch of earth.

A skull poked out.

A human skull.

Marshall walked back over to Keane. 'Thank you.'

Keane couldn't look at Marshall. He focused on the assembled crew digging the soil, led by Kirsten. Any evidence needed to be catalogued and captured immediately. Anything that could lead them to the other bodies was worth more than platinum. Diamonds. Bitcoin. Anything. He switched his focus to Marshall. 'I'm not a liar, Robert.'

'Why do you call me that?'

'Eh? It's your name.'

'I'm Rob. Nobody calls me Robert.'

Keane winked. 'That's what *he* calls you.'

Marshall knew who that'd be.

Jesus Christ.

'Is he in on this?'

'Oh God no. We don't talk shop.'

'What the hell?'

Marshall swung around.

Bruce was about five metres away from the grave. An Alsatian was at his feet, ploughing at the ground. A CSI was digging away with a shovel.

Bruce looked over at Marshall. 'There's another!'

Keane laughed. 'Don't say I'm not good to you.'

CHAPTER TWENTY-ONE

Marshall led out into the clearing at the bottom of the hill, to the forestry road back to the car park. The air smelled better down here, none of the stench of death, even though it was in his head.

Keane stopped in the fading light, flanked by his guards. The handcuffs rattled. That smug smirk filled his face. He was enjoying this game. Enjoying being out in the real world.

Marshall walked up to Keane. 'Thank you. Again.'

Keane frowned. 'What for?'

'You've given the locations of *two* bodies.' Marshall gave him the most genuine smile he could muster. 'I thought it was going to be one.'

'Tough to move two.'

'You said the first was Alexander Quiller. Is the other Stan or Caitlyn?'

'Stan and I went for a walk.'

So they had Alexander and Caitlyn.

One of the victims had been forced to walk with him. Likely the most injured, someone he could control.

Marshall stepped back just as a vehicle approached them. A people carrier stuffed with adults rather than a football team's worth of kids. 'Your friendly podcaster decided to bring along the parents of the victims. They're here, Martin. The families of Alexander and Caitlyn will have closure over what you've done to them.'

Keane looked over at the people carrier. Liana was riding shotgun at Marshall's request. 'Guilt won't work on me.'

'You killed their children, Martin. Please. Last chance. Where is Stan?'

Keane chuckled, like Marshall had just used an old in-joke. 'What makes you think this is the last time you'll see me?'

'Not with me. I'm done playing this game with you, Martin. Please, give up the final location or we are done talking. But thanks again for those two.' Marshall rested a hand on Keane's chest, a gentle caress. 'I mean it.'

Keane stared at the hand for a few seconds. Probably the only time in ten years someone had touched him with something less than violence or just daily routine.

'Take him away.' Marshall smiled at the guards and they helped him into the back of the Ranger.

Keane sat in the vehicle, staring into space.

Marshall watched Bett-Leighton drive them off, pleased he'd had the last word in terms of mind games. That would play on Keane for years. Fester away. Eat at his soul like maggots at flesh.

Liana and the podcaster were both out of the people carrier now, helping the parents out into the autumn afternoon.

Marshall strolled over to Liana, though he felt like running. Everything was keyed up inside his head. 'Change of plan. Take them away.'

'Are you sure?'

Marshall nodded. 'Sorry, I wanted him to see them. This is no place for them. Not now.'

'You need to explain to them what's going on.'

'Fine.' Marshall leaned into the people carrier. 'Hi, my name is DI Rob Marshall. I'm leading this operation on the Police Scotland side and I wanted to update you on matters. We've recovered two bodies.'

An explosion of language, crossing over each other. Hard to figure out who was saying what.

Marshall raised a hand and waited for silence. 'My colleagues will be working to confirm who we have recovered and who is still missing. Of course, it's possible this isn't them, but I've no reason to doubt that it is. Your children's bodies will be processed but I strongly advise against seeing them. It's been over ten years since they died. We will be obtaining DNA from yourselves and dental records to validate their identities. You'll all be appointed a Family Liaison Officer to be with you at this difficult time.'

One of the men got out of the back, a big bruiser in his late sixties. He walked up to Marshall, tears in his eyes. 'Have you found my Alexander?'

'I can't comment on who we have found, other than two bodies have been recovered.'

The man wrapped his arms around Marshall, squeezing him tight. 'Thank you.' The softest, gentlest sound. 'My wife can rest now.'

'It's really nothing to do with me. Keane decided to come clean.'

'You've got two of our children back. That means a lot to all of us.' He gave him one last squeeze then got back into the people carrier, rubbing at his cheeks.

'I'll see you at the station, Rob.' Liana got back in and the vehicle drove back down the path towards the car park.

Marshall stood there, watching the brake lights fade from view. He was surrounded by trees and hills. Keane had killed three people here, burying two of them nearby.

The third had to be here.

Or did he really frogmarch Stan Di Melo down to the car park and take him elsewhere?

No, too risky. Keane wasn't the brightest, which meant he knew when a risk wasn't worth taking. He kept it simple.

'You're the hero of the hour, eh?' Elliot was walking out of the path, giving him a slow, sarcastic clap. 'Finding two long-lost bodies. Marvellous stuff, Marshall.'

'Andrea...' Marshall wanted to sigh, but he swallowed it down. 'You can give me all the snark you want about it. I don't care. This isn't something *I've* done. It's happening to me. Keane's... He's a sick little man who'll die in prison, but at least two sets of parents can grieve.'

'Blah, blah, blah, here endeth the sermon before I lose my lunch...' She pressed her fingers towards her mouth. 'Okay, I've got the dogs unit spreading out, trying to find this other body.'

'Good idea.'

'What's the plan?'

'Other than finding them, someone needs to go back to Melrose to interview him.'

'Happy to oblige.'

Marshall wished that was an option. 'Problem is, I'm the only person Keane will speak to.'

'Oh, you're such a tortured hero, Marshall.'

'That's enough, Andrea.'

She reached over and ruffled his hair. 'I'm just messing with you. Surely someone as average as me can't get under your exalted skin.'

'Now's not really the time.'

'When is?' She got out her phone with a smirk. 'Okay, so

I'm going back to base to speak to this boy. Maybe he'll open up to someone who's a bit different to what you brain boxes offer.'

'Bruce isn't a brain box.'

'You know what I mean.'

'Listen, I'm not sure that's wise. He's... He's a crafty one.'

'Look, I'll take your ex-bird in if it'll help.'

'What are you talking about?'

'Lady Liana. Seen the way she looks at you, Marshall. You're definitely on a promise there.'

'There's nothing going on.' But Marshall's face was burning.

'Aye, aye. I know what I saw.'

A dog started barking.

Came from behind them.

Marshall swung around.

The two dog handlers were on the path leading west, bulging up and down over a hill. Thick with trees on both sides. One of the dogs was barking wild. 'Go on, Al.' The handler let it off the lead. 'Go get it, boy.'

The chunky Alsatian's glorious fur swayed as it swooshed across the ground. Snout to the ground, crossing the woods to yet another steep climb towards a hill hidden by trees.

Elliot shook her head. 'Daft sod probably smells someone's McDonald's bag. Filthy sods dump their rubbish up here.'

Marshall wasn't so sure, though. Keane had led Stan away from the other graves. Or so he'd said.

Al stopped and barked at a tree.

'Good boy, Al.' The handler beckoned people over. 'He's found something.'

Marshall followed them across the path then over the forest canopy.

Not a discarded burger wrapper, but a patch of ground underneath a tree. Marked with another deformed X.

A CSI started digging at the spot Al had pointed at, overseen by a pair of uniforms.

Looked like Kirsten behind the mask. She was focusing on the ground and driving the spade into earth thick with roots. She crouched down and looked up at Marshall, pointing at a skull. 'Rob, it's another body. Similar age.'

Marshall felt a weight topple off his shoulders. 'Stan.' He ran a hand down his face. 'Okay, we need to confirm all three. Can you get your guys excavating this?'

'Excavation is the word for it. Assuming it's him, this is ten years in the ground. Even if he was buried in a shallow grave before, it isn't now. This is pretty deep now. And it's just bones. Thing is, excavating carefully in an archaeological style will take days and I'm not sure what we'll gain from it. You know who did it. Also, the sheer number of bodies here... I think we just need to get them out of the ground.' She smiled at him. 'Sorry, this is a bit morbid but—'

The dog started barking again.

'What's up, Al?' The handler let its lead go and the dog shot off again, sniffing and hunting.

Marshall followed, heading further up the hill, cutting between tightly packed pines that scraped at his face. Heading away from the bodies.

The others were following, spreading out to flank him.

Another dog joined them, a spaniel off its lead, racing up the hill ahead of Al.

The dogs were digging in different spots, about thirty metres apart.

The other handler had his pair too – they focused on a third spot nearby, the sites forming a crooked triangle. 'Come on, Bess. What've you got?'

Marshall watched as the shovels started clearing soil away. Clenching everything until he saw what was inside.

He ran over to the second, then over to the third.

They all contained the same grisly object.

A human body, much fresher than the others.

Wrapped in cling film.

Wearing an oxygen mask.

CHAPTER TWENTY-TWO

Marshall slurped the bitter coffee, the harshness softened by milk. He knew how fresh this carton was because he'd bought it himself from the Co-op. He looked out of the window. Melrose's tear-shaped town centre loop was busy with mums and dads collecting their kids from the school over the road. A few teenagers lurked about. Rugby players practised on the pitch, like a reluctant Marshall had done years ago. Built for the sport, but he just didn't care. And others did – they were welcome to it.

Fucking hell.

He'd gone to Elibank expecting to find one body, but they recovered all three. All four parents in that people carrier would all be able to close that door, or at least start the final grieving process.

Keane had no more ammunition.

But Marshall had three new bodies. And a huge new mystery.

'Here.' Elliot handed Marshall a foil pipe.

He took it from her. Heavy and warm, scrawled on with a black marker. Smelled all meaty and barbecued. 'What's this?'

She smiled. 'A chicken burrito.'

'From Melrose?'

'No, Gala.'

'There's a burrito bar in Galashiels?'

She nodded. 'Not far from the new tapestry thingy. Some lad opened it where Greggs used to be. I forgot Greggs was over by Tesco now and drove there by accident. Lot on my mind. Sure you can imagine. Then I remembered when you came to see me in hospital, how you got talking about that cop you worked with who had a thing for burritos.' She lifted a shoulder. 'So I got you one. And I missed your birthday. Hate it when that happens.'

For such a complete arsehole, Elliot could occasionally have moments of extreme kindness.

'Thank you, Andrea.' Marshall set his coffee on the windowsill and tore open the foil. He hadn't eaten since... Well, a bite of toast first thing before he left with Thea. No wonder he was feeling all stabby. He bit into it and fire erupted into his mouth. 'Wow. That's hot.'

'You not a big Mexican fan?' She didn't have one for herself.

'I can take it or leave it. But I'm starving, so thank you.'

'Don't mention it.'

'Even went into the Co-op and got some milk for coffee and forgot to get some food.'

'We're all a bit thrown, Marshall.' She yawned into her fist. 'Oh. That creepy lawyer was at the front desk so I asked Dave to stall him a bit.'

'Why?'

'Because Mark Davidson isn't so much the devil's advocate as Satan's filthy arsehole.'

So mature...

Marshall finished chewing. 'Any reason to think that?'

'He's an Edinburgh-based criminal defence lawyer so it goes with the territory.'

'Take it you've had many dealings with him?'

'Nope. But I know people who have. Though I thought you —' She swung around. 'Ah. Speak of the devil and he shall appear.'

'Oh, Satan is but one of my lesser demons.' Mark Davidson wore a trench coat that was too long and dragged along the corridor behind him. He swung his briefcase so hard and high it might fly off into orbit. His neck was swallowed up by his collar. His creepy little goblin face was so punchable... How could anyone represent a man like Martin Keane without selling their soul? 'Is my client ready for me?'

'Aye, he's in there with two prison guards.' She raised a finger. 'Don't start! They're staying in there.'

'Very well.' Davidson moved to get past her.

Elliot blocked the door. 'Not sure how much you heard, sunshine, but your pal in there has another three bodies to explain. If you could get him talking, we might overlook the other thing.'

'What other thing?'

'You passing on a message to that podcaster. Got him to bring the victims' families along.'

'I just did my client's bidding.'

'Mark, those poor people have been through enough. What kind of—'

'Martin has finally given you their locations, so I think that should count *for* him.'

'Hardly. He's dicked us about for ten years. Just so happened a dog slipped its lead and found where he'd dumped the last body.'

'Right, well, I shall discuss this matter with him.' Davidson dipped his head and entered the interview room.

Marshall ate some more of his late lunch, but his mouth was now an erupting volcano.

Elliot shook her head at the closed door. 'Guy gets worse every day.'

'Heeeeey!' Siyal strolled down the corridor, bopping his head in time to some invisible beat. What the hell? He spun around and pointed at them. 'Guess who has two thumbs and passed his advanced driver training?' He pointed them both at his face. 'This guy.'

'Fuck off.' Elliot laughed. 'Are you kidding me?'

'Nope.' Siyal reached into his coat and held out a certificate. 'I'm the daddy.'

'Even after you sconed that motor off those cars this morning?'

'According to the tester, police pursuits have a higher tolerance for damage.'

'And I've got a lower tolerance for idiocy...'

Siyal rolled up his certificate and slid it back into a tube. 'Was that Mark Davidson?'

Elliot had her phone out, furiously tapping away with both thumbs. 'Why?'

'I know Davidson.'

She looked up. 'Like, you're mates with him?'

'Hardly. Came across him in my old job, before this. He defended a pub landlord who kicked one of my clients into hospital. Afghan refugee, who was cleaning his client's pub. She was pregnant. Back home, she was a lawyer, but the Taliban persecuted her so she fled.' Siyal exhaled slowly out of his nostrils. 'Davidson got his client off on a technicality. But he grassed her up and she got detained for illegal immigration.

I tried and failed to get her off with it. So, aye. He's a nasty bastard. Doesn't want to win, just wants to destroy.'

Marshall finished his burrito but he had a ball of tinfoil, fingers covered in gloop and a mouth that was hotter than the surface of Venus. 'That's the... work of a bastard... for sure.'

Elliot handed him a napkin and he cleaned up his fingers. 'Thanks.'

'That case broke me.' Siyal walked over to the window and looked out. 'Decided to join the police so I could stop shit like this happening to good people like her.'

'And law's loss is policing's loss too.' Elliot slapped him on the back. 'Sorry to hear that, Shunty. Sounds like a right load of shite.'

'That's an understatement.'

'Listen, I need you to head out to the woods and supervise the recovery of those bodies. Our Geordie chums are out there but we need you to make sure their focus is on these new ones.'

'On it.' Siyal nodded at her, then Marshall. 'See you later.' He walked off with the posture of a man who'd just confronted a demon and not only won but eradicated demons from the world.

Elliot was shaking her head. 'I just saw another side to Shunty.'

'It was there all along, Andrea. You just had to look for it.'

'Hmm.' She opened the door and entered.

Marshall dashed into the toilet and washed his hands and mouth clear of Mexican slime. Kind of her, but really – he wasn't that sort of cop. And he needed to be careful what stories he told her in future.

CHAPTER TWENTY-THREE

The interview was already under way when Marshall entered the room. His mouth was still on fire.

Keane rested both elbows on the table. 'I don't know them. They're not mine.'

'Right. Fine. I believe you. That's this done.' Elliot reached over to the recorder in the middle of the table, then snatched her finger away. 'Or do I? See. I think you do know who they are.'

Marshall took the seat next to Elliot and sat there, arms folded. Not making eye contact with anyone. Just letting Elliot lead this.

Keane was staring at him. 'Not the last time after all, Robert.'

'Want to know why? It's because I thought that was the last time we'd dig up bodies of people you'd killed.'

'They're not mine.'

'I mean, they bear the hallmarks of your killings.'

Keane tilted his head towards Elliot. 'Alexander Quiller. Stan Di Melo. Caitlyn Westerberg.'

Elliot waited for him to finish. 'These others share the same victimology. Young people. All three are late teens, early twenties.'

'I know all of mine. I know who, I know why. I know their names.'

'Cool.' Elliot nodded her head a few times. 'Right now, we don't know the first thing about these people. Could be they're all loaded, like your others. Got to admit the MO is the same.'

Keane was rattled. Big time.

Marshall understood why. His precious message would be diluted by this discovery. He'd be reduced to a bit part player in his own story.

But he'd never lied.

Withheld information, sure.

Tried to minimise, no.

Tried to even plea bargain for a reduced sentence, no.

Could be he was telling the truth.

And Owusu's preliminary findings indicated the new bodies were unlikely to have been out there for a year, much less ten. So he couldn't have done them himself. So – what? Where did that leave them? An accomplice? A protégé of his own?

Elliot leaned back and rested her head in her hands. 'All buried in woodland near your last trio. Come on, Martin, those are textbook killings of—' She paused, sniffing. 'What was it they called you? Captain Gimp? Lord Wanker? Saint Tinycock?'

'I know my name. I know their names. I know the reasons. I know why they needed to die! I am not a liar.'

Marshall gave him a few seconds to follow up. He'd never seen Keane so worked up. The fact that someone was on his patch, doing the same crimes as him...

Or did they...

'You have a collaborator, don't you?'

Keane looked at him like he'd lost it. 'Eh?'

'To kill these three, you'd need someone to help you. They all looked quite recently killed. Last couple of years, maximum. Like you say, you've been inside nine years, but the urge to kill must be burning away at you. Hard to kill in prison, right? Lot of hard bastards in there, much harder than some unsuspecting cyclist or runner. All those eyes watching you.' Marshall left a long gap. 'No, you've got to do it on the outside. Sure, having an accomplice isn't the same as you stabbing them a hundred times yourself, but you do this for control. When you control the life and death of someone, you feel like a god. Even if it's not you doing it directly, and someone on the outside is wielding that power, it's you who's in control. You choose who. You choose how. You choose when. Where. Why. And what they do to these victims.'

Keane stared at him, hard, unblinking, unflinching. Then the rage returned, his teeth bared. 'I didn't need help for any of them. It was all me. Just me. You know who I killed.'

'I'm serious. You've got a collaborator.'

'Nope.'

'What about guards?'

'Guards?'

'A friendly guard could be killing for you.'

'Guards hate me. Don't like killers.'

'Your lawyer, then.' Marshall deliberately didn't look at Davidson. 'You're very friendly with each other.'

Davidson's eyes bulged. 'That's ridiculous! I don't even like this piece of shit, much less take orders from him!'

Keane laughed. 'I have nobody. It's me. Just me.'

Davidson was blushing but looked furious too. He leaned across the table. His breath was rancid. 'You know what I think? I think it must be someone copying him. Think about it.

His story comes up in the press every few months. There was that show on Netflix.'

'Man, don't you listen to me? My message is being ignored. Whoever did these other murders, it's someone feeding off me being a serial killer, not me being a visionary.'

'A visionary.' Marshall smiled. 'Good one.'

'I'm serious here.' Keane smacked the table and made Elliot look up from her phone. 'Am I boring you?'

'Kind of, aye. Just checking the time and wondering if the Sermon on the Mount will be finishing any time soon.'

Keane grimaced. 'Someone out there is copying me. Some sick bastard.'

Elliot raised her eyebrows. 'And you're not a sick bastard?'

'I don't want to be a part of someone else's crimes.' Those ice-blue eyes drilled into Marshall. 'When I saw your story in the papers, Doctor Robert... I... I needed to confess.'

'It's torture, right?' Elliot held the gaze until Keane looked away. 'Wrapping people in cling film. Oxygen masks. Why do that to someone?'

Keane's eyes bulged. His skin turned pale. 'I'm done talking. Take me back home.'

Marshall sat back. No matter which way he cut it, he didn't see a way they'd get any more out of him. 'Okay. That's us done here.' He got to his feet.

'I can go?'

Marshall laughed. 'No, Martin. You're going to be here for a while. A few people will be interviewing you over the next few hours. Then you'll be taken back to Frankland for more. Obviously, anything you could offer us would be treated favourably.'

'Sure. I'll get a better pillow or nicer soap.'

'Don't knock a good pillow, Martin. Key to a good night's

sleep.' Marshall strolled out of the room, then stormed down the corridor.

No matter how many times he sat in a room with a murderer – convicted or suspected – it stayed with him for days afterwards. All those little microscopic gestures, the words. All of it. The way those eyes looked through him.

He entered the obs suite and collapsed into a chair.

Pringle and Bruce were sitting there in silence.

Pringle was staring at his phone like it was the first time he'd seen one. Might explain how he was so bad at answering it. He looked over at Marshall. 'Well, well, Herr Doktor. What do you think?'

'It'll take a while to process it.' Marshall leaned forward, resting his hands on his knees. 'But I think it's unlikely there's someone working with him.'

'Go on?'

Marshall waved at Bruce. 'Jon and I discussed it earlier – he's been in seg unit all the time so it's... It's unlikely. Unless it's the lawyer or the podcaster... Plus he doesn't really have the social skills to gain someone's trust and... And.... There's something bugging me.' He grabbed the remote and rewound the video.

'*—torture, right?*' Onscreen, Elliot was staring hard at Keane. '*Wrapping people in cling film. Oxygen masks. Why do that to someone?*'

Marshall paused it.

There.

The look on Keane's face. Eyes bulging. Mouth hanging open. Skin already fading.

Fear.

'See that?' Marshall waved the remote at the screen. 'When he heard about the cling film... I mean Elliot shouldn't have said that, but—'

Pringle cleared his throat. 'I shall have a wee word in her shell-like, as they say.'

'Okay, but we went in there working on the theory that Keane knew about the cling film and masks. Yet clearly he didn't.'

'So?'

'I need to think this all through.' Marshall ran a hand through his hair. 'The thing is, it would change his psych profile drastically. Keane is a loner. Even if he was capable of establishing a relationship with someone on the outside, sharing the crime with someone would be too much for his fragile ego.'

Pringle nodded slowly. 'Like that David Bowie song, it's been ten years.'

'Five years.' Bruce screwed up his face. 'The song's called *Five Years*. Not ten.'

'Is it?' Pringle raised his eyebrows. 'My point is, a lot can change in ten years. All that enforced solitude.'

He had a point, but Marshall still didn't agree with it. He needed time and space to think it all through.

'Fuck it, I'm going to go for it.' Bruce stood up. 'Really nail his balls to the wall.'

Pringle smirked. 'That's a contravention of the Geneva convention.'

'You know what I mean.' Bruce stepped over to the door. 'I'm having another go. You disagree?'

Marshall sat back. 'I think it's futile.'

Pringle laughed. 'Like resistance to a Borg.'

'What to a what?'

'Never mind.' Pringle tossed his phone in the air. Instead of catching it, he let it rest on the back of his hands, then flicked it around and grabbed it. 'You don't think Bruce will get anything out of it?'

'Why the hurry to do it wrong again so soon? Keane called off the interview. That's it done. Now we do police work. Identify the victims, put the case together the old-fashioned way. Stop looking for shortcuts and do it right this time.'

Bruce narrowed his eyes at Marshall. 'Saying I did it wrong last time?'

'Let's not get into that now.' Marshall cleared his throat. The burrito was starting to repeat on him. Another reason he avoided Mexican food – way too many onions and peppers. 'You do what you want, Jon.'

'I will.' Bruce stepped out and the door slammed behind him.

Marshall got up. 'Listen, I need to clear my head and think it all through. See what comes out of the sausage machine.'

CHAPTER TWENTY-FOUR
GRACE

Grace Paton hopped off the bus first and raced off along the street. Getting dark, but she didn't need to get her torch out yet. The sweet wood smoke reminded her of her granny's old house.

Grace missed her.

Her phone chimed in her pocket – the WhatsApp notification sound, but she didn't check it.

'Grace!'

She turned around and saw Elsa running after her. Blonde hair tied back in a ponytail, flanked by six other arseholes.

Shit!

Grace bombed it, her Converse squeaking as she ran away from them. Mum was so right – these shoes were well past it. The holes in the bottom were so bad her socks and tights were soaked already. She splashed through a puddle and the water ran right up her leg.

'John Wayne Gracy is a killer!'

Guess who'd just watched a documentary on John Wayne Gacy and had an imagination bypass.

Two red-faced old perverts stood outside the pub, eyeing up Grace.

She scurried past them and cut along the lane at the back. Elsa's boyfriend Kieron lived up here. Grace slowed to a walk so she could step between the puddles.

Fucking Elsa. Absolute bitch. She really had it in for her.

Grace kept checking behind her as she walked, but at least Elsa was keeping her abuse virtual or from a distance. All day at school, she'd shouted the same bullshit.

Thing was, if Elsa did catch up with her, Grace didn't know what she'd do. Would take at least those two old men to hold her back and stop her smashing Elsa's face in.

Another chime from her pocket. Then again. And again.

She got out her phone and checked it. WhatsApp was exploding. She tapped on the notification:

> Elsa McGill: So I heard all about what Grace did on Saturday, so I thought I'd let everyone else know.

> Kieron Wilson: Spill, bae!

> Elsa: Not your bae.

> Kieron: Spill

> Jago: Yeah, spill!

> Milo: Spill!

> Ash: Spill!

> Mylo: Spill!

> Elsa: Of course I'll spill! Gimme five

> Tiegan: Were you even there, Elsa?

> Elsa: Calling me a liar, bitch?

> Tiegan: Uh, just asking a question

> Tiegan: Were you?

> Elsa: Course I was there. Saw it all. Pieced it all together tho

> Elsa: Grace is a killer.

Grace stabbed her finger on the top of the group then scrolled down to the red text.

Exit Group

WhatsApp asked if she wanted to just mute the chat. She wished she had a button to turn Elsa into a puddle of goo. She clicked the second Exit Group button.

This was fucked up.

'Bitch!'

Grace swung around and fucking Elsa was there. Storming towards her. 'Killer!'

Grace did what her dad told her to do and just walked away.

'You killed him!' Splash splash splash. 'Gave him meths!'

Grace got faster and faster.

'Tipped it into his vodka! Watched him drink it! John Wayne Gracy!'

Grace could run – she knew from cross-country how much faster she was. Always back in the changing rooms way before anyone. Elsa was always one of the last.

Fuck it.

Grace turned around. 'He didn't die.'

'I saw them put him in the ambulance, Grace. My uncle works at the Borders General. Said he died!'

'That's bullshit. Why are you doing this to me?'

'Because you're a killer. He wasn't at school today because he died!'

Grace pulled back her arm, ready to punch her. But she saw a police car driving through the village.

They were after her!

Shit!

'Fuck you, Elsa.' She turned and ran off, squelching down the lane to the last house in the village. The fields beyond were just blonde scrub, perfect for the family walking their Andrex puppy.

She let herself into their cottage and was welcomed with the smell of chips. Home chips, from Mum's new air fryer and not from the chip shop in town.

'Hi, Mum.' She kicked off her shoes and took her bag upstairs. Her room had been cleaned. Great – Mum would've put all of her shit in weird places *again*. Took a week to find stuff in the most random locations. At least she had clean clothes again. She needed them.

She perched on the edge of the bed and looked out of the window across the field. The family with the puppy were heading across the golf course towards Minto.

They surely wouldn't go that far, or maybe that's where they'd come from and they'd be heading back.

Elsa lived in Minto...

Elsa.

Fuck.

Grace needed to get out of here.

Now. Tonight.

She opened her cupboard and found her dad's old ruck-sack, the army green one he used for camping as a kid himself. Still smelled of his sour deodorant. Still had a few tins of beans in the bottom. Didn't have dates on them, they were that old. Probably poisonous, but who'd care if Grace died?

'Grace?' Mum stormed into the room. 'Where are you?'

Grace dropped the bag and stepped back out of the cupboard. 'Here.'

Mum was clutching a can of Coke. 'Got you this.'

'Thanks.' Grace took it off her. Super cold like it came from the fridge in the chip shop. She sat down at her desk in front of her computer. 'What's up?'

'You didn't say hello when you got in.'

'I did.'

Mum had her hands on her hips. 'What's going on? Has something happened?'

'Nothing.'

'I know there's something going on. What is it?'

'I've got an essay to write for tomorrow.'

'Grace! Did you forget?'

'Remember when we went away two weeks ago and you took me out of school and—'

'To see your father. Yes. Why?'

'The teacher gave us it then. Nobody told me.'

'Ah.' Mum pecked her on the cheek. 'Tea's on. Won't be long.'

'Cool, Mum.' Grace unlocked her laptop. Waited for Mum to leave. Waited for her to thunder down the stairs.

The Coke can was open so she couldn't take it with her. She slurped some of it, then went back into her cupboard.

Her phone chimed a few times.

Two were the same TikTok video. A lot of people in the area liked it – the police had found some bodies at Elibank up near Galashiels. Dad took her cycling there once.

The other was a WhatsApp from Tiegan, her friend at school. The only one who Elsa hadn't infected. The only one she spoke to now.

Tiegan: You left the group.

Elsa's a lying bitch.

Tiegan: Why not say that?

Nobody listens to me.

Tiegan: Elsa said she's called the cops about you.

Fuck.

Grace raced over to the wardrobe and started stuffing jeans, T-shirts and jumpers in. Her battered old Converses, the ones without the holes. Her dad gave them to her. They were precious, a thin thread back to the past. She put on Dad's old walking boots, which were still too big. She went over to her bedside table and stuffed knickers and socks in. The Colleen Hoover hardback went in too. She took the mobile charger out of the wall, then started coiling it up.

No.

Dad told her not to do that. She took her phone out of her pocket and dropped it on the carpet at the bottom of the cupboard.

Then stood there, trying to figure it all out.

Staring at Mr Teddy.

Her little bear with TEDDY on his jumper. Had him since she was a baby. Dad's mum gave her him. And Mr Teddy was making those eyes at her.

'Of course I'm taking you, Mr Teddy.'

She put him right on the top, then pulled the bag's cord tight and slipped the cover over, clipping it tight. She left her room and tried to sneak down the stairs, but it was a loud clump with those wobbly boots on. She grabbed her jacket from the post and left the cottage without another word.

As she walked, she hauled her coat on and the bag bobbled around on her back. Heavier than she expected and the tins clanked together. She got the zip done up then slung both arms over her shoulder.

Heavy.

'Grace!'

She swung back around.

Mum was walking along the path. 'Where are you going?'

Grace turned and bombed it into the field, crunching over the dry scrub.

'Grace! Come back!'

Grace never wanted to see her mum again.

CHAPTER TWENTY-FIVE
SIYAL

DS Rakesh Siyal wasn't used to sitting in an interview with a DI. When he was a lawyer, it'd be a DC and a DS on the cases he ran.

DI Jon Bruce, though, wasn't just in the room, he was leading the interview with Keane. 'You can see how it looks to us, Martin. You told us a body was in those woods. Someone you killed. And of course, you gave us a buy-one-get-one-free deal with the second body. That was good of you. But the third one – you didn't expect us to find him, did you?'

Keane trained his focus on Siyal, rather than Bruce, which was unsettling him. He had the weirdest eyes. Pale like ice. No, something else. Like a marketing executive's idea of ice. How they'd package chewing gum at a supermarket till. Or an expensive watch or aftershave in a magazine advert.

'Alexander Quiller and Caitlyn Westerberg, sure. But you didn't expect us to find Stan Di Melo.'

Keane picked his nose then wiped it on the table.

Bruce swallowed. 'The problem with time is you forget what happened years ago, right?'

Keane chewed on his thumbnail where he'd cut it. A trail of blood had dried. Nobody had given him a plaster. Siyal wasn't going to.

Bruce rubbed at his forehead. 'If *I*'d killed someone ten years ago, I'd still remember absolutely everything about it. Name, location, job, how I killed them. All of it. But Stan was just one of many.'

Keane scratched at his balls.

Siyal leaned forward and cracked his elbows off the table. It hurt. 'Nine victims.'

Keane focused on him. 'Ten.'

'Oh yeah, your friend.' Siyal tilted his head to the side. 'I think it's thirteen.'

'Ten.' Keane shifted his gaze to Bruce. 'Those three aren't mine.'

'Not directly, no. But you know something about them, don't you? You know who killed them. Who buried them there. Why they did it.'

'I'm not a liar. I just don't know.'

'Okay, so you're trying to tell me that someone just so happened to kill someone in the same place you've been dumping bodies?' Bruce laughed. 'Pull the other one.'

Keane opened his mouth. 'Do you want—'

Mark Davidson looked up from making a note, then jostled his client.

So fast.

Siyal wouldn't have noticed it if he hadn't been staring at the creepy lawyer. The worst kind of person in his old profession.

Davidson wasn't a lawyer because he loved the law, with its elegant way of putting everything in the right place and establishing clear rules.

He didn't fight for poor souls like Siyal had done. The

downtrodden. The abused. The left behind.

No, Mark Davidson was all about himself. Working for a firm that had taken over his father's, that subsumed him into a partnership position. Davidson was a lawyer for money, pure and simple.

Why else would he sit next to a man like Martin Keane? A murderer. A confessed murderer. And someone who hated people just like Davidson enough to murder them in cold blood.

But Keane had no money. No friends, no family. Representing him for a guilty plea would've been court-appointed and not very lucrative. But mostly it brought fame – and associated infamy and so more opportunities for him to make even more money.

He couldn't have done enough to have been brought into Keane's confidence – if Davidson knew anything, his history showed he would have leaked it already. All the same, Keane had been about to slip until Davidson said and did something that shut him up.

Siyal knew it.

What, though? What was Keane about to say?

Bruce leaned forward. 'Come on, Martin. You looked like you were about to own up there. What do you know about those bodies?'

'I want to go home now.'

Bruce looked over at Siyal, raising his eyebrows.

Siyal shrugged – he didn't think they'd get anything else out of him, certainly not now.

'Fine.' Bruce spoke into the mic: 'Interview terminated at sixteen fourteen.' He hit stop on the recorder, then got to his feet.

Keane looked up at him. 'Can I go?'

'We're waiting on a judge to extend the return date for a few days.'

'Please. Take me back. I don't know anything. I've given you all of my victims.'

Bruce checked his watch. 'Due in court in about ten minutes. There are another ten senior cops who all want to take a shot at you. With good luck, you'll be back in your cell about three o'clock in the morning. Ready for a nice wakeup call at six.'

'That's torture.'

'You'd know all about that, eh?' Bruce clapped Siyal on the arm. 'Come on, Sergeant, let's leave him to stew.' He led out into the corridor and shut the door, then blew air up his face.

Siyal gestured at the door. 'He knows something about this.'

Bruce looked over at Siyal. 'Are you sure? Because Marshall says Keane isn't a liar.'

'Not Keane. Davidson.'

'What?'

'Didn't you see them? He shut him up.'

'Right, right. What was—'

The door opened and Davidson followed them out, carrying his briefcase. 'I need to get something to eat.'

Bruce thumbed to the side. 'Co-op a few doors up.'

'I need something more substantial than a supermarket sandwich.'

'There are a few nice eateries in this town, Mark.' Bruce clamped a hand on his arm. 'Not sure they'll serve someone like you.'

Davidson brushed his hand away. 'What's that supposed to mean?'

'Someone who makes a living defending monsters.'

'Even monsters are allowed criminal defence lawyers.'

'Mark, whatever it was you said to your pet monster, you made sure he shut up good and proper, eh? Well done.'

'He shut himself up, you numpty. He's been doing that to you lot for ten years. Don't think I have any control over when he talks or what he says... he's his own muppet.'

'Thing is, he won't be prosecuted for the three additional murders he's held back on for ten years. I don't agree with it, but what can you do?' Bruce pointed at the closed door. 'The new three, though... We're very interested in nailing him to the wall for those, balls first.'

'Jonathan, what you do in your own time with hammers, nails and scrota isn't my business, assuming it's with consenting adults.' Davidson ran his tongue over his lips. 'What *is* my business are my client's legal rights. You need to gather evidence, prove the case, then prosecute, or not. If you have evidence he did it, then he's already in jail until he dies. It's not in the public interest to prosecute him again now. You know yourself, Jonathan, that trials are expensive and if the results are inevitable, then why do it? Neither the Procurator Fiscal nor the CPS will sign off on a show trial. And Mr Keane has clearly not killed these three additional bodies. I would've thought a man like yourself, with your personal history, would be very careful about not prosecuting an innocent man. Again.'

Bruce laughed. 'Martin Keane is *not* innocent.'

'Jonathan, you *know* my client didn't do these, so why waste time like this? Investigate then interview, please. And you can't interview him without my presence. The bottom line is he didn't kill these people.'

'True, but Charles Manson wasn't there when his followers murdered Sharon Tate.'

'Martin Keane is *not* Charles Manson.'

'Brilliant.' Bruce laughed again. 'Should make T-shirts with that slogan.'

'Anyway.' Davidson hugged his briefcase close to his chest. 'I shall be gone for about an hour, so please do some police work in that time.' He focused on Siyal. 'Very odd seeing you on this side of the fence, Rakesh.'

'Is it?' Siyal folded his arms. 'Last time we met, you didn't recognise me. Blanked me, in fact.'

'Remind me?'

'I arrested a drug-dealing hairdresser in July. Someone who you represented.'

'Ah, yes. Actually, I did recognise you then, but I needed to make sure you didn't have a twin brother who was a cop before I made a grave error.'

'Hardly a grave error.'

Davidson looked down his nose at him. 'Why did you quit the law?'

'I didn't quit.'

'So it quit you, then?' Davidson flashed his nicotine-stained teeth. 'You're DS Rakesh Siyal now. That's some fall from grace.'

'I chose to change professions because of people like you, Mark. You're responsible for what happened to Afri Shamsuddin.'

'Oh, come on. That was an open-and-shut case. She was an illegal migrant and *clearly* in the wrong.'

'She was desperate. And your client abused that. He kicked the shit out of her. A pregnant woman. A desperate woman.'

'She should've gone through official channels.'

'When your life's on the line, you have to act. Thing is, she'd starting going through official channels. I was putting her paperwork through at the time of her attack. If you hadn't—'

'Listen, I'm just glad there's one fewer woke lawyer sullying—'

'Woke?'

'And now there's a woke cop instead. I'm not sure that's better, but it's less harmful to me personally. Know what they say – go woke, go broke.'

'It isn't woke. It's basic human decency.' Siyal felt his blood thudding in his throat. 'You—'

'Hey, hey.' Bruce got between them. 'Enough of this.'

'Do you know what his client did? He tied up a pregnant woman and kicked the shit out of her.' Siyal jabbed a finger at Davidson. 'You represent subhuman scumbags. It's only because she escaped that she isn't dead.'

'My client didn't perpetrate the violence against her.'

Siyal stopped. Felt his forehead crease. 'What?'

Davidson raised his hands. 'You're preaching to the choir! I'm a member of Amnesty.'

'Virtue signalling. Great.' Siyal held his gaze, long and hard. 'What did you mean? Who did it to Afri?'

Davidson glared at him. 'See you around, *Shunty*. Heard you buggered another car today. Or three.' He scurried off down the corridor like a rat.

'Creepy bastard.' Bruce was stroking his chin, watching him go. 'Maybe he did it.'

'Did what?'

'Worked with Keane to kill those three people. Wouldn't be surprised if he had a cling film machine at home.'

Siyal frowned. 'Are you sure about that?'

'Nah, he's a useless sod. The only thing he's murdering is a pizza and a bag of chips.' Bruce stared at him. 'You used to be a lawyer?'

'Criminal defence. Human rights, mainly.'

'Better off out of it. And don't let creeps like him get to you.'

'I try, but... Listen, I'm serious. I think we should treat him as a suspect.'

'Aye, so am I. Look, we've got a briefing. Let's raise it with Pringle.'

'You want me there?'

'Of course I do.'

CHAPTER TWENTY-SIX
MARSHALL

Marshall stood in the corner like he could hide away. He sipped another cup of that coffee, but this time he had it black – some bugger had swiped his fresh milk and he didn't like the smell of the other stuff. Probably been left out on the counter for hours. Or worse.

Elliot was in the middle, over by the whiteboard, sipping from a teacup. 'My youngest is like that. Just... I can't get through to them.'

'Mine's too young for that stuff.' Jolene sipped from a protein shake in a green bottle. 'It's all David Walliams books with her.'

'Oh, that's a long shift.'

'I stopped buying them for my daughter.' Pringle didn't have a drink, just a cheeky glint in his eyes. 'Couldn't stand *Little Britain*. Can't stand him. And yet the kids go mad for him.'

'Wait.' Elliot tilted her head to the side. 'Your *daughter*?'

Pringle started warming his hands on the radiator at the back. 'Kirsty.'

'You don't have a daughter, Jim.'

'Eh, I do.'

'How old is she?'

'Seven.'

'You've kept a seven-year-old daughter secret from a team of detectives?'

Pringle grasped his elbow and his chin – the thinker's pose. 'Good point. I'll need to cover that at your next annual appraisal.' His phone rang. 'Bums. It's the lord of the dance settee. I'll be back.' He left the incident room but didn't shut the door behind him, so his voice rattled around in the silence.

'Absolute cobblers.' Elliot walked over and closed the door, then scowled at it. 'Got to get up pretty bloody early in the morning to get one over on me.'

Siyal was over the other side of the room, staring out of the window. 'I've heard him talk about her. Kirsty.'

'Shite you have, Shunty.'

'Seriously.'

Jolene's mouth was an O. 'He gave me a used crib when Joe was born.'

'Shut the front door.' Elliot slammed her cup down. 'Jim's a wind-up merchant. This is nonsense.' She glowered at Marshall. 'Professor Plums, what's your take on it?'

'I don't know whether to believe it or not. He's an interesting guy.'

The door burst open and slammed back against the wall, and Pringle waltzed back in. 'Okay, gang, circle the wagons around.'

Bruce followed him, looking like his drug dealer had swapped ketamine for speed.

Pringle perched on the edge of a desk and juggled his phone. 'The bad news, children, is I've officially landed the case, all thanks to you, Marshall. The boss is fuming at me for us taking it on. I'll take the heat on that, but we need to get a result here. Okay?'

For all his abstract jocularity, Pringle seemed to be happy about this. Only so much low-level crime you could subject yourself to as a senior detective before you actually wanted to go out and cause something major yourself.

Pringle shifted his gaze around the room. 'Those three bodies are going to make the media shitshow erupt into... Well. An even bigger shitshow. That'll be my job for the next month – shovelling shite for the international shit-shovellers. Our request to house him here didn't pass muster with the judge so, while we interview him, we're going to have to travel down to HMP Frankland. The Looney Lounge or whatever they call it.'

Bruce sighed. 'Monster Mansion.'

'Right, right. Just think of the petrol. And overnight accommodation.' Pringle threw his phone high and caught it between his middle and ring fingers. 'Bloody hell.'

'We'll be taking lead on it, Jim.' Bruce stood up tall. 'I was in with him for a stint just now. Me and DS Siyal.' He sipped from his water bottle. 'Got nothing out of him.'

'Wonders will never cease.' Pringle stopped messing about with his phone and put it away. 'If he's clammed up, I doubt we'll get him to speak about these additional murders.'

'He kept quiet for ten years, sir.' Marshall looked around the room. 'He's good at it and loves the attention. Cut it off, then get back in touch only when he says so.'

Pringle frowned. 'You think?'

'I think. It's possible he doesn't know anything about them.' Marshall stood up and walked over to the whiteboard. 'But I can't shake the feeling it's not a coincidence. Stan's body was dumped pretty far from the other two. But the new three were near his. That's strange.'

'Do you think he has a protégé?'

Marshall scowled at him. 'How is it possible for him to have a protégé?'

'Okay, hear me out. If Keane's involved, it's clearly not him doing it. So either it's a copycat he doesn't know about, or it's someone Keane trained as a protégé. My question is thus: do you think someone is committing murders for Keane?'

'Let's slow it down.' Marshall's head felt like it could burst. 'Let's start with the possibility of it being a copycat. I don't think it is.'

'Why not?'

'The only thing connecting them is the location. The Shadow Man killed quickly. A blitz attack. Frenzy, complete overkill. Death was his sole objective. He optimised murder. He got very efficient. His sole motive was to show to the world that he was powerful, that he was better than the fittest athletes. The rich ones. He dominated them completely and took their lives before they could even react. This other killer seems to have a different motive. He is physically torturing them over a prolonged timeframe.'

'Death by a thousand cu—' Pringle cleared his throat. 'Cuts?'

'Right. I saw the bodies. Signs of cutting but not violent or out of control. Precise. And he's likely repeatedly sexually assaulting them. Wrapping them in cling film. The oxygen masks. It's about power, domination and control. I'd say he has the physical means or charisma to carry out an elaborate set of attacks, whereas Keane... didn't. He used to attack them with a rope. Knock them over. When they were wounded, he swooped in and killed them. This other killer—'

'The protégé.'

Marshall wished he wouldn't use that term. 'He's abducting them first.'

'Why do you say that?'

'I didn't see a cling film machine in the woods, did you?'

'Ah, I see. So he's abducting them, wrapping them. Then torturing them and abusing them. Then he kills them and buries them.'

'Right. Yes. But the fact he's wrapping them in cling film... It's fucked up, to be perfectly frank. He's delaying their deaths and subjecting them to an ordeal. One he – and only he – controls.'

Pringle looked at each of them in turn, then back at Marshall. 'Okay, sir, how about you run us through the possibilities?'

Elliot grabbed a pen and uncapped it. 'Let me be your beautiful assistant, Professor Plums.'

Like Marshall was some stage magician. 'First possibility is, like the DCI says, that Keane has a collaborator.'

'Or a protégé.' Pringle looked around the room. 'Do we have any suspects?'

Siyal held up his hand. 'Mark Davidson.'

'The lawyer?'

'Right. He's sly.'

'Sly?' Pringle laughed. 'We need a bit more than him being sly, Sergeant.'

Bruce snorted. 'I agree with Rakesh. Davidson *is* sly, but he's... There's something about him. He got Keane to shut up when he was about to say something. I don't know what. I'm suggesting DS Siyal investigates him.'

Pringle's mouth hung open. 'You want Shunty to investigate his lawyer?'

'Why not?' Bruce shrugged. 'Lad's been in the Monster

Mansion every so often. They chat. Stands to reason, doesn't it?'

Pringle looked at Elliot. 'Andrea, what's your thinky?'

'My thinky... Well, investigating him isn't a good look.'

Pringle looked at Marshall. 'And you, Professor?'

'Like DI Bruce says, Davidson is someone who has regular interactions with Keane. Stands to reason he's a suspect. Or the go-between to the actual suspect.'

'Ah, the protégé's message boy.' Pringle stared at the whiteboard. 'Our first action is for DS Siyal to investigate a criminal defence lawyer.' He was shaking his head. 'This is... Just don't get into trouble.'

Elliot scribbled it down. 'Only thing Davidson has to fear is being run over. Long as he's not behind the wheel of a motor, he'll be fine. As will his wing mirrors.'

'I'll be counting the pennies for that little incident this morning until my dotage.' Pringle gave a belly laugh. 'Okay. So are there any others who he's meeting?'

Bruce shoved his hands into his pockets. 'No visitors of note, save for that creepy doyle of a lawyer and the podcaster.'

'Oh, now you've piqued my interest.'

'I've done three quarters of their meetings myself. Keane just sits there, talking about killing all those people.' Bruce scribbled 'VICKERS' on the whiteboard then ran his hand through his hair. 'That guy is a tit. Just wants to enrich himself at the misery of others.'

'Have you checked into his background?'

'We did a deep check when Keane requested access to him. Just in case he had a screw loose. Came back clean.'

'Can you share the results of your check with us?'

'Fine.' Bruce scribbled something on the board.

'Anybody else?'

'Guards don't speak to him. Only other visitor is Dr Curtis

from Durham. First time Keane actually said anything to her was to ask to speak to Goldberg. Failing that, he wanted to see Professor Plums here.'

'I'm not a professor.'

Elliot smirked. 'Aye, but Doctor Plums doesn't sound as good. Wait.' She clicked her fingers. 'Doctor Donkey.'

'An education wouldn't have gone amiss on you.' Bruce grabbed a pen and scored through what she'd just written – 'VISITOR'.

She looked him up and down. 'What about any correspondents?'

'Nope. Keane's post goes through so many eyes, including mine. Besides, he hasn't sent or received anything in a couple of years. All Keane does is sit and read the newspapers. He consumes information but doesn't put anything back out there. That's how he saw the case Rob was involved in. Sorry, Doctor Donkey.'

'Okay, Jonny boy.' Pringle took the pen and scribbled something. 'I need some low-level imbecile to go through the prison logs in detail. Interview transcripts too. And I need people interviewing all of the guards.' He wrote on the board, the marker squeaking loud.

Marshall looked at what was up there. It was the inverse of how he'd approach this. He'd think it all through, attack all the angles. All the board contained was a load of random shit Bruce and Elliot had done in previous cases. No insight or strategy. 'I'd rather we consider it was someone unconnected.'

'Could. Not. Agree. More.' Elliot snatched the pen out of Pringle's grasp. 'I'll show you how it's done.' She wrote something even a forensic handwriting expert or superhuman artificial intelligence couldn't decipher in a million years. 'Okay. Elephant in the room. Could he have a friendly guard killing for him?'

Bruce shook his head. 'Covered that. Nope. Nope. And thrice nope.'

'Why not?'

'They all want to remove his teeth with pliers. Or baseball bats.'

'Okay, but Keane's a manipulative son of a bitch. There's got to be someone he can intimidate.'

'You're talking about a guard letting him escape from prison to kill?'

'I think so.'

'Andrea, that place is called the Monster Mansion for a reason. It houses murderers, rapists, terrorists. The worst of our society. You don't work there unless you're vetted by the best. And they keep monitoring you and your family and friends.'

Elliot shrugged. 'Still think it's a possibility.'

'What?' Bruce threw his arms in the air. 'Listen, there's no way he's getting out of there and back in, is there? Biggest living serial killer in England. Talk about high profile. Besides, that place is locked down tighter than a billionaire's prenup.'

'You're the boss, boss.' Elliot sniffed, like she was hiding a laugh. 'Okay, so how about a cellmate who's now free?'

Bruce was checking his phone. 'In seg unit all his time in there.'

'He was in seg for *ten years*?'

'Well, no. Had a cellmate for the first six months, but they got into a big fight. Other guy was hospitalised. He's been flying solo since, even with the overcrowding in there.'

'Well, well.' Elliot clicked her fingers. 'We've got ourselves a suspect.'

'No, you don't. Alfred Constantine died six years ago, partially as a result of what Keane did to him.'

Pringle twisted his lips. 'Seg isn't solitary. People would come and go. He'd have to interact with others.'

'So let's check them all out. Possible one of those sick puppies is out.' Elliot stared at the board like it showed something other than illegible scribbles. 'I'd put my money on Keane having a copycat and not a protégé.'

Pringle stroked his chin. 'What's the difference?'

'A copycat isn't doing crimes in his name. Someone he has no control over.' Elliot looked at Bruce. 'What about anybody in Keane's friends or family who might know about this?'

'No chance. All of them were spoken to ten years ago. We'll go through the list again, of course, shaking the tree to see what falls out, but every single one disowned him years before he was arrested. And there weren't exactly a lot. Less than the people in this room.'

'Fewer...' Pringle looked at the board. 'So you think it's just a random stranger, then?'

'Could be. We don't know.'

Pringle grabbed the pen off Elliot but didn't write anything. 'Okay. For the sake of clarity, let's go through those friends and family. Marshall?'

He tried to think through the biography he'd stored in his head. Most of it was stuff he worried he'd forgotten – it'd been ten years, after all. 'Keane was an only child. Parents died around the time he started killing. Possible trigger for what he did. No immediate family. No friends from school. Left at sixteen. If I recall correctly, he barely attended in later years. Reports he was bullied, but nothing was actually done about it.'

Marshall managed to read some of the shit on the board. He took the pen and wrote himself an action that humans could actually read. 'Bottom line is we don't have a clue who killed the other three.'

Bruce leaned back against the wall. 'I'd say that's a fair comment.'

Pringle took a deep breath through his nostrils. 'Are you telling me I've taken on a case where—'

The door clattered open and Kirsten stormed in. 'Sorry.'

'No need to apologise.' Pringle rolled his eyes. 'Though when you enter a room like that, Kirsten, I expect you to save the day.'

'No such luck.' She rested against the filing cabinet closest to Marshall. 'Just wanted to give you an update. My lot are combing the whole forest, but it's used by dog walkers, cyclists and the occasional Forestry Commission worker. We are going to be up to our oxters with stuff to process in those six graves...'

'Your old chums in Edinburgh are on their way down for a jolly...'

'Even so. The Forestry and Land guys have been very helpful. Bett-Leighton in particular. He said a lot of other plantations around here will be forested soon. Storm Arwen was a wake-up call to get the wood out of the ground.'

Pringle rubbed his hands together. 'So they would've dug up those bodies?'

'Nope. No plans to cut down those trees. Besides, they're pretty deeply buried. The machines would've just missed them.'

Could be Marshall's imagination but Elliot stood up a bit taller now Kirsten was there. 'My team are going to interview the Forestry Commission team.'

Pringle raised a finger. 'Forestry and Land Scotland now.'

'Whatever they're called, we're going to haul them over the coals.'

Pringle clenched his jaw. 'Andrea, remember that they've done nothing.'

'Still, someone might have knowledge of what happened.'

Pringle huffed out a deep sigh. 'Next steps, then. Marshall, I want you to work up a profile. We've got a serial killer here.'

That was going to mean dealing with Liana.

Great...

'Happy to. But we'll need a lot more data than the bodies. Keane killed nine people we know of. Six we had the bodies for and the three we've just found. But this clearly isn't Keane.'

'What are you saying?'

'That we're starting from scratch with the profile of a different killer. And we need to identify the victims first. Victimology is the first step. I can't do a profile if I don't know who the victims are, where they came from, what their commonalities are. All of that. The original victims were all from the northeast of England, around Newcastle, Durham, Sunderland. Not local to us. These could be from up here. Could be from Transylvania. We don't know.'

Kirsten rolled her eyes at Marshall – subtle, but not quite enough. 'Jim, as for the new victims, we're running DNA tests on them now. Should get some results back in an hour or two.'

Elliot curled up her lip. 'I've worked cross-border before.'

Pringle chuckled. 'And that wasn't something that cost me hours in conference calls, was it?'

'I mean it.' Marshall focused on Elliot. 'We need to know who died. Okay?'

'Okay. I hear you.'

'Excellent stuff.' Pringle was nodding. 'Andrea, I expect your team to be matching the victims against missing persons reports. Age, sex, height, weight, hair, etc. Lots of ways to cross-reference.'

'Teaching your granny to suck eggs, Jim.' Elliot jotted it down on the board.

Pringle swept his gaze across the board. 'But I think Marshall's profile is going to help us focus the investigation.

There will be literally hundreds of people to rule out, so knowing where to look will save time and resources.'

Marshall laughed. 'No pressure, eh?'

Pringle jumped to attention then clapped his hands. 'Let's get to it.'

The room cleared like someone had broken wind.

Leaving just Marshall and Siyal, who was staring out of the window.

'You okay there, Rakesh?'

'Not really, Rob.'

'You not okay investigating Davidson? He's Keane's lawyer, stands to reason he's a suspect.'

'It's not that...'

'Go on?'

'I've got previous with him.' Siyal turned around. 'In my old job. I had a client. Afri Shamsuddin. Afghan women tend to not have surnames. They're a nomadic people, but she had one. Tells you a lot. She was a lawyer back home. The Taliban killed her husband when we pulled out last year, so she fled. Walked over the border to Pakistan. Got a flight to Turkey, then hitched her way here. Got many lifts from dodgy people until she arrived. She knew a woman in Edinburgh who took her in. Worked as a cleaner. Found she was pregnant. Then a pub landlord kicked the shit out of her. She was locked up in his basement but somehow escaped. He was charged but the case fell apart. Problem was, she was done for illegal immigration. Sitting in Dungavel House now, awaiting deportation. An immigration removal centre. I mean...'

'Guessing his lawyer was Davidson?'

'Got it in one. Thing is... Today, he said it was someone else who did it. Not the pub landlord. He knows more than he's letting on.'

Marshall saw some deep trauma in the way he looked at him. 'This is why you joined the police, right?'

'Right.'

'Okay. Do you think he's involved in these murders?'

'He could be, Rob. That's the thing.'

'Okay. Investigate him. But be careful about it. Keep me posted.' Marshall smiled. 'But more importantly, keep DI Elliot posted.'

CHAPTER TWENTY-SEVEN
GRACE

The number of times Grace had sneaked across the golf course to Harrison's house was unreal. Then she had to avoid his dad as she crept up and knocked on Harrison's window. Guy was a green keeper, so he could spot tracks in the grass.

She looked behind her, expecting to see her mum running after her. Surprised her car wasn't parked out front, but it was just Harrison's pocket rocket.

The cottage sat at the edge of Minto, not quite in the village, not that there was much of it, just a few old houses and—

What was it her mum called them?

Steadings. That was it. Old farm buildings that were now people's homes.

She walked up to his bedroom window and heard that band he loved playing.

Crywank. What a name.

She chapped on the glass. Waited, then another two chaps.

She hoped he wasn't having a crywank in there.

His blinds snapped open and he was standing there in his Calvin Kleins. Razor thin and almost hairless, like a shaved monkey, just those circles of wiry hair around his nipples. His fringe swept down and hugged his eyes. Trouble with having a boyfriend a few years older, who had a job on a farm and his own car was...

Well.

He wasn't her boyfriend anymore.

And he shagged anything that moved, when he could.

Harrison opened the window wide enough to let her in but blocked it. He was stinking of Lynx. 'Hey. You okay?'

'I'm fine.' She didn't feel it. 'Has Mum been here?'

'Not since last month. When she made us split up. Why?'

'Harrison, I'm in trouble...'

'You're pregnant? I thought you were on the pill?'

'No, no. Nothing like that. Just... I need help.'

'Babe, I love you but I'm seeing the boys tonight. Going up to Edinburgh.'

'On a Monday?'

'Big house party at the uni, aye.'

'Harrison, I need you to drive me somewhere.'

'Babe, I'm meeting Steve and Dicko in, like, twenty minutes. Dicko's brother's driving us up to Tweedbank for the train.'

'I need help, Harrison.'

'What's happened?'

'The cops are after me.'

'What?' He was looking behind her like they were in hot pursuit.

'I need to get away. I'm leaving. Can you give me a lift to Hawick?'

'Hawick? Baby, that's the opposite direction. We're going to Jedburgh to pick up Dongle on the way.'

'Please.'

'Look, I can't help you. I'd be aiding and abetting a fugitive.'

'I didn't fucking do anything!'

'So why are you running away from home?'

'Because Elsa's saying I killed someone.'

'Woah, woah. *Killed* someone?'

'I didn't do it.'

'Why are you running, then?'

'The cops won't believe me.'

'Why not?'

'Because there's no evidence. It's my word against hers.'

'Elsa?'

'Right. Look, if you're not going to help, I need to get gone.'

'What's she saying you did, Grace?'

'At Kieron's party on Saturday night in Hawick, Deacon Smith was wasted. Elsa poured meths into his glass and he drank it. Ended up in hospital. Stomach pumped. Tiegan heard that Deacon *died*.'

'Shit.'

'And I didn't do it.'

He looked down his nose at her. 'So why's she saying you did?'

She wrapped her arms around herself. The tins clunked. 'Because I was messing about with the bottle earlier and everyone saw it. Elsa videoed it. She's going to put it on TikTok.'

'Grace. You need to go to the cops. Tell the truth. They'll believe—'

'Harrison, don't you ever listen to me? My dad told the truth and that's why he's in prison.'

He leaned back into his room and gave his skinny torso

another blast of Lynx. 'Babe, running away looks guilty as hell. If you didn't do it, tell them the truth.'

'I can't prove I didn't! They're all saying I killed him!' She was sounding like a crazy person. 'Harrison. I'm desperate here. My whole life has fallen apart because of this. All the dicks in school shouting about how I'm John Wayne Gacy. It's all over the WhatsApp group... Nobody believes me. My life's *over*.'

Harrison took a deep breath. 'Don't you think this is an overreaction?'

'No.' She was shaking her head. It was an underreaction if anything. 'Do you want me to suck your dick or something?'

He glanced over at the clock, like he was checking if he could spare the twenty seconds. 'It's just...' He ran a hand through his hair. 'Fine. I'll give you a lift.'

CHAPTER TWENTY-EIGHT
MARSHALL

It was one thing seeing the bones in shallow graves on the site – porcelain against soil – but quite another seeing Keane's victims on the slabs in Pathology. Skeletons laid out. Two young men and a woman, long since gone.

Dr Belu Owusu stood over them, running a hand over her short hair. 'It's going to be hard to do a post-mortem on them, is the bottom line.' Her South African accent was jarring and staccato.

Marshall took in the sight, spotting the gouges the knife had taken from the ribs.

Jolene stood a few feet away from her, hugging herself tight. 'Are they Keane's?'

'That's easy. Martin Keane murdered his victims with knives. Gouges to the throat from the rope he used to knock them over, then stabbing at their chests. With these... I'm seeing marks on the bones, specifically the ribs, which would be consistent with a frenzied blitz attack. And there's no healing taking place, so it's safe to say they died as a result of this.' She pointed at the throat of one. 'Also, since he used a rope at neck height and they hit it with some velocity, he either dislocated or fractured cervical vertebrae. Or both. And two of them, he broke the hyoid bone. Cause of death in all three is... hard to say. Multiple thoracic lacerations inflicted by a single-edged blade approximately three centimetres in width. Probably exsanguination, but could be ruptured heart or lungs. My full report will be ready this evening.'

Jolene stepped a bit closer. 'How closely does that match the other six from that message board?'

'Sufficiently consistent to imply the same killer using similar MOs.'

Marshall stared up at the ductwork on the ceiling. 'How about identifying the bodies?'

'That's not a problem. Assuming these are them, we know Stan and we can tell Caitlyn and Alexander apart, but I'll be working with Kirsten's lot to process the DNA of all three. It'll be a while before we know if these are actually the victims.'

'Even with that new machine up in Edinburgh she keeps going on about?'

'That won't be the hard part. Getting the DNA off these bodies will be. They're so badly decomposed that we might not be able to obtain anything. But the bone marrow should be a good source. It's protected from the elements unless there has been a fracture. So harvesting DNA from a femur or pelvis is still very possible.'

'I appreciate it. What about the other victims?'

'That's where I'm much more on home soil.' She led him across the lab towards another set of slabs. This side of the room was freezing and stank of ammonia. 'Keane's victims were all quick kills, on location, near to where they were found. Overkill, sure, but it all happened there and then. Two minutes, three maybe. Then he buried them quickly and left the scene of the crime.' She pointed at the new bodies. The post-mortem would open up the cling film, but right now, they looked like mannequins waiting to be shipped to a sex shop in Soho or Amsterdam. 'These guys were wrapped from head to toe. After they'd had oxygen masks secured to their mouths.' She lifted the body of a young man and flipped it over. Marshall was sure his penis was missing. The back of the cling film was wide open, revealing pale flesh. 'All three have various openings to permit torture and/or abuse.'

'Sexual?'

'Not sure. Knife wounds for definite. Burns. Cuts with rough edges. The other two victims look like they went through a blender.'

'In this context, piquerism is a close substitute for sexual assault.'

She frowned. 'Piquerism?'

'Sexual interest in penetrating the skin of another person with sharp objects.'

'I see.' Owusu pointed at another victim. 'The wounds on the back of her show—'

'Her?'

'One of them is female.'

'Okay. Sorry for the interruption.'

'No problem. They show that time has elapsed during the assault. Her wounds have healed over. See?' Owusu was pointing at the back of the woman.

Marshall saw what she meant. Though the skin was rotting away, it wasn't a wound that was fresh at the time of death. The skin had been given time to turn to scar tissue. 'And the men?'

'Some healing evident.' She gestured at the flipped-over body, then at the third. Again, his penis was missing. 'They show some signs of cauterising and healing, but not scarring like with her.'

'And the penises?'

'Found inside their mouths. Keane was ambivalent about the gender of his victims. Male or female, they received approximately the same treatment. Overkill. But this guy, there's definitely more violence towards the male victims.' She slapped the nearest body like it was a side of beef. 'He's removed the penis and testicles and placed them in the victim's mouths.'

Marshall didn't want to see but got the sick feeling in his gut all the same. As experienced as he was, some things made even his gut clench. 'He was ashamed to have acted out on males, so he punished them post-mortem.'

'You're the head-doctor, Marshall.'

'I'm assuming it's a he, then. A he who feels a bit shameful about doing this to a man. The fact she was able to scar over shows he didn't have the same feeling of guilt over her.'

'Not something I can really comment on. But I'd say they were stored somewhere beforehand.'

'And the masks gave him a time limit, showed he was in absolute control of them.' Marshall stared at the corpses. 'Keane's were angry acts, but these were calculated – sexual torture or a substitute for it. And they were likely kept alive and tortured. How did they die?'

'Asphyxiation.'

'Not exsanguination?'

'Correct. Different MO to Keane. The masks were wrapped in the cling film, but they weren't hooked up to anything when we recovered them. So I'd suggest they died where they were being kept when the air ran out. And he disposed of them afterwards.'

Jolene cleared her throat. Marshall had almost forgotten she was there. 'The fact they were buried in the woods... It's like they were dumped. So the only connection between them is the location.'

Marshall raised a finger. 'We don't know the victimology yet. The variety of genders is similar to Keane's previous kills. Similar ages, though maybe younger.'

'The cling film...' Jolene scowled at him. 'That's not ten packs of Ashworth's Saver. That's hardcore stuff. Industrial stuff. Rolls two, three, four metres wide. Big enough to wrap a whole cow or a flight case holding a drum kit. You need a factory or farm with that kind of equipment.'

'Good point.' Marshall scribbled it down in his notebook along with a few other salient points. 'Someone with industrial access. And the fact they were kept alive with oxygen, we're looking at someone with medical expertise.'

Owusu grunted. 'Stop jumping to conclusions, Marshall.'

He looked over at her. 'Eh?'

'We don't know it was oxygen they were piped up to. It could've been compressed air. Could also have been how he killed them. Hook the masks up to carbon dioxide or helium or an inert gas. Lights out pretty quickly. Or it could just be he found a load of masks somewhere and he put them on so he didn't have to look at their faces.'

'Thanks.' Marshall was sweating – that was a stupid assumption he could've made and got caught out on later. 'I'll add that to the new profile. Good stuff.' He snapped his note-book shut. 'I'm convinced it's nothing to do with Keane.'

'I'd agree with that.' She clicked her fingers a few times. 'Actually... Your copycat or protégé aren't—'

'Protégé?'

'It could be someone Keane knew, right? Someone he nurtured and encouraged.'

'Could be.' Though Marshall didn't like the use of that word. 'Probably not, though. Anyway, thanks, Belu.' He took a final look at them. 'This has been helpful. When is the post-mortem?'

'I'm discussing with Kirsten. We want to nail down the forensics for when I open the cling film, so we'll have to do that together. Probably be tomorrow.'

'Sure.'

'One thing, though. The levels of decomposition in the exposed skin suggest that these bodies were dumped three months apart. Rob, I need to do some more detailed analysis, but I think you're looking at them being dumped nine months ago, six months ago, then three months ago.'

Jolene stared at the faces of the victims. 'If that's true, whoever killed them has a three-month cooling-off period.'

'And they'll want to do it again.' Marshall sucked in a cold, acrid breath. 'It's possible someone, somewhere is being abducted and tortured right now.'

Owusu's phone went.

She held up her gloves. 'Can you get that?'

'Sure.' Marshall found her phone.

Kirsten calling...

What did she want?

He answered it. 'Hi, Kirsten, what's up?'

'Trying to find Belu, Rob. Why are you answering her phone?'

Marshall looked over and heard some squidgy noises, so he looked away again. 'She's otherwise engaged in the preliminary autopsy.'

'Oh. Right. Well, you'll do. My team has identified one of the bodies.'

CHAPTER TWENTY-NINE
GRACE

This felt better.

Like Grace was doing a normal thing – just sitting in Harrison's car, driving into Hawick like they would've done when they were still together.

And, of course, he was taking the piss out of her.

'You brought Mr Teddy with you?'

Grace stared at the car showroom. She could steal one of—

Don't be daft – she was in enough trouble as it was.

She looked over at him now. 'So what if I did bring him?'

'You're *sixteen*, Grace.'

'And you're twenty.'

When she said it out loud, it started to feel a bit odd. They were only at high school together for one year. Him almost a man with circles of hair around his nipples, her still a child. Didn't meet again until she'd turned sixteen...

'Don't you think you're a bit too old for that kind of thing?'

'I'm fine, Harrison. Totally fine. He helps me.'

'Right, sure.' Harrison pulled up at the Morrisons roundabout. A few cars ahead of them. Left went into town. Where she needed to go. 'What's your plan?'

'I'll get a coach.'

'A coach?'

'It stops at the horse statue. That'll get me down to Carlisle.'

'Carlisle.' Harrison was grinning. 'And then what?'

'I've got money.'

'Right.'

'You think I'm stupid, don't you?'

He shook his head.

Grace hugged her bag tight. She wished it was Mr Teddy hugging her.

'What's your plan, Grace? Where are you going?'

Talking to her like she was still a kid. She was more mentally developed than him. Dickhead worked on a farm! Just because he was older—

Stop!

He was helping her get away. Play nice.

'Birmingham.'

'You're going to Birmingham?'

She made eye contact with him and nodded.

'Where your old man used to live?'

'He's still got friends there.'

'You know where?'

'I'll find them.'

'Birmingham's massive. It's like over a million people or something. It's not like Hawick where everybody knows everybody's business.'

'I'll be fine.'

A police car approached them from the north, heading towards the roundabout they were stopped at.

'Shiiiiit.' Grace slumped down. And waited. The car stank of Lynx, like all the upholstery sucked up the smell.

'Why are you— Oh. Right.'

The car moved again, but Grace didn't get up.

'They've gone past, babe.'

Grace sat up and they were driving along the high street. That pub her dad used to drink in. The horse statue was just up ahead.

Harrison pulled in. 'I really don't like the heat, babe.'

'Thank you.' She reached over and kissed him on the cheek, then grabbed her bag and got out into the gloom. 'See you around.' She walked away from the car without looking back. At him or her old life.

Get to Birmingham. See her dad in prison. He'd help her. He'd know what to do.

She'd be fine.

She got to the coach stop opposite the horse statue and it wasn't anything glamourous. Kept her out of the rain but it stank of cigarette smoke. She saw Harrison's taillights flash on as he pulled in, letting a car slide back into a space.

Grace wanted him to help her. Drive her a bit further on, down to Carlisle. But he'd done all he would for her – they weren't even going out anymore. She needed to do the rest herself.

She checked the timetable. She'd missed the last coach by forty minutes.

Shite.

That couldn't be right – there had to be another bus stop somewhere.

But Carlisle wasn't far. Took an hour to drive there. She could walk there – probably be there by midnight. Find the bus station and sleep there. Get the first coach in the morning. She'd be in

Birmingham in no time. And she'd save herself some money –
that was going to run out, so avoiding wasting it on a coach
ticket she could easily walk felt like a good move. A wise one.

She could hitchhike.

No.

That was stupid. People got killed doing that.

Walking was healthy. She was young, fit and able.

She set off along the high street, weaving through people
doing their shopping. Nobody she recognised, nobody who
seemed to recognise her. Weird feeling, because her face would
soon be all over the TV – the girl who killed the schoolboy and
who ran away.

Over the bridge to the main road now. Just walk along
that and she'd be in Carlisle. The shops here were thinning
out. Homes rather than businesses. Old mills. Sports
ground.

Just focus on one foot in front of the other and keep on
going. Don't worry. Everything will be fine in Birmingham.
Dad will help. He had mates who owed him favours.

She must've zoned out because she was walking in the
darkness at the side of the road.

Cars passed on both sides, headlights catching her.

She was *starving*. And she had no food with her. Some
money – the cash her dad left her – but she'd stop at the next
town. Langholm. There was a good chip shop there. And some
shops. A big bag of crisps would keep her going and be
cheaper.

There.

A plan.

She had a plan to get to Carlisle, then to Birmingham.

A car pulled in next to her, trundling slowly.

Shit, was it a cop?

The window was down. 'Hey, love.' A man was leaning

over, eyes shifting between her and the road. Short hair, stubble. 'You okay there?'

'I'm fine.'

'Need a lift?'

'I'm fine on my own.'

'Sure about that?'

'Sure.'

'Where are you going?'

'Home.'

'I'm heading as far as Carlisle. I could drop you on the way.'

'Said I'm fine.'

'It's going to rain.'

'I'm *fine*.' She turned to face him and tell him to fuck off.

Blue lights flashed behind her, around the bend. Maybe a mile away, but the cops were coming for her.

Shit, shit, shit.

'Fine.' She opened the car door and got in, resting her bag on her lap. The car smelled of tobacco and sickly energy drink. 'Sorry. You're very kind. It's been a long day.'

The police car shot past, pulling out to weave past them.

The man pulled out and drove off at speed. 'Name's David.'

'Hi David, I'm Faith.'

'Faith, eh?'

Why had she picked that one?

'It was my granny's name.'

'Right, aye. Lot of kids your age have old people's names.' He seemed old. Maybe her dad's age. His hair was dark. Stubble was ginger. T-shirt and trackies on. 'Hattie, Olivia, Alice, Elsie, Alfie, Albert, Harry. Better than everyone in your class being David or Sarah, eh?'

He was going to bore her all the way to Carlisle...

She watched the road pass in a blur. Her stomach rumbled. 'Suppose so, aye.'

'That's a Hawick accent, eh?'

'Aye.'

'So why are you walking away from the town?'

'Going to see my dad in Carlisle.'

'Makes sense.'

Jesus, she shouldn't have got in. Her story was falling apart. And getting in his car was stupid. But she was desperate. And maybe she'd get to Carlisle—

The clock said quarter to five. She'd be there before six. Hopefully they had coaches that ran overnight, so she could be in Birmingham first thing in the morning. Find out how to get out to the prison.

Aye, she was going to be fine.

Besides, if David tried anything, she had Dad's hunting knife in the side pocket.

CHAPTER THIRTY
MARSHALL

O ver the border into England and serviced by Bruce's Northumbria constabulary, Berwick-upon-Tweed was just off Marshall's patch. A place he'd visited a few times over the years – the nearest place to get the train to Durham or London from home. Back when it was a bus ride up to Edinburgh before the train back down the coast, it saved a ton of time. Now there was a train up to Edinburgh again, driving across still saved enough time to be worth it.

The day was darkening as he drove along a curving street with huge mansions set back on both sides. Berwick wasn't the poshest of places, but like Galashiels, it had its share of upmarket properties. Probably got a lot more value living here than closer to Edinburgh or Newcastle and you could easily commute to either. Right on the coast too, with some gorgeous countryside nearby and beaches to die for.

Aye, it was a place someone could live a life.

Marshall pulled up at a roundabout at the end. An open view looked across a downhill park over to the mouth of the

Tweed, the river that ran through everything in his life. He glanced at Jolene in the passenger seat. 'So, you've got a kid?'

'Joe. He's three.'

'Difficult age?'

'They're all difficult. Mum's really good at looking after him when me and Fergus are at work.'

'That's good.' Marshall took an immediate left, then turned right into a row of ex-council houses. He couldn't imagine ever having kids. Not that he'd left it too late, but he'd given himself over to his career, to helping others without thinking about himself. Using the work to numb his grief.

Maybe it wasn't too late.

A squad car sat outside a house. A cop was leaning on the bonnet.

Marshall pulled in opposite and waved at him. Old houses with pan-tile roofs. A local pub, a hybrid of Scottish and English ones, which summed up Berwick. He let his seatbelt go. 'You want to lead here?'

'Happy to.' Jolene got out first.

Marshall's phone rang.

Jen calling...

He answered it. 'Hey, everything okay?'

'Just got your text, Rob. Don't worry – Mum's going to pick up Thea.'

'Thank her for me.'

'It's Thea you owe it to.'

'Mum's not that bad.'

'No, she's not. You are. And you promised.' Jen left one of those pregnant pauses he knew would be filled with venomous thoughts about her brother.

Outside, Jolene scowled at him, but at least she was talking to the cop.

'Listen, Jen, I better—'

'Remember to come to my party tonight. Worried nobody will come.'

'I'll be there in my best party frock.'

'Sure you will.' Jen laughed. 'Why haven't you answered my calls?'

'I was driving. Over at Berwick just now.'

'Have fun there. See you later.'

'You will.' Marshall ended the call and got out into the cool air. Always felt that bit colder in Berwick, over on the coast. Must be the sea air. Melrose was an hour from the sea in any direction, so the salty tang was a strange novelty.

He walked up to the attending officer and held out his hand. 'DI Rob Marshall.'

'Aye, she told me.' The local cop didn't look like he wanted to shake hands. 'PC Simon Barker.' His accent would pass for Geordie – Berwick's proximity to Scotland had the weird effect of pushing the accent to being the most English it could get; a few miles up the road in Eyemouth and it was as Scottish as haggis, sporrans and drowning your sorrows in whisky. 'Word is you lot found his body?'

Jolene nodded. 'We uncovered the remains of three victims in woodlands near Galashiels. Our forensics team managed to profile the DNA and identified one of them as Steven Cork.'

'Thought we'd find him alive, you know?' Barker winced. 'Ah, who am I kidding? I hoped against hope we would but knew in my heart of hearts he was dead. When did he die?'

'Dr Owusu thinks about six months ago.'

'Not long after he went missing.' Barker shifted his gaze between them and there was... something going on in there.

Marshall was used to big city cops who dealt with shite.

Barker was a local bobby, a throwback maybe, but a central part of the community. He wasn't just there for murders and stabbings – he wouldn't see anything worse than a pub scuffle in his whole career – but he was the glue that held the town together.

Barker scratched at his neck – he had a nasty looking rash there. 'How did you know it was him, though?'

'He had a criminal record. His DNA was on file from the arrest and you were the investigating officer.'

'I was, aye.' Barker looked up into the sky. 'You meet these kids from a young age when you talk to them at their school, then some of them you just keep seeing. Little sod nicked a car when he was fourteen. Did him for drug offences at sixteen. Served three years of seven, released on parole. Got a job up on the oil rigs off Aberdeen, worked through the pandemic, then they let him go last summer. Stayed at home with his mum. Got into fights and drugs, so I kept on seeing him. Lived off these online scams, like.'

'You're listed as the investigating officer for his disappearance.'

'Aye. Went missing just over six months ago. Twenty-one.' Barker brushed his hands against his cheeks. 'Rumour was he'd absconded to Thailand. Phone was switched off, never went on again. Probably in the Tweed.'

Jolene frowned. 'You thought *he* was?'

'No, the phone.'

'Ah, right. But you didn't think he'd been killed?'

'Not so much. We had suspects. Man, did we have suspects. Trouble is, without a body, you can't arrest anyone.'

'What happened the night of?'

'He went to the pub with some friends, got into a fight and brutally injured someone. I mean, the bone was sticking out. Skull fractured. That kind of brutal. And Steven ran off. He didn't tell anyone apart from a mate. Lad called Neshy. Thirty, been in and out of prison all his life. Obviously, Neshy was very reluctant to talk. He's the one who raised about Thailand, so he was our number one suspect. Trouble was, Neshy had a cast-iron alibi and now we know why. Had to let him go, obviously, and of course *he* ended up in Thailand. He'll be back when his cash runs out, but who knows when that could be.'

'Right. Could do with speaking to him.'

'I can ask around, like. See if anyone's got a number for him.'

'Appreciate it.' Marshall rubbed his hands together. 'We've found his body, so I hope that gives you some closure.'

'It's not for me to...' Barker blinked hard a few times. 'Aye. Thank you.'

Marshall waited until Barker looked at him. 'We don't know why he was killed, though. I'm building up a profile, so—'

'A profile?' Barker's eyebrows shot up. 'You think this is a serial killer?'

'Unfortunately. We've got three unknown deaths with the same MO. So, it'd be helpful if we could speak to anyone close to him.'

'His mother's the one who reported him missing. Come on.' Barker led them up the path and knocked on the door. 'A DI doing profiling, eh?'

'Long story.'

The door opened and a woman in her mid-forties peered out. 'Simon?'

'Hiya, Dee.' Barker took his hat off – he was completely bald on top with some nasty looking moles up there. 'Got some bad news.'

She looked at each of them in turn. 'You've found him, haven't you?'

'My colleagues here did. DI Rob Marshall and DS Jolene Archer. This is Dee Cork.'

She looked between Marshall and Jolene. 'He's dead, right?'

Marshall nodded slowly. 'I'm afraid so.'

She shut her eyes. 'Thank you.'

Strange.

'I need to ask you a few questions about your son, if that's okay?'

Dee stepped outside and pulled the door to behind her. 'Don't want to let my dog out. She's just had puppies. Don't want them out either.'

Marshall smiled. 'I'm a cat man, myself.'

'Oh, I've got cats. The dogs are just a way to pay the bills.'

'I'm sorry about your loss. Tell me about your son, please.'

'What's there to say?' She was shaking her head. 'Stevie was a difficult boy. Always in trouble, ever since his dad left us. Got worse when they found his body...'

'How old—'

'Six. Stevie was six when Danny left. And that rat bag died when Stevie was thirteen. Stopped going to school, didn't he? Never expected him to grow old. When he went missing, I knew he'd be found eventually. He went. You know? Just disappeared. Him and his passport. Always talked about going to Thailand, but he didn't touch the money he'd saved up.' She looked at Marshall. 'Can I see his body?'

'I'm afraid that's not to be advised.'

'Don't you need me to identify him?'

'The DNA did that.'

'Please.'

'His body was in the ground for six months and there's been some decomposition.'

'Oh.'

'Listen. My job is to find his killer. To do that, I need to know more about his life. Was he into sport or exercise?'

'What kind of question is that?'

'An important one, unfortunately.'

'Not in the slightest. He watched boxing on the TV. Had one of those sticks, you know? And he had boxing stuff in his room. Gloves and a bag. Punched it once, that was it. Never ran. Drank a lot with his mates. Went to the football, Berwick Rangers. When they were away, he'd watch Rangers or Newcastle in the pub. His other teams.'

'He online much?'

'Useless with technology. Bought him a computer when he was a bairn, but he never used it for anything other than hitting things with. Think all he looked at on it was... Well, sure you can imagine.'

'I can. Was he into politics?'

'Oh, aye. Never missed a Prime Minister's Questions.' She rolled her eyes. 'He wasn't even on the electoral roll. Never read the front of a paper.'

Marshall gestured at Barker. 'My colleague here says he worked on the rigs?'

'Right. That useless so-and-so Neshy got him into it. My boy didn't have any skills, but he was making a lot of money there for the first time in his life.'

'What happened to that money?'

'Still in his account. Alba Bank.'

Barker nodded. 'We've got a flag on his account for any activity.'

Marshall tried sifting through it all, but he had enough of a picture now to be going on. 'Okay. I think that's been useful.'

'That's it?'

'Can you email me the best photo you've got?' Marshall

handed him a card. 'I've got a file to read through. I'll be in touch if I need anything more.'

'Okay.'

Marshall handed her a card. 'Listen, if anything comes up that you think is important, give me a call.'

'Sure thing.'

'And I'm sorry for your loss.' Marshall held her gaze for a few seconds then walked back to the car.

Jolene caught up with him. 'What do you think?'

He glanced back at the house, where Barker was still chatting to Dee. 'The victimology is very different. Twenty-one, so he's younger than Keane's targets. Working on the oil rigs. Been in prison. Not an athlete.'

'So it's nothing to do with Keane?'

'Didn't say that – being in jail could've turned Keane against working class people. More of them and they tend to be the violent ones.'

'That's a bit judgmental.'

'It sounds it, but it's not. I've got a PhD in Criminology, Jolene. I wish the world wasn't the way it is, but it is and we do all we can, so when the data says something, you have to believe it.'

She didn't seem to agree. 'See what she said about Cork being inside? Could he ever be in the same prison as Keane?'

'Three years served for drugs, which would be Cat B at most, not Cat A.' Marshall looked up into the grey sky. 'Still, things happen in prison. People get moved around for various reasons. Can you dig out his record?'

'Already requested.'

'Excellent work. Let's look at it back at the station.'

'Now?'

'I want another chat with Barker before—'

Marshall's phone rang.

Elliot calling...

'Better take this.' He answered it. 'Andrea, what's up?'

She paused. 'Have you seen Shunty?'

'No, I'm out in Berwick with Jolene, as per Pringle's reallocation of resource.'

'Don't get smart with me.'

'I'm not. And let's be honest, you wouldn't recognise smart, would you?'

'I maybe can't define it, Doctor Donkey, but I know it when I see it. Smart arse.' She sighed down the line. 'I'll ask again. Have you any idea where Shunty might be?'

'As far as I'm aware, DS Siyal is looking into Mark Davidson.'

'What? Why?'

'Andrea, you were the scribe in that brainstorming session this afternoon. Don't you remember?'

'Doesn't mean the rationales didn't bamboozle me.'

'He was heading to Dungavel.'

'What? Where's that?'

'Immigration centre. Is that the only reason for your call?'

'Nope. But I've noticed how Kirsten's not speaking to you.'

'Eh?' Marshall was blushing. Jolene was watching him, so he turned away. 'What do you mean?'

'Refuses to call you herself. Why's that?'

'No idea. Why don't you ask her?'

'I did and she was as weird as you are about it. I'll get it out of you, don't worry.' Elliot's laugh was full of mischief. 'Good news, though. She's got an ID for another victim.'

'The three we—'

'Aye, aye. The one killed nine months ago. I mean, I did most of the legwork on it. Had to call in a favour with the

Garda in Ireland. A violent assault in a pub in Temple Bar in Dublin. No time served but kept DNA on file.'

'Another criminal record?'

'Aye. Funny, eh? Quite different victimology to Keane.'

'I agree.' Marshall tightened his grip on the phone. 'Can you give us his address?'

'His? Marshall, it's the lassie.'

CHAPTER THIRTY-ONE
GRACE

Grace sat back in the seat, pressing against her head rest and glancing over at him as subtly as she could. The dashboard lit up his face. Old, but athletic. Handsome, maybe. He kept on touching himself. Down there.

Ah shite, he is a perv.

She'd got into a car with a perv.

So *stupid*.

Knew she shouldn't hitchhike and she got into the first car that stopped. And he's wanking himself off while he drives.

The wiper cleared the rain on the windscreen. They passed a sign for Langholm, two miles away.

'Can I get out?'

He looked over. 'Eh?'

'Please. Stop the car and let me out.'

'It's pissing down.'

'Let me out.'

'Come on, I'll take you—'

'You're wanking yourself off there.'

'I'm not!'

'You're touching yourself!'

'I've just had a vasectomy.'

'Bullshit. Let me out.'

'Come on, I can't let you out in that!'

Grace reached into the bag's side pocket and eased the hunting knife out of the sheath. 'Just pull over. I'll walk the—'

'Don't be daft.'

She pointed the knife at him. 'Let me out!'

'Okay, okay!' He hit the brake and she jerked forward, the seatbelt biting into her shoulder. 'I don't know what you think I am, but—'

'I appreciate the lift, but you're a sick bastard.' Grace kept the knife trained on him as she grabbed her bag and opened the door. She stepped out onto the grass verge and her jeans were soaked straight away.

'Daft lassie.' He sighed. 'Good luck.'

She slammed the door and he drove off honking his horn. She wrapped the bag over her shoulders. Absolutely ravenous now. God.

He was right about one thing, though – the rain was pretty heavy. Her thin coat didn't exactly keep the rain off. Didn't have a hood.

Still, she'd made a couple of hours of progress down the road. Must be halfway to Carlisle by now.

She eased the knife back into its sheath. Bastard thing wouldn't go! There. She put the bag on both shoulders and set off.

Left, right, left right.

Getting into a car with a guy like that. Wanking himself off while he drove.

Jesus!

Something rumbled behind her.

A lorry.

She jumped off the road onto the verge and it rumbled past. She waited for the splash. Braced for it.

Didn't happen.

She looked up, expecting the driver to pull over – another desperate wanker – but the lorry slipped off into the town in the distance.

The lights were bright. There were shops there. Food. Drink. She needed energy.

She hurried on, pushing herself hard now. Desperate for those chips. Her legs were aching already. Running in PE at school wasn't preparation for this. Mum always said she was skin and bone – she'd kill for some muscles right now, ones that didn't ache.

Still, the town wasn't that far away now. She passed a car park – two cars sitting there, driver to driver. Harrison would do that with his mates. Usually bought some hash or sold some speed. Half the time he was just showing off Grace to them – look at my young bird, eh?

She hurried on past them, just in case they spotted her, then crossed the bridge over some river and – finally – she was in the town itself.

A long high street, but a lorry was parked on the pavement, blocking the road.

The chip shop looked like it was open. And it was actually a Chinese takeaway – she'd remembered it differently when she'd stopped there with Mum. She scanned the menu in the window.

The man waiting inside was staring at her. She tried to ignore him.

They did chips. The best chips were always from Chinese takeaways – that's what Dad told her.

A Londis a few doors down. Over the road was a local paper

shop, but it looked shut. The lorry blocked the way, so she couldn't see past to see if there were any other options.

Crisps or chips?

She was absolutely starving. Skipped lunch. Breakfast was a slice of toast.

Chips.

She went into the Chinese and walked up to the counter.

The woman looked up. 'Yes?'

'Bag of chips please.'

'Salt and vinegar?'

'Please.'

'Two pounds.' But she disappeared through the back before Grace could pay.

'Best chips for miles around.' The man waiting inside was staring at his phone. Big guy. Looked old, about the same age as the wanking perv. He looked exhausted. Big bags around his eyes. Panda man. 'You okay there?'

'I'm fine.' She ignored him. Wished she had her phone on her. So bored.

He put his mobile away and took his time looking her up and down. Not quite sleazy... Something else. Concern? 'Here, let me pay for your chips.' He was Scottish and his accent was local. His hat covered his ears – she was surprised he could hear her.

'No. I've got the money.'

'Love, I know a troubled kid when I see one. Brother used to be a cop.'

Shite.

He'd tell him and they'd find her and she'd go to jail just like her dad.

'Whatever trouble you're in, it's okay.'

'Said I'm fine. *God.*'

'Kid like you needs every penny. It's just two quid but you

need it a lot more than I do.' He reached into his pocket slowly and produced a two-pound coin, then slid it across the counter. 'There. Paid for.'

'Thank you. But I won't suck your cock for a bag of chips.'

'Who do you think I am?' He looked angry. 'Just trying to help you, okay? Because you look like you need help.'

She nodded slowly.

The rain lashed against the window. 'Miserable night. You walking?'

'To Carlisle.'

'Carlisle?' His eyes went wide. 'You'll be hours.'

'I'll be fine.'

'Where have you come from?'

'Hawick.'

'You're soaked. Listen, if you need a lift to Carlisle, I'm heading to Manchester tonight.'

Manchester...

That was more than halfway. Easy to get to Birmingham from there. And she actually knew a friend of her dad's there – Uncle Pete.

She looked him up and down. Could she trust him? He seemed okay, but...

She had the knife.

Sod it.

'Aye. Thank you. A lift would be great. Can I pay you?'

'God no. Not my truck. Not my fuel. Company's always good. Only so many audiobooks you can listen to, eh?'

The curtain rattled and the woman reappeared with two bags. 'Here you go.' She looked at the money on the counter. 'Thank you.'

'Cheers, Tina.' The man took the bags and left the place. 'Name's Archie.'

Grace followed him out into the rain. 'I'm Faith.'

'Nice name.' He opened the passenger door of his lorry. 'Here you go, doll.'

It was some climb to get in there. If this went to shit, how the hell was she going to get out?

What were the odds of two pervs in one night? Ninety-five percent of the world was normal, right? So... one in twenty. She'd take those odds.

She hopped in and put her rucksack at her feet.

He shut the door and walked around.

She tried the door and managed to get it open. Okay. That was fine. She eased the knife out of the bag and put it in her pocket. That was fine too.

Archie hopped in and passed her a bag of chips. 'Like I say, best in the area.'

'Thank you.'

'Don't mention it.'

She opened her bag. The chips were golden and crisp, with the sharp tang of vinegar hitting her nose and waking her up a bit. She stabbed the wee wooden fork into the first one and ate it. Bloody thing burnt her mouth but she just chewed and chewed.

'See what I mean?'

'Aye, they're brilliant.' She ate two next. God, she was *starving*.

'I'm guessing you're running away from home?'

'No. Going to see my dad in Birmingham.'

'Long way to travel on your own at your age.'

'Aye, but I want to do it on my own, if that makes sense. For the achievement.'

'Nothing makes any sense at the best of times. You live your life and you just get on with it.' Archie shoved a handful of chips into his mouth and chewed. He had two bags of them. And some spring rolls in a plastic tub. He gunned the engine, deep and rattling through her seat. 'I'll eat as we go.' He pulled off and chewed his chips as they went. 'Driven down from Thurso today.'

'I don't know where that is.'

'Right on the top of Scotland. Near John O'Groats. You can see Orkney from there. Or the southern islands anyway.' Archie bit a spring roll like it was a sausage. 'Some lads go via Glasgow, but I had to stop in at Penicuik to get some idiot to check the tatties were up to standard. Special ones. Rare breed.' He chuckled then ate more of his spring roll. 'That's pigs, isn't it? Heirloom variety. That's it. Some daft contest or something, needs a lorry full of them. Anyway. They passed the test so I'm driving to Exeter tomorrow. Now, we might not make it as far as Manchester tonight but I'm going to keep going as long as I can.'

'So, maybe further than Manchester?'

'Maybe, aye. Popped a speed just north of Perth so I'll see how long it lasts.'

'*Speed*?'

'Aye. Keeps me alert.'

Jesus, like Harrison and those idiot mates of his.

Grace didn't feel safe, but for a totally different reason this time.

CHAPTER THIRTY-TWO
SIYAL

'You and me, Shunty, we're complete opposites.' DC Jim McIntyre was driving. A big guy whose appearance screamed cop. Tall, strong, dark hair. Calm. And he was right – Rakesh wasn't any of those things. Well, he was pretty tall and his hair was even darker than McIntyre's, but strength and calmness...

They were passing through deepest, darkest South Lanarkshire. Not exactly different from the area he was based in now – forestry plantations on rolling hills rising to mountains – but it had that off feeling Siyal had every time he went within about twenty miles of home. Something felt bad here. Always did.

'In what way are we opposites?'

'I spent fifteen years in uniform and Pringle pushed me into becoming a detective with the promise of a pay rise that hasn't materialised.' McIntyre pulled into the Dungavel House car park and wedged their pool Audi between two minibuses. 'You're a direct entry.'

'So I'm stopping you getting promoted or something?'

'Didn't say that.'

'Do you think it?'

'No, but Jolene does.'

'Yeah, I know all about that.' Siyal was careful when he opened the door – after this morning's incident in Selkirk, the last thing he needed to do was scrape the other vehicle with his door as he got out. Besides, who had to take a minibus to a place like this?

Oh, he knew. He knew very well.

Siyal sneaked through the gap and followed McIntyre across the dark car park, taking in the place. A modern facsimile of a Scots baronial castle, blocked off by twelve-foot fences, like if they made *The Walking Dead* in Scotland and some evil warlord had set up a commune in there. The place itself was dark, but the grounds glowed under the floodlights, the light spreading to the mature woods on the other side of the car park.

Aye, it was spooky as hell, especially at night.

McIntyre stopped at the gate and held up his warrant card. 'DS Siyal here called ahead.'

The two guards wore orange vests. Both sneered at Siyal like someone with his skin tone should be in there as a 'guest'. The older one thumbed them in, then stepped aside.

McIntyre crossed the courtyard to the security door.

Not Siyal's first time there, but his first at night. It had all the warmth of an A&E at four in the morning the Saturday before Christmas, when all the idiots had kicked lumps out of each other. He walked up to the reception desk and showed his warrant card. 'DS Rakesh Siyal. Here to see Afri Shamsuddin.'

The guard had a strong poker face, etched with a precise goatee. He scanned the ID, taking greater care than passport control, especially with Siyal's brown skin. The wall behind him was stuffed with postcards from hot places: Magaluf,

Rhodes, Palma, Antalya, even Sydney Harbour Bridge. He handed the card back. 'Afraid they've countermanded your meeting, Sergeant.'

'Who has?'

'They have.'

'The Home Office?'

The guard nodded.

Shite.

All that way, just to—

'What's up?' McIntyre was frowning at him.

Siyal ignored him. His head was a flood of thoughts, mostly about how stupid he was. He tried to wade through it and get to the other side. And got something. 'Can you check on the system to see who Afri's lawyer is?'

'Sure.' The guard's fingers clattered across the keyboard. 'Okay. Says it's a Rakesh Siyal.' He looked over at him. 'That's you?'

'It is. I'm still a practising lawyer. Afri's my client, so I'm insisting on speaking to her.'

'They countermanded that—'

'This meeting is about her appeal. Please, it's urgent.'

The guard didn't look like he knew which way to jump. One way was getting his arse kicked by his boss, the other by the Home Office. 'Fine.' He pressed a button and a door opened wide. 'I'll get her brought down ASAP. Room three. Just around the corner.'

'Thank you.' Siyal smiled like he meant it, then entered the door and walked down the corridor. Whatever torment they were inflicting on people, the walls still had the air of old Scottish grandeur. Just missed a stag's head hanging there. In fact, you could make out the shape of where it'd been – the cheap magnolia hadn't quite covered the previous layers of paint.

The signs were worse –

Processing.

Interviews.

Onward Travel.

Do you wish to plead guilty or be found guilty?

The place was filled with shouting and crying, haunting the corridors. The constant stream of newcomers would be the ones making all the noise, thinking volume could get them released. After a few days, they'd be used to it. But the prospect of returning to where they'd fled...

McIntyre opened the door to room three and popped his head in. 'Clear.' He entered.

Siyal followed but he couldn't take a seat. Couldn't rest.

'You been here before, Shunty?'

'Not for a while, no. Most of our dealings were in the police station. The way they've treated her... It's barbaric. She's a victim in all this.'

'But she did come here illegally.'

Siyal looked at him. He meant it. 'She was trying to fix that. We were. Doing all the paperwork. Besides, when she left—'

'Still.'

Jesus. McIntyre was a bigot.

'You honestly think—'

McIntyre laughed. 'Winding you up, mate.'

Siyal didn't believe him. Or didn't know whether to.

McIntyre looked around the corners of the room. 'They call this an immigration removal centre... Talk about Orwellian.'

Siyal didn't have anything else to add to that.

'Me and Liam...' McIntyre shut his eyes for a brief moment. 'Last year, we picked up this lad for stealing bread from Asda in Gala. Minor crime as it went. Trouble was, he'd come here illegally from Yemen. We were going to let him go but these people in black suits appeared and took him away. Heard he'd been sent here. Feel pretty bad about it, especially seeing it in the flesh, as it were.'

'You want to talk about Liam?'

McIntyre looked up at him, then away. 'I'm fine.'

Siyal hadn't even started when... what happened to Liam happened, but at least he'd finished it. Did some good. And twatted a car off a bridge badly enough to earn a stupid nickname.

The door opened and a guard led a frail woman in. A hollowness to her eyes, her skin pallid, her hair a frizzy spiral. Took Siyal a few moments to recognise her as Afri Shamsuddin. She'd been here a year and had aged ten in that time. She didn't sit and looked at McIntyre with deep suspicion.

Siyal smiled at the guard. 'Thanks. I'd like a moment with my client in private.'

'Sure thing.' He gave a tight nod, then shut the door behind him.

Afri looked up at him and it took her a few seconds to focus. 'Rakesh?'

'Hi, Afri.' Siyal walked around and grabbed the back of the chair he should be sitting on. He still couldn't bring himself to sit. 'I'd ask you how you're doing, but this place.'

'It's killing me, Rakesh.' Afri sat opposite McIntyre. Looked like she didn't have the strength to remain standing. 'I'm absolutely broken by the way I've been treated.' She tugged at her curls. 'I just wanted a new life where I wasn't being oppressed and look where I am now. Look at this place.'

McIntyre smiled at her. 'On behalf of this country, I'd like to apologise to you.'

She scowled at him. 'Who are you?'

'DC Jim McIntyre.'

She frowned. 'He's a cop.'

'I'm a police officer now, Afri. Jim works with me.'

'You're... After what they did to me?'

'That's part of it. Actually, it's most of the reason I joined up. Your ordeal made me want to change the system from the inside. Right now, I want to get you out of here.'

'Good luck. I'm supposed to be on the first plane to *Rwanda*.'

Shit.

'When that fails in the High Court, I'll be heading to a worse place than home.' She nibbled at her nails, already cut to the quick.

McIntyre seemed a bit twitchy but he kept his mouth shut. Good boy.

'Afri, I'm still registered as your lawyer. Why isn't anyone from Greening and Binnie on there?'

'I don't know.'

'I'll take it up with Owen Greening. He still owes me.'

'I doubt that'll help me.'

'Afri, I'm investigating your case as part of my current role.' Siyal finally took his seat. 'I need to ask you a few questions about that night.'

Her eyes burned with fire. 'Why?'

'It's pertinent to the investigation.'

'What investigation?'

'Darroch's lawyer, Mark Davidson, is a suspect in a serial murder case.'

A steely calm settled over her. 'How does that help me, exactly?'

Good question. Her legal brain was still in top condition.

'Rakesh, I don't think you discrediting him will have any bearing on me. Doesn't matter who reported me. I came here illegally. That's all they care about.' She leaned forward and it was like her elbows were the only thing keeping her upright. 'Have you got some kind of vendetta against Mark Davidson?'

She was right.

This was a vendetta against Davidson – Siyal was self-aware enough to recognise that. But he didn't want this whole thing slipping out of his grasp.

'Look, if we can get you as a witness in a case against Davidson or his client, then that'll defer any deportation.'

She narrowed her eyes at him. Her legal mind was as sharp as any Siyal had met and she could see the logic in what he said. She looked at McIntyre. 'I was a lawyer back home, you know? A bloody good one. When your country and the allies pulled out, the Taliban took over again. They don't like women. They especially don't like smart women. And they certainly didn't like me. At the start, I was helping other women. Thought I was doing good. But they started targeting *me*. They killed... They killed my husband. I had to get out of there.'

'I'm very sorry to hear that, Afri. I can't imagine what you've been through.'

'You'll never have to, will you?' She looked McIntyre up and down. 'Men like you are never the targets, are you?'

'I don't want to get into an argument with you. I support DS Siyal here, one hundred percent.'

That somehow seemed to pacify her. 'Okay, you've got me, Rakesh. What do you want to know?'

'That night. Talk to me.'

'It was all covered in the case. He was masked, I couldn't see him.'

'But it was Brian Darroch. Correct?'

'That's right. My boss. He owned the pub I cleaned.'

'In those interviews, you said it was definitely him.'

'That's right.'

'Was it?'

'I think so.'

'Afri, "think" isn't good enough. What makes you think it was him? Something in your unconscious mind confirmed it and I need to get at what that was, make it tangible. Take me through it step by step. What did you see? What did you hear? What did you smell? What did you feel?'

'Why?'

'Because Davidson let it slip to me that it maybe wasn't Brian Darroch.'

'What? Who was it?'

'The million-dollar question.'

'Look, I've thought about it a lot. In here, I've got a lot of time on my own. And... I get these flashbacks. They say it's PTSD. As a result of what they did, I lost my baby. Can you imagine what that's like? I went through that and the only thing I had left from my husband is gone.' She flared her nostrils, then swallowed something down. 'I don't want to replay what happened but, to answer your question, there were maybe two men.'

'Maybe?'

'Okay, I think there were. They carried me. I mean... I'm not exactly heavy, so one could've taken me. That's what I thought. But I was struggling.'

Crowd control. One to control her head and arms, cover her mouth. The other to do most of the lifting.

Made sense.

'Can you describe them?'

One was hairier than the other. Smelled of some strong cologne. But I don't know who. If it wasn't Darroch, I have no idea who either was.'

Siyal sat back. If it wasn't Darroch, then could it be Davidson?

He needed to find out.

'Thank you.' He stood up. 'Afri, I'm going to get you out of here, okay?'

She looked up at him with exhausted eyes. 'Don't make promises you can't keep.'

'I don't. I *will* get you out of here.'

CHAPTER THIRTY-THREE
MARSHALL

'If he's not here, we're going to have to do this ourselves.' Marshall pressed the doorbell and waited, looking around.

Washington was an old town as much to the south of Newcastle as to the west of Sunderland. Like a lot down here, it hadn't exactly been levelled up during twelve years of Conservative government.

The address was halfway down a long row of Sixties houses, nicotine yellow under the streetlights with trios of lock-up garages spaced out.

Jolene looked around at Marshall, shivering in the cold evening, but she didn't say anything.

The house itself could do with some attention – the masonry was cracked, the paint faded.

Marshall's phone chimed. He checked it – an email from Barker. He opened it and it had no text, just a photo. Steven Cork. An ugly bugger, with blonde hair styled like that daft footballer.

Movement misted in the window and the door opened. A

young man looked out. Plain white T-shirt showing off sleeve tattoos up both arms. Baseball cap. Chains. 'What's up?'

'Police.' Jolene showed her warrant card. 'Looking for Gary McMenemy.'

'That's me. Why are the feds here?'

'Are you married to Layla McMenemy?'

'Found her body, yeah?' His accent was the street patois of west London, with a sprinkling of the northeast.

Jolene frowned. 'Excuse me?'

'My missus ran off nine months ago. Cops show up – stands to reason you've found her body.' Gary held out his arms, clasped at the wrist. 'Cuff me and do me.'

'Are you saying you killed her?'

'Wish I had.' He laughed. 'Fuck it. Want to know the truth? If she'd turned up here, I would've ended her. After what she put me through, it'd be the least she deserved.'

Marshall smiled at him. 'You're pretty blasé about this.'

'Got nothing to hide, kid. Motto of my life now. Transparent honesty all the way.'

Kid...

The guy was early twenties at the most.

'Mr McMenemy, can we come in?'

'You ain't coming in.'

'Something in there we shouldn't find?'

'Not saying that at all. I'll tell you anything you want to know but we're doing it out here.'

Drugs, probably.

Or Marshall was being a judgmental prick.

He wasn't a suspect, so they didn't need inside.

But it was cold out here. Even to a thick-blooded, thick-headed Scot like Marshall. He narrowed his eyes, focusing on Gary. 'We found your wife's remains.'

'Thought so.' Gary snorted. He looked up at the sky and it

seemed like a weight had been lifted from his shoulders. He shifted his focus between Jolene and Marshall. 'Where?'

'In a wood in southern Scotland. About a hundred miles from here.'

'When did she die?

'Nine months ago.'

'Right.' Gary started scrunching his face up tight. Kept doing it. Like he was stifling tears. 'Layla upped and left nine months ago. Pretty much to the day. Last week, in fact. Out of the blue.' His accent had lost the patois and was his native northeast. 'I was at work. Just left us, man. Me and our bairn. What the fuck am I supposed to do on my own with a bairn, eh?'

'Talk to me about her, Gary.'

'She'll be twenty-two next month. I mean, she won't be but you know what I mean. Two months older than us. I knocked her up at sixteen. Did the right thing by her, you know? Been an absolute car crash, like.'

Jolene folded her arms over her chest. 'Why did she leave?'

'I don't know, do I?'

'She never mentioned any frustrations?'

'All the fucking time, man. Constantly. How shit I was as a man. How annoying our bairn was. How little help we got from my parents. Course, hers were perfect, weren't they?'

'Did you worry she'd killed herself?'

'No. Never. Layla wasn't that kind of lass.'

'So what did you think—'

'Thought she'd left us.' Gary's face crumpled like a sheet of paper. 'She... We...' He fell back against the wall and slid down it until he was crouching there, back pressed against the masonry. He looked like a young lad. Someone who'd done too much too young, like he'd sprinted through his life and only just realised it was a marathon and he had a lot of laps to go.

Blubbering like a small kid. Probably the first time he'd been able to feel anything in months.

Jolene squatted next to him. 'Hey, it's okay.'

'No. It's fucking not! The shit she put us through, man. She was abusive. Shouted at us, put us down.' His cheeks were streaked with tears. 'Night before she went, I was looking after the bairn and she was out... And I cracked.'

'What happened?'

'She came back. Mortal. Started shouting at us. Woke the bairn. Then she told her off for it. Wasn't her fault, was it? Kid's mam comes in, banjaxed and shouting her head off, dancing to Taylor fucking Swift. I calmed the bairn down and I had a word with Layla. Told her to quit her nonsense, like.' He shut his eyes and clenched his jaw. 'Then she hit us with a vodka bottle. Knocked us clean out. Must've scared her. Thought I was dead. So she ran away. Never heard from her again. The police looked into it, but never found her.'

And the investigating officer couldn't even be bothered to turn up...

Marshall tried to connect Layla McMenemy with the victims of Martin Keane but nothing was tying together.

She did, however, share something with Steve Cork up in Berwick. Anger issues. Violence. A difficult life. A criminal record that let them identify her remains.

'I need to ask you some questions. Let's start with her routines. Daily, weekly, monthly.'

'Sure. Em. Not much. Barely left the house, like. When she did, it was a Friday night to get wrecked with her mates. Sometimes didn't come home until Sunday.'

'And you never went out?'

'How could I?'

'How did she get around?'

'Walked most places. Couldn't drive.'

'Cycle?'

'Nope. Got the bus, like.'

'Was your wife into exercise?'

Gary scowled. 'Never. Why?'

'What about jogging? Sports?'

'No. Told you – during the week, she didn't leave the house. I was out at work, like, but I knew she was in.'

'How?'

'Got security cameras on the doors. Never left. Nobody came round.'

'Did your wife take any drugs?'

'Like, illegal?'

'That kind of thing.'

'Probably. I don't know, though. Kids she hung out with, let's say it's likely.'

'And you said she drank.'

'Right.'

'Did you have reason to think she was promiscuous?'

His Adam's apple bobbed up and down. 'You don't stay out on the lash for two nights straight without doing something like that, right?'

'Thank you. I know it's difficult. Did you have any evidence?'

'She didn't shit where she ate, if that's what you're asking.'

'Did she have a debit or credit card?'

'Both here. She cleared about sixty quid from my wallet. No idea how much she had on her, like.'

'Did she take risks?'

'Not with the bairn, no. But... Well... It's how we've got her, right? I wanted to wear a rubber or get her on the pill. She wasn't that good at remembering to take it, like.'

'Did she suffer from any mental illnesses?'

'Nothing diagnosed, but I think... I mean... She was *nuts.*

Angry as fuck, like. Don't know what that was but it was something.'

'Did she talk about her fears or fantasies?'

'She hated being stuck, like. Trapped. Used to wake up screaming, saying she was trapped in a burning house. Wanted to run away.' He scratched his cheek. 'And she did.'

'Did she use her phone or computer a lot?'

'How do you mean?'

'The kids describe it as being "very online". Was that her?'

'Not really. Bit of social media. Schoolbook, Twitter, Instagram. Posted photos on there.' Gary stood up tall and got out a fancy Samsung phone. Brand new and expensive. One of those folding ones. He snapped it open and held out a Schoolbook profile page.

Layla McMenemy.

Nothing posted in nine months, seven days.

The last post was a video of her in a karaoke bar, mic in hand. Before that, lots of drunk photos of her and her mates. No sign she was married with a kid.

'Her phone's still here, like.' Gary thumbed behind him into the house. 'Police took it but gave us it back. Like I fucking want it. What am I supposed to do with my dead wife's phone? See all the texts to blokes she was fucking behind my back? Hardly. She just fucked off out of my life. Nobody's heard from her since.'

Jolene looked at him. 'We understand she was arrested in Dublin?'

'Fight on her hen night two year ago. Can you believe it? Someone started on her and Layla could never not finish things. She got arrested after they had a scrap. That's what she told me, anyway. Mates backed her up. I don't know the truth. Could be bollocks, like.'

'She was arrested and charged. That's how we obtained her DNA to match it against her remains.'

'Fucking hell.'

'Dad! Daaaaad!'

'Back in a sec.' Gary barged into the house, leaving the door open.

'Daaaaad!' A small girl in a wheelchair. Dressed in pink and yellow clothes. Maybe five years old. Could be MS, cerebral palsy or MND.

It punched Marshall in the stomach. Poor kid. Both of them. She'd lost her mother, and he had to raise a child with special needs on his own.

Jolene leaned in close to Marshall. 'The investigating cop who was supposed to meet us here has finally shown up.' She gestured at the squad car making a dog's ear of parking by a garage. 'Worth me looking into what they found on her?'

'I think so. If they did a better job than Barker up in Berwick, we might have some sightings of her. Get an idea of how she got from here to Elibank in a couple of days.'

'We should head back to their HQ and see what I can gather. What about you?'

'I think only a profile is going to help us here. Really need all three victims to do an effective profile, but I know enough that we're dealing with a new killer. The differences from the Shadow Man are massive.' Marshall looked inside the tiny house, worried about being overheard. 'I need to get the best in the business to help.'

CHAPTER THIRTY-FOUR
GRACE

The lights on the motorway were swooshing in front of Grace's eyes. Green cat's eyes on the left became red during the...

What were they called? The bits where you turned off the road?

She had no idea, but she was knackered. The chips were sitting heavy in her stomach but being tired was much better than being hungry. The truck's cabin was absolutely melting, like when Mum roasted a chicken.

And Archie's audiobook was *so* loud too. And irritating as. Why did that guy have to keep saying "Dale" every time he talked to the character called Dale?

She noticed he was saying something. 'Can't hear you.'

'Sorry!' Archie reached over and turned it down. 'Bottles of water in my fridge back there, if you want.'

'Told you, I'm fine.'

'Still think you need to drink something. People don't hydrate enough these days.'

She didn't want to think what he did when he needed to pee.

'How you doing over there, Faith?'

'I'm okay.' Grace smiled at him but it hid the turmoil burning away underneath. Her hand was still resting on the hilt of the knife, greasy fingers still just about gripping it.

He yawned into his fist. 'That speed is wearing off. Thinking I might pull in at the truck stop just after Penrith.'

'Oh.'

Not even eight o'clock.

He'd taken her past Carlisle at least, but she was hoping to get to Manchester tonight. Then she could look up Pete. She thought her dad's mate was called Pete, anyway. Something like that.

'Sorry, but I've driven all the way from Thurso, and I'm cream crackered, so I think I'm going to get a few hours here. You're welcome to stay in the cab.'

Staying in the same place as some old dude? Ew.

'When will you—'

'I'll try and get on the road about four in the morning. Beat the Manchester rush hour.'

'Where are you heading?'

'Exeter. Told you.'

'Right, right. But you're going to Birmingham.'

'Not *to* it, no. I could drop you at the services at Walsall.'

'Where's that?'

'On the outskirts of Birmingham. Kind of. Truck stop there. Decent fry-up. Nice selection of...' He yawned. 'Cold drinks.'

She didn't have her phone anymore, but she reckoned she was only fifty miles from home. While she'd made much more progress than by walking, sleeping in a lorry in the north of England felt like she'd be staying in the same place too long...

She needed to keep moving.

'I think I want to keep going tonight.'

'Sure? Listen, I've got two cribs here. One in with all the tatties. I can sleep in the back, you can sleep in here. I'll give you the keys.'

Tempting. 'Thank you, but I'll take my chances with a coach.'

'If you're sure...'

The brakes hissed and he pulled off the motorway, twisting around a looping road, then steered into a truck stop. A wide-open area, all floodlit. Ten lorries, maybe, all parked away from each other. Felt like he was going way too fast but he hissed to a gradual stop and parked about as far away as he could get from anyone else. He let his seatbelt go and seemed to collapse. 'Watch yourself, Faith. There are a lot of bad people about.'

She unplugged her seatbelt but it just sort of flopped over her. 'I can handle myself.'

'Don't kid yourself. Remember the rule for men picking female hitchers. Cash, grass or ass.'

'Ew, gross.'

'I'm serious.'

'Which one do you want?'

'Oh, I'm the rare example of someone who buys you chips.' Archie held out his hand to shake. 'It's been nice knowing you, Faith. Hope you get yourself where you need to be.'

'Thanks, Archie.' She shook his hand. He was palming a twenty-pound note, like her uncle would do. 'I can't take this.'

'Please. Get yourself a nice meal. Or several bags of chips. I don't care, just look after yourself.'

She should refuse it. But she needed money. Any amount. 'Thanks, Archie.' She eased the knife back into her bag, then opened the door and hopped out onto the tarmac. 'I do mean it. Thank you.'

'Just be safe.' His eyes were looking heavy, like he really needed to crash.

She shut the door carefully and trudged off across the lorry park. Felt much bigger out of the truck.

Where the hell was she going?

No plan, really. Penrith. She needed to head into town and find the bus station. Or train station. Get on down to Manchester and Birmingham.

She did have money, but she didn't want to waste it on a hotel or a B&B. She'd do what Mum did and sleep in the car. If she had a car. She hoped she wouldn't regret turning down a bed for the night.

Bloody hell, she was so lost without her phone.

Then again, it had a chance of betraying her like Dad's had him.

She stopped at the edge of the truck stop, by the road. A sign pointed into the town centre. Penrith was a much bigger place than Hawick. The bus station had to be open all night. She'd be fine. Totally fine.

She walked along the pavement at the side of the road, much busier than the one she'd left at Hawick. Cars on both sides of the road. That was good. Less likely to get abducted. Still, she was back to walking.

She needed something to get through this. Getting to see Dad in prison was only going to be so much...

She needed more than that.

A truck like a fat SUV slowed as it approached and flashed its lights at her.

She flicked the Vs at it and walked on, head bowed, heading into the darkness as the streetlights ended.

Archie was right – the roads were full of creepy bastards.

The truck was next to her now – it must've turned around.

Slow, matching her pace. Window down. She caught a Batman symbol on the side.

She looked over but couldn't see the driver. 'I'm not a sex worker.'

'No, but you look like you're hitching.'

'I'm fine.'

'Listen, I'm going to Bristol. That any use?' He sounded English, but she didn't know where from.

'Said I'm fine.' Grace kept walking.

The creepy bastard was still driving after her. 'Seriously, I'm a good guy. It's dangerous around here.'

'Just supposed to take your word for it that you're a good guy? Bye bye.' She gave him a one-handed wave and hurried up.

Where the hell was the town centre?

'Look, I'm serious. Where are you going? Listen, I can drop you in Manchester or Preston.'

'I'm fine.'

'Tough gig, running away.'

'Haven't run away.'

'Sure, okay. I mean, that's what I told people... When of course I had. Like I had a choice. Abusive dad, drunk mum. Brother left home. Just me and them. Had to get away. No option.'

He knew what she was going through. Maybe she could trust him.

'Fine.' She was tired. She needed to keep moving.

Besides, she had the knife.

She opened the door and got a good look at him. If he was dodgy, she'd run and he'd have a door hanging open.

He looked okay. Mid-thirties, maybe? Clean shaven. Nice haircut. Short and precise. Flannel shirt, black walking trousers. 'Name's John.'

'John. I'm Faith.'

'Nice to meet you, Faith.'

She got in. The front smelled of pine and something sweet. Was it WakeyWakey energy drink? 'Thank you.' She stowed her bag at her feet and snapped on her seatbelt. Then gripped her knife. 'Sorry, it's just—'

'I get it. Hitch-hiking's a dangerous game. Don't know who's out there.' John pulled off, then swung into a U-turn. 'So, Faith, where are you going?'

'Birmingham.'

'What are you doing there?'

'My dad lives there.'

'Right, right. That a Hawick accent?'

'Aye.'

'Can't your dad have driven up to pick you up?'

'It's complicated.'

'Family, eh?' John drove them onto the motorway and floored it past a lorry. 'Heard about some bother with a lorry driver a few months back. Picked up some lad, tried it on with him. Big fight. Someone lost an ear.'

'An ear?'

'Aye.' John laughed. 'Don't know who it was. Messy stuff. Better sticking to cars and vans.'

'I don't do this often, but I know what I'm doing.'

'You're young, right?'

'Twenty.'

'I don't believe you. Hey, it's okay. I was sixteen when I ran away from home. Managed to sort myself out, though.'

She just nodded into the dark.

Something felt wrong though.

He was in the inside lane and indicating left, the light flashing against the side of the road. His headlights caught the sign.

Junction 41
Wigton

'This isn't the way to—'

Something caught her in the mouth. Hard. Snapped her head back against the seat rest. Felt like she'd lost a tooth.

The truck took a sharp left at the roundabout.

His hand grabbed her hair and smacked her head against the glovebox.

She reached for the knife, but he jerked the wheel and all she did was spill the bag. It toppled over and the end popped open. 'What the fuck?'

He took a left down a country lane and parked up. He got out of the truck.

She scrabbled at the door, trying to find the release. There.

He was there already.

She tried to rush past him. The seatbelt sliced into her shoulder.

Stupid!

Finally got the seatbelt to go. But he'd trapped her. She got the knife out of the bag and pointed it at him. 'Let me go!'

'You're threatening me?' He laughed. 'Do you know how many people actually have the guts to plunge a knife into another human being? Or to slash them, or to even draw blood? Go ahead, Faith. Cut me, put the knife in right here...' He pointed at his left pectoral. 'My heart's right there. Get it right and I'll be dead. You'll have stopped me.'

She wanted to just plunge it deep. Then this fucker wouldn't—

She couldn't.

She couldn't do it.

He was right – she couldn't kill someone else.

He grabbed her wrist and bent her arm back. Fire burnt all

the way up to her neck. She dropped her knife and it dug into her shoe.

He grabbed her by the hair and pulled her out of the truck onto the road. He yanked his arm around her neck, choking her, and lifted her off the ground. The corners of her vision started to close in on the centres.

He threw her in the back of the truck and punched her hard in the breast, knocking every gasp of air from her lungs.

'Thing you don't have, Faith, is the confidence of a killer. I have it. You don't.' He slammed the door.

Dark.

She couldn't breathe. Felt like he'd snapped a bone or two.

Shit.

Stupid.

So fucking stupid.

Why hadn't she stayed with Archie?

Why did she have to keep on chancing it?

The door opened again and she tried kicking. Missed, caught clean air.

Something hit her. Her rucksack.

He grabbed her and pushed her face down. Something slid around her wrists and she couldn't move. Then her ankles. She kicked out again and caught something.

'Bitch!'

Her feet were stuck together and she couldn't move.

Then something covered her mouth. 'Mmmmmf!'

The light caught Mr Teddy, lying there, but even he couldn't save her.

He grabbed her hair again. She expected him to smash her head against the floor.

Something ripped. She looked down. He had a knife and was slicing her clothes, right down the middle. He hauled them off and tossed them to the side. Her bra slid off and she was naked in the freezing air.

'Just remember one thing, missy. I'm in charge here. Okay?'

Something went over her eyes. Everything went black. He'd taped her eyes shut.

CHAPTER THIRTY-FIVE

MARSHALL

Marshall knocked on the door and stepped back, breathing in familiar cleaning smells that hadn't changed. Somewhere nearby, someone was vacuuming, the drone sounding distant like traffic.

He hadn't been here in such a long time. Felt like a lifetime, but ten years wasn't that far off.

Prof. Liana Curtis
Chief Profiler
Centre for Criminal Profiling Excellence

She'd done well for herself.

And she wasn't here. Great.

The world was full of lying PAs, desperate to get off the phone and—

'Come!'

So she was still here. Thank God.

Marshall opened the door and stepped in. It had been his office for a few days after Goldberg's abrupt retirement, but the place was now unrecognisable. Gone were the bookshelves groaning under the weight of hundreds of egos. The walls were now filled with two giant TV screens filled with a spreadsheet and what looked like a freeform mind-mapping app. Ten whiteboards, all with her immaculate handwriting.

A meeting room table had four chairs around it and another, larger one was stuffed with piles of books and papers.

Marshall waved a hand at it. 'If I didn't know any better, I'd say that's Goldberg's horizontal filing system.'

Instead of facing the corner, the giant oak desk was now in the window, facing into the room. 'It actually works. And really well.' Liana was sipping from a tall coffee cup. The room smelled of smoky stuff, which Marshall traced to the espresso pod machine over by the door to the bathroom. 'You're lucky I'm still here, Rob.'

'Always were the night owl.' Marshall stepped into the room but he didn't know where to sit. Or what to do. 'Glad you're still here. I drove all this way because your PA said you'd be working late.'

'Need to focus on a profile for a case in Nottingham. Serial rapist. My drive up to Scotland hasn't exactly helped progress that.'

'Right. Sorry.' He thumbed at the door. 'I can come back.'

'No, Rob, it's fine.' She sighed. 'So. What brings you here?'

'I need your help with the profile.'

'Funny, because Bruce told me your lot have "got a guy" who does all that. Presume that's you?'

'My boss is keen on overselling what I do.'

'Pringle? The guy with all those whistles and weird phrases?'

'Sadly. He's okay, I guess. Just lets me get on with it. Well. He's supposed to. With a colleague out, I've had to run his team.'

'Quite the cop now, aren't you?'

'For my sins, aye.'

She grinned, but he couldn't read much into what she meant by it. 'So why are you here, Rob?'

Marshall took the seat opposite her desk. Durham's night blinked through the window behind her. During the day, it'd be blinding. 'I need your help.'

She was frowning. 'Listen, I spoke to Goldberg on my way back. He told me about what happened... With Anna.'

Why the hell was she bringing this up?

'I didn't know, I'm sorry.'

'I didn't tell anyone. Just Jacob. Sat and worked up a profile on her death together. Never got anywhere. Turned out to be a bit too close to home.'

'You solved it?'

'I did. I've had therapy. A ton of it. Some people say "buttload" but I don't know what that means. For the first time in years, I feel at ease with what happened.' Marshall winced. 'Not at ease, but I realise there's nothing I can do about what happened to her. The man who's responsible is behind bars. Awaiting sentencing. If you believed in ghosts needing to move on, then Anna's would finally be able to. I've done more than my fair share of grieving over her.'

Her mouth hung open. 'That's a bit crass, isn't it?'

'No...' Marshall slapped a hand to his forehead. 'Not a day goes past where I don't wish Anna had lived, but *I* stopped living because of what happened. Things are different now. I've had therapy and I've had resolution and closure to it. And I can move on with my life. That's what I mean by it – I grieved for twenty years and I owe it to myself to get on with living. And I owe it to her, as well. I can't stay wedded to a ghost.'

She raised her eyebrows, partially obscured by her glasses. 'That's... Still... It sounds good that you're over it, I guess.'

'Good's stretching it, but it lets me focus on what's important.'

She held his gaze for a few seconds, giving a kind smile. 'Okay, so why do you need my help?'

'Like you said, I've been a cop for ten years. Sure, my experience makes my mindset different to most, but my profiling skills are really out of date.'

'You practised with Goldberg for longer than me, Rob, so you should know all of his tricks.'

'I do, but... Last time I tried... I fucked it up. Liana, you've kept up to date with it. You've built this thing from us dicking around with the cops into a centre for excellence. Twenty people on staff, right? That's amazing. And you're talking at conferences all over the world.'

She laughed. 'Thank you for blowing smoke up my arse, Rob, but I was asking why you needed a profile for finding Keane's three victims?'

Marshall looked over at her. 'Didn't Bruce tell you?'

'Tell me what?'

'Christ. He *can* keep some secrets, after all. It's not just Keane's three. After you left, we found three other bodies, murdered and buried there. Three months apart. The oldest one was just nine months ago.'

'Christ.'

'Aye. I think you were talking to the parents of Keane's victims at the time, but... Aye, three new victims. Not far from where Stan was buried.'

She got up and walked over to a blank whiteboard and started scribbling. 'When were they buried?'

'Three months ago, then six and nine.'

Focusing on the whiteboard. 'A cooling-off period of three months.'

'Give or take, but you'll know—'

'—from American studies, that they don't always stick to it.' The pen squeaking as she drew a long arrow connecting two words he couldn't read from there. 'To start with, most would cool off for a year or more. So this offender may have honed his craft to a point where he's convinced he can get away with it every three months or less... There could be victims in between, just buried somewhere else. Do you think it's a copycat?'

Marshall got up and walked over to join her at the board. 'Pringle keeps saying it's a protégé.'

'Ouch.'

'Aye. But to me, it's not. It can't be. Martin Keane executed them with blitz kills. He inflicted sterile deaths on them. Stab, stab, stab, then he buried them. Whoever killed Steven Cork and Layla McMenemy abducted and tortured them for up to a week before burying them.'

'You've done a post-mortem already?'

'Preliminary exam only. Bottom line, there are strong sexual overtones to these new murders, whereas Keane—'

'Steven Cork and Layla McMenemy.' She wrote their names in her careful handwriting. 'You've only identified two of them?'

'Sorry. I'll try harder next time.'

'No, it's good.' She was writing down the various dimensions she could slice and dice the victimology. 'Talk to me about them. What do they have in common?'

'Both young. He's twenty-two, she's twenty-one. And these victims were blue-collar, at best. Criminal records. Drugs for him. Drunken violence for her.'

'Violence?'

'She was charged with assault in Dublin. DNA still on file, hence being able to identify—'

'Okay. And him? Any violence?'

'Cork was arrested for drug offences. Served time. Worked on the rigs.'

'Violence?'

'The night he left, he got into a fight and thought he'd killed someone.'

'Okay.' She drew a line between them. 'Similarities to Keane's victimology?'

'No exercise, not much online use. No interest in outlandish political conspiracy theories. She was a risk-taker. Heavy drinker. Despite having a kid, she was a party girl. Mum during the week, then she was out all weekend. Possible domestic violence, probable psychological torment. No cards on her, small amount of cash. Talked a lot about being hemmed in.'

Liana stepped back and those manga eyes scanned across the board. 'I agree with you. Different victimology to Keane. Younger, different stations in life. Different personalities.'

'Thing that gets me is the locations. They lived in Berwick and Washington. And were found at the same place as Keane's last three.'

'Interesting. Could be coincidence.'

'I don't like coincidences.'

'So? It's not about you, Rob. I saw where they were found. It's a ten-minute drive along a back road in either direction to even get to the car park. Then a good twenty-five minutes hike up to the start of the trail up to where the graves were. It's a place few would bother going. Great place to hide a body. Where you live isn't exactly sparsely populated, but it's much less than down here or up in the central belt. Thing is, to get people to the burial sites, you'd need a vehicle capable of running off road. Four by four or an ATV.'

'A dirt bike wouldn't be able to carry anyone, but a quad would be fine.'

'Right.'

Marshall had missed working with a sharp mind. The best he got on a daily basis was a sharp tongue or wit. Or Pringle's inanity.

Her eyes scanned across the board. 'To have a hope in hell of profiling anything, we need to identify the third victim.'

We.

He'd snared her interest. 'I know. We're working on it. My team. But I want to see if there's—'

'You want to do geographic profiling, don't you?'

He shrugged.

'I don't believe in it these days.'

'What about with Keane?'

'That was those days, Rob. Nowadays, things are... See, the problem with geography is... What business does geography have in an online world? The tendrils of the world wide web don't translate one to one with any geospatial map. The definition of the word "community" has to include the "online community".' She tapped at the whiteboard. 'An online community breaks the dimension that links a real-world one – location. You can be better friends with someone in Omaha, Nebraska than anyone in this country. The internet has, for better or worse, broken geography.' She smiled. 'Thanks for listening to my TED Talk.'

Marshall returned the grin. 'I get that. But there's something here. I know I need to identify victim three, but both Layla and Steven seem to have left home.'

'Like run away?'

'Aye.'

'Wastrels and runaways... Okay.' She turned and looked at her whiteboard. 'I agree – I don't think it's Keane. The MO's too different and he was at Her Majesty's Pleasure, God rest her soul. But whether there's a copycat or a protégé...' She gave him some side eye. 'I'm afraid you do need victim three to draw it out. You've got two data points and we're starting to see something in this, but your assumption could be blown open. There could be something in the third one that explains it all and links it all back to Keane. There could be missing victims that smooth out the differences.'

'I don't see how.'

She stared hard at him. 'I've missed working with you, Rob. You think about things in a different way to anyone else. Very unexpected outcomes stem from your angular thinking.' She was frowning. 'Angular? Is that what I mean? I'm searching for a word that's on the tip of my tongue. My brain hasn't quite recovered from Covid.'

'Sorry to hear that.'

'Negative two weeks ago. It's not long Covid, it's just…'

'I understand. Thanks for listening, Liana.'

'Rob. Leave this with me. I'll work on it tonight.'

'Okay. Are you sure?'

'I want to.'

'I'll call you in the morning.'

She bit her lip. 'Or we could work on it together. You could stay in a hotel?'

For a criminologist, she wasn't exactly subtle…

'Look, I've got to head back to the station in Washington to collect a colleague. She might have more data for me. Then I'll head back to base and see what's what.' And he had to show his face at his sister's divorce party… 'But I'll call you first thing.'

'Okay.' She walked back over to her desk and sat down. Looked pissed off with him.

'Liana. It's been good doing this. Working with you… You're way better than I ever was. Than I ever could be. And I think we do need more data, so I'll focus on acquiring that. Agreed?'

'Fine.' She gave him a pregnant look. Then clicked her fingers. 'Got it.'

'What?'

'The word. It's... Ah crap, it's gone again.'

'Oblique?'

'Yes!' She laughed. 'See? Covid messes with your brain. The other day, I forgot the word for "word". I mean...' She smiled. 'The important thing is your guy's cooling-off period is up. Assuming this sticks with the pattern, you've potentially got a live victim.'

'We've got teams combing the woodland.'

'Good. But that's assuming he'll use the same dumping ground again. If he works in threes, these could be victims four, five and six, and seven goes somewhere else. Or he's got somewhere else. Particularly with all the heat of discovering the bodies – he won't come within miles of that spot.'

'That's good thinking. I'd hate there to be another Steven or Layla out there right now.'

CHAPTER THIRTY-SIX
GRACE

Grace woke up and felt like someone had dropped her on her head.

Fuck.

A massive lump on the back of her skull. Felt like a few teeth had been knocked loose. Her whole head was thumping.

Where the hell was she?

Total darkness.

Getting into that truck.

Stupid.

Fucking stupid, Grace.

She tried to move but she couldn't.

He'd tied her up. John. He'd tied her up with something.

Her wrists and ankles.

But no.

Worse than that. Felt like something covered her whole body. Like... Like she was wrapped in a tight blanket. Felt cooler in places, though. Weird.

Something was stuck in her mouth.

A mask.

What?

Like when they had that one holiday to Tenerife three years ago and she went snorkelling with her dad. That time he actually had some money. The best time.

Focus on that. You'll see your dad again. You'll go somewhere hot again.

'Faith.'

That voice made her jump. If she could've moved, she'd be halfway to the moon. Everything in her clenched up tight.

A light switched on.

John was standing there. Naked. But he was blurry, like her eyes were smeared with butter.

Shit.

The room was metallic, all dimpled surfaces. Dark blue. A lightbulb swung in a gentle breeze.

Not a blanket – she was covered in cling film. Like a leftover turkey after Christmas, that they'd live off for days until it started smelling.

Nothing wrong with her hearing, so maybe it stopped at her ears.

Was it really cling film?

'I am your God, Grace.'

Shit.

He knew her name.

Her real name.

He was smiling, grinning wide. In goblin mode. 'I've been through your wallet, Grace. I like the idea of you swapping your name to another... What's the opposite of a sin? A virtue? Aye, another virtue.' He crouched down near her. 'Here's what's going to happen to you, Grace. Your next few days are going to be miserable. There's no getting away from that. I just want you to know that this isn't personal, okay?' He held up a knife and the blade glinted in the light.

Her knife.

Her dad's one. The one he'd left her, with his camping bag.

'This is a good blade. Old school. Early Nineties, I think.' He pressed his finger against the edge. 'Still incredibly sharp. Suspect this has killed a few rabbits in its time. I'm glad you didn't manage to get it anywhere near my skin.' He leaned over.

She shut her eyes.

Felt something cold. Something sharp.

Under her ribs, below her breast.

She sucked in breath.

The fuck was cutting her.

'Careful now, Grace. I don't want your air to run out too soon. That stuff's expensive.' He held the knife up and a thick droplet of blood fell from the blade onto his other finger. He touched it to his tongue. 'You don't eat enough, Grace. That's your problem. I can taste it on your blood. Real lack of iron.'

She tried to drown him out, making her ears do this hissing thing, make it sound like the seaside.

She wanted this to end.

She wanted her mum.

God.

Mum...

She'd be fucking scared, wondering where the hell she was. Why she hadn't gone after her? Just thought she was going to see Harrison Palmer again.

The police would report to her that Grace was dead.

That's if they even found her body.

God, if you're listening. Please. Let me get away. Please. I'll do anything. I'll... Please. Just...

But God wasn't listening to her, was he? She'd not been to church since with her gran.

All she had to do right now was lie still and wait.

Let him do what he wanted.

'Here's what's going to happen, Grace. The oxygen will keep you alive but don't think I'll keep it topped up. I allow myself one tank and one tank only. After the oxygen runs out, you'll die. Suffocating. I'll be here to watch it. That's the greatest thrill of this, Grace. The power I have over you. I am completely in charge of you. I've got about forty hours of pleasure here. Sorry. I've been busy lately, not had the time to get a refill or I might have enjoyed your company for longer. It's for the greater good. Really, it is. We're both sides of the same coin. Your pain is my pleasure.'

He sliced into the film around her abdomen and down towards her vagina, a shallow cut that stung like that time she picked up a dying wasp.

'So let's get started here, shall we?'

She clamped her eyes shut and tried to ignore the indignity of it all.

Fortunately, the pain gave her no time to think of that.

CHAPTER THIRTY-SEVEN
SIYAL

A few wide blocks of the old Southside Edinburgh mansions and they'd be at the Commonwealth Pool and Siyal's flat. Being a landlord didn't sit easy with him. He hated to think of anyone else living in his home, especially not while he was renting a poky one-bed flat in Galashiels. Still, if he sold the flat, he could buy a massive house down in the Borders.

But he'd be stuck in the Borders.

'Have to say, Sarge, I'm feeling a bit weird about this.' McIntyre was behind the wheel, expression level. 'We've done a lot of driving around this evening and I appreciate the OT, but we're spending a lot of fuel and are we really getting anything on Davidson?'

'This is important. Davidson's a suspect.'

'Afri asked you if this was a vendetta against Davidson.'

'It isn't.'

McIntyre glanced over, eyebrow raised. 'Isn't it?'

'Listen. If we can discredit Davidson, that's potential leverage in these murders.'

'I've been a cop for years.' As McIntyre was prone to bang on about. 'And I just don't see your logic.'

No.

Because Siyal *was* on a personal vendetta here. He really wanted to make Mark Davidson suffer for what he'd done. The realisation made Siyal sweat.

But he wasn't going to stop.

'Sorry if that's talking out of turn, but there it is.' McIntyre seemed to think red lights were optional and blasted through another as it changed. 'I don't see how Davidson being involved in this violent assault gives us any leverage over Keane.'

'A man who's capable of that is capable of killing with Keane.'

'Come on... Really? Grassing someone to immigration is very different from—'

'Constable, we're doing this.'

'You're the boss.' McIntyre squeaked through the next set of lights onto Lothian Road. 'Still think this is a bit too personal.'

Siyal didn't deny it. Just shut up.

'Playing it like that, eh?' McIntyre chuckled as he pulled up at the lights, indicating right. 'You okay there, Shunty?'

'Just thinking it all through.'

'Lot of that going on... Seriously, if—'

'Look. I'm not denying there's a personal element to this but put yourself in my shoes. That partner of yours who died in January. Liam. If you could change that, would you?'

'Of course I would.' McIntyre set off along West Port, heading deep into Edinburgh's Old Town, the underbelly lying beneath the castle up on the hill, overlooking the whole city. This area had been totally renovated in the time Siyal had lived this side of the country, the seedy and rundown buildings being replaced by upmarket office blocks and apartments. The slow descent to the Grassmarket, though, was still full of cheap bars for the students at the nearby art college.

Like the Debonair.

McIntyre parked up a few doors along from it.

Might be a Monday evening but it looked like Friday night in there. Sounded like it too – booming techno blasted out, the lights flashing in time with the solid rhythm. Too early for a noise complaint but one would surely be coming from the flats on the lane behind.

His phone blasted out.

Owen Greening calling...

He answered it. 'Thanks for calling back.'

'What's up, Rakesh?'

'Just visited Afri Shamsuddin in Dungavel.'

'Shite. How is she?'

'Shite would be an improvement. Thing I wanted to ask you is why I'm still her lawyer on the system. I left in December last year.'

Greening sighed down the line. 'We're so stretched, Rakesh.'

'Fix it, please.'

'Woah, you're actually saying how you feel!'

'Damn right I am. I'm disgusted by what she's going through.'

'We all are.'

'So, please. Fix it. I shouldn't be her solicitor.'

'Okay. Will do. And let's grab a coffee at some point, aye?'

'Sounds good. Bit busy just now.'

'Sure, sure. Catch you later.' Click and he was gone.

Siyal doubted that'd fix anything.

Two big lumps approached the car and got in the back seat.

'DS Rakesh Siyal.' He craned his neck around. 'This is DC Jim McIntyre.'

'DC Jason Craigen.' Siyal recognised him – not exactly difficult when he had a scar running diagonally across his face, deep and long-since healed. Couldn't remember where he knew him from. His shaved head didn't hide how bright the ginger hair was.

His pal was tall but thinner. Sandy brown hair in a perfect quiff. 'DC Michael St John.' The kind of accent you got a lot of in Edinburgh – upper-middle-class English – but they usually buggered off back south after university. Quite what he was doing as a detective...

Siyal knew perfectly well what could drive someone to join up. Most of the people he worked with were *cops* through and through. The kind of people who'd been good at PE at school, but not much else. Not the kind of sentiment he'd say out loud, but they were mostly decent people like McIntyre. Honest, but questioning.

And then there was DI Elliot...

Sometimes, Siyal was glad they were making the police a much broader church and letting in people like himself and Marshall. Other times, he realised just what he'd let himself in for.

He smiled at them. 'Thank you for meeting us here, gents.'

Craigen wouldn't look at him. 'Don't mention it, Shunty.'

Bloody hell. No escaping that name...

Craigen cleared his throat with a sickening howk. 'Anyway. Why are we here?'

'We're looking into Mark Davidson's background.'

Craigen frowned at him. 'The lawyer?'

'That's correct.'

Craigen snorted. 'Scumbag.'

'You got previous with him?'

'Not personally.'

'But professionally?'

'Of course. Lawyers are all the same.' Craigen looked at him with venom in his eyes. 'Heard you used to be one.'

'Emphasis on "used to be one". Try and keep up with the conversation, Constable. DC McIntyre here could give you a "Previously on The Adventures of Shunty" recap if that'd help?'

Craigen grinned at the side of his mouth. 'Lawyers, though... Especially criminal defence ones.' He looked back out of the window. 'So, this is about those bodies in the Borders, right? DI Elliot's team, right?'

'I report to her, yes.'

'Struggling to see why this is part of the investigation. Care to enlighten us?'

Everyone was digging into Siyal's rationales for anything. He'd no doubt get the third degree for using crunchy peanut butter rather than smooth on his toast. 'We want to build up a picture on Mark Davidson.'

Craigen arched an eyebrow. That was solid ginger at least. 'Davidson's a suspect for those murders?'

'Martin Keane might have a collaborator on the outside.'

'The Shadow Man. Aye, heard all about that clown.' Craigen leaned forward. 'Listen, I know you, Rakesh, but you don't seem to recognise me.'

'Sorry, I don't.'

'I worked the case last year. Interviewed you.' Craigen ran a hand over his head. 'Before I shaved the ginge off.'

Siyal had no memory of it. 'What case?'

'Afri Shamsuddin.'

Siyal had spoken to the cops, giving her a character reference he would've stood up in court and repeated. It didn't get that far. Case dropped, Afri dropped in it, next stop Rwanda.

'Sure we should be opening old wounds, Shunty?'

Cops never wanted their work looked at, but usually for benign reasons like personal pride. Other times, though...

'We're not raking over the coals of your work, Constable. Just want to find out what we can about Davidson's possible involvement.'

'Seems a bit of a stretch, but okay.' Craigen sat back in the seat.

St John leaned forward like they were connected by a length of string. 'The conviction seemed solid enough at the time, but then evidence and a witness both went missing so we had to drop the case. PF wasn't best pleased.'

Craigen laughed. 'She was spitting teeth.'

'You both worked it?'

St John nodded. 'I was sure we'd get a conviction. Cases like that hinge on witness testimony, but in the end it was just Afri's word against Darroch's. Sadly, nobody would take those odds.'

'Okay.' Siyal looked at them in turn. Craigen, St John, McIntyre. 'Here's what I want us to do. We'll scope out the area, see any avenues that weren't fully investigated back then.'

'Mate, this is ridiculous.' Craigen took a deep breath. 'Don't do this. You'll look like even more of a clown than you already do.'

'Constable, can you and DC McIntyre here take the left side of the street. DC St John and myself will do the other.'

'You're the boss, Shunty.' Craigen got out and stormed off.

'Rakesh...' McIntyre got out and charged after him.

'Come on, then.' Siyal opened his door and waited for a bus to pass, then walked over. He looked around the quiet street and let out a slow breath. 'Craigen's a piece of work.'

'Not backwards in coming forward.' St John was licking his lips. Seemed like a nervous thing. A twitch, almost. 'I'd say he's a good, honest cop, but he's just back off suspension.'

'What did he do?'

'A suspect's arm got broken during an arrest. He claims it was reasonable force. I'll let you decide whether it was or not.'

'There was an investigation, right?'

'Correct. Deemed it inconclusive. Trouble is, he's angrier than ever. Thinks the world's out to get him. You coming up from the Borders, looking through a case he worked... It's upsetting him.'

'Poor thing.'

St John laughed.

The Debonair had a rear entrance on a little lane that ran in a curve, leading to a big block of council flats, probably all sold off now. The lane's only occupants were bins, but the lorry wouldn't get anywhere near it, so it'd be someone's job to wheel them around twice a week.

St John stopped to look at the Debonair's rear entrance. 'Sickening what happened in there.'

The level here was about six foot lower than the street at the front – whoever moved the bins every week had their work cut out for them. Even with that difference, there was still a basement.

Where Afri was held for six hours.

Before she escaped and ran out that door.

Someone saw her being chased.

'Who was the witness?'

St John pointed at a block of flats, where the fronts were open to the street. 'Woman who stayed in there in an Airbnb. Gave a statement of what she saw. Afri scurrying away. A man chasing her. Afri hailing a cab and going to the station.'

'But you couldn't track her down again?'

St John shook his head. 'She wasn't the named occupant of the address in there. He refused to talk.'

'An affair?'

'Maybe. Some people put their own lives above those of others, right? If she had a husband and kids back home.' St John rolled a shoulder.

Siyal managed to spot a camera. 'Did you get the footage from that?'

'We did. Backed up the witness statement.'

'But?'

'The video went missing.'

'How?'

'Deleted from our server. The backup too.'

'That doesn't sound right.'

'No, it's not. Takes a lot to wipe both. Especially the back up.'

'Is it a council camera?'

'Rolled off their servers too. They don't keep backups of these. Princes Street, Royal Mile, Lothian Road, yes. Here? No chance.'

'So someone on the inside wiped the footage?'

'I wouldn't say we have evidence of that.'

'But you suspect it?'

'True.'

Siyal had one suspect – Craigen. 'Come on, we're going inside to speak to the owner.'

St John dragged him back. 'Wait, wait, wait. Well, that bar's notorious. The previous owner kind of ran things in Edinburgh.'

'What happened to him?'

'You don't want to know, but it ended in a couple of cremations. He had cops on the payroll.'

'So you're saying Darroch is—'

'No, I'm not. But it stands to reason. Right?'

Sod this.

Afri didn't have the time for it.

Shite.

Siyal needed to get her out of that place and he was clinging to reopening this case as a way of doing that.

'Come on.' He charged back around to the street.

Craigen and McIntyre were lurking by the car. Both looked over, completely conspicuous.

Siyal stopped by the car. 'You get anything?'

McIntyre shrugged. 'Not entirely sure what we're supposed to be looking for, Sarge.'

'Aye.' Craigen's glare was like a pair of knives. 'No wild geese recovered.'

Siyal pointed at McIntyre and St John. 'Can you two try and get hold of anyone in the council CCTV unit?'

Craigen was frowning. 'What are we going to do?'

'We're heading inside.' Siyal strode off. 'Come on.' He walked into the bar like he was looking for a drink. Taking in the place. The long oak bar. The taps against the wall rather than on the bar. The lack of optics, but a stacked wall of bottles of spirits. The thud of the music was vibrating around in his chest.

Not much of a queue to get served, just a woman trying to assemble two glasses of white wine and two shots into something she could carry while she tottered through to the back room. Not actually a disco, but some experimental band playing a gig on a Monday night.

Siyal could keep an eye on Craigen in the mirror above the till. Keeping cool.

Brian Darroch was serving, his gaze focused on the customer's progress through to the back room. Looked and dressed younger than his age. That footballer haircut was dyed a few shades too dark for his skin. Would've been good looking about twenty years ago; now he just looked seedy, but thought he still had it.

He shifted his focus to them. Didn't seem to recognise either of them. 'What can I get you, lads?'

Craigen walked up to the bar and rested against it. 'Don't recognise me, do you?'

'Know that scar anywhere.' Darroch pulled a pint from a tap at the back. 'Jim! The Northern Monk's gone off! Can you replace the keg?'

'On it!' The disembodied voice came from somewhere below them.

The basement, where Afri was held.

'Cops, eh?' Darroch looked at Siyal briefly, but Craigen got a long, hard stare. 'Listen. Pal. Whatever you're going to ask me, you can piss off. Any questions, I want my lawyer here.'

Siyal took over. 'Just want to hear that story about the night in question. Again.'

'Why? Are you lot so stupid that you don't remember what I said? Might be an idea to write it down next time.'

'Afri Shamsuddin's being deported. First plane to Rwanda.'

Darroch picked up a beer towel and dried a glass. 'Sorry to hear that. She was a good worker.'

'She's in Dungavel House. Heard of it?'

'Aye. Brutal place. Still.' Darroch switched to another glass. 'Can't do the time, don't do the crime.'

'She was raped downstairs.'

'Aye. I know.' Darroch swallowed. 'Think about it every time I go down there to change a keg of beer.'

He wasn't denying it.

Craigen smirked. 'Haunted by your wank bank, eh?'

'Fuck off.' Darroch slammed the glass down on the bar.

'What happened to her was a tragedy. Like I told you, I wasn't even here.'

'We know.'

Darroch looked at Siyal. 'Eh?'

'We believe you.' Siyal splayed his hands on the bar and leaned across. 'Thing is, Afri told us two men raped her. If it wasn't you, who was it?'

This hadn't come up in the case.

Darroch just started drying another glass. 'If there were two, I wasn't one of them.'

Siyal held his gaze. 'So who did it?'

'No idea.'

Craigen thumped his fist off the bar top. 'A cabbie found her in the street outside. She escaped from your basement. So either you know or one of your staff knows. You got off with it. Fair enough. But someone here knows.'

'Sorry, lads, nothing to do with me. Like I say, she was a good worker, but a bit unreliable. Had that PTSD, you know. Don't blame her after what she went through.' Darroch leaned forward. 'But if you want any more, I want my lawyer here.'

Siyal looked him up and down. He didn't have a witty retort.

Darroch waved at them. 'Night night, boys.'

In the mirror, Siyal spotted the security guys moving through from the back room. Not quite blocking their exit, but not far off it.

Siyal turned and left the bar just as a roar of applause came through, back out into the cold air.

The security watched them leave, eyes flicking over to the bar for any sudden incitement from Darroch.

None came.

Craigen stopped outside and looked back in. 'My mate suffers from it.'

Siyal frowned at Craigen. 'From raping someone?'

'No. PTSD. He's on meds and talking therapy. He was a squaddie over there. Afghanistan. Where Afri's from. Absolutely brutal. Hope the oil was worth it because so many people died so they could get at it.'

Maybe Siyal had misjudged Craigen.

Or maybe he was virtue signalling. Easy to read the room and act accordingly. Cops were masters at it.

Siyal got in the passenger seat.

McIntyre and St John were sitting in silence.

'Have you got the CCTV?'

St John shook his head. 'Like I told you – the council lost the CCTV footage too.'

Siyal shifted his gaze between Craigen and St John. 'Did either of you watch it?'

Craigen nodded. 'Showed Afri getting abducted on a fag break and taken back inside.'

That seemed weird.

'Why wait to do that outside?'

'What do you mean?'

'She was in the pub, cleaning, but they waited until she was on a break, outside, before they abducted her and took her back in.'

Craigen smirked. 'Separate door for the basement. Roll the beer barrels down there. They had to take her outside out of the pub.'

Made sense to Siyal. He looked at each of them in turn. 'Thanks for your time, lads, but that'll be all tonight. Myself and DC McIntyre will get back to base and we'll take it from there. Thanks again.'

CHAPTER THIRTY-EIGHT
MARSHALL

Melrose station wasn't the biggest in the world so Marshall had to share an office with Elliot. He sat behind his desk, at right angles to hers but at least she wasn't there, just like for the last few months. And they didn't have the whiteboards or Durham grandeur of Liana's office, but Elliot had left the TV on, showing the evening's news. The bleakness of the shitshow in Westminster was softened by some surprisingly good news from Ukraine as they forced the invading Russians back. He switched it off and unlocked his laptop.

A gazillion emails that would have to wait.

No. Might be something important in there. He scanned through all the unread.

Nope. Sod all.

He pulled up his old criminal profile template and started filling it out. He got stuck on the title.

Killer of three unknown victims in Elibank

God, he was useless. They knew two of them. He deleted 'unknown'.

Pringle would want something sexy in there. Clingfilm Man. Bacofoil Bill. The Wrap Man.

The door opened and Pringle stormed in, hands in pockets, a giant bulge in his left cheek. Speak of the devil. He gave a big slurping noise and exposed the gobstopper he was sucking on. The kind Marshall would've taken ages to get through as a kid. 'Marshall.' Another sook. 'There you are.'

'Here I am.' Marshall sat back, but just wanted to get on with his work. 'What's up, sir?'

Pringle's left cheek bulged with the gobstopper. 'Two thongs.' He held his thumb. 'First thong. I've sent Elliot home after she finished with Forestry and Land. I'm impressed she lasted that long on her first day back after—' He made bunny ears with his fingers. '—the incident. She's got a scar the size of Kansas on her undercarriage. Anyway. Bett-Leighton's boss is flying back from his holibags tonight, so Andrea will interview him tomorrow.' He slurped his gobstopper again and moved it to the other cheek. 'What was the other thong?'

'You tell me?'

Pringle swapped it over again. 'Oh, aye. How's the old Vulcan mind meld going?'

'The profile?'

'That's what I said, diddle I?'

Marshall snorted. 'I need to do some more thinking on it. But identifying two of the three victims is great progress. I have a general take on age, sex, size, clothes, possessions. And I spoke to Dr Owusu on our way back—'

'Our? You took the good lady doctor away from her post-mortem?'

'No. Myself and Acting DS Archer visited Washington, sir.'

'DC?'

'No, she's an Acting DS, sir. You promoted her.'

'No. I meant you were in Washington, DC?'

'Washington in Tyne and Wear. South of Newcastle.'

Pringle slurped his gobstopper again. 'Isn't that *Ash*ington?'

'That's north of Newcastle.'

'Right, right. And the good doctor was with you?'

'No. Dr Owusu was on the phone, sir. At home, I think. She told me she found the presence of semen on and in the victims.' Marshall held up a hand. 'If we're dealing with multiple perpetrators, then one is male. But I'd say that's unlikely.' He jotted that down on his notebook as something he needed to cover off. 'Our perpetrator is either large enough to be able to overpower both male and female victims, or they're charismatic enough to lure them in. And they have a job so they can afford a vehicle for transport.'

'I don't follow.'

'Unlike with Martin Keane, we're dealing with live victims being stored somewhere, where they're being tortured and abused, and likely killed. The bodies are then dumped elsewhere. So our killer needs a place to house them before dispatching them and transport to get them to and from.'

'I see, said the man with new corrective lenses.'

Marshall gritted his teeth. 'There's a slight pattern, though, just from the two. Both victims were troubled individuals who'd been arrested in the past and who upped and left, seemingly after incidents where they thought they'd be in further legal trouble. Steven was in a fight in a pub, Layla hit her husband with a vodka bottle. So, while we maybe lucked out with our double identification, criminal records aren't a surprise.'

'I don't follow?'

'I'm starting to think whoever killed them is murdering

runaways. Easy to target, already missing, trying to leave no traces. People living on the fringe of society or within a narrow margin of acceptability. Very easy to prey upon. Who knows them, who cares? And if they've gone missing already and the police haven't found them, nobody will be actively looking for them.'

'Colour me impressed, Marshall. Goldberg's been helping you?'

'No, sir. His replacement in Durham. Liana Curtis.'

'Ah. She was the... The woman with the parents, no? The lassie in the canteen.'

'That was her, sir. She's working on the profile too.'

'I thought I told *you* to do it?'

'I'm not a profiler, sir.'

'Marshall, I pay you all the magic beans because you are one.'

'I *was* one. I'm a DI now.

'Cool your jets!' Pringle held up his hands. 'Listen, I've been on a conference call with the dean of her university and the Chief Constables of Northumbria police and our shower. Liana's not on the case. You're my guy. Okay?'

Like Marshall had a choice in the matter. 'If you insist, sir. But I think she should be.'

'She's not, okay? I've already had DI Bruce call me up to chastise me, but I need full accountability for her actions. Her dean insists it all falls elsewhere. Namely on our shoulders. So it's you, okay?'

'I don't think I've got a choice in it, so I'll just say fine and get on with the work.'

Pringle didn't take the hint. Just stood there, making sickening noises with that gobstopper. 'Are you *sure* it's not Keane?'

'We've discounted his direct involvement, sir.'

'But a linked copycat, an accomplice or a protégé.'

That bloody word again...

'We'll know more once Dr Owusu completes the pathology work, sir, and when we identify victim number three. If we do.'

Slurp, rattle, slurp. 'Okay, so the headlines at ten are?'

Marshall sat back and sighed. 'The bottom line is Keane was committing complete overkill. We don't know why – he's never explained that part. We've all hazarded guesses but until you get them to speak you just don't know. And even then, they can be playing you.'

'Bang.' Pringle punched his right fist into his open palm. 'Blitz. Anger, show of power when he has none. We live in the shadows and all that jazz.'

'Correct, sir. Keane is a small guy so he overcompensated with his anger. At least that's my theory. Nowadays, some would call him an incel, but his motive wasn't sexual.'

'Keane was on the fringes of society himself.'

'Good point, sir.'

Bloody good point.

Marshall scribbled it down as something to consider. 'The way I see Keane is he had to reassure himself through his actions that he was, for want of a better word, manly. I think it's something he prizes. He was physically bullied as a kid. Stopped going to school because of it.'

'Okay.' Pringle prodded his gobstopper with a finger for some reason. 'The protégé takes his time.'

'I don't think we should say he's a protégé, sir. We don't have any evidence.'

'Okay, so whoever he is. What do we know?'

'He is calculated in his actions. Instead of blitzing them, he's capable of winning people over who are on the run. He gains their trust and then overpowers them. He holds them somewhere. He holds all the power and he's confident. He has the size to overpower or the charisma to coerce his victims. And he tortures and sexually assaults his victims because he enjoys the suffering aspect. He seems to want to repeat that high over and over again, whereas Keane wanted it over and done with as quickly as possible.'

Pringle's eyes widened. 'Burying them alive is—'

'No evidence of that, sir. All we know is he has them wrapped for freshness with an oxygen mask on. That's it. We'd need Dr Owusu to say the cause of death was suffocation with soil fragments found deep inside the victim's lungs and some supporting analysis to show they were consistent with the area where they were found.'

'Of course.'

'But he is burying them, sir. And in doing so, he's burying his own trauma. Two of the victims were male and he cut off their genitals. So, while he does let himself be a slave to his desire, once he's killed them, he's full of revulsion at his actions. He needs to bury the shame.'

'God.' Pringle was grinning like a kid with the gobstopper in his mouth. He slurped again. 'I love working with you. This is... This is *magic*. I never knew policing could be such fun.'

'These are people's lives, sir. Murder victims who have suffered greatly.'

'I know, I know, but the usual brand of murders we get here revolve around who pissed who off to start a pub fight, so it's just professionally interesting to have something different to— Hello?' Pringle jerked around.

Kirsten entered the room, head tilted to the side.

Siyal was with her, yawning into his fist.

'Aha, the bold and the brave are here.' Pringle winked. 'Not saying which one's which.'

Kirsten smiled, but it was merely to humour him. 'Just wanted to update you on my work before I head off, sir. No dice on the third victim yet. The DNA is drawing a blank.' She looked pissed off at herself, like she'd failed them.

Marshall waited for eye contact. 'I'm absolutely blown away we've identified two of them so quickly. I'd expect one, maybe, and after a few weeks of shoe-leather work. You've done two in a couple of hours.'

'Thanks.' But she wouldn't look at him for long.

'Can you make use of any additional databases?'

She frowned at him. 'I used the Garda in Ireland. Isn't that enough?'

'No, that was great.' Marshall was smiling wide, trying to encourage her. 'I meant private companies. Genealogy databases.'

'Oh. Right. I think there's some access through the NCA that might help. I'll email my guy.'

Pringle crunched into his gobstopper. 'Christ!' He spat it into the bin. 'Cinnamon!' His lips were all purple. 'Okay, Elliot is going to focus on missing person reports around three months ago and try to ID this other victim.'

'Good idea.' Marshall noted it down. 'Thing is, we know there's a three-month window, but we don't know if Layla was the first victim. Could be others elsewhere. Aborted attempts. Times where he abducted someone and couldn't kill them.'

'I'll ask her to add that to the groaning pile.'

'Sir.' Siyal couldn't stop yawning. 'Sorry. I wanted to update you on the lawyer.'

'Lawyer?'

'Mark Davidson.'

'Ah, yes. Well?'

'Something went down.'

'Oh, did it?' Pringle rolled his eyes. 'Something was affected by gravity?'

'No, sir. We spoke to Afri. She said there were two assailants. I'm thinking one was Mark Davidson.'

'Here comes Johnny in again...' Pringle pointed at Siyal. 'No vendettas on my watch, please.'

'It's not a vendetta, sir. I... The police in Edinburgh lost some evidence, hence the conviction being dropped. She was attacked outside the pub she worked in, but someone deleted the video from their servers.'

Kirsten scowled. 'They *what?*'

'According to the two guys I—'

'Right. I'll have a look at that.' Kirsten jotted something on her phone.

'Sir, Afri's being kicked out of the country. Sent to Rwanda. Evidence going missing, plus two men and not one? Davidson said it wasn't his client. So who was it? Doesn't feel right to me. I think something happened here.'

'Have you got any suspects?'

Siyal nodded. 'Davidson.'

Pringle's tongue was working overtime. Even deeper shade than his lips. 'Based on what?'

'There's something here, sir.'

'Is there any connective tissue here? Because all I see is you trying to litigate a case from the opposite side.'

'You weren't in that room, sir. Davidson has a power over Keane. A serial killer. One of the worst in UK history. I strongly think he's involved or knows who is. I want to see if we can find some leverage on him.'

Pringle peered into the bin at his discarded gobstopper like he regretted discarding it. 'Okay, well. I approve you digging into it further. Just not too much longer, okay?'

'Sir.'

Pringle stood up tall. 'One final thong. If Marshall's right, our guy's possibly doing it again after a three-month cooling-off period. Timing-wise, we could be looking at a fresh victim right now. I don't want to land with egg on my face.' He ran a hand over his mouth. 'Okay, gang. Knock off for the night, get back at it tomorrow. I've got to spend time with my daughter.' He gave a big theatrical wink. 'Marshall, you do the thinky, okay?'

'On it, sir.'

Kirsten couldn't get out of there quickly enough.

Marshall needed to mend those fences.

Focus.

Get on with the thinky.

He opened his laptop again and the empty profile stared back at him. The stuff he'd discussed with Liana and now with Pringle was all fizzing around his head, but it wasn't congealing on a person he could stick in a room and interrogate until they confessed.

It wasn't saving any lives.

His phone buzzed. A text:

> Whre fuck am uy?

Well, at least Jen was sober enough to spell the swearword right.

Maybe a glass of wine would help his brain do the thinky on its own.

CHAPTER THIRTY-NINE

Marshall could just so easily walk on by and get on home to his mother's. Cup of tea if she was still up. Feed Zlatan and give him a big cuddle.

But he couldn't let Jen down, could he?

So he walked into Taylor's and made his way through to the bar at the back of the hotel. The place was pretty busy. The screen showed some post-match football analysis on Sky. Looked like Newcastle had beaten Brentford or Brighton two-nil and the pundits were dissecting the play on those giant iPads, but their chat was lost to the din of a Nineties Britpop anthem Marshall couldn't quite name.

One person who wasn't really aware of where they were was Jennifer Armstrong.

Marshall corrected himself. Jennifer Marshall. Jen. His twin sister.

She was propping up the bar, waving a twenty-pound note in the air, but struggling to stay vertical. She wore a skirt shorter than any she'd have dared to wear as a teenager on one of their underage nights out when they'd bomb up to Edinburgh in a mate's car and go clubbing in the big city. Or the even shorter ones she'd wear to the club in Gala. At least she wore tights.

Marshall perched on the edge of the bar. 'You okay there?'

'Rob!' She wrapped him in a big hug and smelled of sweet cherry perfume mixed with vodka and wine. White wine – the fast train to Oblivion Central. 'You came!'

'Sorry I'm late, got held up at work.'

'Aye, she was just saying.' Jen pointed along the bar.

Kirsten was standing there with the look of someone who'd had to deal with the absolutely shit-faced for longer than she wanted. 'Hiya, Rob.'

Jen leaned in. 'Rob, get us some prolapses in. Carlos won't serve me.'

Wonder why...

Kirsten was frowning. 'What's a prolapse?'

'A Jaegerbomb but instead of energy drink, it's white wine.'

'Fuck.' She turned away and started speaking to someone else.

'No way am I order—'

'Pleeeeeeeeeeeease!'

'Fine.' Marshall locked eyes with Carl the barman. 'Get me two glasses of that Malbec and a prolapse.' He winked.

'No!' Jen stuck up a drunken finger. 'Three of them. Some people have some catching up to do.' She pointed at him and then over at Kirsten, obliviously chatting to a female CSI Marshall vaguely recognised. Sally?

Marshall raised his hands. 'Fine.'

'Right, Jen. This is your last round.' Carl brought over two glasses of red wine and pointed a finger at her. 'Okay?'

'Fine!'

'Right. Prolapses. Coming right up.'

Marshall took the two glasses of wine and slid one along the bar to Kirsten.

Jen had to unsubtly tap her on the shoulder.

Kirsten looked back at him. 'What's that for?'

Marshall raised his shoulder. 'You to drink?'

'Okay.' She took it with a smile. 'Thanks.' Then turned and spoke to her pal again.

At least Marshall had tried. Act the big man, the only advice his dad had ever given him.

Carl brought over three tumblers of amber wine with shot glasses resting inside, each filled with dark liquid – Jaegermeister. 'Thirty-six eighty-five.'

No wonder he was still serving Jen...

Marshall tapped his phone against the card machine and got a beep.

'Cheers, man.' Carl handed him a receipt and slipped him a twenty back, along with a crafty wink, then buggered off, probably to escape Jen's blast radius. And get the sick bucket ready.

Marshall sniffed his drink and was relieved. Grape juice and cold coffee. He just hoped Jen was too blasted to taste the difference.

Kirsten turned back around and took one of the glasses. She leaned in close. 'Fuck sake, Sally in my team is guttered.'

'Good pal of mine.' Jen dribbled a bit of hers down her blouse. 'Whoops.'

'Okay, let's do these.' Kirsten took her drink, locked eyes with Marshall, then held her glass in the air. 'One, two, three.'

Marshall threw his back and it was absolutely vile. Even worse than what it was supposed to be.

Jen necked hers. At least it wasn't alcoholic. Might even sober her up a bit. Or take the worst edges off tomorrow afternoon when she woke up.

Kirsten slammed her glass down with a grimace, then took her glass of wine. 'Smells good.'

Drunken Sally grabbed her arm again and took her attention away.

Marshall leaned into his swaying sister. 'Jen, have you eaten anything?'

'Eating's cheating.' Her voice was a low slur.

'How old are you?'

'Same age as you, little brother.' She wrapped an arm around him. 'You were supposed to collect Thea.'

'I was down at Durham. Bit of a commute to Peebles from there.'

'Still stinks that you didn't turn up. Mum had to go and get her.'

'Did she come here?'

'For about like five minutes.'

'Oh.'

'Not her scene. Honestly. She met up with some pals in Gala to go to the cinema and watch some black-and-white Swedish shite with subtitles. She's *seventeen*, Rob. She should be drinking.'

'She told me what happened.'

'What happened?'

'With you and Paul. How she found—'

'Rob. Shut up.'

'You haven't told me. Why?'

'Because it's none of your business.'

'You tell me off for not talking about—'

'What do you expect me to say? My husband was shagging someone in our hot tub? Rob, I've got a therapist for that.'

Marshall wanted to press her, but she was right – this wasn't the time.

She held up her empty glass. 'Here, Carlos, can I—'

'Nope.'

'Oh, come on.'

'No, Jennifer. You've had your lot. I'd call the police, but they're all here.'

'Wanker.'

He handed her a pint glass of water. 'Drink three of these and I'll let you have a vodka.' He held out a finger. 'Single. With a mixer. A lot of mixer.'

'Spoilsport.' She took a big glug of her water but didn't seem to be able to finish even half of it, let alone three pints of the stuff. 'Thank you for dropping her at her dad's this morning. Absolute lifesaver.'

'We had a good chat. I'm sorry about how you found out.'

'Fuck him, Rob. This is about me and my new life.' She tried more water but barely managed a sip. 'Here's to being Jennifer Marshall again. Here, Carlos, another prolapse please!'

Marshall grabbed her sleeve. 'Jen, you're too pissed.'

'M'not.'

Marshall held out his phone. 'You sent me "Whre fuck am uy?" three times.'

'Well, here fuck am uy.' She threw her head back and laughed.

The music was so loud nobody seemed to notice.

'Need to chat to you about something.'

'Anything.'

'House. I'm so stressed, Rob. So stressed.'

'Why? You've got a ton of cash. You'll be set.'

'Only half the mortgage will be paid off. The way energy bills and mortgage rates are going... I just don't know if I can afford it.'

'You have bought it, right?'

'Agreement in principle.' She held her hand out and shook it like it was still in the balance. That or she was trying to show she was sober. 'Still with the lawyers. You know that thing where they stick loads of stupid missives in the proposed deal to buy yourself time? That.'

'I don't, sorry. I bought mine off plan. And it was in London.'

'Right.'

'I mean, if the house isn't for you, you could stay with—'

'Rob! I've got to move. I'm sick to death of Mum. She's lovely but she's doing my nut in. I need to get away.'

'She's not that bad.'

'*Rob.*' Jen looked at him like he was crazy. 'Anyway. You and Kirsten.'

'What about her?'

'Get her pissed and snog her.'

'Jesus, Jen.'

'Seriously. She likes you.'

'Bullshit.'

'Don't even start denying it. Remember on our birthday when you got twatted and you told me all about what happened.'

'Right.' Marshall picked up his glass of wine and sniffed it like the posh wine git he was. Fruity and rich. He sipped it and sluiced it through his tongue to get the full flavour.

Lovely stuff.

Helped this hotel was owned by the local wine merchant.

'So. Why were you in Durham?'

'Seeing someone about the case.'

'That ex-girlfriend of yours?'

'What?'

'Leanne?'

'Liana? She's not an ex.'

'No, but she's the one who got away, right?'

'No. She's not.'

'Was she hitting on you again?'

'Not in so many words, no.'

'So she was! All those birds, eh? Don't know what they see in you, Rob.' Jen shook her head. 'Could do with a bit of romance in my life but who wants a single mother, eh?' She managed another centimetre of water. 'Right. I'm going to the toilet. After that, I'm doing my speech.'

'You haven't done that already?'

'Nope.' She punched his arm so hard it'd bruise. 'Back in a sec.' She staggered off, bouncing against the doorframe and spinning around until she faced back into the room. Which seemed to confuse her. She righted herself and tottered away towards the toilets, hiccupping in a way that was usually a precursor to vomit.

Marshall smiled at Carl. 'Thanks for the alcohol-free version.'

'No sweat, man. She's shit-faced. I mean, good on her for divorcing that arsehole, but she's been taking the piss tonight. This isn't some Rose Street hen-do hellhole. This is a respectable bar.'

'I'll get her home safely.'

'Not exactly far, is it?'

'Nope.' Marshall sipped the wine and could just die right there. 'This is great stuff.'

'Dean put it on especially for you, but he did say Malbec's a shit drink for wankers.'

'He'd know.'

'True.' Carl nodded at drunken Sally. 'What can I get you?'

Marshall walked away from the bar to get some space.

No such luck.

Kirsten followed him over, clutching her glass tight. 'So that was helpful?'

'Those two identities? Sure. Massive help.'

275

'Didn't feel like it.'

'Why?'

'Pringle wants the third.'

'He's a—' Marshall reached for a word, but all that came out was one Elliot would use. '—clown.'

'I know, but still. He's the boss. Your boss.'

'Sorry if I made you feel crap, Kirsten.'

'What about?'

'The databases thing.'

'Oh. Don't sweat it. I was going to do it anyway. Just made you look good in front of him.' She took a sip of wine. 'Was he really eating a gobstopper?'

'Aye. No idea why.'

'It'll be for his daughter.'

Marshall winced. 'Does she exist?'

'No idea but everyone's talking about her like she does.' She sank her wine and he smelled her sweet perfume. Made his stomach flutter. 'Do you want another?'

Marshall checked his glass. Still a load left, but it was going down nicely. 'Sure. Just one more.'

She caught Carl's attention and pointed at Marshall's glass then two fingers up, the right way round and together.

Carl went back to stopping drunken Sally getting any more alcohol.

Kirsten looked back around. Face flushed already. Staring at him. Staring at him hard. 'Listen. I didn't handle you turning me down that well.'

'Come on, let's not make a big thing out of it.'

'I was crass. I didn't understand what you'd been through. Me and your sister... We're pals and she told me what happened.'

'She has, has she?'

'So. Here's an apology.' She handed him another glass of Malbec. 'Sorry.'

'Apology accepted.'

She tapped her card off the reader. 'I shouldn't have run off like that. Should've waited while you talked to Pringle.'

'I should've spoken to you afterwards.'

'I shouldn't have avoided you for months.'

'Look, I thought we'd have to do that long-distance thing. You up here, me in London, but... I've been here almost four months now.'

She frowned. 'What do you mean?'

'Well.' Truth was, he didn't know. He was here, but not really. Him and his cat staying at his mum's. He took a drink of wine, a big one. 'Thing is. What I thought would be a long-distance relationship... It wouldn't be.'

She looked away from him, sipping her wine. 'Oh.'

'Kirsten, you were great that night. We sat in here for a bit. I talked. You listened. And it's taken me a long time to talk about what happened with Anna to anyone. I... Thank you.'

She leaned over and kissed him on the cheek, brushing him with her perfume. 'Come up to my room if you want to talk more.'

CHAPTER FORTY

'I'm sorry.' Marshall perched at the edge of the bed, resting his feet on the same carpet as when he'd stayed here. Somehow she'd moved into the room he'd vacated – felt weird. But not as weird as—

Kirsten rested her hand on his back. 'Why are you apologising?'

'It didn't exactly last very long, did it?'

'Does it have to?' She leaned in close to him. 'Rob, you don't need to worry about me in that sense.'

He looked around at her. The faint light from the window caught her face, her eyes, the curve of her breasts. He couldn't deny the attraction to her. She was gorgeous. The way his heart bounced when he saw her. The way she looked at him.

'Tell me that isn't...' She swallowed hard. 'Oh God, Rob, I'm so sorry. That's the first time in years, isn't it?'

He turned around to look at her again, her eyes twinkling in the faint light. 'It felt good, Kirsten.' He leaned over and kissed her on the lips. 'This feels good.'

'But?'

'But nothing. I... I probably love you. Or I could love you.'

She grabbed a pillow and hugged it. 'First thing. Nobody's talking about love here, Rob. This can just be fun. And I didn't know this was the first time in, what, twenty years?'

He nodded.

'Rob...'

'Sorry, this is a lot to take in. I don't... I feel... I... I feel like I'm inflicting this on you?'

'Inflicting? What?'

'You know. This... I...'

'Fuck's sake, Rob.'

Marshall broke away from her. 'I should leave.'

'Is this how you deal with all your problems, Rob? Running away?'

'No, it's just...'

'Stay.'

He looked around at her again but he couldn't make out any features. 'Are you sure?'

'Of course I'm sure, Rob. I'm thirty-six. Got through a lot of scrapes all by myself, thank you very much. I don't ask people to stay unless I want them to.'

He smiled – couldn't help himself. 'People?'

'It's a turn of phrase, Rob. I haven't had sex in a while myself. Okay?' She leaned into him again, but somehow pushed him over, then somehow she was lying on top of him, her soft skin pressed against his. 'Let's not make this a big thing. Let's just enjoy the here and now. Good sex, good friendship, good fun. Let's see where it takes us, okay? And we've both got separate spaces for when we need time out.'

It seemed like it was just sex to her, but to Marshall it felt like a lot more.

He grabbed her and stood up, carrying her in his arms.

Time to live life.

CHAPTER FORTY-ONE
THE NEXT DAY

'It's been a while.' Marshall was bleary-eyed but at least he wasn't hungry any longer. His plate sat between them, the special cooked breakfast half-eaten. The second cup of coffee was starting to nibble away at his lack of sleep. 'Three months ago and now I'm back here.'

'You can stay again any time you want.' Kirsten put her knife and fork together then pushed her plate away. 'And I mean it.'

'Thanks.' Though Marshall was sore. Bits that hadn't been used in a long time, at least not in that way. And not three times in a single night.

'There we are, guys.' Dean Taylor rested a second coffee pot on the table. He was growing out his lockdown suedehead into a quiff, but the bushy beard still remained. 'I'll take these away.' He grabbed Kirsten's plate. 'This boy will do anything for a free breakfast, eh?'

'Do anything?' Kirsten glowered at him. 'Like me, you mean?'

'God, no.' Dean's mouth hung open. 'Sorry. That's not what I meant.'

Kirsten gave him a fierce glare. 'Just because we're cousins, don't think you can get away with that kind of chat.'

'It's fine, Dean.' Marshall finished his cup of coffee. 'I'll pay for my breakfast.'

'God, no. You stayed in my hotel overnight. You're my guest as much as hers.' Dean nudged Kirsten with his elbow. 'Just glad my sneaky ploy to get you two on a date finally paid off, even if it was months late.' He scuttled off lugging the plates and barking orders at a passing waiter.

The other diners didn't seem to mind.

Kirsten topped up his coffee and her own. 'I'm glad you stayed.'

'Me too.' Marshall locked eyes with her and stayed there until she put her cup to her lips. 'You were right to insist on me staying last night. I... I just need you to be patient with me.'

'Of course. And you me. I can be a bit of a dickhead at times.'

'Can't we all... I was nervous about our first time. And it being my... first... as an adult. And I'm a bit spooked by letting this happen.'

She frowned. 'This?'

'Aye. I'm overly protective of myself. I don't let people close. I'll be an arse to people. Be snarky. But you saw through that bullshit.' He took a sip of hot coffee. 'And a big part of me wants to settle down with a wife. Two point four kids. Cat. Dog. White picket fence...'

'Sounds amazing.' Kirsten was smiling. 'Would your wife mind if I came by while she's out?'

He laughed. 'I'm not being serious.'

'So why say it?'

'I sort of am. I... Thing is, by hiding away from the world

like I have... I've missed so much of life. And I want to experience it all. To live. I've no idea what I'm doing here so I'm worried I'll make a big mistake.'

'Let's just start by having fun, okay?'

'Also...' He looked around the restaurant. 'Isn't it inappropriate to have a relationship with someone at work?'

'How else are we supposed to meet people? It'd be inappropriate if you were my boss or the other way round. Just because our cases overlap doesn't mean we shouldn't be doing this. I've checked the rulebook and there's nothing stopping us.'

'One thing you should know, Kirsten, is most psychologists are screwed up in the head. I'm not daft enough to claim to be the exception.'

'Sounds like you're talking from experience?'

'No.'

'What about the one that got away?'

'What?'

She leaned across the table. 'Rob, me and your sister are good pals. We go to the same gym in Tweedbank to do circuits classes. Found out we both live in Melrose, albeit temporarily. Went for a glass of wine in here. Met up a few times.'

'And you've clearly talked about me.'

'Is that so strange? We both know you.'

'I suppose not.' Marshall took a sip of his third coffee. That'd have to be him for the day after this otherwise he'd be going to the toilet constantly. Who was he kidding? He was going to be doing that constantly as it was.

'So who is she?'

He pushed the coffee away. 'Her name's Liana... Professor Liana Curtis.'

'Wait, *her?*' Kirsten's eyebrows almost reached her silver hair. 'She's a bit out of your league, Rob.'

'And you aren't?'

'Come on, she's way hotter than me.'

'One, she's not. And two, that's not what's important to me, Kirsten. Thing is, she's the kind who'd like the white picket fence.'

'There you go. You can play husband and wife together.'

'I suspect she will mind if you pop round.'

'Ha bloody ha.'

'Thing with her is... I could've done that whole thing if I'd ever wanted to. When we both worked the Shadow Man case, we kissed. But that was it.'

She gave him a distant look. 'You ran away from her, aye?'

'Just like you did in July.'

'Touché.' She gave a flash of eyebrows. 'Thanks for telling me.'

'Well, Jen did.'

'No, but you could've denied it. Said your sister's a lying idiot.'

'I mean, she is. And a drunk. But I'm trying to be honest with myself and that means being honest with other people. Especially someone like you.' He reached across the table and took her hands. 'You're the first person who I've wanted to try something with, Kirsten. Okay?'

'Okay.'

'Like you say, I usually just ignore my feelings. Bury them. Run away from them. But I left Liana's world because of my frustration with the cold science of profiling. I had this fire burning inside me and I needed to do something about it. I wanted to stop the crimes myself. Directly. It's been an incredibly tough road, personally and professionally, but the reward has been peace with my past.'

'Rob, I'm glad but you... I...'

'What?'

'I've been ordered to return to Edinburgh.'

'Oh.'

Now she tells me.

He broke a long run of abstinence because he thought there might be something to explore with her.

Wasn't exactly a million miles to Edinburgh, but it was different to a few doors down.

She tilted her head to the side. 'What, you're not happy with that?'

'None of my business, is it?'

'Rob, there's a role available here in the Borders if I want it. Worse for my career. I don't have to go. I could stay here in the Borders. But here we are. I'm sorry. I don't know which way to go with this.'

'What if you take me out of the equation?'

'I've been veering towards going back to Edinburgh. This case is pretty interesting but there's much more interesting work up there. More opportunities for promotion. Besides, it's not like I'll be a million miles away from you. An hour on the train into Waverley.'

He grinned. 'But to get to your flat, I'll need to get a *bus*, Kirsten. A bus!'

'Snob.' She laughed. 'But you won't. The tram goes past my door, pretty much.'

Marshall sat back and sipped his coffee. 'To be honest...'

'Go on?'

'Never been on the Edinburgh tram.'

'Come on, really?'

'Really. Not been to Edinburgh in years...'

'Seriously? How can you... You've been here four months and haven't been up there?'

'Managed to avoid it.' He sighed. 'Whatever you choose, okay? It's fine with me.'

'I'm sorry. My timing is lousy.'

'It's pretty good, actually.' Marshall pushed his chair back. 'Look, I need to get back and feed Zlatan.'

'You don't strike me as a cat man, have to say. But at least you're part of the way to your white-picket life.'

'I'd stay, but Mum has a habit of forgetting to give him his biscuits.' Marshall leaned over and kissed her cheek. 'I'll see you at work and we can maybe talk it all through later?'

'There's nothing much to talk about, is there? This is just a bit of fun. We both know that. If I go back to Edinburgh, we'll be fine. You come up, I come down. I'd suggest meeting in the middle, but... Gorebridge isn't exactly happening, is it?'

He laughed. 'We'll make it work.'

CHAPTER FORTY-TWO

Marshall put his key in the lock and twisted, then took his time going inside. Creeping. He hadn't sneaked in like this in twenty years. That time Anna's parents were away to a party on Skye and he stayed at hers overnight.

Not long before his world exploded.

'Meow!' Zlatan stood just in the door, chest puffed out, eyes wide, staring up at him. Stern, disappointed. '*Meow!*'

'Hey, boy.' Marshall knelt down and stroked his thick fur. Looked like Thea had brushed him again. He was all prim and proper, which went against his rough and ragged demeanour. He picked him up and cuddled the tabby monster.

'Meow!' Zlatan wriggled a bit so Marshall put him on the end of the counter.

'Let's get you fed, big lad.' He tipped some food into a bowl and laid it in front of him.

Zlatan started purring as soon as he bit his first biscuit.

'Just like the old days.'

Marshall swung around.

Jen was sitting at the table, fingers around a cup of tea. Still wearing the same get-up as last night. Make-up smudged. But smiling. 'Sneaking back in, eh? Walk of shame. Dirty shagger.'

'Mum and Thea not up yet?'

'Nope.' She slurped her tea. 'Not that I know. Just got back myself.'

'And you're calling me a shagger?'

'I wish I was a shagger, clean or dirty.' Jen rolled her eyes. 'We had a lock-in.'

'In the bar? Carl stopped you drinking.'

'Managed three pints of water, didn't I?'

'Seriously?'

'Hardly. No, we all went back to Sally's room. She's in a suite somehow.'

'That's not a lock-in. A lock-in is in the bar.'

'Whatever. I don't think there's any white wine or Jaegermeister left in Melrose. Not that you can talk. Didn't even turn up, did you?'

Marshall laughed. 'We had a chat, Jen. For about fifteen minutes.'

'Oh.' She frowned and it turned into a smirk. 'Of course. You, me and Kirsten had a prolapse.'

'Right.' Marshall didn't tell her the truth about that. 'You were very insistent.'

'Thing is.' She leaned forward and spoke quietly: 'Sally's room is next door to Kirsten's. Sounded like she had company. Headboard banging in the dead of night!'

That old joke from when they were kids, twisting the words to the Beatles' *Blackbird*.

'Lucky guy.'

She held his gaze. 'It was you, wasn't it?'

Marshall only had eyes for Zlatan, still crunching at his biscuits.

'You spent the night. Wow.' She came over and wrapped him in a big, squishy hug. And stank. And not just of booze. 'I'm so pleased for you.'

'Jen, have you been smoking?'

'Just a couple of cigarettes. We had the window open.'

'Jesus. I thought you'd quit.'

'Aye, well. I won't start again. Promise.' She held up crossed fingers on both hands. 'Listen, I planned to spend the day in bed enjoying this stinking hangover but I got a text this morning. Upshot is I've got a meeting with my solicitor.'

'The house?'

'How did you know?'

'Almost like we discussed it last night...'

'Oh. Well. The sellers are pushing me to close on it today.'

'And despite all those missives your lawyer's stuffed in there, you're not sure?'

'Correct.'

'Talk me through the pros and cons.'

'Thing is. Clovenfords would be perfect for Thea. It's on the bus route back to Peebles and her old school, which would take a lot of strain off me. Like you did yesterday.'

'But?'

'But it's slightly more than I can really afford now. Worried about mortgage rates and heating.'

'Which will stabilise over time. That war can't go on forever. You could put a heat pump in. Solar panels.'

She stared at him, her eyes twinkling. 'Rob, I really want that house.' She passed him the schedule from the table and flicked through it. He'd been to see it with her. Twice. 'It's lovely, but... It's expensive.'

The granny flat over the garage. He could live there – bedroom, kitchen, bathroom, separate entrance so he could come and go as he pleased.

On the plus side, he'd be able to get away from Mum's clutches, and he'd have his own space.

It'd help Jen out of a bind. God knows he owed her for twenty years of being a shit brother.

'I thought you were going to Airbnb the granny flat?'

'I was, but it's not exactly stable income, is it? Or I don't know if it is.'

He pushed the schedule away. 'I've really got to get to work.'

'You running away again, eh?'

'Aye, need to go and earn my corn.'

CHAPTER FORTY-THREE

Marshall checked his watch as he ploughed along the corridor. Already bloody late for the briefing. He should've declined Kirsten's invite, just gone home and slept.

Because if Sally and Jen knew, then everyone would.

Get over yourself.

Someone shows you some affection and you hide in your work. Best thing that's happened to you in years, you idiot.

Aye. The voice inside his head put up with no nonsense because the rest of him tried to get away with so much of it.

The incident room door was shut so he'd be conspicuous going in. Pringle would give him a right doing, set an example of him – like being back at school.

Hang on.

Voices came from an interview room.

He stopped and listened.

Elliot.

Couldn't tell who she was talking to. A man, though.

Was it Siyal?

What was she up to?

Marshall knocked on the door and waited.

No answer. Elliot kept talking.

He knocked again.

'Sorry about this.' A chair scraped back, footsteps stomped then the door opened to a crack wide enough for Elliot to peer out. 'Marshall.' She looked him up and down. 'Briefing's on.'

'Aye, but I want to know what you're up to in there.'

She folded her arms. 'Do you now?'

'Come on.'

She shut the door.

Jesus Christ!

He knocked again.

It opened again. Elliot stepped out into the corridor and kicked the door shut behind her. 'What are you playing at, you clown?'

'What are *you*? Who's in there.'

'Adrian Robinson. The Forestry Commission boss.' She huffed out a sigh. 'Forestry and Land, isn't it? I'm interviewing him.' She looked away from him, down the corridor, shooting daggers at the door. 'The boy's being very abrasive, but I've got this.' She slipped back into the room.

Marshall checked his watch. Ten minutes to the briefing. Sod it. He went into the obs suite and turned on the telly. Absolutely freezing in there. Some sod had left the window open.

Adrian Robinson was a big bear man. His wild hair was on the verge of thinning and needed trimming. The deep tan of someone who worked outside all day, every day, even in Scotland. Or had just been somewhere hot.

'So. Where were we?' Elliot frowned. 'Oh, aye. We find out that someone's been murdering people on the ground you manage. Mr Robinson, it'd be useful to know of any people with familiarity in the forest... Any of your staff, any regulars, landowners. Problems, people with negative history.'

'I mean... Not really. I know all the landowners. It's good income for them. Better than sheep.'

'Get a lot of people walking the trails, aye?'

'And cycling them. They don't mind. I don't mind. It's good for tourism in a deprived area. Few people walk their dogs there because it's that bit further away from the main roads, so it's quieter. Don't get a lot of cyclists – they prefer the bigger places like Glentress or Innerleithen, with marked-out courses. Even Thornielee as it's on the A72.'

'We want to search the whole forest.'

Robinson laughed. 'You do know how big an area you're talking?'

'I do. But we've found six bodies there. There could well be more.'

'Right, well, of course you can do that. I mean, there shouldn't be *any* bodies there. The fact you've found six is... Well, it's awful, isn't it?'

Elliot leaned back. 'Is there a plan to... Sorry, I don't know the technical term, but cut down the trees?'

'Let's just call it forestry. Part of what I'm responsible for is devising forestry plans for everywhere we manage. When we harvest the timber, and the subsequent site treatment. Problem with that place is, between us two, there's decent money in those trees but we've got the issue of the red squirrel population there. Any forestry work has to maintain their habitat.'

'How much money are you talking?'

'Oh, not a lot really. Thing is, all that land was a tax swindle back in the Sixties and Seventies. Loads of rock bands sunk money into it way back in exchange for tax breaks. But the price of imports plummeted, so they lost so much money.

Decent for their tax returns, I suppose. The price of timber skyrocketed in lockdown. Everyone wants their decking, don't they? That ship getting stuck in the Suez Canal started it and it was like an avalanche. Gap in the market that never got filled and started eroding everything else. Everyone's playing catch up. So they're felling trees all around here.'

'But not at Elibank?'

'No. And we won't until the native woodlands are back to a healthy level. Glenkinnon's a great example – oldest native forest in Scotland and we're growing it out, replacing the old pine plantation with birch, oak, you name it. Elibank's already got a good level of beech, birch, oak and so on growing amongst the evergreens. Need to keep them unscathed to protect the red squirrel population. Great seeing the little buggers around again since the zero-tolerance policy came in.'

Marshall got it.

Adrian Robinson was a tree hugger. Any antagonism from him towards Elliot was to protect wildlife and conserve native trees.

Of course, she took any actual objection as a sign of guilt and acted like a feral animal. 'See if you're doing your forestry operations, wouldn't you uncover the bodies in the ground?'

Robinson thought it through. 'No. We've got— I'll not use the technical term. These big machines come in and chop them down in a few hours. Kind of our version of a combine harvester. They fell them, then they're loaded into lorries. Besides, we cut them at the base and leave the rootstock in the ground. Eventually it all rots away.'

'So you'd never find the bodies?'

'Right.'

Elliot took a deep breath and scribbled something in her notebook. 'I see.'

'Look.' Robinson raised his hands. 'It's been a bugger of a

year since Storm Arwen. Not had a day off since last November. Ten days in the sun and I've almost forgotten my own name, so I'm not on my A-game.' His grin widened. 'And getting woken up by your lot at half five this morning was a bit much, especially as my flight back from Lanzarote was delayed by three hours. But aye. Of course my lads will help out. They're at your beck and call today.'

That seemed to placate Elliot. 'Okay. Thanks for your time, sir. Suggest you get back to Elibank and get them all ready, because today's going to be a long day.'

'Used to them...' Robinson got up and walked over to the door. 'Just along the corridor and down the stairs, right?'

'Correct, sir.' Elliot smiled at him. 'Do you need a hand out?'

'No, I'll be fine.' Robinson left her to it. A man who was used to nature and clearly struggled with the built environment.

Marshall left the obs suite and went into the room.

Elliot slumped back in the chair. 'There you are.'

'Here I am. You get anywhere?'

'My wound's nipping me something rotten today so I was acting like a bit of a cow there.' She sighed. 'Anyway. That's my day sorted out. Got the dogs ready to go.' She stood up with a wince. 'How was Jolene yesterday?'

'Jolene? She was okay. I mean, we just sort of drove around and spoke to people. You know how it is.'

'Aye, but we need to push for her promotion to be made permanent.'

'I've worked with her for three months and I'm not sure she's ready to be a DS yet.'

'And Shunty is?'

'Andrea, that's whataboutery. I've got no skin in the game

for either of them. DS Siyal's got a lot to learn but she's got a bit more. It's up to you and me to sort those two out.'

'Christ, you're a bundle of joy today. What happened to you last night?'

Did she know?

How could she?

'Nothing. Just got a lot of work on.'

'Aye, aye.' Elliot walked over to the door and opened it then ducked back in. 'Bollocks.'

The door opened and Pringle waltzed in, pointing at them both. 'Found the pair of you!' He shook his head. 'Bit embarrassing trying to run a briefing when both of your DIs aren't present.'

Elliot jutted out her chin. 'I've just got a result.'

Pringle tilted his head to the side like they'd solved the case. 'Oh?'

'Got approval to scour the whole site today.'

'I'm very pleased for you.'

'If we find any more bodies, we'll have more data for Marshall to unpick.'

'And if you don't?'

'Listen, I'll get DS Siyal to lead it.' Elliot got out her notebook and scribbled something down. 'See if he can do something right.'

Pringle pressed his tongue into his cheek. 'See, this is why you need to attend briefings, Andrea. I've asked the Shuntmeister to focus on the prison stuff.'

'Prison stuff?'

'Keane was interviewed several times by a podcaster.' Pringle reached into his pocket but all he produced was a gobstopper packet, which seemed to be a surprise to him. 'I want Shunty to see if we can get anything on Keane that shows he's got a protégé.'

'Why Siyal?'

'Because it transpires that Mark Davidson was in all of those recordings.'

'Cool beans, Jim. Anything else happen at the briefing I should know about?'

'No.' Pringle frowned. 'Oh, well. Bruce's got time with the podcaster down in Newcastle. Marshall, go and have a word with him.'

Elliot tilted her head back. 'Is there something you're not telling us?'

'No, but it's the same old story. Vickers and Davidson were in all those interviews. Vickers as he was the laddie doing the interviewing, Davidson as he was the lawyer. If one of them's the protégé then we need to know. So your pretty face is going to Hell, Marshall. Or rather, Newcastle.'

'Sir.'

'Go on, then.' Pringle focused on Elliot. 'Now, you're going to come with me to finish the briefing.'

CHAPTER FORTY-FOUR
SIYAL

Siyal didn't know when it started, but in ten months he'd gone from never having drunk anything with caffeine in it to needing it every day. And always having it. Even got quite into it – especially the pot of black coffee Kirsten's team had on the go in their office, kept a secret from the cops. All except him.

The door clattered open and Kirsten fizzed in, her face twisted up. He knew not to mess. 'Tell me that's decaf?'

Siyal shook his head. 'Full fat.'

She grunted. 'Had too much coffee already. My heart's thumping.'

'You okay?'

She smiled at him. 'I'm fine.' The smile wasn't touching either eye but Siyal didn't want to pry. 'Why do you ask?'

'Just...' He looked away. 'No reason.'

'I'm fine. Thing is, I've got to somehow get CCTV for she who shall not be named. From Newcastle. Or Newcastle-shire.'

'Jolene? What does she want with it?'

'Search me.' Kirsten picked up the packet of coffee beans

from behind the machine, like she was tempted to have yet another cup. 'Oh, Bruce sent me those prison logs. I think they were meant for you.'

'Thank you.' Siyal leaned against the wall. 'Have you thought about your decision yet?'

'No, Rakesh. Got a lot on my mind with this case.'

'Fair enough.'

The door opened again and Elliot appeared. 'What the hell are you two up to in here?'

Siyal held up his mug. 'Drinking coffee.'

'You don't drink coffee.'

'I do.'

'Eh?' She was scowling. 'When you started, you made this big hullaballoo about it.'

'I didn't drink it back then. I started since.'

Elliot didn't seem to believe him. 'Good that I've caught you both, actually.' She entered the room and let the door shut, but her steely focus was on Kirsten. It was like an enemy boat's searchlight had moved to another patch of sea and Siyal could resurface. 'How are the crime scene forensics?'

'You mean the woodlands?'

'No, I mean in Shunty's soiled undercrackers.' Elliot rolled her eyes. 'Of course I mean the woods.'

'The good news is it's slow and laborious.'

'Eh? What's the bad?'

'I've been focusing my team's time on identifying the victims first.'

'Why the hell would—?'

'Don't, Andrea.' Kirsten raised a finger. 'I'm not in the mood for this. My team, my choice. Our initial findings are that the bodies are forensically inert – whoever did this knows what they're doing. So you won't get a lot from them.'

'But the graves must—?'

'What do you expect to get from them? Hairs or prints? Don't be so stupid. There's nothing in there. Not even Roman coins or Anglo-Saxon spears. Or Celtic... I don't know. Scabbards?'

Elliot raised her eyebrows. 'Who crapped in your porridge?'

'Andrea, I'm very busy and not in the mood for this. Those graves are closer to archaeology than what I do. DCI Pringle was pretty bloody clear that *our* highest priority is on identifying them. Which I've done two thirds of. Now. Is there anything I can actually help you with?'

Elliot stared her down. Siyal wanted to hide. 'It's just to say we're going to scour the woods for other bodies today with help from our best friends from the Forest Comm— from Forest and Land Scotland. I'm leading that, so I'll need as many of your team as you can spare.'

Kirsten laughed. 'No.'

'What do you mean, no?'

'First you're harassing me about forensics and now you're asking me to give up my resource for some menial donkey work. Which is it?'

'Okay, give me Sally and—'

'She's called in sick today.'

'Fine. Then the lad with the mullet.'

'Trevor?'

'Aye, Trevor.'

'Fine. You can have Trevor.'

'That's a bit too quick, Ms Weir. Makes me think he's shite.'

'He's good. All of the team down here are.'

'That'll be why they're moving you back up to the big city, eh?'

Kirsten's nostrils flared. She tilted her head to the side. Smiled with a grin that would've melted steel. 'If you've got issues with me, please take it up with James Anderson.'

Elliot smirked. 'He still won't answer the phone to me.'

'Wonder why. I'll go and fetch Trevor for you.' Kirsten barged past into the corridor.

Leaving Elliot's searchlight with one target to focus on. 'Shunty, Shunty, Shunty... Talk to me about this investigation into the lawyer.'

'What do you mean?'

'I mean, why are you doing it?'

'DI Marshall approved it.'

'Just so you and I are perfectly clear, Shunty, you report to me, okay? And I'm not happy with you arsing about like this.'

'Arsing about like what?'

'Big Jim McIntyre said you'd put in the miles yesterday. Over to Ayrshire then up to Edinburgh. Better be worth it.'

'We spoke to two related parties.'

'I just want you to know that that amount of travel doesn't sit right with me. So I'm stopping it. Okay?'

'No.'

'No?' Elliot laughed, but it was short and sharp like gunfire. 'You don't get to say no to me, Shunty.'

'No, but DCI Pringle does. He followed up on that request. Said it's a priority.'

Elliot hefted a sigh like someone would a knife. 'He honestly thinks that creepy weirdo Mark Davidson is capable of murdering people? I mean, sure, wrapping someone in cling film I can see. The guy is a total pervert, but the abduction part? He's just not capable of it.'

'DI Marshall said there may be multiple parties involved in these murders and I've identified Davidson as a possible suspect in an abduction and rape.'

'Aye?'

'Aye.'

'Before these victims?'

'Before the three we've found, yes.'

'That's interesting.' Her fury seemed to vanish, replaced with a raised eyebrow. 'See, I heard Marshall banging on about there possibly being trials of this MO. Him giving it a shot before he started killing. When was this abduction?'

'Eleventh of August last year. Case collapsed—'

'Aye, I remember it. I was up in Edinburgh at the time. Craigen and St John were on it, doing the donkey work. Kirsten said the witness data has been deleted off the system. Overwritten the record. Can't go back to the historic version either. Means someone on the case did it.' Elliot started counting on her fingers. 'This Layla from Washington lassie was killed in January.' More counting. 'August is five months before that. It's not three months, I'll grant you, or even two times three months, but... Okay. Stick to this, Shunty, but you come to me first, okay? Not Marshall. Not Pringle. Got it?'

Siyal hadn't got into this game to become embroiled in office politics and yet here he was, wedged between two DIs. 'Fine.'

'What else are you looking at for him?'

'Nothing for Rob. But for DCI Pringle, he's asked me to review all the interview transcripts for messages passed between Keane and Davidson. Or gaps when messages could've been passed. And to see if there's a connection with Alexander Vickers.'

'The podcaster. Right, right. Excellent. You have a wee shufti, Shunty, but remember that you're mine. Okay?' Elliot checked her watch. 'Okay, if you need me, I'll be out at Elibank.'

Siyal gave as close to a smile as he could muster. 'Sure thing.'

'That coffee smells nice, though. Where did you get it?'

'Dean's Beans.'

'Seriously? Mine always tastes like warmed-up piss from there.'

'Might be because they're weeing into yours.'

'Aye, very good, Shunty.' She gripped his shoulders. 'We'll make a copper of you yet.'

'Thank you.' He watched her go. Waited for the door to shut. Then let out a deep breath. And took a drink of coffee. Cool now, but he still drank it. Needed a few more of these, so he topped it up from the filter pot hiding behind the paper box.

The door opened and Kirsten stormed back in. 'What did the ballmuncher want?'

'Usual. But she's on manoeuvres against Marshall, so keep an eye out.'

'Always do.' Kirsten reached for the pot and filled up her mug. 'Sod it.' She put it back and it hissed. 'Long as she doesn't find out about this, we'll be fine. But still, second day back and she's already playing politics against Rob. She never stops, does she?' She drank her coffee in silence, staring at the wall which had that old poster where a wallet was being taken out of the pocket of a hanging-up coat by another jacket's sleeve.

'You want to talk about why you're upset?'

She didn't look around at him. 'Not just now.'

'Okay.' Which meant it was serious. 'Could I ask you a favour?'

'Another one?'

'No, it's more about the last favour.' Siyal took a drink of slightly warmer coffee. 'The one last night. Have you looked through the contents of the evidence store for that case?'

'I had a rummage first thing this morning. I didn't work on it, but... Bottom line is that evidence... Well, it went.'

'Elliot said someone deleted it?'

'I think so.' Now she was looking at him. 'Why would they delete it?'

'Somebody's up to no good, Kirsten. The case fell apart because they lost CCTV from the server and now a contact record for a witness. That stinks to high heaven. Any idea who?'

'The previous owner of the Debonair is known to have bent cops on his payroll.'

'Now *that* I remember. Trouble is, they were booted off the force.'

Siyal drank some coffee. 'All of them?'

'Well...' She twisted her lips together. 'I don't like the feeling that someone else is screwing about with my evidence.'

'The council lost the CCTV too.'

'That's shite.'

'Eh?'

'Their data retention policy is a shambles. They never delete anything.' Kirsten tapped her phone's screen and put it to her ear. Took a slug of coffee as she was waiting. 'Mr Naismith, how the devil are you?' She smiled. 'It's nice of you to say but you don't get away from me that easily.' Another sip. 'You get the email I sent you this morning?' Her eyebrows shot up. 'Okay, well you're very patronising too, but it'll be easier for both of us if you still have access to the tape back-ups. Aye, that's covered by the existing warrant. Thank you. I'll be in touch if I've not got them by, oooh, two o'clock. Ciao.' She stabbed a finger off the screen and pocketed her phone. 'He's arranging for the tape backups to be restored.'

'Tape?'

'I know. Went to the storage facility once – it's like that bit at the end of that Indiana Jones film. All you need to know is he'll send those video files to me this afternoon.'

'Thank you, Kirsten. I owe you big time.'

'I know.' She finished her coffee and rested it on the table. 'You've got a lot of hope placed in this, right?'

Siyal nodded. 'I think Jason Craigen's done it.'

Kirsten screwed her eyes up. 'Nasty bugger.'

'You know him?'

'Oh, I know him. Angry man. He broke someone's arm. Told me I'm useless, but that's just him all over, eh?'

'Thanks, Kirsten. I'll go back to getting my arse kicked by Elliot.'

Kirsten scowled at him. 'You don't need to take it from her.'

'Oh, it's fine. I'm getting pretty good at managing her now.'

'If that's the case then you've just forgotten that you told her you're looking at those prison transcripts I sent you.'

CHAPTER FORTY-FIVE
MARSHALL

Marshall still didn't have an answer to Elliot's question.

How *was* Jolene doing?

For a start, she was driving them. Without too much fuss, just took the keys and got behind the wheel.

Now, she was driving them through the pain-in-the-arse road system around Newcastle without a moan.

Still, that's the sort of thing he'd expect from a uniform constable straight out of...

What was the Scottish police college called? Tulliallan? Something like that anyway.

To prove she was worthy of being a DS, Jolene needed to do something more than be Elliot's drinking buddy.

Or was he being too harsh?

They passed a trio of lads walking along the side of the road, all topless. On a Tuesday morning. In November. In Newcastle.

'Did you get my message this morning, sir?'

He looked over at her. 'Which one?'

'There was only one. Neshy.'

'Remind me?' Marshall snapped his finger. 'No, I remember. Steven Cork's mate. Last person to see him?'

'Right.' Jolene overtook a bus and powered on too fast for a thirty. 'I followed up with the local lot, got his number. Spoke to him late last night. Don't think he was entirely sober. And it was very early in Bangkok. His take matched Steven Cork's mum's take. Thought he'd gone to Thailand. Kind of sweet, really – he went there to try and find him.'

'And what does that make you think?'

'That we shouldn't—'

Her phone rang. The only pool car in Melrose you could pair a mobile with.

Big Boy Bruce calling...

Marshall laughed. 'Big boy?'

'Andrea sent me her contact info for him and I didn't check it.' She was blushing as she hit answer. 'Hi, Jonathan.'

'Jolene, Jolene, Jolene, Jo-leeeene, how many times do I have to tell you? Call me Jon?'

His joke didn't land. Or rather, it landed behind enemy lines, surrounded by divisions of tanks. 'Okay, *Jon*. First, you're on with DI Marshall too. Second, we can see you.'

Just along the road, Bruce was a hulking mess in a fighting suit standing on the streets of Newcastle. At least he had his top on.

Jolene parked up and started searching the car. 'Where's that bloody sign...'

Marshall got out into the downpour. 'Hi, Jon. You okay?'

'I'm a police officer, Rob. I could never be described as being okay.'

Marshall chuckled. But it died in his throat when he recognised where they were. Northumbria University. 'This is where...'

Bruce winced. 'Where we picked up Michael Shaw.'

Marshall let out a slow breath. 'Is the hosting company still here?'

'Nah, all that's dried up. Most people host with Amazon or Microsoft nowadays, rather than a reputable local firm. Cheaper and more reliable.' Bruce thumbed behind him. 'This building is now twenty podcast studios, would you believe?'

'There are that many in Newcastle?'

'Five of them just on the Toon. Wor Mags and all that.'

Marshall felt like he was talking Swahili. 'What?'

'Football, man. Jesus! Newcastle United? Team are doing well, like.'

'Right. Not a football man.'

'Your cat's called Zlatan, isn't he?'

How the hell did he know that?

'He is but that's from the previous owner.'

'Ah, well. Aye. Lots of podcasts in this part of the world.'

Jolene got out of the car and gave Bruce a big hug. 'Been a while, Jonathan.'

'Aye, wish it'd been longer like.' But he was grinning. Maybe they were old friends, or just frequent acquaintances.

Jolene tilted her head towards Marshall. 'Boss here's been a grumpy sod all the way down the road.'

'What else is new?' Bruce shot Marshall a wink. 'Okay, so your pal Kirsten Weir called about the CCTV. We've put our heads together and got a spark of flame.'

Jolene rested her fist on her hip. 'Any chance you can spell it out for us?'

'Okay. So far, we've got video of Layla McMenemy getting on a coach in Newcastle, heading to Carlisle.'

Jolene's forehead creased. 'Carlisle?'

ED JAMES

'I know. Why anyone would go there's beyond me. We've requested the CCTV from our colleagues in Cumbria, but they can be a bit slothful.'

Jolene gave a flash of her eyebrows. 'Andrea's got a mate there. Foxton.'

'Oh, God. I know him. Bit of a bell end.'

'Takes one to know one, I suppose.'

Bruce smirked. 'True.' He clapped his hands together. 'Reason I'm here and waiting for you is my lot have uncovered a little nugget of information. Our friendly neighbourhood podcaster Vickers previously trained as a respiratory therapist.'

Jolene frowned. 'What's one of them?'

'Varies, like, but he was a nurse, specialising in invasive ventilation. Including tracheal intubation.' Bruce pointed at his windpipe. 'Whoever's been killing these people has been keeping them alive. If the dress fits...'

Forget what Siyal was up to with Davidson – Marshall had to shift Alexander Vickers to the top of the suspect list. 'Obviously, Vickers was in all of those interviews with Keane too. And he actually had the skills to keep them alive while he did what he did to them.'

Bruce grimaced. 'And he knew how to end their lives too.'

Jolene snorted – she hated to be left out. 'I think we need to speak to this guy.'

'Okay, okay, okay.' Bruce held his hands up. 'Plan is to get him down to the station. I've got a DNA warrant on Vickers to compare with the semen found in the recent three. Trouble is, we also kind of need all of his recordings and we don't want him deleting them. So let's get in there, get him away from the machine and someone with a brain like a dinosaur egg can get the files.'

'Fine with me, Jonathan.' Jolene winked at him.

'Come on, then.'

CHAPTER FORTY-SIX

Bruce walked along a dark corridor that skirted under a staircase, the walls filled with gold discs that looked fake, then rapped on a door.

Marshall recognised the face who answered.

Alexander Vickers. Tall and balding, wrapped up in a couple of fleeces. 'Look, mate, I told you on the phone. I'm too busy.'

'And I heard you on the phone.' Bruce stepped right up to him. 'My colleagues have travelled the best part of two hours to bask in your company, Alex. Least you—'

'It's Alexander. Please don't shorten my name.'

'Okay, Mr Vickers. How about we have a little chat inside, eh?'

'I'm being hassled to turn over my own, personal correspondence to the police. If that doesn't infringe on my civil liberties, I don't know what does.'

'Come on, Alexander, I've asked nicely.'

'I've said no.'

'All we want is a little chat. How about we do it here rather than somewhere a lot more police station-y.'

Vickers looked him up and down. 'Fine.' He held the door open for them. 'I'd offer you a coffee but the machine's broken and I have to bring mine here in a sodding Thermos.' He took a seat in front of a giant laptop hooked up to two even bigger screens, with massive speakers either side. Two microphones, one on the desk, another pointing in at an angle. A few cameras. A pair of headphones was stuffed onto a mannequin's head – creepy.

Bruce walked into the room but couldn't get close enough to the computer.

Jolene took the only other seat in there.

Marshall followed her in, not that there was anywhere to sit, so he went over to the window.

Christ, he could see where he'd taken down Michael Shaw. Where Shaw had drawn his knife and established his guilt in the eyes of DI Jon Bruce.

Poor bastard.

The world had conspired against him. Another skeleton in Marshall's closet – one he'd actually managed to exorcise the ghost of.

Bruce was looking at the pictures on the wall – footballers in black and white wearing black and white strips. 'How many staff do you have?'

'Staff?' Vickers laughed. 'I do it all myself. The dream is to employ editors and marketers, but I have to do it all for now.'

Jolene pointed at the screens. The left-most was filled with some waveforms, the right with a text document. 'What are you working on?'

'Episode five of the podcast. I'm editing together audio of interviews with the victims' parents after the discovery of all three bodies.' Vickers carefully folded his arms. 'I've done a lot of reading over the years about dramatic theory. How best to tell the story in a compelling way. Planning on writing a book about it. Going to call it *All I Do Each Night Is Prey*. But prey as in opposite of a predator. But that's for next year. This episode's due to drop next week.'

Bruce pointed at him. 'We've not cleared that.'

Vickers shrugged. 'It's a free country.'

'And that's evidence for a murder investigation.'

'You're not going to prosecute Martin Keane for them, though. They're not—'

'What makes you think that?'

'His lawyer told me.'

'Mark Davidson?' Bruce looked over at Marshall. 'Interesting.'

Jolene shot Bruce a sharp look – she was taking over and running this chat. 'Talk to me about what you've assembled.'

'Well.' Vickers exhaled deeply. 'The pitch for my podcast is the British version of *Serial*. Seeing as how they're not really doing it anymore, someone needs to do important work. I mean, last month Adnan Syed was freed because of their efforts.'

Jolene sat back, arms folded. 'So you think you're going to get Martin Keane freed?'

'Look, all I do is report. Print journalism is dead, but in audio and on YouTube... it's alive. Thriving, even. I've met Martin a few times in prison and I've recorded hours and hours of audio and video. No money changed hands. I just want to get Keane's story out there.'

Jolene gave a polite smile. 'What story would that be, Mr Vickers?'

'There's something in his message. You know. We do live in

the shadows. Someone like Elon Musk can just buy Twitter to suit his own narrative. A crown prince of a sovereign nation can get a critical journalist killed on a whim. It's up to people like us four to stop that.'

'How does Martin Keane fit in to that?' Even her frown was polite. 'He killed, pure and simple.'

Vickers was pursing his lips. 'There's the possibility he might be innocent.'

'Even though Keane confessed? Even though he bragged about it?'

'Even so.'

'The only loose end was the undiscovered victims. He maintained public interest in his story by withholding locational information on three victims. He kept the authorities interested by not revealing where he buried them until now. And you don't think he's killed these people? Why?'

Vickers smirked. 'I'm just asking the questions here.'

'Thing is, I've seen your YouTube channel, Mr Vickers. It's monetised. That means you're making income from ads that Google serves against your content. So, from where I'm sitting there's moolah here for you.'

'Moolah.' Vickers moved his chair a little bit closer to the laptop. Unlocked – he could trigger a single-click wipe mechanism. 'Sure.'

'I'm serious. You get hundreds of thousands of views for your videos. Do you share any of that money with the victims of the crimes?'

'I do, as it happens. I set up a fund which my sister manages for me. There's over a hundred grand in my account. Talking therapy, funeral costs, travel expenses. Anything they need.'

Jolene was nodding along, a kind look in her eyes. 'None of that money goes to you?'

Vickers glanced away. 'Didn't say that.'

'But after you've taken out a grand or so for talking therapy, funeral costs and travel expenses, you'll have the best part of a hundred for you. For your IT equipment. For this place.'

'It's not a crime.'

'Morally, though, you're exploiting the trauma of innocent people for your own personal gain. And helping the word of a convicted killer get out into the public domain.'

'Still not a crime.'

'Mr Vickers, you know that Martin Keane led us to the graves of three victims. You were there. You brought the parents along. You collected them from their homes at super-short notice.'

He looked around at his laptop. 'Still not a crime.'

'You know he's guilty. He confessed to killing them and he showed us the graves.'

'Still not me that's committed a crime.'

'Mr Vickers, I think your interest in this is veering into that territory.'

He looked around at her. 'What territory?'

'Of it being a crime. Of you being involved.'

Vickers pushed his chair forward a few paces from the desk. 'What the hell are you talking about?'

'You sound like a fanboy. Or maybe a protégé. Or maybe you know Keane is actually innocent because you killed those people and he took the rap for them.'

'That's preposterous!' Vickers shot to his feet and pointed at her. 'I was working in the States when he was active!'

'Sure.' Jolene flipped open her notebook and noted something down. 'Great. See, that's something we can look into and confirm, Mr Vickers. I appreciate the co-operation.'

Vickers looked like the place he was running to was the door, not to his computer. 'Do that.'

'What you don't know, Mr Vickers, is we found three further bodies at the site.'

His eyes went wide. 'What?'

'They were killed much more recently. Three, six and nine months ago.'

'You expect me to give alibis for them?'

'Are you saying you need to?'

'That's... This is... When?'

'We'll never get precise times of death.'

Vickers looked around at them in turn. 'Whenever you're after, I will either have been recording material or editing. All of my time goes into the podcast. Costs me a fortune to host it too. I'm not a killer. I'm just providing entertainment in diffi-cult times. That's it.'

'You're exploiting people.'

'I'm a content producer. People love my work.'

'But you are exploiting the torment of these people for financial gain. Your podcasts contain adverts, which gives you income. You've got a Patreon so people can pay you directly.'

'It all gets swallowed up by my hosting!'

'I'm sure your accountant can vouch for that.'

'Fine! I'll send it all on!'

'Alexander.' Bruce folded his arms. 'We know what you did before you started this podcast.'

'What?'

'What you were doing in America. You used to be a respira-tory therapist. Came back here when your dad got sick, but you got struck off, didn't you?'

'Bullshit.'

'The truth you're seeking, Alex, is how you accidentally killed three people at Newcastle General. How you got fired. Faced a big tribunal. Lucky not to be charged with anything. Down and out, so you did a podcast about it, protesting your innocence. It's all there. Had a lad listen to it. We've got copious notes, possibly enough to reopen the investigation.'

'I don't know what you expect from me.'

'Just the truth. How about we start with you giving us all of the video and audio from the prison interviews with Keane.'

Vickers glanced around at his laptop, still awake.

Jolene stood up and walked over. 'I'm not accusing you of anything here. I think you're not in bed with Keane, that there's an innocent explanation for it all. You're trying to exorcise your own guilt at those tragic deaths that maybe weren't really your fault by getting close to a real murderer. Or another killer anyway.'

'That's bullshit.'

Bruce pushed away from the door. 'Come on, Alex. Let's do this down the station.'

'What?'

'I'm taking you to be formally interviewed.'

'I haven't done anything!'

Bruce leaned back out into the corridor and beckoned a few people in. All plainclothes. 'Take him back to HQ. Grab his computer and any notebooks.'

Jolene pushed her away between them.

Vickers was reaching for the laptop, his fingers clawing at the machine. 'No, you can't do this!'

She smiled at him. 'Yep, we can.'

The two big lumps in suits grabbed hold of Vickers and dragged him out of there. 'Please!'

Bruce watched him go. 'Well done.'

Jolene frowned. 'What did I do?'

'You got him talking. More importantly, you kept him talking. Few bits and bobs I hadn't quite bottomed out, like the money stuff.'

Her frown deepened. 'That's basic, Jon. Always follow the money.'

'Good advice, but you knew where he was hiding his pot of gold. How he was topping it up. Look, if he's involved in this, great. We'll get it out of him. But if he's been coining it in, I'm sure there's dirt somewhere. Like this bent charity set up to funnel dosh elsewhere.'

Jolene was staring hard at him. 'Do you really think he's murdering people?'

'Me?' Bruce laughed then looked at Marshall. 'Your boss here's the expert on that score. I'm just pleased I've got something to do. Been feeling a bit side-lined since your man Pringle swooped in to save the day. This is good stuff.'

A pair of Northumbria CSI officers walked in, carrying all the necessary equipment to take Vickers' machine and document the whole story.

'Come on, Sergeant.' Marshall gestured at the door, then followed her out with a wave to Bruce.

She walked alongside him, her shoulders slumped. 'That's it? That's all we're going to do?'

'For now.'

'We've driven two hours to get here and we're just buggering off?'

'We've got profile work to get on with. That stuff is going to take a while to process and longer to analyse. We're going to head back to their HQ and review the files they've got. Excellent coffee there too. Or it was ten years ago.'

Jolene put her hands on her hips. 'And what will I do?'

'Help me. Seriously. And that was great work there.'

'What was?'

'Leading that. Tearing someone apart on their own turf isn't easy. Not quite a confession but I think they'll get there in the station. Much easier to intimidate someone in an interview room, but you did it here in his podcast studio. And we were able to get his laptop, unlocked too, so we can start to get all of his prison interviews.'

'Thanks, sir.' She stopped by their car. The squad car containing Alexander Vickers trundled past. He sat with his head between his knees. 'That respiratory thing, though. I mean, it fits.'

'If the shoes fit, we need to prove they were worn.'

She frowned at that, like it was something profound and meaningful.

Marshall's phone rang. He reached into his pocket for it and checked the display:

Kirsten calling...

Last thing Marshall wanted was Jolene overhearing stuff. Personal stuff. Before the words had left his mouth, they'd be back with Elliot.

'Better take this.' He stepped away from the car and kept walking. 'Marshall.'

'Rob.' She left a pause. 'Just came up to your office to have a chat, only to find Elliot getting changed into her outdoor gear.'

'Sorry, I'm down in Newcastle.' Marshall couldn't help but smile. 'Sorry you had to see that.'

'I'll recover. Okay, so Bruce has sent Shunty a ton of AV stuff from the prison. What needs to happen with it?'

'I've asked DS Siyal to get his team to run through all of the recordings from prison and match them with the logs to check it's complete and there are no gaps.'

'Bruce's team have just got hold of the podcaster's laptop so his original recordings will be coming too. If there are any discrepancies, then we know he's involved. Like if the interview is two hours but we've got ten minutes of audio missing, that could be when they discussed how to kill people. So I need forensics to—'

'—prove there are no cuts or edits. Got it. Tall order, Rob. Audio forensics are with the NCA, not us. But I'll get on with it and see if they'll play ball.'

'Thanks. Listen, Bruce's team are—'

'Hang on, one of my machines is beeping. Rakesh is sitting right here.'

The phone rattled and wobbled in Marshall's ear. 'Rob? It's Rakesh. Just overheard what you're asking. Already doing that.'

'Good work.' Even though he was working for Elliot...

'Got a list of people to speak to. Seven people visited him inside.'

Marshall looked back at the podcast studio. 'Bruce told us about two.'

'They're all people on our radar, except one. A Sharon Shaw.'

Marshall felt everything clench. 'She's the mother of Michael Shaw. A suspect who... He killed himself on remand.'

'Ah, right. Why's she speaking to Keane in prison?'

'Search me. But I think we should leave her until the end.'

'Fine. I'm going to speak to the rest of them today.'

'Good work. And please, make sure you keep Bruce's lot updated on what you're doing.'

'Okay. Listen, I'm still waiting on some CCTV back so I'll head out to Elibank and help DI Elliot.'

'Okay. Keep me updated.'

'Will do. Here's Kirsten.'

She came back on the line. 'Rob...'

'Look, let's talk about stuff when I get back to Melrose. Dinner?'

'Sure, fine, whatever.' She sighed down the line. 'Thanks to your suggestion last night, the NCA gave us access to the Schoolbook Family DNA database.'

'Schoolbook? A social network is doing DNA? That doesn't sound like a great idea.'

'Yeah, I know. But they let us have access. And I've just identified your third victim.'

CHAPTER FORTY-SEVEN

Marshall took his turn behind the wheel, not least to occupy his brain more than being in the passenger seat. And it was a massive relief to pull off the A19 into one of those slower dual carriageways that served as arteries for northern cities. Still, heading into Sunderland on a Tuesday morning was something he'd rather not be doing.

The satnav guided him up the first left from the roundabout, passing an industrial estate that was halfway through transforming into a retail park. An Aldi sat next to a factory that wasn't too clear about what it made, but fumes belched from a tall chimney.

He needed to turn right at the next roundabout but had to stop – a middle-aged dad pushed a pram across, followed by two very young kids swigging from bottles of blue drink. The dad stopped to berate his kids and a dog popped its head out of the pram.

'What the hell?' Marshall waited for them to clear the roundabout. 'Did you see that?'

Jolene looked up from her phone. 'What's up?'

Marshall swung around into the housing estate of post-war brick houses. At least the satnav knew where it was going. 'Just saw a dog in a pram.'

'A what?'

'Someone was wheeling their dog in a pram.'

'Probably taking it to the vet.' She shook her head and went back to her phone. 'You're being really quiet there.'

'Am I?'

'All this time alone in the car and you're not talking to me.'

'Because you're playing *Indignity Online* or something on your phone.'

'Hardly. I'm chatting with Siyal about this prison stuff. Can that guy not think for himself?' She put her phone away. 'What's going on inside your head, sir?'

'Just thinking about the case. About how Vickers thinks Keane's maybe innocent.'

'Whereas you think Keane's as guilty as a puppy in a puddle?'

'Correct.'

'You don't think he's doing it for the attention?'

'Maybe. But I don't see why.'

'If you listen to his podcasts, like I have, he's doing that "playing all angles" trick.'

'You've listened to it?'

She pulled an AirPod out of her ear. 'What I'm doing while you're not talking to me.'

'Aha.'

'What I mean is he's got two experts on there with him. One was wrongly convicted and campaigns against aggressive policing; the other is a former criminal lawyer. Much like your-self, but she's adamant about Keane's guilt. He plays a bit of an interview with Keane, then he speaks to them, but it's structured in a way that makes Keane seem like he might not be guilty. He holds a lot of things back.'

A common technique in broadcast media, so no wonder it had translated into the modern world of podcasts and YouTube videos, without the same guardrails.

'Okay, that's interesting. What's your take on Vickers?'

Jolene sat there for a few seconds. 'I think he's interviewed a serial murderer and is smarter than Keane, with a higher emotional intelligence, which he's exploiting for his own gain.'

Marshall could understand the logic. He followed the satnav's guidance but it seemed to be leading them into a retirement community, low-slung bungalows hiding away from the road behind fences and mature trees. 'Are you pissed off with me?'

'Eh? Why would you think that?'

'You seem it.'

'No.'

'Come on, the way you act is—'

'Fuck it. Aye, I am.' Her breathing was fast and harsh. 'The way I see it, sir, is you've taken my job. After you joined up, Pringle sat me down and told me there's no budget for my promotion to be made permanent. So I'm in this limbo of being an Acting DS for however long that takes. And now I'm your sidekick, when it should be Shunty.'

Marshall appreciated the honesty, at least. 'If you want my opinion, I don't think you're quite ready to be a full DS.'

She laughed. 'Brilliant.'

'Listen, I've been a DI for ten years. No likelihood of me ever getting promoted, so I know those feelings. The resentment, the anger, the doubt of your own abilities. I think you've got some strong skills. Your drive and determination are pretty solid foundations for a career as a senior officer. Back in that office, you took charge of a room with a pair of DIs and you got the result we went in there for, plus more. A lot more.'

'Thank you, sir.'

'But you're impatient and desperate to get promoted. What's all that about?'

'My mentor worked with someone in Edinburgh like that. Said he was pushy from the get-go. And he's now a DI.'

'I suspect he had to learn to not be like that to become a DI.'

'What's that supposed to mean?'

'Just do the job to the best of your abilities and things will happen for you.'

'Easy for you to say – you were a direct entry at DI.'

'Don't kid yourself it's been easy. Ten years, not been promoted, shoved off to the margins. And everybody knows I've been brought in at that level. They don't let you forget. But I do this job to help people, not to get rich. If you want that, work in a bank.'

'My boyfriend does and the pay's shit nowadays.'

Marshall laughed. 'You've got potential, Jolene. DI Elliot and I will help you fulfil it.'

'Thank you, sir.' Her voice was dripping with sarcasm.

Marshall followed the road between a Chinese takeaway and a corner shop. Definitely did not feel like the way to a garage. Just some more houses.

Wait.

On the right, a gap between two blocks of flats was marked with a hand-painted sign:

BEARDOS MOT'S & TYRE'S

Marshall pulled up and got out. 'You want to lead in here?'

'I'll try my hardest, sir.' Jolene stormed off into the din. Clanking, clattering and chart pop.

Marshall took it slower, keeping an eye on the place. Two ramps, both occupied with cars and mechanics underneath. The radio switched to blasting out a sad girl piano cover of The Darkness's Christmas song, at least a month too early. It kept Marshall's Whamageddon alive.

Jolene was already in the office to the side, talking to someone.

Marshall followed her in, steeling himself – never easy giving someone a death message.

Jolene thumbed at him. 'This is DI Rob Marshall. Sir, this is Jonah Beardsmore.'

'Call me Beardo.' A giant shovel of a hand, covered in oil and dirt. 'What's this about, pet?'

Jolene gestured at a sofa. 'Suggest you—'

'What's this about?'

Jolene fixed him with a hard stare. 'It's about your son.'

Beardsmore perched on the edge of the sofa like he was going to spring off and attack at any moment. 'Kris?'

'You have another son?'

'No, no. Just... You've found him?'

'Sir, I'm sorry to have to tell you this but, unfortunately, we've recovered his remains.'

Beardsmore stared into space. He swallowed hard. 'Aye.'

That was it. Some men were so emotionally damaged they couldn't begin to process anything, so it was all just nipped in the bud. A whisky or ten pints would sort all those feelings out later.

'We recovered them in a forest in southern Scotland and we were able to identify Kris from a heritage DNA kit.'

'Right.' Beardsmore ran a hand down his face. 'Lad got us it for Christmas last year. Made us both do it. I joked about how his bairns would love to know where he'd come from when he has them.' He swallowed again. 'Fucking ironic, eh?'

'I understand, sir. The loss of a loved one is so much—'

'You don't know, do you?' Beardsmore's laugh was like a shotgun. 'Three months ago, I caught him shagging a lad in the office here. Young Dean. Had to sack him on the spot.'

'Your son was gay?'

'Dropped him at the bus station in town.' Beardsmore kept swallowing. 'Last time I saw him. Fuck.' He looked like he wanted to hit something – those giant hands could probably punch through steel. 'I mean, seeing their boy with another lad? How can anyone accept that? Eh?'

The world still had its share of homophobes.

Jolene held his stare. 'Why is it any different to you catching him with a girl?'

'Fuck's sake...' Beardsmore shot to his feet and stomped across the office to an ancient computer. He hammered the keyboard with the grace and precision of a pool typist. 'He's...' He stopped typing. 'Because he's *gay*.'

Jolene wandered over, slowly. 'Can you explain?'

'Don't you get it?'

'No.'

'So I'm supposed to just change my views because some woke Scottish lass comes in here and has a go at us? Get out of it!'

'I'm not having a go, sir, and I'm sorry if you think that. We're trying to under—'

'It was a shock is all. I wanted to be a granddad one day. Selfish, really, that's all.' Beardsmore looked at her. Steel and fury. Then his lip quivered. And shook. He collapsed back into his chair and seemed to collapse internally. Rocking with tears.

Jolene frowned over at Marshall.

Rather than raise his hands, he extended his fingers. Let it play out.

Jolene caught the message. She stepped away, arms folded. Waiting. Waiting. Waiting. And couldn't help herself. 'I'm sorry for your loss, sir.'

'My loss?' Beardsmore looked up, tears flooding his cheeks. 'It's my fault my fucking son's dead! I forced him away. I couldn't sit with him and talk. I couldn't. I... I just dropped him on the bus with five hundred pound in his pocket. Told him I never wanted to see him again. And you know the worst part of it?'

Jolene held his gaze.

Beardsmore swallowed again, but it seemed to be one final attempt to get whatever it was down. 'I'm gay.' Even though he whispered them, the words were loud above the din from the workshop. 'I'm... I... I meet fellas on Grindr. Wife doesn't know. Doesn't care. But when I caught my lad at it in here... I thought I'd given him it, you know? Passed it on. That DNA kit, must be my fucking *bender* genes in there.' He brushed tears from his eyes. 'And I felt so fucking angry because my son's never had to be in the closet. He's lived his life like that. He told us he was bent when he was twelve and I smacked the crap out of him. Never told us again. Never had lasses back but... He must've had lads. Him rubbing it in my face like that was too much... Soon as he went, I... I didn't know what to do. I'd give anything to have him back. Just to have that chat with him.'

Marshall reached into his pocket and took out a card from his wallet. He rested it on the desk. 'This is the card of a grief counsellor based in Kelso. She's the best in the business. Helped me through a lot myself. Suggest you speak to her.'

Beardsmore picked it up and stared at it, scratching the back of his neck. He looked up. 'Thank you.' His voice was like ground glass.

Marshall waited for eye contact. This was starting to fit the same pattern, but he was wary of leaping to conclusions. 'Do you know where he was going from the bus station?'

'No, sorry.'

'Was your son outgoing?'

'Not really, no. Kept himself to himself. Had a few mates he texted. Occasionally go out and get blasted with them in town and up in Newcastle, but... That stopped. Stopped going out.'

'Was he much of a risk-taker?'

He looked up at Marshall. 'Don't think him and that lad were using any protection.'

'What about money?'

'Spent all he got, didn't he? Clothes, mainly. Shoes. His phone.'

'He use it a lot?'

'Constantly.'

'You gave him some money to get a coach. Would he hitch and keep the cash?'

'Possible. Like I say, kid took risks. His work here was shoddy.'

'Did he have any friends? Any enemies?'

'Told the cops this when he went. None that I know of. Turns out my lad was as much of a stranger to me as I am to myself.'

'Thanks for your time.' Marshall left the office.

Jolene caught up with him. 'You're not going to ask him any more?'

'No, we'll get it all from the police files. All Beardo there knows about his son is his name, date of birth and sexuality.'

'Okay... Do you need me to speak to his mum?'

'I'll drop you at her work. Make sure you get the local plod out to help you.'

'Plod is hate speech, sir.' At least she was grinning.

'That's the second one who hasn't shown up to deliver a death message, so they deserve all the derision. After that, I need you to dig out the CCTV from the Sunderland bus station for that night. See if that story checks out. Right now, Beardo in there thinks we're on his side, but you never know... He could've killed them all.'

She nodded slowly. 'Where are you going, sir?'

CHAPTER FORTY-EIGHT
SIYAL

Kirsten opened the door and looked Siyal up and down. 'Bloody hell, are you hiking up Everest or something?'

Siyal was already sweating. The outdoors gear wasn't mandatory but it'd been really cold in the woods the previous day and was set to be even colder today. He wasn't built for this temperature. Then again, who was? 'Any coffee on the go?'

'Trev put a pot on before Elliot grabbed him.'

'Thanks.' Siyal went over to the back of the room with his mug and filled it from the clandestine coffee pot hidden behind a stack of printer paper. 'Hate having to work with her.'

'Who doesn't?' She sat back down at her workstation. 'Did you get those audio files I sent you from the podcaster?'

'Aye, but I'm drowning under the weight of other stuff. I've squared off the other prison interview stuff, but then Elliot came a-knocking.' Siyal drank some coffee.

'Why are you so frustrated?'

'I'm not.'

'You are. Spill.'

'Okay. Mark Davidson... it is personal. Nasty, nasty bastard. He screwed me over. A good woman is in a bad situation because of him. Kirsten, you should see the detention centre she's in. It's barbaric. And the toll it's taken on her. This whole thing underlines why I became a cop. At least this way I can do something about it. I can stop Mark Davidson. Take him down a peg or two.'

Kirsten was smiling. 'I'm impressed by your fire, Rakesh. Harness that.'

'Trying to.' Siyal downed the rest of the coffee but it wasn't touching the sides, so he reached over and topped it up.

Elliot entered the room, dressed up like she was going to a riot. Or playing in goal in a feisty ice hockey match. 'Is he here?'

Siyal put the pot back and spilled hot coffee on his hand. Had to swallow down his swearing as he slid the paper boxes back in front. He hid his mug behind it too. 'Over here, ma'am.'

Elliot pulled up her goggles. 'So you are. Listen, this is for both of you. Jolene called me up. Her and that clown Marshall have got a lead on the most recent victim. Dad dropped him at the bus station in Sunderland on the night of. Trouble is, the local cops are very short-staffed today. Some shite about a Sunderland match tonight meaning we're going to need to wait until tomorrow to get their help. Or do it ourselves.'

Kirsten rolled her eyes. 'So you're now expecting me to get CCTV from Sunderland bus station?'

'Nope. Jo's already got CCTV of Kris Beardsmore getting on a bus in Sunderland to Newcastle, where he caught a coach to Stranraer.'

Kirsten frowned. 'Why would anyone go there?'

Elliot rolled her eyes this time. 'Ferry over to Northern Ireland.'

'And you want me to—'

'No, she's got access to that CCTV. Coach got there, but he

never got off. So we've got the coach leaving Newcastle and arriving in Stranraer. Stopped in Carlisle on the way.'

'Oh come on, I—'

'I know you've got access to their CCTV, Kirsten, because I spent half an hour pestering a superintendent down there to approve your access.'

Kirsten looked at her machine. 'Okay. Still got way too much to do before I can even think about that.'

'So have we all. But seeing as how we're friends, I'm giving you a chance to get ahead of this, Kirsten.'

'Ahead of what?'

'Pringle put a call in with your boss.'

'No he—'

'Aye. We're short on resource, but you've already got access to the Cumbrian CCTV. So I need you to look into it.'

Kirsten laughed. 'You're buggering about in a wood and you're asking me to devote *my* resource to this?'

'Aye. I could applaud you for identifying the third victim, but the thing you lot forget is my lot are trying to solve a triple murder here.' She smiled like a snake about to eat a mouse. 'Please. Take one for the team.'

'I could do with Rakesh's help on it.'

'Nope. He's done his time in the trenches on that shite. I need him to demonstrate his leadership qualities over at Elibank. We've got three dog teams, half the Forestry staff, most of the Borders uniform and virtually all of the plainclothes.'

Kirsten folded her arms. 'You're expecting my team to sift through hours and hours of CCTV footage?'

'Better get started, eh?' She clapped Siyal on the arm, hard as a punch. 'So, come on – let's go.' She pointed at him but didn't leave. 'Seriously. Where are you getting that coffee from?'

Kirsten sighed. 'I keep telling you. Dean's Beans.'

'Every time I go in there, I get what tastes like instant.'

Kirsten shrugged. 'Dean's my cousin so maybe I get the best stuff.'

Elliot stared hard at her for a few seconds. 'Come on, Shunty.' Then she left.

Leaving Siyal sweating in a tiny office, dressed for the North Pole.

Kirsten was smirking at him. 'I told Dean to give her the worst coffee. No chance she's getting the good stuff.'

Siyal trudged over to the door.

'Chin up, Rakesh.'

'Why?' He looked around at her but turning in this many layers was a real challenge. 'Elliot's treating me like her pet dog.'

'Just do it, Rakesh – she'll think better of you.'

'Hard for her to think *less* of me.'

'Jesus Christ.' She scowled at him. 'Look, she's giving you an opportunity, whereas she's bullying me into doing work I shouldn't be doing. If staying in the Borders means dealing with her, then St Leonards here I bloody come.'

CHAPTER FORTY-NINE
MARSHALL

Despite the cheesy name, the Delly Grind was a pretty swish café. Where it wasn't wood, it was white. The whole place. The walls, the chairs, the china. And immaculate, as clean as the day it was opened twelve years ago – Marshall could only surmise it was because the smell of the coffee overpowered the constant repainting.

Liana didn't see him approaching, just sat there, fingertips placed together, staring out of the window at the Wear down below.

'Hey.'

She didn't move.

'Liana.'

She jerked around to him, her forehead creasing then smoothing out again. 'Oh. Rob.' She sat up and sipped her coffee. 'What are you doing here?'

'Best coffee in the northeast.'

'Yeah, but you live in Scotland.'

He took the seat next to her. 'Your PA said you'd be in here.'

'I've got a lecture.' She checked her watch. 'In twenty

minutes. I like to top up on caffeine beforehand. The poor saps don't know what hits them when I turn up with three of Del's super-strong lattes flowing through me.'

'So you're getting into the groove for first year criminology?'

'No, Rob. I'm obsessing about your bloody case.'

'Thought you refused it?'

'That's what I was told. "Marshall is our profiler. We don't need you." Way to make a girl feel welcome.'

Down below, some swans were caught in a vortex but seemed to get out of it pretty quickly. 'Sorry, I didn't know about that until last night.'

'I'm not the sort to just give up, Rob. The three-month cooling-off period... You and I both know there's a possible abduction happening now. Someone wrapped up in cling film, going through all of that, about to be buried. Or someone we can find before they're abducted. Either way, it adds up to someone we can stop.'

'There's a lot of assuming going on here and it's melting my brain as much as yours.'

'Nothing wrong with mine, Rob.'

'Sure about that? Because you sitting there—'

'You want to talk about brains melting?' Liana laughed. 'Those three victims. I didn't find them.'

'They were already dead. You didn't not save them.'

'I know. But Keane tormented me. You. Jacob. Bruce. And an innocent man killed himself because of me.' She shook her head. 'That was my fault. I work every day to make sure I do what I can to stop there being another Michael Shaw. And I see you doing the same.'

Marshall shrugged. 'We do it in different ways, I suppose.'

She stared into her latte for a few seconds, then up at him. 'Rob, why have you driven all this way to see me?'

'Because I was in this neck of the woods. Sunderland, to be precise. Liana, we've identified the third victim.'

Her forehead creased. Then uncreased. 'Come on.' She grabbed her coffee and walked over to a giant map on the wall just outside the toilets. 'Give me the locations.'

Marshall folded his arms. 'I thought geo profiling was old hat for dinosaurs like me?'

'It is. But so is psychological profiling and we still do that. I keep telling my students this – the more techniques we try, the better our chances of catching the killers.' She clicked the end of her propelling pencil until the lead popped out. 'Besides, I've been thinking about how you found Keane because of it. It's worth a shot.'

The barista looked over at her.

Liana waved. 'Two Americanos, Del. To go.'

'You got it.'

Liana turned to the map and marked an X with her pencil. 'Nine months ago. Layla McMenemy. Early twenties. Mother from Washington. South of Newcastle. West of Sunderland. North of here.' Another X was a lot further up, on the coast as it curved around. 'Six months ago, Steven Cork. Single lad from Berwick.' She looked at Marshall. 'And victim three?'

'Okay, so three months ago, we've got Kris Beardsmore. From Sunderland. Dad... It's a long story.'

'But he ran away?'

'Right. Dad dropped him at the bus station. From what Jolene just told me, he was going to Stranraer.'

'Where's that?'

Marshall pointed to the far left of the map, not far from the thin sliver of Northern Ireland coast. 'Arse end of nowhere Dumfries and Galloway. Takes hours to get there from anywhere, but it's the main ferry port to Northern Ireland.'

'Why was Kris running there?'

The way she named the victims – they weren't just data. 'No idea. But he didn't get there. Got a team of people working on it, but he seems to have got off in Carlisle. We've requested CCTV from the bus station. Hopefully it'll show Kris and give us a clue as to where he went.'

Her arms dropped to her side. 'Why did you want to leave this and become a cop? Seems like all you do is go through CCTV?'

'When I worked with you and Jacob, waiting for the cops to do their bit was... It was impossible. I came to realise it's getting stuff done. Assembling the data for a profile. Now, I've got people working for me who are pulling this all together. I can make sure it's done in the correct way. Organised, methodical.'

'Very pleased for you.' Liana looked at the map, her eyes darting around it. 'Similar locations for one and three. Berwick's a bit of an outlier. No obvious way he's targeting them.'

Marshall tracked the map across to Carlisle in the west. Kris Beardsmore was the only one with an active trail like that, where they had an inkling where he went. Both Layla and Steven had vanished, though there was a ton of work left to do.

'This shows us nothing.' She flicked her hand at the map. 'Sunderland and Durham could be important, but so could... Glasgow and Dunfermline. Or London and Paris.' She was biting the inside of her cheek. 'But... There's something in this, I just...'

Marshall felt like it was almost there too. Some little detail that he couldn't quite see... 'Okay, listen to me here. This isn't like the previous cases I've successfully deployed geographic profiling on. Those were abductions.' He tapped the map, pretty much in the middle of their homes. 'These three victims all ran away from home. Layla either from her obligation to her child or from a relationship where she was the abuser and things went a bit too far. Steven thought he'd killed someone and ran away to a new life elsewhere. Kris was free from his unsupportive dad. And now they're all dead. Where they lived isn't important as they weren't kidnapped.'

'Okay, Rob, so focus on the psychology, not the geography. They're all runaways but that's a dead end. Hundreds of people every week fall into that category. They'll go where they won't be found by who they're running from. Like Northern Ireland. But we know these three found trouble.' Her pencil traced all over the map. 'Were they headed to the bright lights of London? So many kids go there and end up homeless. Or somewhere they feel safe?' She dug the pencil into Stranraer. 'Why would Kris head to Northern Ireland?'

'I don't know. Jolene's following up for me, but his old man doesn't know. Mum called in sick and isn't answering the door. She's seeing if any of his pals knew of anyone there. Fairly common for people to have internet friends they've never met.'

'True. Thing with people on the run like this... The two we've talked about already. Layla and Steven. They want to avoid discovery, so getting a coach and paying with cash makes sense... Or hitch hiking and paying by some other means. Bottom line is, if we can pin them down in the same way you have with Kris, it can show a direction or a route through a locale. This isn't just geographic profiling. This is about their psychology, Rob. Their goals. Their thoughts. She starts here and ends up there. He starts in a different place headed somewhere else. But does it all draw an X in the place where the protégé is meeting them?'

Marshall winced. 'Please don't use that word.'

'It's official, Rob. DCI Pringle called it Operation Protégé.'

'Jesus wept.' Marshall shut his eyes. 'He's... unreal.'

'You have three data points. You have the start of a profile.'

Marshall stared at the map. 'Washington, Berwick, Sunderland, Stranraer, Carlisle. There are other places I've asked to search for CCTV. But...'

'Rob?'

He looked around.

Liana had her coat on, clutching two coffee cups. 'Got to dash to that lecture. Here.' She handed him one. 'Just like old times.'

'Thanks.' He took it. 'Doesn't the owner mind you using that map?'

'The amount I spend on coffee in here?'

'Fair point.' Marshall led her over to the door and held it for her. 'Thanks.'

'What for?'

'Helping me with that.' He eased along the street next to her. 'I'm looking where I dropped my keys now. I could never cut it as a profiler.'

'What are you talking about? You had so much potential as a profiler. You and I could be doing this job together. You abandoned the science because—'

'I abandoned inaction. I was stifled. The inaction. Being reactive.'

'Okay, but you abandoned it because you're an impatient sod.'

'That's true. And it's not something I can really change about myself.' He stopped on the bridge. 'But now, I feel like I can make a difference. I can find this missing victim, assuming there is one.'

'We both know it's likely.'

'That's the thing. Your world is dealing with probabilities and data. I have to speak to the mother of someone who's run away because his dad couldn't handle the fact his son was gay.

When secretly he was too. It's...' He stared down into the water. The swans were back in their vortex.

Her hand ran across his back.

He flinched.

She leaned in close.

He turned away but she wouldn't let him go, so he turned to face her but stood up tall.

'Rob, I see what you've become and... I like it.' She leaned in for a kiss.

Last night with Kirsten... That felt like it meant something.

He pulled away. 'Sorry, I—'

'Huge mistake. Sorry.' She ran off, skittering up the hill towards the university.

Marshall watched her go.

What a disaster.

CHAPTER FIFTY

Marshall knew these roads like the back of his hand. All the rat runs he could cut up and round to get home. When home was in Durham. Now it was a flat in London nobody wanted to buy and his old bedroom at Mum's.

He couldn't stop thinking about Liana...

Shit, he'd let that happen. Should've been clear. Or clearer.

Especially after last night with Kirsten. And this morning.

What a mess.

Twenty years of being frozen and he was starting to thaw. He could make all the mistakes an eighteen-year-old Rob Marshall should've learnt from. Instead, he'd lived like a monk.

His phone rang through the dashboard. He'd no idea how it had paired, but there it was, blaring away.

Elliot calling...

'Oh, magic...' Took Marshall a few seconds to figure out

how to answer it – strangely enough, the big green button in the middle worked. 'Andrea.'

'Marshall.' Sounded like she was outside, somewhere windy. 'Just calling to check on how the Brains Trust are doing.'

Like Jolene hadn't been reporting back every two minutes...

'We're getting there. Lot to think about, as I'm sure you know. How's your investigation into the missing persons?'

'Turns out you already have all three, Marshall, so you should be finished with your profile, right?'

'Not as simple as that.'

'But you do have a third victim?'

'That's right. Looks like they're all runaways. Or on the run, at least.'

'Huh.'

'Does that mean something to you?'

'No. It's just... Feels like I'm doing all the work here, Marshall. My team are investigating the bodies. Finding out who they are and where they came from, but I can't get a handle on what you're actually doing.'

He took a few deep breaths. She had a bloody cheek. 'Are you at the forest?'

'Quit changing the subject. How's your profile?'

'Look, I am working on a theory. It's quite loose, so I don't want to share it yet.'

'Very coy. I've already shown you mine, Marshall.'

'I'm thinking the home locations of the victims aren't important.'

'So what is? Where they were buried? Because I've got a team ready to go over the whole forest.'

He could hear the glee in her voice. 'There might be a common abduction location. But I've got no data.'

'What about Carlisle?'

'Not necessarily.'

'You heading there now?'

'No, I'm heading to pick up Jolene in Newcastle and see what she's got from the Northumbria lot.'

'Good luck. Those lot have arseholes tighter than a camel's in a sandstorm.'

Charming...

She paused, long enough for the car's speakers to rattle with the wind buffeting her phone's microphone. Not often Elliot shut up long enough for that to happen. 'Listen, Marshall. I've been thinking about what you said about trials. Earlier attempts where he didn't or couldn't kill them?'

'Okay?'

'Okay what?'

Marshall shook his head. 'What have you been thinking about it?'

'Nothing much. Just that you should be thinking about it. Let us all know when you've got some more data points, you fud.'

'Don't talk to me like that.'

'It's just banter.'

Marshall sighed. 'Right, sure.'

'Not saying anything. I'm in charge of finding the bodies. Your job is to pin the stabbing tail on the murdering donkey.'

Marshall couldn't handle any more of her childish attitude. 'Best of luck there, Andrea. Let me know if you find any more bodies.'

Or when you don't because it was a waste of time...

'Will do. Ciao!' And she was gone.

Marshall was now hurtling up the A19 towards Newcastle. Somehow the car's display showed his phone's caller log, so he thumbed down to select Jolene's number and hit the green button.

The dialling noise was so bloody loud, like an air raid siren. And the volume wheel did nothing.

Marshall picked up his coffee from the Delly Grind and sipped it through the lid as the phone rang like church bells pealing right by his head.

'Sir?' Sounded like Jolene was in a café. 'What's up?'

'Just on my way up to Newcastle. You still there?'

'Getting a coffee just now.'

'Oh. Sorry. Don't let—'

'It's fine. We're kind of finished. I'm with DS Williamson of Bruce's team.' She paused, sounded like she thanked someone, then walked off. 'You know how Kirsten found the CCTV showing Kris Beardsmore getting off the bus in Carlisle?'

'Right, you said.'

'We've just got the street CCTV. It shows him walking off and getting picked up by a lorry.'

Shite.

A runaway picked up as a hitch hiker.

'Find the driver, please.'

'Already done it.'

CHAPTER FIFTY-ONE
GRACE

Grace lay there, unable to move. Like she had for... days? She had no idea how long she'd been there. Could be a week, could just have been a few hours. Time seemed to fold in on itself.

Everything hurt.

Her back. Her thighs. Her—

She didn't want to think about that.

The light flashed on again. So bright, it stung like someone had squeezed lemon juice in her eyes.

Then off again.

Then on. This time it stayed, dulling only when he moved in front of it.

Grace couldn't keep her eyes open for long. But she knew how to play it. Just like she was dealing with Elsa in Geography – laughter was the best form of attack. Defuse him like she'd done to her.

Grace waited until he appeared. Until he looked at her. Until he looked at her again and stayed looking at her.

She laughed at him.

'What the fuck is so funny, Grace?'

The mask was stuck to her mouth, so all she could do was keep on forcing herself to laugh. Locking eyes with him. Shutting them and laughing harder.

'Why are you laughing?!'

She kept them closed. Kept laughing.

'Fuck's sake!'

She opened her eyes again.

His knife flashed in the light.

She shut them again, bracing herself for another savage cut.

He pulled her mask off.

The air tasted metallic.

The room smelled damp. Like a public toilet at a festival.

He pressed the blade against her throat. 'Why the fuck are you laughing?'

'Why should I tell you? You're just going to kill me.' Her voice sounded hoarse and shrill.

Good.

'You bitch!'

She braced against the knife slicing into the flesh on her arm. A deep bite.

'That fucking hurts.'

'It's meant to.'

'Good job.'

Something flickered in his eyes. Intrigue?

She hoped it was.

'Go ahead, *John*. Do what you want to me.'

Her plan, as much as it was, was to take what he gave her. Don't beg, don't plead. Don't show enjoyment. Just play off his desires, maybe be worthwhile keeping around...

'These breaths are going to be your last ones without the mask.'

'Just do it. Or,' she whispered, 'Can't you get it up.'

'What?' He leaned closer. 'What did you say?'

'You can't get it up. Your cock. It's useless.'

'Of course I can.'

'No. You *could*. You raped me when we got here. But now you just cut me. Was it the cutting that aroused you? Because you can take pills for—'

'Fuck you, Grace.' He sliced deeper into her arm.

She jerked forward, trying to bite his ear but it was too far away.

He stepped away, laughing. 'Nice try. Got to admire that.'

'Lend me your ear.'

'Oh, Grace. Come on. Dad jokes are beneath you.'

'You try to cut and poke things into me. Is that until you can get it up again?'

'Fuck you!'

'I want you to fuck me. Come on. Do it. Fuck me.'

He reached over and grabbed her throat. She gurgled. He pressed the mask onto her face again. She tried to avoid biting the breathing apparatus but she had no choice. He wrapped tape around her mouth. Around and around and around and around.

'This is your last tank, Grace. Enjoy it while it lasts.' Then he walked off. And the light went out.

She was still alive. Dazed, but still alive. For now.

And she knew his weakness.

CHAPTER FIFTY-TWO
MARSHALL

Back on home turf.

Marshall felt much easier driving along the country lane between St Boswells and Selkirk, open views across rolling hills and lonely paddocks. No cars visible. He passed the only golf course for miles around and rolled up to the junction with the A7. The main road between Carlisle and Edinburgh, running through Selkirk and Galashiels.

Lorry drivers.

Could it be that? Felt too prosaic.

'Williamson says he's been a DS for twelve years.' Jolene was still resting her hands against the heater like she'd never get warm, even thought they'd been driving the best part of two hours. 'How's that right?'

Marshall checked the fuel gauge – could do with a top-up from the petrol station around the corner, but he wanted to get this questioning out of the way first. 'You heard of the Peter Principle?'

'The *what*?'

'People are promoted to the point of incompetence.'

'Never heard of it.'

'But you've seen it in action, right?'

She smirked. 'Sometimes they're direct entry to the point of incompetence.' She raised her hands. 'I'm not talking about you.'

'But you're talking about DS Siyal.'

'Not really.' She sighed. 'Just trying to have a laugh, that's all.'

'It's not funny to keep picking on the same officer.'

'Aye, aye, I get it.' She pointed at the street past the school. 'Right here.'

Marshall followed the road around into a crescent of ex-council houses. Blocks of four with decent gardens, all raised up on one side so they'd get good views across into the park opposite.

Pringle Park.

Marshall had to smile at it – the surname was synonymous with the area, but not all of them were landowners. Some were DCIs promoted to the point of incompetence.

'There.' Jolene waved at a garden and Marshall pulled in between two cars.

She was out by the time he'd checked he was in the space properly.

Marshall got out into the freezing air and buttoned up his coat. Just as well it wasn't raining as it'd be snowing.

Jolene was waving at a man struggling to push his mower up the lawn's steep bank, the dirty fug of petrol fumes mixing with cut grass.

He stopped and took off his ear defenders. 'Aye?' Selkirk accent, not as out there as Hawick but closer than the locals would admit.

'Archie Fairbairn?'

'That's me, sweetheart.' His hungry eyes looked her up and

down. Even in November, even in this cold, his cream T-shirt was soaked with sweat. Jaco Pastorius, a man with a ponytail, playing bass guitar without a care in the world.

Marshall had more than enough jazz fusion from working for Jacob Goldberg.

Archie tore off his hat and revealed a chewed-up ear, like a toy a dog had got at. Then he clocked Marshall. 'Cops, aye?'

Jolene raised the corner of her lips. 'Afraid so.'

'Judging by that accent, you're local.' Archie kicked his mower and came down to the fence. 'This one of those discussions we need to do inside?'

'Afraid not.'

Archie let out a deep breath. 'There's a bastard relief, eh?'

Jolene was nodding. 'Gather it's your day off?'

'Tell me about it, hen. Trying to get this lawn mowed the day. First clear run I've had at it in weeks with all that rain. Still looking like my hair just before it's cut so it'll need another go after I finish.' Archie laughed and ran his hand through his damp hair, spraying sweat into the air. Looked like he needed to run the clippers over it again. 'Busy as fu— *hell* just now, like. Just drove a lorry full of tatties from Thurso down to Exeter last night. Got there at dawn this morning, then brought a load of stones back to Hawick. Not an easy drive, I tell you!'

Her eyes were wide. 'You drove from Exeter to Hawick?'

'One go.' Archie swept his hand through the air. 'Felt like Moses parting the Red Sea, ken? Seven hours, twenty minutes. Norris McWhirter's putting us in the Guinness Book of Records.' He chuckled. 'Two days off the now, then I'm driving to Amsterdam. Not too keen about getting over to France, like. Queues are massive down in Dover.'

'Shouldn't you be sleeping now?'

'Too buzzed, love. If I sleep, I'll just see the bloody M6

when I shut my eyes. Once I've finished this, I'll be heading to a pal's to sink some tins of cider I was given down there.'

'This is maybe a long shot, but hopefully you can remember picking up this lad.' Jolene held out the photo of Kris Beardsmore she'd got from the boy's mother.

Archie inspected it closely. 'I mean, I pick up a lot of waifs and strays, you know? Few dodgy fu— folks out there, so I try to do my bit to help them out.'

He wasn't denying it, at least.

'Do you remember him?'

'Think so. Picked him up in Carlisle.'

Jolene frowned. '*In* it?'

'On the outskirts. Bus stop just off the A69.'

Marshall knew the road system around there. The way the M6 curved around the city, with the A69 shooting off towards Newcastle from two converging roads. Neither made sense for a lorry driver.

Upshot was he smelled a rat. As prosaic as it was, a lorry driver who admitted to picking up waifs and strays... Well, it wasn't too much of a stretch for him to murder them, was it? Especially as he lived within spitting distance of where the bodies were buried.

'Do you remember where you were travelling, sir?'

'Usual route. Take empty pallets from Hawick up to Thurso. Fill them up, then down to wherever they're going. This week it was Exeter. Think it was the same back then, too. It's bizarre, but don't really know why they do that. Think it's for crisps or something.'

'So why did you leave the M6?'

'Good question.' Archie ran a hand through his hair again. 'Think I had to follow a diversion. Roadworks there for eight weeks. Absolute nightmare if you timed it wrong.'

Marshall stared at him for a few seconds, watching for any ticks. 'We will check that.'

'Sure.' Archie shrugged. 'Look, I definitely didn't go into the city or town centre. Just saw that lad at the bus stop and asked if he needed a lift. I let him in the cab and we got on our way again.'

'And where—'

'Stopped at the next truck stop in Penrith. I was driving on fumes, so I pulled in to refuel. Then it hit me. It was late and when I do that run, I like to get past Preston before I kip. But I'd been late leaving Thurso and the A9 was a bastard. Made it out of Scotland in one piece, mind. Told the lad I was going to sleep for a few hours. Plan was to get an early start, get down past Birmingham before rush hour.'

'He didn't want to go there?'

'Nope. Kid was heading to London, probably went and asked around the other cabs.'

'You see him get in another vehicle?'

'Was asleep pretty much by the time the door shut.'

'He say anything to you?'

'Gave the lad some good advice. Told him his dad will come around.'

'About what?'

'Him being gay.'

There it was.

Proof it was Kris Beardsmore.

Marshall saw it a bit clearer too. A truck driver picked up a young effeminate lad travelling solo. Or even a macho lad.

Coded signals passed between them.

But he had no idea what happened next. How he'd get them from there to a lonely death before being dumped at Elibank.

Then again, a lorry would be a good place to store someone.

'Get them all the time, you know? Supposed to be enlightened times.' Archie shook his head. 'That lad was from Sunderland, I think. Dad hated him for being gay.' He laughed. 'Offered to suck my cock for money. Fuck's sake. I'm helping these kids, not, not... Who did he think I am?'

'What *did* you do?'

'Like all of them, I gave him twenty quid. Tried to talk him out of going to London, but he wouldn't listen. Seemed desperate to get there, but I've heard tales of how bad that can get. Sleeping rough. Getting into drugs and prostitution.'

Marshall had seen it happen in his time down there. As much as he loved the city, its dark underbelly would swallow anyone's soul.

Archie held up the photo. 'Told him to call his dad and let him know he's safe. Promised me he would, soon as he was someplace safe.'

Jolene took the photo back. 'His folks didn't get that call.'

CHAPTER FIFTY-THREE

Marshall raced up the A7 heading back to Melrose and the station. Some kids were playing football on a pitch carved out at the edge of a field. No signs of a village nearby.

'So what do you think?'

Marshall looked over at Jolene. 'I think there's two possibilities. One, he's on the level and he did pick up Kris Beardsmore and did the whole Good Samaritan act.'

'Or he's picked him up and killed him?'

'Correct.'

'We don't have anything pointing to that, do we?'

'Don't have anything pointing to anything, though.' Marshall sighed. 'Sort of person who commits these crimes is someone who spends a lot of time on his own. He can't discern reality from fantasy. Fact and fiction blur. Spending all that time in a lorry, driving up and down the country, especially the routes he was doing, means he was probably taking amphetamines to keep going.'

She folded her arms. 'My dad was a lorry driver.'

'I'm not saying they all are. Or that our killer is a lorry driver. Just that he could fit the loose profile I'm forming in my head.'

Jolene looked up from her phone. 'Andrea keeps bouncing my calls too.'

'Glad it's not just me. Can you try DS Siyal?'

'Did. Same.'

'Okay.' Marshall drummed his thumbs on the wheel. 'Call Kirsten Weir.'

'Her? Why?'

'Just do it, please.'

The phone rang through the dashboard.

'Jolene, what's up?' Kirsten sounded annoyed.

'Kirsten, it's Rob. We're driving back just now. Looking for DI Elliot.'

Kirsten yawned. 'Think she's at Elibank.'

'And DS Siyal?'

'Shunty's at Elibank too.'

'Is anyone doing their job?'

'I am. What's up?'

'Elliot's team was supposed to be looking into the CCTV. Where they went.'

'I'm doing that.'

'You are?'

'Most of the team are at Elibank.'

'Right.' Marshall couldn't see the logic in it, but this was the wild south. 'Need to see if they went hitchhiking.'

'O-kay... That Cumbrian CCTV came through and I've done a bit of it. Found Layla at the bus station in Newcastle, tried getting on a bus but she had no money so she got turfed off. Bus was heading to Birmingham.'

'What happened to her after that?'

'No idea. Dead end trail after that. But Steven Cork. Got him hitching at a truck stop in Penrith.'

'Penrith?'

'Is there an echo on the line?'

'The same one as Kris Beardsmore.' Marshall felt his heart thudding in his throat. 'Kirsten, can you check that location on the date Layla McMenemy ran away?'

'What?'

Jolene leaned forward. 'Fifteenth January, Kirst.'

'I mean, you'll need to give me a few minutes to even access that. And Rob, you owe me. Big time. Okay?'

'Of course.'

'I'll be a few minutes. Got orders from on high to focus on some CCTV footage from Edinburgh.' Click, and she was gone.

Jolene looked over at him. 'What's going on?'

Marshall floored it and powered on towards Galashiels. 'Office politics. I'm going to have a word with Pringle. Face-to-face. But I think we've found out where he's abducting them.'

CHAPTER FIFTY-FOUR
SIYAL

The light was fading, but Siyal daren't stop walking through this infernal forest. The trees were so tightly packed together he kept having to step around and do the dance with the two guys either side of him.

Jim McIntyre and Euan Moir, a uniformed officer from Eyemouth, both dressed like they knew what they were doing yomping across a moor in late November.

The ground was so uneven that Siyal had to slow down and walk a step or two behind his neighbours. At least they didn't notice him stumble every couple of paces.

There, again, his foot caught in a hollow.

Shiiiiiite.

He fell over, just his hands catching him from hitting his teeth off the tree stump.

McIntyre stood over him, grinning away, hand held out. 'You okay there, Shunty?'

Siyal didn't take it. He managed to get up to standing all on his own. 'Cheers.'

'Watch yourself, Shunty.' McIntyre chuckled to himself. 'Don't want you impaling yourself on a rogue branch.'

'Good advice, Jim. I don't want that either.'

This was the last place he wanted to be. Forget about everything else, walking across a freezing woodland at a glacial pace when you're cold, sweaty and hungry... And needed a pee...

At least he could keep an eye on Elliot, a hundred metres and twenty people away. She was walking with a dog handler. The Land and Forestry boss – or was it Forestry and Land? – caught up with them.

Anyway, a pair of dogs were doing their work for them, chasing ahead.

Siyal kept walking, heading ever onwards.

His phone blasted out and Elliot shot him a glare. 'Shunty, I told you to pay attention!'

A few laughs burst out around him.

'Sorry, thought it was on mute.' Siyal took out his phone and checked the display.

DCI James Pringle calling...

He looked over at Elliot. 'Ma'am, it's the boss.'

'Pringle?' She broke formation and stormed over to him. 'What does he want with *you*?' Practically spat out the last word.

'I'd better answer it to find out.'

'No, you—'

He answered it before she got there. 'Siyal.'

'Ah, young man. There's no need to feel down. It's Jim. Jim Pringle, AKA the big boss man. I'm with DI Marshall. We're hanging out in his—' Whistle. '—office.'

Elliot held out her hand. 'Give.'

Siyal turned away again. 'How can I help, sir?'

'Rakesh, it's Rob. Listen, I need to ask you about the missing persons work. Specifically the CCTV.'

Siyal had to step away to keep Elliot from grabbing the phone out of his hands. 'Sorry, Rob, I'm out at Elibank with DI Elliot, so I haven't had a chance to look at any of it.'

'Okay.' A sharp sigh. 'Where did you get to?'

'Nowhere, sir, I—'

'Shunty, my boy.' Pringle laughed. 'You were supposed to be looking into the missing persons, were you not? Vis a vis Layla, Steven and ... the other one. Their CCTV.'

'I believe DI Elliot had Kirsten progress it.'

'That's it?'

Elliot finally grabbed the phone off him and stuck it on speaker. The wave of police officers was progressing, almost out of earshot of them. McIntyre kept looking back the way. 'Sir, it's Andrea and—'

'Rakesh says you're not progressing the CCTV?'

'Aye. Well, I was but I had to take them off that. Got Kirsten's boss to tell her to do it.'

'That's our role, Andrea. I told you that work was a priority.'

'The stuff in Edinburgh is, aye. All that crap in the bus stations is a needle in the haystack.'

'And using half the force to comb a forest isn't?' Marshall grunted. 'Look, Andrea. I need Rakesh back here. Okay?'

'Jim, he's my resource.'

'That's not important.' Marshall sighed again. He wasn't giving up. 'Andrea, we need to focus on a truck stop in Penrith. It's possible our guy's targeting people there.'

'That's miles away from here.'

'We've got sightings of both Steven Cork and Kris Beardsmore there.'

Elliot shut up and stared at the phone, like it was a live grenade.

'So I need DS Siyal and at least another two people to run through hours and hours of footage to see if Layla McMenemy was at the same place.'

'Fine.' Siyal set off back towards the parking area. At least a mile and a half, though there was a shortcut he could take if he was brave enough.

And he'd left his phone.

He turned back and walked over to her.

Elliot was glaring at him. 'DS Siyal is key to this operation. That CCTV is a waste of resource.'

Pringle laughed. 'Andrea, we're not asking.'

'Why can't you do it yourself, Marshall?'

'I will be.'

That shut her up.

Siyal held out his hand. 'Can I have my phone, please?'

'You can shove it where the sun doesn't shine.' Elliot tossed it through the air.

Siyal tried to catch it but it dropped into the undergrowth. He picked it up and the call was still live. 'Rob, I'll be back in about half an hour.'

'Please hurry.' Click and Marshall was gone.

Siyal gave Elliot one last look, then set off towards the shortcut past the ruined castle and the ponies.

A dog started barking behind him. Really close behind him.

'What have you got there, Bessi?'

Siyal turned back around and watched the line of cops break ranks and follow a dog handler towards him.

The spaniel was off the lead and sniffing the ground, tracing an arc around him, then it set off down the hill through the thicker trees. It stopped to bark, pointing a paw at the ground.

Another dog barrelled past Siyal and stopped at the same spot.

Siyal raced off after them, heart thumping as he trudged through the thick bracken. He tripped up and went flying, landing on a patch of grass in a field of ferns and bracken.

The dog was pointing at a bone sticking out of the ground.

CHAPTER FIFTY-FIVE
MARSHALL

Another body.

Marshall hadn't expected that. Looking around the woodland, as he walked, at the hundred or so people out scouring the landscape, he realised he'd expected Elliot's mission to fail for one reason – because it was her.

A barking dog snapped him out of his reverie. No signs that it had caught any fresh scents, but...

Elliot was lording it over everyone. Surrounded by a team of twenty cops all doing their jobs, or at least appearing to.

She'd only been back a day and she was already inside his head. The complete opposite of him – a cop who'd worked her way up from uniform and clearly still had ambitions. He was just doing a job, serving a mission, so of course he was a threat to her. Those months she'd been off recovering from her wounds had been time he'd been able to get his feet under the table, so inflicting herself on every single aspect of the investigation reminded everyone she was still there.

But he couldn't figure out why she annoyed him so much. He knew all the psychological theories and could dissect it in others as soon as click his fingers, but when it came to himself? Forget it.

Elliot was walking over to him, struggling to hide her grin. An eyebrow kept rising and falling. 'Marshall.'

'Andrea.'

'This is...' She just stood there, for once lost for words. Maybe he'd misjudged her and her motivations. Maybe she was just doing her job, like he was trying to.

A crime scene was in place, with two suited figures erecting a forensics tent around three other suited figures. Marshall identified two immediately: Kirsten waving her hands to establish her team's forensic search patterns; Dr Owusu's slumped shoulders showing how unlikely she thought it was they'd gain anything from a pile of bones.

And the third figure – Pringle, standing still.

Marshall looked over at Elliot. 'Any clues to the age, gender, time they've been in the ground?'

'All I know is they've been here a while.'

He frowned at her. 'You're not one to use gender-neutral pronouns.'

'I'm not.' She raised her eyebrows. 'I mean, I am. My Sam is an enby, as we're supposed to call non-binary kids these days, but...' She swallowed. 'There are two bodies in there.'

Marshall's gut churned at the prospect of two further murder victims. Part of his brain clung to having another two data points.

'Owusu thinks there are two bodies, anyway.' Elliot winked at him. 'Or someone with four arms, which would mean they're from Hawick.'

Humour was good, even the dark form of local gallows humour, so Marshall smiled at it. 'Let's stick with two bodies, then.'

'No, there definitely are.' Elliot looked over at the tent and swept her fringe out of her eyes. 'And both have been there a long time.'

'Longer than Keane's?'

'Just bones now. Owusu thinks one's been there fifteen years, give or take. Skull on one is cracked, blunt force trauma, probably how he died.'

'He?'

'Big lad too. Rugby big. Like yourself, Rob. Not much to get a DNA trace on, but Owusu and Kirsten are working towards it.' She looked at Marshall. 'Fifteen years would be around the time Keane was killing people right here.'

'Too early. Besides, if it's Keane, he would've told us.'

'But if it's, say, his lawyer...'

Marshall needed to have a word with Siyal about it.

Elliot was still trying to get her fringe all the way over. 'Doc reckons it's going to be difficult to get anything from them.'

'They were in the same grave?'

'Buried next to each other, she reckons.'

'At different times?'

Elliot finally got the fringe to stay. 'Right.'

Marshall was frustrated at having to get this all second-hand from Elliot but he wanted Owusu providing guidance over at the actual crime scene. 'What about the MO?'

'Hard to tell if it's the same killer. No initial signs of knife wounds to bones in the chest.' Elliot's fringe caught the breeze and flopped down over her eyes. 'Christ on a bike!' She got it back in place. 'But they're just bones now.'

'So we'll only know if it was Keane's overkill once Dr Owusu does her detailed investigation.'

'You're good at this, Marshall.' Elliot rolled her eyes. 'Not much flesh means the signs of shackles or bonds like the other new ones have rotted away. Can't tell if they were buried alive but, as far as I know, there's no sign of cling film. Or masks. And there would be.'

'So there's a possibility of a third killer.'

Her laugh was a scoff. 'Doesn't feel likely, does it?'

Marshall snorted. 'Not writing it off.'

'Well, hello there.' Pringle was tearing his crime scene suit off like it was an evil symbiote that would control his mind. 'Okay, gang, what do we need to do?'

Elliot was staring into space. 'Hoping you would be able to help us, sir?'

'I'm a bit confuddled, to be honest.' Pringle kicked his suit away. 'Two more bodies...'

Marshall realised it was up to him to provide leadership. 'First, we need to identify them, if at all possible. Is it possible we'll get something from the bone marrow of either victim for DNA?'

Pringle was nodding. 'Doubt it.'

'Andrea said they'd been in the ground fifteen years?'

'Well, aye, but...' Pringle seemed really out of his depth. Then again, this wasn't a golf course so that wasn't a surprise.

'This is nothing! They've got DNA from Egyptian mummies.' Elliot waved over at the clump of officers fanning out in a grid. 'And we're continuing the search – there may be more bodies here.'

'Excrement suggestion.' While he actually meant 'excellent', the prospect didn't seem to give Pringle any enthusiasm. 'The Edinburgh forensics team are on their way down, so I'll leave that with Kirsten to progress.'

Elliot jutted her chin at Marshall. 'We were just talking about Keane. We should interview him again. See what he's saying about these. Is he still in Melrose?'

'Back at the... Animal House?' Pringle stared at Marshall. 'What are your thoughts?'

'I think it's fair enough. Keane might know what's going on here. Hell, maybe Vickers is right and he is innocent, but he just knew where the bodies lay. But you can reduce it down to Keane either knows about these or he doesn't. If he knows anything about this, then the sooner we get him talking, the better.'

'You want to go first?'

Elliot raised her hand. 'I'll do it.'

'That's weird.' Pringle rubbed his hands together vigorously. 'Because previously he only talked to Marshall. Why on God's green earth would he suddenly divulge anything to you, Andrea?'

'Because I've been a cop the worst part of twenty years. I do know how to talk to people, sir.'

'But he's a serial murderer. DI Marshall here is the expert.'

'All I'm asking is for a shot at him. That's it.'

'It's two hours each way to the… Freak Farm?'

'Monster Mansion. And not the way I drive, it's not.' But she was still scowling. 'So what are you going to do, Marshall?'

He couldn't look at her. Sod it. He did. Stared right at her. 'While you've been working here, DS Archer and I have uncovered a potential lead on the three recent victims. Two of them were spotted at a truck services at Penrith. Thing is, given the cooling-off period of our killer, there's a—'

Elliot shook her head. 'I'm very sceptical of that. Absolute mumbo jumbo, if you ask me. Think about it. Just so happens this guy strikes every three months and the clock's about to strike midnight again? Do me a favour.'

'Hang on.' Pringle rested his hands on his hips. 'Andrea, part of the reason you were given approval for this dig was because you said there might be someone here. "Very real chance of a live victim, sir. Someone who's been taken recently.

Maybe they've been buried here with a mask on." Words to that effect, anyway.'

'Didn't say it was daft to not treat it seriously.'

Pringle frowned at her mangled words. 'Look, whatever, we need to get on top of this—' He whistled then smacked his hands together. 'When they crossed streams in *Ghostbusters*, the Marshmallow Man appeared.'

Elliot laughed. 'What's your point, sir?'

'I'm the SIO on this, so I want three clear work streams here.' Pringle raised his thumb. 'First, Bruce is the Ghost of Christmas Past, who will be responsible for finding and identifying the victims here. Marshall is the Ghost of Christmas Yet to Come, who can work towards identifying the killer's profile. Andrea, you can be the Ghost of Christmas Present and, in your own special way, find a potential live victim. Let's call them Tiny Tim. Or Tiny Tina.'

'My own special way?' Elliot gave a wide smile. 'What's that supposed to mean?'

'Your leadership qualities are distinct and unique, Andrea.' Pringle couldn't stare at her for long. 'Look, it's as simple as Mom's apple pie. Someone needs to be tracking down the dead. Makes sense it's Bruce given his historical involvement in the Keane case, but also the victims came from his patch. Doesn't matter if they were heading to London, Northern Ireland or Narnia, he knows the people.'

Elliot looked up into the grey sky. 'Here's a better suggestion.' She looked back down again. 'I'll take one for the team and focus on the past. I'll keep on identifying these poor bastards. See if there were any others in between them. Any trial runs.'

Marshall got it – Elliot was trying to pin it all on Mark Davidson. The dodgy criminal defence lawyer who represented a serial killer. She knew Siyal's case in Edinburgh was related, despite the lack of evidence.

Pringle was thinking it all through. 'So you're suggesting DI Bruce works on finding Tiny Tim or Tina, if they exist, and Marshall looks for the ghost of Christmas Yet to Come, vis a vis the killer's identity?'

'Pretty much.'

'That's all Ebeneezer Goode… Okay, Marshall, you're the Ghost of Christmas Yet to Come.' Pringle sighed. A deep and resonant one. Others would argue back, but he'd just folded.

Marshall smiled. 'Makes sense if I help Bruce with the missing persons' work too. It's all related to the profiling.'

And it'd keep him well away from Elliot.

She smiled and cracked her knuckles. 'I'm going to have a wee word with Martin Keane about this.'

CHAPTER FIFTY-SIX

Marshall couldn't think of anything worse than a lorry rest stop after dark. He got out into freezing air with the smell of spent diesel hanging on it. The rumble and swish of distant cars and trucks on the M6, just the other side of a long strip of tall trees. He counted eleven lorries on the tarmac, parked pretty much equidistantly away from each other, apart from two separated by a space – presumably friends catching up.

At least, he hoped it was innocent.

The pair of detectives going around each one would determine that. A bleary-eyed driver answered questions while scratching his thinning hair.

Marshall spotted a familiar face coming their way – DI Shaun Foxton, as ever in his dark suit, white shirt, black tie, face like he was attending the worst funeral ever. 'Marshall, isn't it?'

'That's right.' Marshall shook his hand. 'This is DS Archer.'

She shook his hand too. 'Call me Jolene.'

'Sure you've heard all of the jokes.'

'They just keep on getting funnier and funnier.'

Foxton tilted his head to the side. 'Mr Marshall, you're causing a lot of havoc here.'

'Can you cause a lot of havoc?'

Foxton grinned. 'You're giving it a good shot.'

Marshall returned the grin. Bloody hell, it was freezing here. 'Look, I appreciate you helping us with this. So we need to know two things. One, do these drivers recognise any of the three we sent through? Two, which is a longer shot, is who's been here in the last few days who meets the victim profile, male or female.'

'The first is just about impossible... The second?' Foxton laughed, but his eyes were dead. 'We'll need a new word for that. Something much worse. Much less likely.'

'Must be CCTV here, right?'

'I mean, yeah, but the camera checks if people drive off without paying for fuel.'

Jolene bristled. 'I'd still like to review the footage.'

'Why?'

'My team have pulled together a list of twenty-five missing persons who match the profile of the abducted.'

'You think he's done someone recently?'

She nodded. 'It's always a possibility.'

'None of them could've come here.'

'Still like to cross that out.'

Foxton scratched at his head. 'What makes you think there's anything there?'

'Profiling.' Marshall smiled at him. He was sick fed up of having to defend something he didn't even do anymore, but at least he was well-practised in it. 'The only good thing about having three victims is we start to see a pattern. The victims are all young people running away from their lives. Skint. Desperate enough to get in a lorry with a stranger in this day and age, despite the warnings. Those twenty-five fit the profile.'

Foxton looked away, exhaling slowly. 'And you've requested my lads stay and question anyone who stops here?'

'For the next week.'

Foxton slapped his hand to his head. 'You owe me one, Bobby.'

The name made Marshall freeze. He tried to laugh it off. 'Could be someone who works here. Or used to.'

'Shitting where you eat, eh?' Foxton glanced over to the side. 'Here's your chance to ask.' He strolled off across the damp tarmac. 'Thomas!'

An older man was resting on a vintage cane and staring at a brand-new iPad. Tall and dapper – not the kind of guy you'd expect to run a service station. 'DI Foxton, I hope you and your men will be buggering off soon.' He might've dressed like a Victorian gent but he spoke like a miner.

'Will do, guv. After a few days.'

Marshall joined them, flanked by Jolene. 'Guv?'

Foxton slapped his arm. 'Sergeant Thomas Craven, as was. Taught me everything I know.'

Craven had the eyes of a hardened cop, scanning everyone a few times over. 'Don't blame me for whatever he's fucked up.' His face stayed straight as Foxton creased himself laughing. 'Got my papers not long after this idiot made detective. Now look at him, bungling murder inquiries left, right and centre.'

'Speaking of which...' Foxton gestured for Jolene to take over.

She cleared her throat. 'We're looking into missing persons who've been here in the last few days. Male or female. Late teens, early twenties.'

'Thing you should know about this place is, as ex-Job myself, I keep a close eye on what goes on. Drugs, people trafficking, you name it.' Craven flicked a hand over towards the pair of lorries next to each other. 'If it's happening here, I don't want it. And nothing gets past this beak.' He tapped his red nose.

She passed him the prints of missing people. 'Here are the people who match the profile.'

'Profile.' Craven rolled his eyes as he tucked his iPad under his arm. 'Headshrinkers were a bloody nightmare in my time.' He started flipping through the pages. 'This prick over in Durham used to sit in his ivory tower and dictate all these fruitless searches.' More pages. 'We'd be knocking on doors all over the Lakes and over to bloody Newcastle. American nonsense. Police work is the only—' He stopped. Then flipped between two pages. 'Thing is, there was a girl hanging around for a bit last night. Looks a bit like these two.'

Jolene looked over at Marshall with wide eyes.

'I watched her on the CCTV, wondering what she was up to. Dropped off by a lorry. Young lass like that, well, I'm thinking prostitution. Not here. Not on my watch. Weird thing, though, she just walked off towards town.'

Marshall was piqued by this. 'Can we see the CCTV?'

'Sure.' Craven unlocked the iPad and swung it around to show them. 'This is her.'

Jolene frowned. 'You just so happened to have that?'

'No, I've had two detectives in my office quizzing me for half an hour and this is what I showed them.' Craven looked at Foxton. 'Didn't seem to be too interested in it, mind.'

Foxton glowered at him. 'I'll have a word with them.'

Marshall took the tablet and stared at it. She fit the profile, no question – the shifty look of a runaway. Definitely at the low end of the age scale, though. And definitely a waif, barely anything on her. He set it playing and watched her leave the lorry park, rucksack slung over her shoulders, traipsing over onto the main road that led into the town centre. The time stamp was 20:34 the previous night.

'Still don't see—' Marshall stopped.

A truck drove alongside her and kept following her. A discussion that lasted a few minutes, then she got in.

'Someone picked her up.' Marshall had an audience now as he wound the video back.

The truck actually approached on the other side of the road. Must've pulled a U-turn when they saw her.

The plates were misted out.

'Shite.'

As cold as he felt from the weather, Marshall got a shudder from what was running through his brain. 'This is him.' He passed Jolene the iPad and snatched the list of missing persons out of her hand. 'It's possible she's not been reported missing, but...' He flicked through the pages, through the seven males then the older females. 'Okay. These two young women match the age of the girl on there. One near Hawick, the other in Halt-whistle, between Carlisle and Newcastle.' He looked at Foxton. 'Let's split them – can you find her parents?'

CHAPTER FIFTY-SEVEN
SIYAL

Though he'd been a cop for the best part of a year, Siyal hadn't been in too many interviews, and now he was in his second with a convicted serial killer.

Martin Keane should've been in an interview suite where the facilities reflected the magnitude of his crimes. Where all the guards knew him and his behaviours, especially the pair who were lurking around in the room here like they were frightened of him. But he was sitting in a glorified cupboard in HMP Frankland, with a sneer befitting the place.

Or just the way Elliot was talking to him. 'I don't care about your childhood, Martin. I just want to know why I've recovered the remains of five people in the same place you buried your last three.'

Took a lot of balls to sit in a room with a man who'd caused that much pain and torment and treat him like she was doing. Or maybe it took no balls, and you just needed to be Andrea Elliot.

Keane ran a hand through his hair. 'Didn't just bury them

there. Killed them there too. But these other murders you're trying to pin on me... Nope.'

Mark Davidson leaned over and whispered something in his ear.

Keane snorted, grinning.

Siyal had no idea what he'd said. But just being in the same room as Davidson made his stomach clench and gurgle that little bit worse.

Elliot sat back. 'Go on, then. Tell us about your childhood.'

'You wouldn't know how to process it.'

She laughed. 'Martin, your sort always wants to talk about your childhood. Now I'm letting you do that. So go on, fill your boots – talk about how little your daddy loved you.'

'It'd be wasted on you.'

'What's that supposed to mean?'

'You're just a cop.'

'Just a cop?'

Davidson grabbed a hold of Keane's top then let go. Very strange. 'Listen, my client needs to be taken back to his cell. You can't keep him here.'

'No, Mark, we can.' Elliot leaned across the table. 'We can keep him here as long as we need him.'

'It's taxpayer's money you're wasting.'

Elliot twisted around to look at Keane from a different angle, then swept her fringe over. 'Aye, you're right.' She scraped her chair back and stood. 'Still. Your client's been itching to talk about his past. Might want to just talk to us, Sonny Jim. Get it all off your chest.'

Keane wasn't looking at her. Just focused on his shoes.

'If it's not you, it's someone killing for you.' Elliot was staring at Davidson. 'How about you open up to us about that, eh?'

'My client wishes to return to his cell.'

Keane nodded. 'Not read the papers today.'

Elliot stared at Davidson for a long time. Siyal felt uncomfortable. 'Come on, Shu— Sergeant, let's leave this pair to conspire in private.' She walked over to the door and slipped out into the corridor.

With all the malarkey out at the woods, Siyal had almost forgotten the possibility of Davidson being directly involved in the case...

Elliot hadn't. She'd ranted about it all the way down.

If she was right, she'd just left Siyal in a room with *two* murderers, not one.

The guards would help, but still. He didn't like it.

Siyal smiled at Davidson. 'See you around, Mark.'

'Yes, I hope not.'

Siyal walked over to the door and left them to it. Whatever they were cooking up.

Elliot was standing there, not staring at her phone for once, but at a poster on the wall, one of those ones local primary school kids did to advertise road safety. He couldn't figure out what it was doing in a prison, other than to bring a tear to the eye of the hardiest of killers. 'You weren't much help in there, Shunty.'

'Wasn't aware I was supposed to be.'

'How about being good cop to my bad cop?'

'That only works if you agree it's the strategy before you go in. And if you can stick to which role you were supposed to play.'

'Hey, I didn't know I was getting an audience with the renowned god of policing.'

'Seriously, Keane's just way too wily to fall for it.'

Elliot's mouth hung open, then it snapped shut. 'For starters, the guy's a moron. A village idiot. But you, Shunty...

You were useless in there. Just sat back and let me do all the work.'

'I don't know why you're having a go at me for your perceived failure in there.'

'No kidding, Shunty. You wouldn't know a...' She tailed off and let out a sigh. 'Forget it.'

'Ma'am, Keane's a narcissistic psychopath. Why would he speak to you or me? He doesn't know us. Doesn't value us. We can't get him anything.'

'He spoke to Marshall.'

Ah, there it was. Professional envy.

'Ma'am, Rob worked the original case.'

'If he's so bloody good, he should've taken the task of interviewing Keane, eh? But no, Doctor Donkey is off searching for a missing girl, who might or might not exist, who might not even be missing. Or be a girl. I don't even want to be here, but that's the division of labour we agreed.'

'You insisted on this! And we've driven down here, a lot faster than I'd have liked, to achieve nothing.'

'Aye, sure.' Elliot shifted her focus to her phone. 'Speak of the devil. The good doctor isn't prone to leaving just one voice-mail, is he? Twelve missed calls from DI Rob Marshall. Well, I'll take it on lucky thirteen. Maybe. See, I've just got the one from Weirdo. Can't stand her, but that shows respect.' She looked up at him. 'Can you deal with her when we get back?'

'We're leaving?'

She sloped off. 'Aye, this was a complete waste of time.'

CHAPTER FIFTY-EIGHT
MARSHALL

Marshall pulled up in the gloom. The address was a green keeper's cottage just south of Minto, itself a few miles east of Hawick, then a few miles north of Denholm. During the day, you'd feel like you were in the middle of nowhere, surrounded by hills, fields and trees.

Nobody around, though. Two cars and lights burning inside the small cottage.

The headlights caught one vehicle and the dual language words lit up:

POLICE

POILEAS

The door hung open. And raised voices erupted out.

Marshall shot over to the house. 'Hello?'

No response.

Marshall motioned for Jolene to go first.

'Ms Paton?' She stepped inside. 'It's the police.'

'How *dare* you suggest that?!' The voice came from upstairs. Female. Local. Loud.

'Please, just calm down.' Male. Irish. Quieter.

Marshall followed Jolene up the narrow, winding steps.

A bedroom door was open and a cop stood there, cap in hand. No sign of any partners. Big guy, stubble growing out at this late hour. 'Please, just wait for—' He clocked them and relief filled his eyes. 'Alexandra, my colleagues are here.'

Marshall stepped into the bedroom. Typical teenage girl's – BTS and Ariana Grande posters on the walls. A bookcase filled with hardbacks. All the usuals: *Harry Potter*; *Hunger Games*; as many Colleen Hoovers as you'd like. A sleeping laptop resting on a desk.

It could be Thea's room...

Jolene had her warrant card out.

The cop turned around and caught a glimpse. 'Liam Warner, how're you?' He didn't offer a hand, instead focusing on the figure bent over in the walk-in cupboard. 'Alexandra, my colleagues here would like a word with you.'

She tossed a bunch of clothes over her shoulder, landing on the floor at Warner's feet. She got up with a sigh and turned around. Late thirties, blonde hair tied back, skin vampire pale. 'I can't *find* it.'

'Alexandra, it's okay.' Warner approached her. 'My colleagues here—'

Her right hand lashed out and slapped his face with an almighty crack.

Warner stood there, stunned. A big lad like him was probably used to the punch of a drunk football fan but didn't expect the slap of a missing girl's mother. 'Alexandra, that's the final warning.' Both of his cheeks were red – that wasn't the first slap, but it was the last she'd get away with.

Marshall got between them, hands not exactly in a defensive position but able to move quickly if he needed to. 'Ms Paton, I need you to be calm.'

She turned to face him, looking like she was going launch that hand. 'Have you found her?'

'No, but we—'

'Then I'll keep looking!' She turned back around.

'It'll be a great thing for us if she's in that cupboard.'

Alexandra looked around at Warner. 'Of course she's not. How could you joke about that?'

'Mrs Paton, we need to have a chat with you about your daughter.'

Alexandra shut her eyes. 'I'm not looking for *her* in there. I'm looking for *him*.'

'Him?'

Alexandra swallowed hard. 'She came home from school last night. We sort of had an argument, then she left. It wasn't really an argument, just... Grace being Grace... But she didn't come back after an hour, like she always did when we've argued. She's taken Mr Teddy.'

'Mr Teddy?'

'Little bear with TEDDY on his jumper. Had him since she was three. Her dad got her it.' Her voice was tiny, just little fragments of sound.

'Has anything else gone?'

'A book. Her phone charger. But her phone's here.'

Marshall nodded at Jolene. 'Get some forensics done on that. Messages, calls. See who she's been in touch with.'

'On it.' Jolene snapped on a pair of blue gloves then set about her task.

Marshall focused on Alexandra, staring hard enough to calm her down – she knew he was in charge here. 'Did she take any clothes?'

'I think so. I can't find her dad's rucksack.'

The girl from the Penrith truck stop was lugging one.

Marshall got out his phone and checked the photo. Greyscale so he couldn't tell the colour. He held it out to her. 'Is this her?'

Alexandra examined the screen. 'Sorry, either your phone's broken or my eyes are too bad to tell if it's my daughter.'

'But it could be?'

'Aye, it could be.' Alexandra raced over to the window and peered out into the lane. Then clenched her fists. 'That wee shite!' She barged past Warner and charged down the stairs.

Marshall was first out, following her down the rickety stairs. A cold draught hit him in the face as he went outside.

A little blue Renault idled outside. Window down.

'Where is she, Harrison?'

A spotty face peering out, sheepishly avoiding Alexandra's fists and open palms. 'No idea, Mrs Paton.'

'You lying bastard! You've killed her!' She lashed out to slap him but Harrison was too quick and ducked his head back into the car.

Her wrist clonked off the door surround and she yelped in pain.

Warner was quick enough this time – he grabbed her and shuffled her away from the car, back towards the house.

'Let me go!'

Leaving Marshall with a clear run at the car.

The window started winding up.

'Harrison?'

The window stopped.

Marshall rested on the doorframe, popping his head into the car. It stank of deodorant and sweat. 'Is Harrison a first name or a surname?'

'Name's Harrison Palmer.'

'Are you Grace's boyfriend?'

'Was.' The lad was a lot older than Grace's sixteen. Twenty-five, maybe. Still had spots and his haircut was the current fashion of football-obsessed teenagers – a skin fade, blended from hair to baldness over a few inches. 'She broke up with us a few months ago.'

'Why are you here, Harrison?'

'Her mum called us, aye?'

'What about?'

'Didn't she say?'

'Not yet.'

Harrison sniffed. 'Said Grace's run off. That right?'

Marshall nodded. 'Last night. You know anything about that?'

'No.' He turned away.

'The way you said that then immediately looked away makes me think you do know, Harrison. Now, we can—'

'She came to my bit last night. I was heading out with the lads, up to Edinburgh.' Harrison looked a bit tired and hungover. 'Asked me to drop her off in town last night.'

'In Edinburgh?'

'No, man. Hawick.'

'Right. 'Where did you drop her off?'

'Horse statue.'

Slap bang in the middle of the town's high street. One of the two sets of coach stops was opposite. If Marshall remembered rightly, that was just used during the day, but the one over by Morrisons had service all night, certainly until late.

He stared hard at Harrison, locking eyes with the kid. 'Did she say where she was heading?'

'Not to me.'

'That true, Harrison?'

'I'm not lying.'

'Did she say if she was running away from home?'

'She did. From you lot.'

'The police?'

'Aye. She was wanted for some kid dying from drinking meths.'

'*Meths?*'

'Aye. Someone had it at a party. This bitch at school, Elsa. She reported Grace.'

'For giving someone meths?'

'Said she poured it into his glass. Dared him to drink it.'

'Grace told you this?'

'Aye.'

'Harrison. Is this true?'

'Swear on my car's life.' He tapped the steering wheel. 'It's on TikTok. I think.'

Another runaway. Another daft kid fearing repercussions for something.

'She must've told you where she was going.'

'Mentioned something about her dad.'

'Where does he live?'

'England.'

'Where?'

'Ask her mum.'

'I will do. Okay. Thank you. So, as far as you're aware, she's on the run because someone died after she made him drink meths?'

'Right. Not even sure she made him, to be honest.'

'Thank you, Harrison. Don't go anywhere.' Marshall walked back, keeping an eye on the kid and turned just in time to see Liam get slapped by Alexandra once more.

Marshall grabbed her arm and pressed his thumb into her wrist. 'Enough!'

She looked at him like he was the one who'd abducted her daughter. 'What the— Let me go!'

'No.' He slackened off the grip slightly but it was still pretty tight. 'You've hit him twice and tried to hit Harrison. No more.' He gave a squeeze and she yelped. 'Where is her father?'

'Birmingham.' She frowned. 'You think she's gone there?'

'I need to find out. What's his address?'

'His Majesty's Prison Birmingham.'

'Oh. Right. I see.'

'Ten years for armed robbery.'

'Okay.' Marshall looked at Jolene then jerked his head towards the house. 'Can you take her inside, please?'

Jolene grabbed Alexandra's wrist in a similar way and led her back into the home.

Marshall focused on Warner. 'Okay. I'll need you to get a statement off the lad.' He waited for a nod. 'Was there an incident at a house party in Hawick on Saturday?'

'Aye, I was on. We went in and broke it up. Some kid was in a really bad way. Totally banjaxed, you know. Had to go to BGH to get his stomach pumped.'

'Had he been drinking meths?'

'*Meths*?' Warner cackled, loud and high-pitched. 'Nobody drank meths. He had half a bottle of vodka. Drove him up to Borders General myself. Sat there while they pumped his stomach. He was a bit embarrassed afterwards, parents wanted to kill him but nobody *died*.'

'Are you sure?'

'Aye. That's all that happened.'

The truth didn't matter as much as Grace's perception. Marshall had a girl running away from home, heading south…

He hoped she'd made contact with her father.

CHAPTER FIFTY-NINE
SIYAL

S iyal opened Kirsten's office and got the moist fug of a freshly brewed pot of coffee.

She was sitting at her workstation, head in hands.

'You okay?'

She looked over and made him wish he hadn't gone to work that day. 'Shut the door. Elliot's around.'

Siyal hurried in and nudged it behind him. 'Just spent two hours each way to HMP Frankland with her driving at American speeds, only to sit with Keane for about ten minutes and get nothing.'

'Right.'

He took the seat next to her. 'What's up?'

'Just heard that we won't be able to identify the new victims from DNA.'

'I thought we'd be able to—'

'So did I. Owusu's struggling to get any decent marrow from the bones. Animals have been at them. Probably why the dogs smelled them. She's sending it to Gartcosh, who might fare better. Failing that, the Met lab in Lewisham might be able to do it. Either way, it's way beyond my capabilities.'

'You can't win them all.'

'Feels like an even longer shot than Elliot being nice to you.' She leaned out across her desk. 'Oh, Kirsten, you're being a bitch. She baked me a cake, after all.' She smiled at him. 'You want a coffee?'

'I've had enough to last me until Christmas.'

She sprang to her feet then went over to the filter machine. 'It's good stuff. New beans. Guatemalan.'

'I'm fine. What did you want Elliot for?'

'Elliot?' She frowned as she topped up her mug. 'Nothing.'

'But you called her?'

'Oh, and she sent you. Oh, aye. Right.' She tipped in some oat milk from a beige carton. 'It's about those tape back-ups of CCTV.'

'You've got them?'

'Sorry. My guy in Edinburgh said Elliot's old team are prioritising his time for a murder up there. If he's lucky, we might get them back tomorrow morning.'

'Great. I could really do with that stuff now.'

'Believe me, I've tried pleading but there's nothing I can do.'

'Is there anything Elliot can do?'

'Not even the great Andrea Elliot could fix this, no.'

CHAPTER SIXTY
MARSHALL

Marshall stopped outside the office door and kicked it open.

Someone kicked it shut.

Elliot?

He nudged it open again.

Pringle was in there, phone to his ear, waving Marshall to back out.

So he left him to it.

What was the point in having an office if the boss nicked it from you?

Marshall checked his phone, but he had nothing back from HMP Birmingham. Hopefully Jolene would get somewhere. He called Foxton and leaned back against the wall.

Trouble with a station this small was every room was occupied, even the cupboards. The area was too small to have an MIT, but Pringle had somehow—

'Foxton.'

'Shaun, it's Rob. How goes it in Haltwhistle?'

'Over county lines like this, mate, it's…' Foxton breathed

hard down the line. 'It's an active case. Abi Crossland. Mother realised she'd gone first thing this morning. Called it in then and my colleagues in Northumbria have been getting to the bottom of it all day. Looking like the same old sad story of a girl being abused by her stepfather.'

'Any leads on her whereabouts?'

'Working with a DI Bruce. Gather you know him?'

'We're both working this case.'

'Ah cool. We *might* have a lead on Abi going to Newcastle.'

'Newcastle?'

'Sister's mate lives there. Student.'

'Have you recovered her phone?'

'Abi still has it.'

'Are you—'

'Aye, aye. We're tracking it. Got it getting on the bus in Haltwhistle and heading to Newcastle. Turned it off after Corbridge.'

'So it's not likely to be Abi in Penrith, then?'

'Don't rule it out, mate.' Foxton sniffed. 'Oh, Bruce wants a word.'

'Rob?' Bruce sounded out of breath. 'Good effort on this one, mate, but I'd say this lass isn't the one you're looking for.'

'Okay but keep on digging. Could be nothing in either. Could be someone else. But we should find her if we can.'

'True. Take it Pringle spoke to you, Rob?'

'Aye, we'll need to put our heads together soon to see what's what.'

Bruce yawned. 'Tomorrow work?'

'Was thinking now?'

'Mate, we've got a head of steam just now with this lass, so let's keep on this path for now and see where it gets to.'

'Are you still looking into Vickers?'

'That daft sod... Aye.' Sounded like Bruce was flicking

through his notebook. 'Right, we've been going through his phone records to pin down his movements. Thing that sticks out is a lot of travel to the Lakes and he won't answer why.'

'Where in the Lakes?'

'Eh, would need to check.' More flicking.

'Penrith?'

'Nearby, anyway. It's on the way to where he's been going anyway.'

Marshall grunted. 'That's interesting.'

'Not as interesting as this. Turns out Vickers was a teenage runaway himself. Abusive uncle, mum who didn't listen. Found and returned home but this time she did listen. Things got sorted out. Uncle arrested, charged, topped himself on remand. Vickers sorted himself out, even went to college, where he trained as a cardio-respiratory occupational thera-pist. Few years in the States, then he came back home.'

'That's... interesting.'

'Fits, doesn't it?'

Marshall let his breath go. 'It's not incompatible.'

'Anyway, Vickers hated working here. End of life stuff. So much death on his watch. But he got into listening to podcasts and thought sod it. Did one about working in health – lots of deaths in the hospital he worked at. But you know that. Then he starts doing this one about Keane.'

Marshall jotted it all down. Typical Bruce – just dumping information. Still, at least he was structured with it, unlike some...

'You still there?'

'Aye. I agree – the runaway thing is interesting. It's possible he could see what he's doing as a way to control his own past.'

'Thing is.' Bruce sighed down the line. 'Him jumping to Keane's case is out of the blue.'

'So you think he has a personal connection?'

'Would explain it, wouldn't it?'

Marshall was starting to see Vickers as a suspect. It all slotted into place. It all fitted the profile. 'This is good stuff.'

'His family history gets murkier. Uncle was a delivery driver. Local door-to-door stuff. But had a team of people. Place near Ponteland by the airport. Get freight shipped in, they packed it up and bingo, he'd shift it on.'

'That checks out with the cling film. Possibly.'

'Firm shut down about ten years back when the uncle was arrested. Not on normal courtyard exercise and all that.'

'Is the building still there?'

'Still owned by the family. Probably a ruin now.'

A perfect place to keep a body after you've abducted them...

'Okay, is Vickers still in custody?'

'Let him go at lunchtime.'

'You let him go?'

'Not my call, Rob.'

Marshall glared at the door. Pringle would've known. 'We need his whereabouts for last night.'

'Why?'

'Suspected abduction.'

'Oh, this one Shaun here's working on?'

'One of them, aye.'

'Saucy. Vickers wouldn't say where he was. Says we're framing him to stop the truth getting out.'

Marshall ran his hand down his face. 'Send me his file over, would you?'

'Will do, Rob. Our boffins have been going through his laptop. Cheeky rascal has deleted some files, which they're recovering but it's messy. Only going to get partials on them as they've had some stuff overwritten on top. Looks like audio.'

'More interviews?'

'Hope so. Just our luck it'll be like dummy files or something.'

'Aye, that'd be about right.'

'Absolute brass monkeys here, mate, so I'm heading back to HQ. Catch you later.'

'Cheers. And I hope you find her.'

But the line was dead.

Marshall needed to throw all of that down on the page. He'd been rushing around looking for a victim who might or might not be missing. But Vickers was a suspect. Maybe he should head over to Newcastle and track him down himself.

Sod it.

He pushed into his office.

Pringle was sitting on Elliot's desk, staring at his mobile. 'I'd apologise for that, Robert, but I don't really care.' He laughed. 'I was just talking to your officemate. DI Elliot.' He scowled. 'Complaining about her children and the lack of childcare this evening.' He raised a finger. 'I can sympathise with that situation.'

Marshall held his gaze. 'You don't really have any kids, do you?'

Pringle winked at him. 'DI Elliot's uncomfortable with you, Marshall.'

'She is?'

'You're taking over too many things.'

'That's not my intention.' Marshall shrugged off his suit jacket and hung it over the back of his chair. 'Besides, she's been off sick for three months, so you and I have both shouldered a lot of her workload. It's natural for—'

'Haven't we just!'

Marshall sat behind his desk. 'Look, I'll speak with DI Elliot and make sure it's not an issue.'

'Good man!' Pringle smacked him on the arm. 'Anyway. Elliot spoke to Keane again and got nowhere.'

'I'm not sure what she was expecting, sir.'

'Mm.' Pringle snorted like he had a cocaine problem. 'What's your take on him?'

'My take? It doesn't fit. Keane would've been too young back then. All the psychology around the shallow graves and the markers show he wanted to be found out, ideally by his father. Those older bodies were properly disposed of. A lot like the three most recent ones. I don't think it's Keane.'

'But what if it was his mother he was sending the message to? What if he was being abused by his father? If she wasn't listening, maybe that's why he felt he lived in the shadows.'

Marshall tried to let the sigh go slowly. Everyone thought they were psychologists now. 'Listen, sir, we've got a likely for the live abduction.'

'Enlighten me?'

'A girl from Hawick went missing last night. Possible sighting in Penrith where two of the others were spotted.'

'Is this true?'

'We... We don't know. It's possible.'

'Marshall. The reason you're employed is so we've got a profiler on staff and we don't have to rely on someone like Liana Curtis. Little madam told the Geordie big cheese that she can't help us.'

'I thought you told her she wasn't needed?'

'There's that.' Pringle gave Marshall another squeeze. 'Need you to go and do your thinking. Okay? Tell me if it's her we're looking for.'

'Okay, sir.'

'Good. I'll see you in the morning.' Pringle rapped the door on his way out for some reason.

Marshall slumped back in his chair.

The problem was, he couldn't think. He needed something to eat. Absolutely starving. He grabbed his jacket and left the room.

He could smell fresh coffee, so he followed it to the forensics lab. He knocked on the door.

No answer.

He nudged it open. 'Hello?'

Kirsten was hunched over her workstation, hands clasped around a coffee mug. She looked over. 'Rob?'

'Hey. Listen. I was just going to get something to eat. Wondered if you—'

'Too busy.'

'Oh.'

'Sorry. Just... Way too much on.'

'Rain check?'

She smiled. 'Rain check.'

CHAPTER SIXTY-ONE

The haar had settled in Melrose, rising from the Tweed and making the place feel even more Dickensian, especially in the darkness.

Every step Marshall walked through the town, his head thumped that little bit more. He was starving. He hadn't eaten since... breakfast?

Aye. That breakfast with Kirsten when he'd been too polite to eat much.

He needed something now. There was that new sushi place in Galashiels, a little corner of metropolitan chic in the Borders. Or a few good restaurants here.

Sod it – haggis supper.

He walked around the block towards the chip shop and stopped outside. That time of year when it smelled perfect, the hot grease set against the freezing cold air. He went in and smiled at the wee old man behind the counter. 'Haggis supper.'

'Be five minutes, son.'

'No problem.' Marshall put a tenner down on the counter. 'Can of Irn Bru too.'

'Cheers.' He waddled off to the fryer at the back and stirred something.

Champions League football was playing on the telly. Two teams Marshall couldn't figure out but he watched them anyway. Zoning out at the metronomic rhythm of the passing.

His phone rang.

Liana calling...

Oh, bloody hell.

He answered it. 'Hey.'

'Hey. Just... Wanted to clear the air.'

'About earlier?'

She didn't say anything.

'It's okay, Liana.'

'No, it's not. I... Look. I'm sorry I've been pushy, but I'm... not getting any younger. I want to settle down and... I'm sorry I forced that on you. I feel mortified.'

Marshall felt everything squirm inside. That need to settle down. He knew it, but... 'Liana, I want to clear the air too. Maybe we should sit down and—'

'Rob, I really have got so much work on just now. This case in Nottingham... It's eating me alive.'

'Happy to listen to all of that too.'

'Okay, Rob. Look, I'll maybe call you next week. Alright? But think about it. We'd be good together.'

Jesus, she was still pushing.

He laughed. 'I like your confidence.'

'I know what I want, Rob. Bye.' Marshall hung up and sat on the ledge in the chip shop's window.

This was all new to him.

The one he wanted – who he'd spent the night with – was too busy to do more than grunt at him, while Liana...

Jesus.

'Here you go, son.' The man behind the counter put his package down next to some change.

'Thanks.' Marshall picked it all up and walked out into the cold. The heat almost burned his hands as he walked up the hill towards Mum's.

During the day at work, he felt like an adult. Investigated serial killers, for God's sake, but at night... He was like a seventeen-year-old idiot, trapped in amber. He should stick on some Embrace and Stereophonics when he got back in. Or Korn and Slipknot.

He unlocked the door and stepped into the kitchen. No sign of Mum or anyone else, so he grabbed a plate and tipped his food onto it. The vinegar stung his eyes. Glorious. He grabbed cutlery from the drawer then sat down at the kitchen table. As much of a barbarian as he could be at times, Marshall always tried to eat like a civilised human being. Even stuff from the chip shop.

It'd be nice to have his own space.

Bollocks.

He'd left his can at the shop.

Sod it.

He bit the end of the haggis supper and shut his eyes, enjoying the peppery fire and the creamy batter and the harsh salt and—

'Jesus, is that your come face?'

He opened his eyes.

Jen was standing in the doorway, still in her dressing gown. His vision was so blurry from the vinegar and coffee that she looked seventeen again.

A very, very hungover seventeen.

'You look like death cooled down, Jen.'

'Charming.' She tugged her dressing gown tight. 'I feel like it. Mum's out at her therapy group. Thea's with her dad.'

'Where's Zlatan?'

'Sleeping on Mum's bed.'

'Bless him.' Marshall stuffed some chips into his mouth. 'How are you?'

'Feel like I died last night.' She sat next to him, stole a chip, then prodded him with a finger. 'I'm blaming you for ordering me a prolapse.'

'A decaf one.'

'Eh?'

'That was grape juice and cold coffee in that.'

'Wanker.'

'You were in no fit state to drink a real one.'

'I'll be the judge of that.'

'Not sure you can be, to be honest.'

She narrowed her eyes at him. 'Listen, Sally was messaging me earlier. Asking what's going on with you and Kirsten.'

Marshall felt his cheeks burn as hot as a deep-fat fryer. 'What did you tell her?'

'Nothing.' She reached over and hugged him. 'I'm so pleased.'

'You are?'

'Aye! I know how difficult things have been for you. She's great.'

'I don't know if I'm good for her. I'm a bit of a bloody mess.'

'There is that.' She stole another chip and ate it. 'God, these are so good.'

'Go and get your own.' He could talk about Liana and how he found her laser-like focus on him unnerving. But that was a story for another day.

'I really am so pleased for you, Rob. She's a good person.'

He was blushing again. 'How was your meeting with the solicitor?'

She reached over for another chip.

'Mine.' He brushed her hand away with his fork. 'Solicitor?'

'I delayed it a day. Said I'm ill. Lied, basically.'

'Too scared to commit?'

'Too right.'

Marshall took his time chewing the mouthful of fiery haggis. 'Jen, how about I stay in the granny flat?'

Her mouth hung open. 'Are you serious?'

'Sure.' Marshall took another bite of haggis. 'I'm doing it for Thea, not for you.'

'She does deserve to see more of you.'

'That's not the same thing as free babysitting.'

'She's not that young.' She laughed. 'What about your flat in London?'

'Renting it to a mate. If you want me in your life, it'd be good.'

'It'd be a bloody lifesaver.' She leaned over and kissed his cheek. 'Though I'm keener on your cat than you.'

'It'll be a mission prising him from Mum's bed.'

'I know.' She hugged him tight, squeezing him hard. 'Thank you, Rob. It means the world to me.'

'Don't mention it.' He waited for her to let go. 'Listen, I'm supposed to be working all night but I wondered if you fancied drinking a shitload tonight?'

'Fuck off.' She looked green. 'I mean it.'

'I'm winding you up. But I do have a lot of work to do tonight.' He tapped his laptop bag. 'I'll finish this then disappear up to my room.'

Jen twisted her lips up. 'Actually, I'm not sure having two moody teenagers in the house will be a good thing...'

CHAPTER SIXTY-TWO
THE NEXT DAY

The station's tiny unmanned canteen, with its sticky drum of instant, might've been a better option for privacy, but Marshall had settled for a table in the window of Dean's Beans to ruminate over his profile with a very decent coffee. Outside, Melrose languished in darkness, cars swooshing around the one-way system, spots of rain dotting the glass.

His phone buzzed on the table. A text from Jolene:

Bruce found Abi Crossland in Newcastle.

That was good news for Abi. But did it adjust the odds in favour of it being Grace at the truck station? Marshall didn't know.

Then another:

Oh. Forgot to say. Can't get into her mobile. Got her records tho. Grace wasn't much of a texter. Typical Zoomer. Never called anyone. Probably all in WhatsApp or Snapchat. Have to get into the phone to get at them. Mum doesn't know the code. Stalled. Soz.

Well, that was how he figured it'd play out – Grace Paton was a typical teenager. Wedded to the portable pocket computer people called a mobile phone, but more secretive than your average forensics IT officer.

Kirsten walked past the window. Glanced at him then looked away.

She *was* avoiding him.

She came back, waved at him and smiled. Then entered the café and collapsed into the chair next to him with an almighty yawn. 'You okay there?'

'Not really.' Marshall swore his laptop screen was blinking out of time with reality. Either that, or the machine was buggered. Could be his eyesight, of course. He took another glug of coffee and tried to smile at her, but he couldn't. Must've looked like part of his brain had stopped working.

She was a mirror of him, just with her dyed silver hair and without his two-day stubble. While her long face was a different shape to his, her eye bags were just as bad.

They were a pair of idiots who put their jobs before their own wellbeing.

'Tell me you've got something else I can use, Kirsten. Some hard science.'

She let out a deep sigh. 'I wish.'

Marshall took another sip of coffee. 'You okay there?'

'I'm just fine, Rob. Fine and dandy. Because who doesn't want to spend all night helping Elliot with technology...'

'That isn't your job, is it?'

'Nope. She doesn't see it that way. Keeps playing all these cards. Ow, my scars. Oh, the case. Oh, my childcare. Hard to say no.'

'Heard she had a bit of bother with her kids last night.'

'Aye. Her husband got caught at a meeting up in Edinburgh, so she had to stay at home a bit later to cover the school run. And I was just leaving the station when she came back... Good thing is, she doesn't know about the illicit still.'

'The what?'

She tapped her nose. 'We've got a sneaky coffee pot in our room. If you're a good boy, you can share it with us.'

'And if I'm a bad one, I can grass to Elliot now you've told me.'

'Ah.' She waved over at the counter. 'Dean, get us a long black, would you?'

'On it.' A wall of beard turned away to work at the espresso machine.

'Nothing like a fresh one from here in the morning, though. Small pleasures, eh?' She rested on her arms. 'So, Rob. Who are you waiting on?'

'Nobody. Why do you think I'm waiting on someone?'

'Sitting in the window like that, putting yourself on show. Most of our colleagues walk past or get a coffee from in here.'

'I'm a less appealing window display than a butcher's that's been shut for two weeks.' Marshall waved a hand at his laptop. 'Working on my profile.'

She let Dean place her coffee in front of her. 'Cheers.' But her stare sent the message to her cousin that they didn't want to be interrupted. She waited until he tamped down the espresso maker again before leaning forward again. 'Thought that was Liana thingy's job?'

'Long story, but... She's not doing it. Pringle expects me to. I'm out of practice, but Pringle doesn't see it that way.'

Marshall took a sip of still-burning coffee. 'I've been up most of the night working on it and... it's shite.'

'I very much doubt that.' She laughed. 'You've done all this before, so you can do it all again. Even if it's not perfect, it might have all the steps we need to walk on the way.'

He could sort of see her logic, but that emptiness gnawed away at his stomach. The hollow left by not yet finding the killer or rescuing Grace Paton. If she even needed rescuing.

She brushed her hand down the side of his laptop screen. 'Talk me through it.'

'Okay. So... Where do I start?'

'Summary level.'

'Right. Bottom line is we're looking for someone who is probably a loner, but I need more data to confirm that. Someone who spends a lot of time on their own.'

'Sounds a lot like you.'

He smiled for the first time that morning and actually meant it. 'Our killer's solitude means he spends a lot of time in his head. There's nobody to argue back against him, so he's learnt to justify what he does.' He raised his hands. 'Which does sound like me.'

'It does. Where does it differ, though?' She paused, holding her coffee in front of her mouth. 'Does it differ?'

Another involuntary smile. 'I'm not that bad. I do talk to people. Like now.'

'But you have lived a solitary life, Rob. Until the other night, you hadn't been intimate with someone in like twenty years.'

He met her eyes.

She held his gaze for a few long seconds. The light in here and the colour of her hair made her eyes seem grey rather than the soft green they were.

Marshall glanced away, back to his laptop, but the screen

was swimming again. 'Given the victimology, it's possible we're looking for someone who ran away from home himself, who is obsessed about the possibility of being kidnapped himself. Back in the day. Maybe he was and this is his way of controlling it. Inflicting his worst fears on others shows he can get away with it now. Shows there's nobody he can't over-power. He needs to also show that his escape back then was an inevitability for the same reasons.'

Kirsten nodded.

The laptop screen came into sharp focus.

'Then there's the offender behaviour... He overpowers and immobilises. And he controls everything. Narcissistic, psycho-pathic, no guilt, no remorse. High-functioning too.'

'Why do you think that?'

'This isn't some on-site murder like Keane. He needs to organise an abduction, not to mention transporting and housing his victims, then killing and disposing of them. And not just once, but many times. So he has access to a vehicle, a truck, a van or even a large car with a boot and a place to keep them. May even have access to medical equipment.'

'Right, we found big traces of engine oil on the victims.'

'Engine oil?'

'Like you'd find in a vehicle engine. Or a generator. There was also diesel.'

'So, a lorry? He's holding them in a lorry?'

She shrugged. 'Not sure, yet.'

'Okay, well I'll park that for now. But the abuse is... Well, it's physical and mental. And it's sexual – piquerism, where a knife is a penile substitute. Could be he penetrates them in other ways because he is impotent or needs to cut to get aroused or stay that way.'

'Elliot said this podcaster is a suspect. Vickers, is it?'

'Right. He sort of fits the profile. What he does now is a

lonely profession. Sure, he's interviewing people, but most of it is editing stuff together. Listening to hours and hours of murderers talking about their crimes. To bereaved families going through their losses and traumas all over again.'

'Which would twist anyone's melon.'

'Exactly. But I can't figure out if I'm trying to match him to the profile or it to him.' In his head, that phrase made sense. 'But... the thing is, I know that missing girl has been taken. Grace Paton.'

'You know it, do you? You know she was abducted? That someone's got her?'

'No, but... The probability's fairly high. Kept me awake last night. Every time I shut my eyes, I pictured her in a grave. Dead. Or covered in cling film, wishing death upon herself.'

Buried like Marshall's emotions.

'It's not you killing her, is it?'

Marshall laughed. 'Would make solving it easier.'

'Do you need a damsel in distress to solve this?'

'No, but the stress of thinking there could be someone out there...'

'Rob, that girl you saw getting into a truck could be entirely fine. Grace could be meeting her dad in prison today. That girl could be someone else, who could also be fine.'

'And she could be dead. Or dying.'

'True.' She took a long drink of her coffee. 'I'm saying this as your friend, but Grace Paton isn't Anna.'

That hit him like a double-decker bus.

As much as he tried to kid himself that his therapy was fixing him, he was getting deeper into his own obsession.

'I'm... I've been obsessed with the past. I know I can't let go of things, but—'

'Nor can he, Rob.' She leaned over. 'Maybe he's obsessed too. All that stuff you said about him controlling his narrative about his past. He's burying his feelings as much as the bodies.'

Marshall woke up his sleeping laptop. 'The reason he's burying them with the masks on... He didn't feel like he could breathe as a kid. He felt suffocated. Couldn't breathe. So, like me, he buried his emotions.'

'Has Vickers done that?'

'I'll need to get Bruce looking into that. Assuming we can track him down.'

'He's missing?'

Marshall nodded. 'Let him go yesterday and he's gone to ground.'

'Wow.' She was staring at him. 'Listen, I'm sorry I brushed you off last night. The stress gets to me too. We've still got no way of identifying either of these new victims. I was trying all these tricks and techniques I knew would work.'

'But?'

'But there was nothing, Rob. Might come later but we are talking months of DNA cultivation, extraction and manipulation... Like they did with King Tut and other pharaohs. This is archaeology, not forensics. Still can't shake the feeling that I'm letting everyone down.'

'Not just me who's obsessed...'

'No, but... Rob, about Monday night, I...' She glanced away, sipping coffee. Something else going on there. She looked back at him. 'Rob, are you seeing someone?'

'Me? No.'

'I thought...'

'Nobody.'

'Listen, Jolene came in and spoke to Elliot last night. Didn't think I heard them, but my hearing is amazing. They were gossiping about you and Professor Pert.'

'Liana Curtis?'

'Well?'

'Well what? There's nothing. I kissed her once, a long time ago. But it was a one-off thing.'

'Sounds like you still hold a candle for her.'

'No way.'

'Spending a lot of time with her. Went to her office twice.'

'Only because Pringle ordered me to.'

'Rob, I can get out of the way. You can have your white picket fence life with her.'

'She might want something, but I don't. And maybe it could've been something back then, but I'm a lot wiser now. I know myself.'

She locked eyes with him. Didn't speak. A lot of processing going on behind her gaze.

'Monday night was... I'd like to see you again, Kirsten. Go for a date. Get to know each other.'

'Something's jarring about the whole thing.'

'Eh? You don't—'

'Your worst fear is coming true. A live victim, all the while most of the team are looking into Elliot's attempt at glory with old bones.' A change of subject and not a very subtle one at that... 'Does Elliot have a suspect?'

'She does.'

'Who?'

'Mark Davidson.'

'The lawyer, right?'

'Right. I approved Rakesh investigating an old case he was involved with. I think it got a bit personal for him, but Elliot glommed onto something that she could solve. If Davidson was the killer, she'd be the hero. I'm sick of people going off on their own like that. Policing is a team sport.'

'Isn't it just.' Kirsten finished her coffee. 'So you think Davidson is working with or for Keane?'

'No. Keane would take credit for them. He's already inside for six murders and has another three on record now. Plus one from his childhood. Why not just own up?'

'To protect Davidson. Or Vickers.'

'Don't really buy either of them, to be honest.'

Kirsten crumpled her coffee cup up and dumped it into the recycling. 'I'm worried about Rakesh.'

'Me too. He got himself a bit obsessed over that case. Thinks he can somehow spring her from immigration detention.' Marshall shook his head. 'Should I say something?'

'Maybe. He was in until after midnight, working on stuff about Mark Davidson. I told him to leave. Then he was back in at half four.'

'You were in all that time?'

She shrugged. 'I've got good coffee.'

'Kirsten, you can't do all-nighters.'

'I can. I'm good at it. But he's not. Would you have a word with him?'

'Pringle made it quite clear he's not my officer. But your officers are always your officers. I'll have a word with him.'

She scraped her chair back and got up. 'Thanks, Rob.'

'What has Elliot got him doing that means he's in all that time?'

'Everything.'

'But specifically?'

'I sent him that video from Edinburgh.'

'What video?'

CHAPTER SIXTY-THREE
SIYAL

S iyal sat up to give his eyes a rest, but they got worse if anything. A pulsing wave of heat ran across his face. He was struggling with this laptop – it had one angle where the screen didn't warp and the low sun didn't blind him. Both external monitors in the office didn't recognise the machine either. That or it was the other way round and the laptop was the culprit.

Pretty stressful working like that. And his eyes were bearing the brunt of it.

Worse, he was getting nowhere. Or certainly not where he needed to get to so Elliot would be off his case.

Coffee.

Another cup would help. Focus on the task at hand.

He checked his phone, but Kirsten hadn't replied to his last message. Too soon to chase – after all, it was her team's coffee maker. And he only got it when she was there.

Another ten minutes, then he'd brave Dean's Beans.

He assumed the position where he could actually see the laptop screen and hit play again. The sound filled his ears through his headphones – the sound of nothing. Martin Keane sitting in a room, thinking. The background hum of electricity, the drone of chatter in another room.

Mark Davidson perched next to him like a vulture. In all of the hours of video he'd watched, Siyal still hadn't seen any signs of notes or messages passing between them. The extremely remote possibility of some Morse code shit going on haunted him. The tapping of a pen, maybe. The clicking of shoe heels off the chair. Toecaps on the tiled floor.

Absolutely insane to even consider it.

All the same, Siyal knew he'd be reviewing the video again at Elliot's instruction to search for exactly that.

A hand grabbed his shoulder and he jolted upright, tearing off his headphones and getting ready to fight.

Marshall was standing there, frowning at him. 'You okay there, Rakesh?'

'Sorry, just got a bit lost in this task.'

Marshall looked at the screen. 'CCTV?'

'Right.' Siyal paused the video and rubbed at his eyes. They felt like someone had scoured them with sea salt. 'So tired.'

'Don't push yourself too hard, Rakesh. A police investigation is a—'

'—marathon, not a sprint. Aye, I get it, but... It doesn't help when Jolene tells Elliot about this missing girl down in Hawick and Elliot starts piling the pressure on me to find her...'

'It's okay. It's not on you or me if we don't find her. But we need to work hard to see if we can do anything.'

'I'm trying, Rob.' Siyal dug the heels of his hands deep into his eyes and got some mild relief. He pointed at the laptop. 'Got hold of the video files of the interviews with Martin Keane, but they're pretty useless so far.'

'The ones from the podcaster?'

'Right.'

'When you say "pretty useless", does that mean there might be something?'

Siyal had to wade through fatigue to get to an answer. 'Oh, aye. Aye.' He found another file. And set it playing through the speakers. Nobody around to complain.

'Last time we met, Martin, we got to a really good point but we had to finish up. I want to pick up where we left off. You were just about to open up about the trauma at the hands of your father, right?

Keane laughed. 'Not going to talk about that.'

'I thought that's where we were.'

'Forget about it. Said all there is to say.'

Marshall hit pause. 'You should've told me about this.'

'Why?'

'He's never talked about his parents.'

'I'm telling you now.' Siyal hit play again.

'Martin, people out there would listen to your message more if they understand why you do it. Where it's coming from. What drove you to it. There might be stuff that resonates deeply.'

A long pause.

'Okay.'

'Thank you.'

'My father was a bully. Forced me to run every day from the age of eight. Had me doing a marathon-length run every weekend by twelve.'

'That's a lot of running.'

'I know. He was a monster. We all have that side to us. But my father... There wasn't a warm side at all. He just wanted me to run. To be good at running. To keep running.'

'He ran too, didn't he?'

'Every day. Fifteen miles to work and back at night. By the

time I was fifteen, he made me do the same thing to school. Moved us to somewhere further away.'

'Did you ever talk to anyone about this?'

'A friend.'

'You going to name him?'

'Of course not. I don't name names. I'm discreet.'

'Of course you—'

'He made me listen to Oasis. That album. *Morning Glory*. All the time. Never any of the others. That line, "we live in the shadows", it's etched into my brain.'

'Was your dad a fan?'

'Obsessively.'

'You ever—'

'I don't want to talk anymore.'

'Come on, Martin, this—'

'No. That's it.'

Siyal reached over and stopped it. 'That was the end.'

'He just stopped?'

'Right. Did it on all the previous ones too. He gets to a point where he just stops talking. And he leaves. This is the last one. Don't have anything after that.'

'Huh. That's... weird.'

Marshall was an enigma to Siyal. He wished he could see inside his head, how he'd figured out life and policing and everything. How together he was. How he could isolate some microscopic aspect of Martin Keane and blow it up. Explore that in *nanoscopic* detail.

'This is... Keane's never mentioned a friend before. Someone he confided in.' Marshall was grinning wide enough to drive a car through. 'Stay on this, Rakesh. It's great work.'

'Thanks, but Elliot's asked me to work on something else.'

'What?'

'The other case.'

'That rape in Edinburgh?'

Siyal nodded. 'She thinks it's connected. She thinks Mark Davidson's involved in these murders. She told me to keep it from you.'

'And yet you haven't.'

'Because I can't stand stuff like that, Rob. But I'm the champion of lost causes. I'll do whatever it takes to find out whether he is involved.' He waved a hand at the screen. 'Like this CCTV that finally came through. I'll go through that all three times just to satisfy myself he wasn't involved.'

'Show me.'

'What, you think there's something in it?'

'No but being able to shut Elliot's crusade down will be useful.'

Siyal pulled up the video and showed Marshall the precious little he had.

A back alley in Edinburgh, an old pub and modern council flats.

'Rakesh, that screen is terrible.'

'I've complained, but this is all I'm allowed until April.'

Marshall crouched even lower to get a better angle at it. The only passable one.

A woman left the pub's back door and sparked up a cigarette, staring into space and easing off her aching back.

Afri.

Minutes passed. The cigarette became a stub. She hadn't known she was pregnant until she miscarried.

A masked man grabbed her from behind and took Afri inside the basement.

'That's it.' Siyal couldn't look at Marshall. 'All that hassle and that's it. Can't even see him.'

'Okay.' Marshall crouched next to him. 'Show me just the abduction. Slowly.'

'Right.' Siyal wound it back.

Afri sucked on her cigarette again.

A man stepped behind her.

'Stop.' Marshall rocked forward, screwing his eyes together. 'Where does he come from?'

'I don't know.'

'You don't know?'

'No, he just appears.'

'He doesn't come down the lane. So it's either of those two doors.'

Siyal felt a trickle of sweat run down his back. 'He bundles her *into* the basement one.' He played the video to prove it.

Didn't seem to pacify Marshall any, judging by the way he was breathing. 'But does he come from there?'

'I don't know.'

Marshall stood up. 'You don't know...'

'Rob, don't get arsey with me.'

'I'm not. Believe me, I'm not. It's... It's frustrating, that's all.'

'It is what it is.'

'I hate it when people say that.' Marshall waved at the laptop again. 'Does anyone go inside the basement before?'

'Not on the video I've got.' Siyal tapped at his notebook. 'There's a list of people walking up there. Could canvas the flats and see.'

'Okay, that's interesting. How long have you got?'

'Been through eighteen hours.'

'Yourself?'

'Nobody else around, is there?'

'Jesus, Rakesh. You need to learn to delegate.'

'I tried to but Elliot's taken McIntyre with her.'

Marshall snorted. 'Forget that. Do you have anything of her getting away?'

'Okay...'

The timer shuffled three hours later and Afri ran out of the door leading down to the basement, then along the street and away.

Siyal sat back. 'Happy now?'

'Have you got anything from the front?'

Siyal nodded. 'Have a look.' He played the corresponding file from the same timestamp.

Afri appeared at the bottom, slipping around the frame. Three seconds, then she was gone.

'That's it.'

'Okay.' Marshall stood back up. 'You've got the front door there, though.'

'What do you mean?'

'Right. Here's what I'm thinking. You've got eighteen hours of nobody going into the basement, so it's fair to assume that whoever took her came from the upstairs door. You've got eighteen hours of nobody going in that door, either, so we can assume whoever took her went in the front door. Therefore, you can see who goes in before she was taken and who leaves after. That'll give you a population to—'

'Shite.' Siyal slouched back in his seat, face burning. 'See? I'm just not cut out for this job.'

'What? What are you talking about?'

'I'm serious. I've never done this work before. It's all second nature to you.'

'Rakesh, I've been a cop ten years longer than you. That's all. Remember that Jim McIntyre or Jolene Archer wouldn't damage their eyesight by spending all night reviewing eighteen hours of video. Just start going through it all with that in mind. You'll maybe get something.'

Siyal put the video back to the start and let it play. 'Don't tell Elliot.'

Marshall laughed. 'She's the last person I'd mention this to.'

'Right, good.' Siyal stared at the screen with aching eyes. Three hours until the abduction. 'Thank you for listening, Rob. I appreciate it all.'

'Don't mention it.'

Siyal caught something. He stopped it and wound the video back.

Two men went inside the bar.

One had his head bowed and Siyal couldn't make out his face.

The other one, though... He recognised him.

CHAPTER SIXTY-FOUR
MARSHALL

Marshall stepped into what passed for an observation suite in the station – a cupboard with an ancient telly and enough room for two to comfortably stand or one to sit, incredibly uncomfortably.

The screen woke up and showed an empty interview room. He brought up the menu and took a few seconds to—

There it was. Zoom. Took a bit longer to enter his credentials, but it went straight into the meeting.

And sure enough, there they were – Bruce and Williamson were interviewing Martin Keane. Again. Looked like Keane was stonewalling them. Still.

'Martin, DI Rob Marshall is dialling into this.' Bruce waved at a camera. 'You can hear him, but you can't see him.'

Marshall leaned forward and spoke into the microphone: 'Good morning, Martin.'

Keane shook his head, as if he was marvelling at the wonder of modern technology.

'If I was you, Martin, I'd be talking to my colleague.' Bruce was on his feet now. 'But then, I realise what you've got to lose.

Nothing. You've got life sentences stacked up like other people would have pints in a bar. They're going to take you back to prison anyway. So why help us. You don't care what happens out there, do you?'

'Answered your own question there.' Davidson smoothed his hand down his face. 'My client has no reason to help you.'

Marshall cracked his knuckles, took a deep breath and leaned into the mic. He focused on Keane and cracked his knuckles again. Sore. 'Martin. Sorry you haven't decided to work with us but, like my colleague said, you don't really stand to benefit from us solving the crimes. Or from them being committed. I mean, you claim not to know anything about these additional murders and—'

'It's not a claim.' Davidson gave a slow blink.

'If that's true, Martin, then it diminishes your fame. Your notoriety. Your reputation.'

No reaction. Just the same wall of steel. He dug into the other thumbnail, the one that had escaped chewing.

'Let's talk about truth, shall we? Cast your mind back to the night of the fifteenth of August 2021, Mark.'

Davidson looked up at the camera. 'Excuse me?'

'Fifteenth of August, 2021.'

'Is that date supposed to mean something to me?'

'You were in a bar in Edinburgh. Yourself and a friend. Strangely enough, a woman was attacked that night. Afri Shamsuddin. Abducted from the lane at the back of the bar and taken down into the basement, where she was raped and held for a few hours until she escaped.'

'This is preposterous!' Davidson laughed, but his inverted eyebrows betrayed how rattled he was. 'You can't accuse me like this in front of a client.'

'The reason I'm asking you this in front of your client is I want to know the truth about your relationship with him. Mr Davidson, you were raping for him, weren't you?'

'Rape?' Keane raised his hands. 'I never raped anybody!'

Bruce smiled at him. 'Okay, so murder is fine, but rape isn't okay?'

'I don't rape. That's not me.'

'Are you on the level here?'

'If he's...' Keane turned towards his lawyer and Marshall saw the full fury of a killer, long since dormant and buried beneath a cool exterior. Nothing had got to him since his arrest until now – the knowledge his long-term advisor was a rapist. 'I don't rape!'

Davidson had to angle his body, never mind his head, to look at him. 'Martin, this is—'

'You're sacked! Get out of here before I fucking kill you! I can tell you did it, you lying raping bastard! If I see you again, I will cut you into little pieces!'

Marshall's blood was pumping hard now. He could feel it in his throat.

Only now did he notice that Siyal was in the room with him.

Bruce got between Davidson and Keane, then waved a hand at the two prison guards. 'Please take him away and process him. Our colleagues in Edinburgh will be more than interested in spending time with him.'

'On it, sir.' One of them took him by the arm and dragged him out into the corridor.

'This is nonsense!'

Leaving Keane with just one guard. He tilted his head towards the camera. 'Didn't know.'

Marshall took his time trying to get his breathing under control again. 'We didn't either. My colleague suspected and it was a long shot. A one-in-a-million connection that paid off.'

Keane popped a spot on his chin. 'Dirty raping bastard.'

Bruce sat back, twisted side on. 'You honestly never raped anyone?'

'No.' Keane brushed it off with a flick of the wrist like he was dismissing jam before cream on his scone. 'I never raped anyone. I wouldn't. I *couldn't*, I...'

'A lot of people who kill escalate from rape to murder.'

'I didn't.' Keane stared at Bruce, a spider considering a fly. 'I kill people. That's it. I do it quick. I don't like touching people or having them touch me!' He scratched his head, vigorously enough to release chunks of dandruff that fell like snow. He crossed his legs, turned away and hugged his arms close to his body.

Marshall waited a few seconds. 'The other escalation path to murder is violence. You started out attacking people. Punching them. Hitting them with pipes. Attacking with knives. Then you figured out about the rope. It was perfect. Trapped them.'

'Right.'

'Listen. As I'm sure you can imagine, we've got a lot of questions outstanding relating to these fresh bodies. We believed there was a copycat there. Someone who took what you did and twisted it for their own ends. But it looks like there were victims there before you murdered three people there. Do you think it could be Mark Davidson?'

Keane rested his fingers on the edge of the desk. He didn't say anything.

'Martin.' Marshall raised his eyebrows. 'You're a man with a message to spread. Other people just want to make people suffer. Torture them. Torment them. You're different, Martin. If it was Mark Davidson copying you, then—'

'I don't rape people. That's not my thing.' Keane looked like he meant it too. Forehead creased, eyes gleaming. 'It's... Kidnapping and raping and torturing. What... How...'

Marshall let his thoughts play out. He was confused and he wanted him to stay that way. 'Did you ever talk to Davidson about how you killed people?'

'No. Just... Um, he told me when to shut up, how to get more out of you lot.'

'What about Alexander Vickers?'

Keane stopped. He twisted his head to the side. 'Alex?'

'You ever talk to him about it?'

'No. He asked. I didn't want to talk.'

'But he's someone Mr Davidson knows, correct?'

'So?'

'He put you both in touch regarding the interviews for his podcast.'

'But?'

'We're looking for two men. We suspect Mr Davidson is one of them. The other's still a mystery.'

'You think Alex was raping with Mark?'

'It fits. And it's not just that sexual assault. The three bodies we found subsequent to yours. Whoever did those, they were abducting men and women. Holding them somewhere. Torturing them. Sexually assaulting them. Then burying them where you killed your last three victims. That seems like a big coincidence to me, Martin. Someone who knew where—'

'I never told anyone where they were. That's what kept me important. That was my weapon.' Keane leaned back on his chair and sniffed. 'I didn't tell Alex where. Didn't tell my lawyer. First time was with you lot.' He snarled. 'You should've told me they'd been raped.'

'We didn't know when I spoke to you last.'

'That woman knew. Elliot. She knew.'

Marshall could see something in Keane. Not an innocence,

but a naivety. Like a part of him hadn't fully matured. He'd been young when he killed those people. Immature in so many ways. 'Martin, we found another two other bodies there last night. They were buried there at the same time as you were active. Buried together, intertwined.'

The blood drained from Keane's face, his eyes wide. 'Not me.'

'But you know who it was, don't you?'

The way he looked away, with a knowing expression and a hesitancy...

He knew.

He fucking knew.

'We've been going through the interview recordings of the chats you had with Alexander Vickers. Not what was broadcast, but the raw interviews. Unabridged. One of the things Vickers asked you about was your father. About how he made you run—'

'I thought I killed him.'

'Your father?'

'It was my fault.' Keane dug into his nose and yanked out a hair or three. He set them on the table and arranged them end to end. 'I killed him.'

'You denied it at the time. When you were interviewed on remand.'

'I did it. It was me.'

'He died when you were in prison.'

'Coma. Never woke up.' Keane looked up at the ceiling. 'He forced me to run. Pushed me. Pushed me too hard. I... I... couldn't take it anymore.' The colour returned to his cheeks as the rage rose again. The eyes of a killer returned. 'I let him go by me and I pushed him back even harder. He fell, hands didn't even go out. Head hit the kerb. Blood, lots of blood!' He looked around the camera, not at it, but through it, remembering... 'I fucking panicked! I ran! He deserved it but I ran.' He looked at the camera with the eyes of a teenager. The first time in years he'd felt something. Those feelings he'd buried, they were coming out now.

'I understand.' Marshall wished he'd been in the room to acknowledge the bridge they'd crossed together, or just to stand on Bruce's foot to stop him interrupting. But all he had was a microphone and speakers. And words. 'You told us it was your friend, Martin. But it was your father?'

'It was.' A tear fell down Keane's cheek, but he made no effort to move it. He stared at the middle of the table between them, quieter now but calmer than ever before. 'Thought I'd make it to London, but only got as far as a service station near Penrith.'

Oh shite.

Oh shite, oh shite, oh shite.

Marshall felt everything clench and tighten.

'Truck pulled up. Guy inside. Offered us a ride to Manchester. I hopped in. We drove. He pulled out a knife. Said he was going to kill me. I told him to go ahead. Knocked me out. Woke up, couldn't move, air mask on my face.'

Marshall could hear his own breathing. Hear his heart hammering. 'Martin, did he sexually assault you?'

'I had no choice.'

There it was.

Some would flock to it like moths to a flame, blaming their crimes on their own traumas, whereas Keane's aversion to rape was because he'd been a victim himself.

'Did he torture you?'

'I begged him to kill me but he wouldn't. I wanted to die. I *needed* to die for what I'd done to my father. What I thought I'd done.'

'You acquiescing must've thrown him.'

'Don't know that. But when someone deserves to die, you should kill them quick and get it over with.'

Marshall was on the path here. Keane was one of the first victims. So he knew who the killer was. Someone who had murdered five people there. And more. Probably more. 'What happened next?'

'He kept me but he didn't hurt me anymore. But he made me hunt with him, father and son. For a few months. We killed two more, but no more raping.'

Goldberg's theoretical protégé was actually the master. Already an established killer... Keane's rapist.

'This was eighteen years ago?'

Keane nodded. Then he was suddenly interested in something in his ear canal, giving it a good dig, then a sniff. 'So I went home. Dad was in a coma but nobody knew. Nobody blamed me. Figured I got what I deserved and I never told anyone. I just did what I could to get by. But I saw that if you didn't have power those that did would hurt you with it. Those people deserved to die, quickly. No raping.'

Marshall stayed quiet. Mercifully, so did Bruce.

Keane rasped the stubble on his throat. 'I was addicted to running. If I didn't run every day, I'd feel like shite. Absolute shite, man. Not a couple of laps around the park. At least ten kilometres. Sometimes twenty. I found an extreme running message board. Found there were others like me.' He swallowed hard. 'But they weren't. They were all rich. Looked down on us. But I had the locations of everyone. I could trap them in isolated locations and kill them, then dispose of the bodies. And it worked.'

'More than we know of?'

'The bodies at Elibank Forest were my last. Those three missing bodies... Kept my name in the public all these years.'

'But your master returned to his old life in anonymity. Did he continue killing?'

'I don't know.'

Marshall didn't want to tip his hat too soon and get him to clam up. 'When did you last speak to him?'

'Not since he let me leave.'

'Are you saying you didn't know this killer and rapist had actually returned to his previous MO somewhere else, yet he was using the same dumping grounds as you?'

'I didn't.' Keane smiled. 'How could I? You know who's been visiting me.'

'That's true, Martin. Mark Davidson and Alexander Vickers are too young to be your friend. So maybe the person who's committing these crimes isn't Alexander Vickers or Mark Davidson, though he appears to be guilty of something. But your master was confident his older crimes would be attributed to you, Martin Keane, the Shadow Man. Who is sworn to silence. He made you. So he's back killing with impunity. Who is he, Martin?'

'I'm not telling you that.'

Honour among thieves was nothing compared to secrecy among murderers.

'Martin, here's the thing. You were in a master-protégé relationship. We assumed you were the dominant partner. And you did your own murders. You were the Shadow Man, after all. But the truth is you...' Marshall tailed off.

The thoughts were jumbling up inside his head now.

But Marshall was on the right path here.

The other player was the leader and Keane was the mere pawn.

But that was then.

Those crimes were back then. The two murders.

'Martin, the two bodies we found there last night. Were you involved?'

Keane shook his head.

'Did you know about them?'

'He promised me! He told me he'd stop!'

'Returning to his raping ways after he promised you. You kill people who deserve it. You've got a code. But how do you feel about raping people who don't? Martin, you staying silent means he is free to rape more people... we actually think he's doing it right now.'

Keane drummed his fingers on the table, like he was bored.

'Her name is Grace, Martin.'

The shaking got even more vigorous.

'Martin, I believe you when you say you never raped anyone.'

'I never would.'

'But your master has been.'

'What?'

'The three recent victims were all tied up in cling film. Someone had repeatedly raped them and cut them.' Marshall left a long pause. 'One last time, Martin. Who is it?'

CHAPTER SIXTY-FIVE
SIYAL

S iyal hated driving on the south bank of the Tweed. Single lane with passing places. Passing places you were supposed to stop at, unlike this cheeky sod who shot towards them in a grey Volkswagen. Would've been much easier for him to just stop and reverse back.

But no, he didn't.

Siyal acted the big man, as McIntyre would say, and slipped the pool Audi into reverse and slid it all the way back to the one he'd passed a couple of hundred metres ago.

'What are you playing at?' Elliot was in the passenger seat, arms folded and scowling like he'd crapped in her sandwich. 'Force *him* back!'

'This is easier.' Siyal stopped and let the red-faced man past, getting a very polite wave for his trouble. A black greyhound was standing up on the back seat. 'See, courtesy costs nothing.'

'Just you wait. I wanted to say, Shunty... Back at the station, but I never got the chance to...' She swallowed hard, making him brace for whatever was coming. 'Well done.'

'What for?'

'For catching that dodgy lawyer.'

'There's a lot of work left to do on it.'

'Even so, excellent work. My old team in Edinburgh will prosecute him.'

Siyal kept shut about how Marshall had saved the day on that one. 'He'll have to admit it first. We'll have to get evidence.'

'All the same. Great work.' Elliot sucked in a deep breath through her nostrils. 'You know Davidson's mates with Pringle, right?'

'As in our boss?'

'As in him. Go back a long way.' She leaned over and patted his arm. 'Good work, Shunty.'

He drove on in silence as the road descended down to the river level. Maybe he was finally in her good books now.

'Thing is, though, we don't know who the other lad in your video is.'

Siyal shrugged. 'I'm sure they'll get Davidson to crack, right?' He pulled into the car park, that stiff bank climbing up into the woods.

Nowhere near as many cops around today as yesterday or even Monday, but the place was stuffed with Forestry and Land four-by-fours. Didn't seem to be doing much, just standing around chatting. Laughing, even.

Siyal pulled in, blocking their exit, and got out. He made his way over and held out his warrant card. 'Hey, I'm looking for Adrian Robinson.'

Siyal recognised the main guy there. Bett-Leighton? Leighton-Bett? One of the two. 'Why are you asking?'

Because he's a serial murderer...

Siyal got a bit of a thrill from the realisation he wouldn't have done this when he started just a few months ago. 'We just need a word with him, that's all.'

'Look, we're doing all we can to support you guys here. Maybe there just aren't any more bodies here?'

Siyal smiled at him. 'We appreciate all you guys are giving.'

'Right.' Bett-Leighton sighed. 'Haven't seen Ade today. Left in his truck last night at sunset.'

'Okay, thanks.' Siyal walked back to the car. The others had arrived. Four squads of uniforms and two sergeants.

Elliot was corralling them to organise a search.

Siyal got out his phone, calling Marshall. 'Rob, he's not here.'

CHAPTER SIXTY-SIX

Marshall was taking no prisoners during rush hour – the day felt like it had been going on for weeks, let alone just starting. He pulled up, indicating right. A van led a long queue of cars heading north on the A7 through Selkirk. He'd be sitting here for hours.

He went for it, shooting across the path of the van, and sped around the bend, past the same mill buildings as the other day. That was a weaver, not a distillery, after all. He took the next right and parked between two big work trucks and got out into the thin rain. He set off over to the office building, a six-storey mill that seemed to have a ton of tenants. Still marked with the Forestry Commission signage, the same styling as at Elibank a few miles northwest over those brutal hills.

Two mornings ago, he'd been here to help stake out the brewery a few mills along.

'Let me get this straight...' Jolene was walking alongside him. 'Adrian Robinson buried victims at a site he was in control of?'

'That's right. First we need to find him, then we can worry about whether he's killed anyone else.'

'Do you think he has Grace?'

'I'm starting to see a pattern forming here.' Marshall held the door for her. 'But it could be confirmation bias.'

Jolene didn't enter. 'Confirmation bias?'

'Finding what you want to, rather than what's there.' Marshall walked past her and strolled up to the reception. He smiled at the silver-haired rascal behind the desk. 'Looking for Adrian Robinson.'

'Adrian? Adrian, Adrian, Adrian...' He frowned. 'Oh. Aye. Sorry, but the laddie isn't here. Been out all day at Elibank. Police found some bodies there.'

Marshall held out his warrant card. 'We are the police. And he's not there.'

'Oh.'

'Any idea when he last clocked on?'

'Just a second...' He tapped away at a computer. 'Here we go. Last night just after four o'clock.'

'Where was that?'

'Looks like he was here. Funny that. And before that, he was on site at Elibank. Like I said.'

That matched what Elliot and Siyal had found. And her being her, she didn't believe anyone so was checking the site personally with a big team.

Jolene leaned across the desk. 'Have you got a home address for him?'

CHAPTER SIXTY-SEVEN

Jolene pressed the bell again, her impatience making her skin whiten around the edges of her thumb. 'He's not in, is he?'

Marshall did another scan of the area. One of those Peebles estates that hadn't even existed when he was young, all post-millennium stuff. Boxes pushed too close together, the rooms squished to fit even more into the plot. At least they looked nice.

Robinson's house was show-home empty, though. Double-car garage. Big lawn that could do with its last mow of the year. The biggest of three trees was a beech smaller than Marshall. Whatever passion Robinson put into the natural world, it didn't translate to his home.

Marshall peered into the living room. Battered leather sofa opposite the window. No telly, no hi-fi. Not much furniture. If you got your kicks from abductions, you had all the entertainment you needed in your head. 'No, I agree with that assessment.'

Two driveways, one empty, a work truck sitting in the

other. Not Forestry and Land, but a white Ford Ranger pickup with windows in the back. Not dissimilar to the one on the video from Penrith.

Marshall's phone rang.

Liana calling...

That could wait. He didn't want that drama right now.

'I'll check around the back.' Jolene squeezed between the garage wall and the neighbour's.

Marshall got out his phone and called Elliot.

'Finally.' Elliot was panting down the line. 'Decided to call me back, eh?'

'What are you talking about?'

'Been trying for the last ten minutes, Marshall.'

'Well, my phone hasn't rung. Whatever. We're at Peebles now and there's no sign of him.'

'Huh. Well. We're still at Elibank, scouring the place for Robinson and this victim.'

'I told you to spread out, Andrea...'

'And we have.'

'How many is we?'

'Forty.'

Fuck's sake.

'Andrea, we need to—'

'Tell a lie. Forty-three.'

'Andrea, you need to get people out going door-to-door all across the Borders. Especially around here. Me and Jolene doing all of the legwork isn't going to cut it.'

'So you don't think he's here?'

'At Elibank? No, I didn't say that. But I want at least twenty of that lot running down leads at his workplace. Get Rakesh to build a strategic framework around this.'

A long pause, filled with the sound of Elliot licking her lips. 'You think you can give me orders?'

Marshall didn't have time for this. 'Andrea, I'm helping you do your job. Which is catching a serial killer.'

'I'll send a few of them over to you but I'm putting my money on him being here.'

'A *few*? I need at least twenty.'

She laughed.

'Are you winding me up?'

'Aye, of course I am, you daft bugger. That's what you get for not picking up. They're on their way already.'

'It didn't ring...' Marshall's heart was thudding – he needed to stop letting her get at him like that.

'I've got twenty out running down leads in Selkirk. A ton at Elibank, with all of his lads, just in case he is actually there. I'll send the others to you. Shunty's running his telephony now with Weirdo.'

'Fine. We're at his home just now. I'll report back.' Marshall killed the call and pocketed the phone. He hated being played like that. Walking into her trap.

The master psychologist wound up by someone who did crosswords in crayon.

Either way, it didn't look like Adrian Robinson was home, so he crossed onto the neighbour's drive and knocked on the door.

'Just a second!' The door opened and a big black dog's face loomed out, all slobbers and kisses and sniffs. 'Get back!' The dog disappeared inside and was replaced by a guy in his fifties. Belly and long dark hair. 'What's up, pal?' Gentle Glasgow accent. Ginger beard. Pink apron covered in flour.

'Sorry to bother you so early, sir.' Marshall showed his warrant card. 'Looking for your neighbour.'

'Adrian, aye?'

'Adrian Robinson.' Marshall put his ID away. 'You know him?'

'Not well, no. Lad's a bit of a loner. Keeps weird hours, but his job takes him across Scotland. Bonzo!' He tugged at the dog's lead, then shoved him back into the house and stepped outside. 'Sorry. Just got the big lad and he's a fair amount of work. Anyway. Where were we?'

'Your neighbour.'

'Aye, aye. Like I say, don't know him well.'

'Anybody else in the street—'

'Jim and Fi over the road had him in one Hogmanay. Must be... five years back? Six.' He scratched his hair, face scrunched up, like the exact year was of critical importance, then snapped out of it. 'Anyway, Jim's a *demon* with the drink, tell you that for nothing!' He laughed. 'His measures are something else! Ade next door, he was slurping gin like my grandson drinking juice. Mullered. Wrecked. Absolutely cu—' He coughed. 'Started crying and he went home. Barely spoke to him since.'

The loner thing was playing out. Maybe that volume of alcohol let the demons out.

'He's still got my strimmer!'

'Your strimmer?'

'Aye, my lawn strimmer.' He was outside now, bare feet on the slabs. 'Borrowed it last summer to go over his edging. Never returned it, eh? Still got my battery too.'

'When was the last time you saw him?'

'Then!'

'No. I mean, when was the last time you were aware he was here?'

'Last night. Car came back about half ten.'

'At night?'

'Aye.'

Weird.

433

Last spotted at the Forestry and Land office in Selkirk just after four. More than six hours unaccounted for, but less than half an hour of that would be driving over here.

Made Marshall think he had someone.

Was it Grace, though?

Or was that just confirmation bias?

Marshall looked over at the pickup. 'Was that what he came back in last night?'

He scowled at Marshall. 'What are you talking about?'

'The truck?'

'Are you corned beef? I said car. That's a truck. It was gone first thing, mind, when Sheena went to her work. Had to defrost the motor for her. I didn't see him leave.'

'Okay, sir. Thank you for your time.' Marshall handed him a card. 'If you hear from him, please call me on any of these numbers.'

'Aye, just listen out for the phone ringing, eh?'

'One last thing. Do you know where he went on holiday?'

'Holiday?'

'Aye, he's been away for two weeks.'

'Nope. That motor's been here all that time.'

'You're sure?'

'Not all that time, like. He'd be out for a few hours at a stretch.' He went back inside. 'Come on, you. Let's get you out for your walk, eh?'

Marshall didn't know any other way to process it but that Robinson had been lying to colleagues about where he was going so he could build up a head of steam on his latest abduction. Probably drove down to that truck stop several times a week, like a desperate man scouring the reduced section in a supermarket, waiting for a tempting offer. Out patrolling his hunting grounds.

Marshall couldn't escape the feeling that she might be inside the house. And he didn't have a warrant.

'Sir?' Jolene tapped the back window of the pickup. 'There's something in the bed there.'

Marshall peered inside the window. A Batman sticker was stuck to the window, partially obscuring it. The truck bed was immaculate, considering it was a forestry worker's vehicle.

Empty, save for a doll.

No, a bear.

With a red jumper.

Mr Teddy.

Grace's doll.

She was here.

Marshall charged over to the house. 'Call Kirsten and get a team out to catalogue and dust that truck.'

'What are you doing?'

'We've got probable cause here.' Marshall kicked the door open. Quiet inside, just the squeaking of the door on the hinge.

Jolene followed him in. 'Had a wee look around from outside. Nobody's in.'

'Let's see, shall we?' Marshall raced up the stairs, two by two.

Three doors.

First was a bathroom. The tub was empty, nowhere else to hide in there.

The other door was an office, with a single bed next to the window. Where Keane would've slept. That computer was gold dust, assuming it wasn't encrypted to buggery.

Marshall opened the other door. The master bedroom. Immaculately made, like a hotel. A bag lay on the bed. Open, clothes spilling out.

Robinson was planning on leaving.

But he hadn't escaped yet.

CHAPTER SIXTY-EIGHT
SIYAL

'Tell you something, Shunty.' Elliot was driving like a maniac on a road that needed absolute sanity. 'That call from Marshall about not finding him at his home... Feel it in my water. We're going to get him here.'

Siyal looked up from the text message, still not sure how to break the news to her. Sod it – out with it was the only way. 'Sorry, ma'am, but the trace on his phone just came back. It's been off since before four yesterday evening.'

'Figures...' She snorted. 'We'll get him here.'

'Wish I had your confidence.'

'Shunty, when you do a search of someone's phone's location history, we can build up a picture of where it's been in the past.'

'Sounds like the sort of geographic profiling Ro— DI Marshall would do.'

'Does it, aye? Question we're going to answer is, does he turn it off every time he goes to his lair to rape his victims? If not, we'll get where his lair is. If so, we'll see where he turns it off and where he turns it back on again. Either will give us a broad location. Come on, Shunty. This is basic stuff.'

He should've been back at base, coordinating a manhunt across the whole county. Something like two thousand square miles they had to cover, most of it hills or woodland. And that was assuming he hadn't just left the country.

'You into ice hockey, Shunty?'

Siyal looked over. 'Not really, no.'

'My stepbrother played semi-professionally in Canada for a few years. Much colder there than here. Warmer in the summer, mind. We've got this pretty much constant climate but theirs is like minus thirty to thirty. Anyway. Wayne Gretzky said this thing, which was his favourite quote. Still is, even though he's a bit of a snooty wanker. Ideas above his station, that one. Runs a bar in Niagara. Big Jim's. He's neither big nor a Jim, but hey ho.'

Those months off hadn't curtailed her ability to spin an anecdote out into absolute tedium.

'And this saying?'

'Right. Right. It's something like, "I skate to where the puck's going to be, not to where it's been". That's what we're doing.'

'No it's not.'

'How not?'

'It's the complete opposite of that!' Siyal gripped the handle above the door extra tight. 'Kirsten sent us a list of all the locations Robinson's phone's been over the last six months. You're literally heading to where he's been, not where he's going to be.'

'Told you, Shunty – I feel it in my water.'

Who needed forensics when you had her gut instinct?

She flicked the indicator left and pulled into a rain-soaked car park. An actual car park, rather than some logging site. Similar Forestry Commission sign post as at Elibank:

Cardrona Forest

Empty in the rain and this early hour. No dog walkers out. Too early for cyclists or horse riders. Puddles pocked the empty spaces. The gate leading to the path was locked.

Elliot sat there, engine running. Tapping the steering wheel with her fingers. 'He'd have a key.'

'Excuse me?'

'These gates. One at Elibank. One here. They're all locked. Bett-Leighton had a key for that one. Stands to reason Robinson would have one for here. If we could get through, we could drive down and see if he's there.'

'Ma'am, there's no evidence he's here, is—'

'Or we could get out and walk.' She ducked around to look outside. 'Don't fancy it much, but he's here. I just know he is.'

'Seriously. I think we need to get back to base. Devise a strategy around this. Rally the troops. Get—'

'Fuck that.' She reached over to the cradle and snatched her phone off with a sharp crack. 'This is how you do it.' She hit a number and put her phone to her ear. 'We're fucking about here, Shunty. Marshall and Pringle are pussyfooting around with warrants and DNA and search strategies, so I'm going to — Hello, Adrian.'

Siyal swivelled around. 'What the hell are you doing?'

She was clicking her fingers at Siyal, mouthing 'Trace it!'

He texted Kirsten:

> Trace Robinson number now

> Elliot on call with now

She turned away from him. 'I don't think it's daft, Adrian. Just you and me, chatting.' She laughed. 'DI Andrea Elliot. You might remember me from such crime scenes as Elibank, where you killed and buried three people in the last nine months. Talk about shitting where you eat.' She sniffed. 'Let's have a wee word about Grace Paton, shall we?' She reached over and turned the stereo on. 'I know you've got her.' She laughed again. 'Because you left her teddy in your truck, you fud!'

'—she'll die,' Robinson's deep voice boomed out of the speakers. 'No matter what you do, she will die because I'll never tell you where she is.'

'Listen here, dickhead, we know it's you. We are coming after you.' Subtle as a bag of hammers. 'We know where you are right now.' The way she could lie just like that... 'We have a team of armed officers on their way there right now. Your only way out of this, Mr Robinson, is to give us Grace. Alive.'

The line went quiet.

Siyal's phone was ringing on silent.

Kirsten calling...

He got out into the rain, nudging the door shut, and put it to his ear. 'Hi.'

'It's Kirsten. I've got a trace on that number but he's moving. On the A7. South of Hawick. Heading towards Carlisle.'

'Thanks. Keep on it. She's still on with him.' He hung up and called Marshall. 'Rob, it's Rakesh. Elliot's on the phone to Robinson just—'

'She's *what?*'

'Kirsten's got a live trace. He's on the A7 heading to Carlisle from Hawick.'

'On it.' Sounded like Marshall was running. 'Keep me updated.' Click and he was gone.

Siyal got back in the car.

'—the deal is no sentence for Grace's life.' Robinson's voice was ice cold. Eerily calm. 'I want your boss at the station when I get there with a deal already inked...'

'You and I both know how difficult that's going to be, Adrian.' Elliot looked around at Siyal, shifting her thumb between up and down then back again.

He gave her the thumbs up.

'Here we go, Adrian. One last push. The only offer I can make. Grace's life in exchange for a fifteen-year sentence.'

The line clicked and crackled.

'Adrian, that's a really good deal. You won't get any better. Guarantee that now.'

'You're going to have to live with the fact a tasty little girl died because of you.'

'Don't be an idiot, Adrian. When we catch you, you're going to rot in His Majesty's prison for the rest of your life. Will you be able to live with the fact your "tasty little girl" died because of you?'

The line went silent.

Siyal had to check it hadn't died.

'And you can still save her. Come on, Adrian. You seem like a good guy. You're forty-six now. You'll be out before you retire, maybe earlier if you're a good boy. What's it to be?'

CHAPTER SIXTY-NINE
MARSHALL

Marshall stood in the station car park, phone to his ear. 'Aye, we're still waiting.'

Siyal was driving. 'Are you sure you don't need me?'

'It's fine, Rakesh. You've been great. You head on up to Edinburgh. Sounds like they'll need your expertise to prosecute Davidson.'

'Not so sure.'

'Why?'

'Kirsten thinks one of the old team wiped the evidence.'

'And you know who, right?'

'Got a good idea, aye.'

'I'll cover it off with Elliot. Let me know how it goes, okay?'

'Cheers, Rob.'

Marshall put his phone away.

Still no sign of Pringle, but the light was on in Marshall's office. He had no idea what was going on up there, but the core truth was a lump of coal in his stomach, burning his flesh —

Grace Paton was still alive and only Adrian Robinson knew where she was.

He spotted the lights on the main street leading into Melrose, a presidential motorcade for a serial killer.

Two squad cars wrapped around Adrian Robinson's Mitsubishi. The first slowed and blocked the entrance at an angle, lights flashing. Robinson pulled in and parked just metres from Marshall. Engine off. He got out and sank to his knees.

Four armed cops trained their weapons on him. Even in provincial Scotland, guns were a necessity when dealing with someone like him.

A serial killer. Not the first Marshall had encountered, but possibly the worst. Probably. Five victims they knew of. Three decomposing bodies. Two bundles of bones. Years apart, so who knew how many there were between. Keane had given them an idea there were none. Marshall didn't believe it.

Grace Paton was out there. Alive. Waiting.

Probably.

Talk about pressure.

Marshall nodded at McIntyre. 'Protect him.'

'Sir.' The big lump knew what he was doing. He grabbed hold of the serial murderer. Cuffed him. Walked him inside. Everything above board. McIntyre led the troop of uniforms inside Melrose nick.

Another car pulled up on the kerb and Elliot stormed out. 'Where is he?'

He blocked her off. 'Lawyer's inside. Waiting for us.'

'Marshall. Do you mind getting out of my way?'

'I do, aye.'

'What are you...?' She laughed. 'You're stopping me getting in there?'

'Keep your voice down.' He grabbed her arm and walked

her away from the rest of the team, over onto the grass of the park. 'What the fuck were you playing at?'

'It's called getting a result. You might've heard of it?'

'It was extremely dangerous, Andrea.'

'Come on. He was halfway to Carlisle when I called him. Running away. And he fucking answered.' She prodded a finger in his chest. 'See, this is the difference between you and me, Marshall. You think too much. It's all psychobabble bullshit with you. You don't have enough heart.'

'Heart? That's great. Andrea. I'm a professional. You should think about acting—'

'Aye, and professionalism doesn't get results, does it? Sometimes you need to bend the rules.'

'You're out of control.'

She barked out another laugh. 'That's good.'

'I'm serious. That was incredibly risky. You alerted him to the fact we'd identified him as the killer.'

'And because of me, we've got him in custody.'

'But we don't have Grace Paton.'

That shut Elliot up.

'Andrea. We have no idea where she is.'

'We'll get her.'

'Because you offered him some bullshit deal?' Marshall shook his head. 'I wish I had your arrogance.'

'You've got your own arrogance, Marshall. Three bags full of it.'

'There's a whole list of things I want to address with you, Andrea.'

She laughed again. 'Oh, aye.'

'Now's not the time. We've got to find Grace.'

'Or her body.' He thought she'd be furious, but she was grinning.

'Whatever happens to you, Andrea, it's all on you. I hope you can deal with that.'

She held his gaze this time. Chewing her cheek.

'Don't kiss!' Pringle got between them and chuckled. 'Christ, you could cut the sexual tension with a knife! Almost had to!' He made a slicing motion through the air.

Marshall stepped away onto the rugby pitch markings. 'Sir, that's completely inappropriate.'

'Sure, but it got you to stop bullying her.'

'*Me*? She's the aggressor here.'

'Okay, okay.' Pringle raised his hands, palms facing Elliot. 'Look, us three need to sort out whatever this lover's tiff is before I find you smashing each other's back doors in behind the bins.'

'Jim!' Elliot prodded a finger into his chest. 'How dare you? I'm a married woman. Happily married. With three kids. I'm not interested in the forty-year-old virgin here.'

Pringle cackled. 'Ex-squeeze me.' He held up his hand. 'Look. We've got our guy in our clutches, not on crutches yet, but he's got the girl. Our priority's recovering Grace Paton.'

Elliot tugged at his jacket sleeve. 'If you'll listen to me, Jim, he's going to tell us!'

Pringle coughed. 'The PF won't take the deal.'

'Wait, what? She won't take fifteen years? He fucking agreed to it, Jim. I got that. *I* got that. And she's... Fucking hell!'

'It's not as simple as that, Andrea. This is a cross-border issue. Scots and English law are both in effect until we settle on charges. It's not just the PF, we've got the bonnie lad, AKA the Geordie Crown Prosecutor, to boogie with.'

'So which one's put the kibosh on this?'

'Both. It's not on, Andrea. We've got a serial killer who's topped five people we know of. Who conspired with Martin Keane to—'

'We've also got a live abduction, Jim! Didn't you tell them that?'

'I made them aware of the operational emergency, but we can't set precedents like this or any serial killer will just make sure they've got a live victim somewhere in case they get caught. Lo and behold, pheep pheep pheeeeeeep, fifteen years precedent or I don't disclose where they are.'

'For fuck's sake.'

'You can swear all you like, but Robinson's in custody, meaning we've got a chance.'

'And Grace fucking Paton? What about her?'

'That's in our gift.'

'Our *gift*. Jesus Christ. Secret bloody Santa bollocks.'

Another car pulled up, stopping on the corner.

Marshall expected press but this wasn't London or Edinburgh, so there was no big city media to leak to. At least none who could get here that quickly.

Bruce and Liana got out at the same time. She wore a thick winter jacket. Grey, furry hood. He just wore a suit.

Marshall walked over and stopped them getting into the station. 'What are you doing here?'

'Nice to see you too.'

'Eh, we're both part of the investigation.' Bruce barged past him and headed towards Pringle and Elliot's barney.

Leaving Marshall with Liana. 'I thought you weren't working this case?'

She pointed at Bruce. 'His boss spoke to mine. They agreed something. I had no choice.'

'That happened to Goldberg.'

'And I could do with a whisky right about now.' She held up her hands. 'Sorry, that's not funny.'

'No.'

She swallowed. 'Bruce got a call from Pringle on the way up. It's Adrian Robinson, right?'

'Right.'

'So, *you* caught him?'

'We... Well, it's not that simple.'

'But you got Keane to identify him.'

'That's true. But he's got another missing victim. Wait.' Marshall frowned. Something didn't feel right. 'You were coming here already?'

'Tried calling but you didn't pick up.' She brushed a stray hair out of her face. 'We had him down as a suspect.'

'Robinson?'

'Right. I was with Bruce's guys, going through the laptop they recovered. Robinson had been interviewed for the podcast.'

That didn't make any sense. 'Why?'

'Because he manages the site where the last killings happened.'

'We didn't know about Elibank then?'

'No, Kielder Forest. He was in charge of an operation to protect the red squirrels there. Half of England's surviving population are there. He gave background on the area. Local colour. But those were the files that were deleted.'

Why delete some seemingly innocuous files about squirrels? 'When was this?'

'Ten months ago.'

Marshall slotted that into the timeline. 'This is before he started killing again.'

'Could've been a trigger to do it again. Talking to Vickers about the crimes of his protégé.' She held up a hand. 'Sorry, I know you don't like that word, Rob; neither him nor Keane will kill again.'

'If we recover Grace.'

Liana tapped her fingers off her chest in a nervous pattern. She stormed over to Pringle. 'Here's what's going to happen. Marshall and I are going to interview Robinson.'

Elliot laughed. 'Hold on a minute, sister. Last I heard, you're not even on this investigation. I'm the one who got him to give himself up.'

'Andrea.' Marshall took over, hands raised. 'The problem is, as soon as you let him down, he won't want to deal with you.'

'So it's you and Professor Pe— Curtis here?'

'I think that should be the first plan of attack, aye. But if we fail, you can go at him with Jon Bruce. How does that sound?'

'Sounds like a punch in the tits, but it feels like a grope on my arse.' Elliot folded her arms. 'Fine. You two get your glad rags on, a bit of lippy, and make an arse of it.' She punched Bruce's arm. 'Me and this one will figure out how to recover it from your disaster.'

'Let's do it.' Marshall headed inside before anyone objected.

CHAPTER SEVENTY

Marshall put his coffee cup in the sink and filled it with water. 'Okay. Let's do this, then.' He held the door for Liana.

She didn't go through the door. Just stayed there, arms folded. 'Your friend's a piece of work.'

'Elliot? She's no friend of mine.'

'What was she going to call me? Professor what?'

Marshall looked at her but didn't know whether he should spell it out or not. 'Professor Plums used to be her nickname for me. Then it became Doctor Donkey. Yours is Professor Pert.'

'Could've been worse, but my arse is pretty saggy at the best of times. Sorry you have to work with her, Rob.'

'To be honest, I haven't had to so far. Worked with her as a consultant for a couple of days, then she got stabbed. She's just back two days now and is acting like I've taken her job.'

Liana started off along the corridor. 'Have you?'

'Hardly. I'm a specialist. I've got a team and I had to cover for her but... She's an experienced cop. Something I'm not. Not in the same way.'

'If she's that experienced, why the hell did she phone a serial killer?'

'I can't believe she did that. Absolute cowboy. Cowgirl.'

'Maybe you could be a bit more cowboy, Rob?'

'Can't find chaps that fit me.' Marshall stopped outside the interview room and took a deep breath. 'Okay. So we're going to interview a serial killer. We've got to recover a missing victim, who may or may not be dead. No pressure, eh?'

'Half an hour chatting through strategy over a crap coffee in your canteen isn't enough. We could do with a few hours.' She entered the room.

Marshall followed her in. Just like old times.

Adrian Robinson sat on the other side of the table like they were at a business meeting. All jovial. Smiling. Red-faced. His ginger stubble was almost a beard, but not quite. 'Where do I know you from, princess?'

Liana slipped off her coat and rested it on the back of the chair, then perched. 'Surprised that patter works when you're picking up strays at truck stops.'

'It's not a case of charming them, it's just a case of offering enough of them a ride. Twenty, thirty, forty. Eventually one will get in. All about probability versus expectation. Do something enough and it'll happen eventually.'

'I thought you were going to be cagey with us.'

'That a technical term?'

'No. But I did think it and yet you're sitting there like this is all fine, confessing to your murders.'

'I do recognise your face.'

She smiled at him, like she was away to give him a sports massage. 'My name's Professor Liana Curtis. I run the Centre for Criminal Profiling Excellence at the University of Durham.'

'Sounds impressive.' Robinson waved across the table at

Marshall. 'I don't really know this guy, but he seemed very interested in me when I arrived. Is he a janitor or something?'

'Detective Inspector Rob Marshall.'

'I'm Adrian Robinson. I look after thousands of acres of plantation. This is my lawyer. Alistair Reynolds.'

Reynolds still looked like he needed a babysitter – smooth skin, baby-blue eyes and perfectly weighted dark hair. Yet here he was defending a serial killer.

Robinson's focus was on Liana, though. 'Still don't know where I know your pretty face from, my darling.'

'Let's get this out of the way, first.' Liana leaned forward, resting her arms on the table. 'There's no deal.'

'Sorry?' Robinson tapped his left ear. 'Thought you said there's no deal.'

'That's right.'

'Reason I'm here is because I was promised one.'

'Sorry about that. It's really bad when you go somewhere on false pretences. Like, say, into someone's truck when, say, they tell you they're actually a good guy, but really they're, say, a rapist and murderer.'

Robinson threw his hands up in the air. He didn't say anything.

Reynolds cleared his throat. 'In that case, I have to caution my client that he is here under false pretences and it is in his best interests to say nothing.'

Robinson nodded slowly.

Marshall kicked the base of Liana's chair, instructing her he was going to take over. At least, that's how they used to play it. 'Trouble is, Adrian, you're in here. A police station. With no deal. And a charge sheet covering five bodies.'

'And your trouble, DI Robert Marshall, is you've got someone you need to recover. How badly do you want to find her?'

'Adrian, just tell us where she is.'

'Fifteen years. Not served. Sentence. Then I'll talk.'

Marshall leaned back in his chair until it creaked. 'Not going to happen. Meanwhile, you—'

'I'm getting out of prison in eight years with good service. I'll be a good boy. Head down, thumbs up. You won't need to worry about me. My killing days are over. But if you think you're going to get me to give up that girl's location without a deal? You're dafter than you look.'

Marshall felt a thud on the base of his chair.

'Let me spell out the situation for you.' Liana rested her hands on the table, facing upwards. 'You've worked for the Forestry Commission for over twenty years. Now called Forestry and Land Scotland. Got yourself into a senior position there. Managing tens of thousands of acres of woodland, like you say. But that's your day job. At night and on your holidays, you target young people. One in twenty, thirty, forty, fifty will get into your truck. You abduct them then rape and kill them. You bury them with virtual impunity as you are in charge of all that land. You know where the bodies will decompose best, so that by the time the trees are forested, not even their bones will be an issue.' She leaned forward, smiling. 'But it's the reason we're interested in. Why are you doing it, Adrian?'

Robinson licked his lips. Crossing and uncrossing his arms. Twisting his lips now. Shifting his focus between Marshall and Liana. 'Why not?'

She smiled. 'Not a difficult question to answer. Thing is, I don't kill. Never even thought about it. Rob here doesn't. Alistair, do you?'

The lawyer's eyes widened. 'Excuse me?'

'Do you kill?'

'No!?'

'Do you think about it?'

'Of course not!'

'But your client here thinks it's okay to kill. And to keep on killing. He's a serial killer.' She leaned forward again, cracking her elbows on the table. 'And he's like the Bruce Wayne of serial killers. From what I gather, he took in a Robin. Martin Keane. The pair of them abducted and killed multiple victims, pretending to be father and son.'

Adrian's eyes shot out on stalks. 'What?'

'Maybe it's more Hannibal Lecter crossed with Batman and Robin?'

'Don't be facetious.'

Liana shrugged. 'You're both psychopaths. Keane confessed to his crimes. I wonder how many more there are where we haven't found the bodies.'

'Those were nothing to do with me. He killed them and kept quiet for ten years.'

Marshall stepped in. 'The three at Elibank were.'

'Excuse me?'

'Layla, Steven and—'

'I don't know their names, son.'

'There are undiscovered remains from the time Martin was staying with you.'

'No, there aren't.'

'Funny thing about Martin Keane is he's honest. Doesn't seem to be capable of lying. Sure, he withheld the location of the graves of his final three victims. But you... You can't seem to tell the truth.' Marshall held his glare. Reflected it back on him. 'We will find them. Eventually. And you'll be charged with every single one. What you won't get is a fifteen-year sentence.'

'Then you won't get Grace.'

Unstoppable force meets immovable object...

Robinson sat back. The garrulous man was gone, replaced

by the angry inner demon. Nostrils flaring. Angry. Raging, even. But saying nothing. He knew the power of silence. Or he was remembering it.

'What made you start killing in the first place?' Liana was coiling her hair around her fingers. 'When, even?'

'I'm not going to tell you that.'

'Why not?'

'Because it's none of your business.'

'It's my job, Adrian. That makes it my business. Killing is. Serial killing, especially. Like you and trees and squirrels.'

Robinson just shook his head. 'There's a lot more to it than that.'

'Yes. Burying bodies where you worked. Why did you do that?'

Robinson sighed. 'Because I could.'

'Martin buried them in shallow graves. He staked them out. You were burying them in deep graves. Why?'

Robinson stared at her. Then at Marshall. Then up at the ceiling. He sniffed. And again. Then at his lawyer, but he got nothing from him. 'You want the truth?'

'No, lies is what we thrive on.' She smiled. 'Truth, please.'

'My father abused me as a kid. My own dad. My own flesh and blood. Both me and my brother. I was five. John was seven. Kept going on for years. Years and years. John... When he was fourteen, John ran away and escaped it. But I stayed. I bore the brunt of it.'

'That's why you attack runaways?'

Robinson ran a hand down his face.

'What happened to John?'

'I don't know.'

'Did he die?'

'I swear, I don't know. Never saw him again.' Robinson

swallowed hard. 'But I killed and buried my own father. Twenty years ago.'

'Those remains are his?'

Robinson nodded.

'And the other?'

'No idea of his name. The one before I took Martin. Found him in Carlisle. Walking where he shouldn't. Got him in the truck. First boy I'd killed.'

'What about your dad?'

'He was a man. This one was a boy. Sixteen, seventeen.'

Marshall could see it. He had closure on his father's fate, but not on his brother's.

'Women were easier to get in the truck, strangely enough.'

'How many did you kill?'

'Six.'

'Where are they buried?'

'Galloway Forest. Tweed Valley. Kielder Forest. Can't remember where else.'

'Your first victims and you can't remember where you buried them?'

'That's correct.'

'Why did you switch from women to men?' Marshall raised his hand. 'Sorry, girls to boys.'

'Because I wanted to see if I could. That first one fought me off. Bit me. They all tried. The girls would scratch and spit. But he punched. I hit him hard but he kept on fighting so I smashed his head in with a hammer. He didn't fight back then. Which was a disappointment.'

Marshall remembered his chat with Owusu. 'He was a big lad, right?'

'Bigger than you, aye.'

'Was he really the one before Martin?'

'No.' Robinson smirked. 'There were others.'

'I know why you switched, Adrian. Why you stopped killing girls and started targeting boys.'

'You think I'm gay, right?'

'No. Your crimes have a sexual nature to them, but they weren't sexually motivated. You were looking for closure on your own trauma. When you killed your dad, you thought that would be it. Like Bruce Wayne stopping the man who shot and killed his parents. But it didn't end, did it? Because you needed to know what happened to your brother.'

'I started staking out places where runaways would go. I saw lots of girls but fewer boys. I... That's when I took him. To see if John would've been able to fight off an attacker. I was... Jesus. Look, I liked killing. Having power over these people. Being able to decide where they died. When. How. But I'm not telling you where I buried them. I mean, part of me thinks you'll find them. But the rest of me knows you won't. So much land to search. And these will be extremely decomposed by now.'

He was right. But they would look. Some would never stop.

Robinson was talking. Opening up about why he did what he did. Those vicious crimes. And Marshall had to keep him talking.

'Let's talk about Grace.' Marshall put her photo on the table. 'You recognise her?'

Robinson stared at the photo. 'I'm not giving you anything. All this will be inadmissible due to the lies I was told.'

Reynolds pinched his nose. 'Adrian, that's not true.'

'Eh?'

'The police can use any trickery they like to obtain a confession. The only thing they can't really do is deprive you of counsel. You should've shut up when I told you. And kept your mouth closed.'

Robinson's face was glowing red. 'Get out of here!' He

pointed to the door. 'I've got victims older than you. Although I would've liked to have met you five years ago...'

Reynolds grabbed his stuff and shot off.

Marshall waited for Robinson to look at him. 'Come on, Adrian. You picked her up like the other three. Wrapped her in cling film. Raped her. Cut her. But you can't look at her photo?'

Robinson shook his head.

'I spoke to her mother, Adrian. Name's Alexandra. She told me Grace is a good girl. Dad's in jail for armed robbery. Mum doing her best. You know how it is. Grace got into trouble. Ran away from home. Difficult background, but you prey on that, right? Exploit weaknesses in the desperate.'

'Fine. I did it. I took a girl. Grace? Maybe. Don't really know her name. Had some ID with that on. Told me she was called Faith. Besides, they fucking lie to your face about everything.'

'Your victims aren't important to you, are they?'

'Why would they be?'

'Martin Keane killed specific people. But you... It's not about them, it's about your fantasy.' Marshall nodded along with it. 'But these victims. Two bodies from the old days. Then three now, plus Grace. There's a big gap there. Why did you start again?'

'Since you took that deal away, why should I co-operate? I mean, I've taken her, sure, but I will die before I tell you where I've hidden her. Now you get the head lawyer or head cop in here, co-sign a deal with me and we both win. Grace gets to live. You do it soon enough, she'll still be alive.'

'Here's how we see it.' Marshall gestured at Liana. 'You spoke to Alexander Vickers. No idea how he heard of you, but he did. Didn't you wonder about that? Must've made you suspicious... scared maybe? He was asking about Kielder Water. Squirrels, right? I mean, it was just about the location, wasn't it? But even so, he strayed over the lines a bit when you spoke to him and... Well, it must've been a bad interview because he deleted the files.'

Robinson scratched at his neck.

'But you were clearly triggered by it, right? You got the hunger again. Like a dope smoker getting the munchies, you just had to kill again. Layla McMenemy. Steven Cork. Kris Beardsmore. Grace Paton. Thing was, this time when you raped them you couldn't get it up. So you cut them and that helped. The boys were difficult, right? So much shame there so you cut off their penises. Did you wish they were girls? Or were you secretly glad they were boys?'

'Fuck you.'

Marshall had him, like a boxer against the ropes. 'When I spoke to Martin Keane earlier, there was no messing about. He told us your name.'

The room was deadly silent.

'As soon as I mentioned the raping and the cling film, I barely got your name written down quickly enough for his liking. See, Martin was disgusted by the reversion in your MO between then and now. To him, it was all about the purity of the kill. Murder as message. When he learned about how you raped them, that's when he gave you up. Of course, you raped Martin, didn't you? And after you killed together you promised you wouldn't rape again. Keane saw killing those that deserve it as acceptable. It's quick. Robin turning on Batman. Ironic, eh?'

Robinson couldn't look at him. 'Girls were easy. They trust more, they fight less. I want the fight, which is why I've kept Grace alive... "Bring it on. Oh, that was a good cut. Fucking got me with that one, you bastard." It's exhilarating.'

'We could speak to Martin Keane again, Adrian. Ask him where you'd hide a live victim. Give him a chance to ruin you, to become the master, instead of your protégé.' Marshall smiled. 'Maybe you mentioned where you kept them, so you can re-victimise them over and over again. He didn't have to wrestle with where to keep them, but you do. I'm guessing it's someplace underground. A vault, crypt, bunker.'

Robinson was tapping his foot on the ground.

'Come on, Adrian. What's it going to be? Who is the master in this, you or Keane? Not going to lie, getting Grace back will count in Martin's favour or yours. One of you will have the Procurator Fiscal's consideration at some point in the future. Are you going to be the big boy in this or are you finally going to let Martin win?'

'I've got a friend. His family business was in logistics. Went bust a while back. He still owns some of the properties. Including an old mill building in Selkirk.'

CHAPTER SEVENTY-ONE

Marshall hurtled down the A7 towards Selkirk. What still passed for daylight lit up the Ettrick as it headed for its confluence with the Tweed just downriver.

'We work well together, Rob.' Liana was in the passenger seat. Serene, like his granny out on a day trip not someone racing towards a dramatic rescue. 'Like old times when we interviewed offenders in prison. Just with a clock ticking away, right?'

Maybe she was right and it'd be calm. Just get inside the building and find her. Bingo.

Aye, right.

'You made a good choice by becoming a police officer.'

Marshall kept at seventy even when the speed limit changed down to forty. The flashing blue lights of the two squad cars pulled in ahead pushed the traffic up onto the verges. He had to slow when he took the right turn past the timber frame factory, but he didn't go below thirty for the rest of the way. 'I'm a better cop because I was a crap profiler?'

'No, because you recognised how you personally could make a change in the world. And here you are.'

'Let's not count our chickens until they've hatched, eh?'

Another two squad cars parked across the road ahead of the mill, letting Marshall slip into the car park.

Around the corner from Robinson's Forestry and Land office. The same complex as the almost-botched raid two days ago. The craft brewery was busy, with a bearded man enjoying a smoke in the fading light. Lights on inside.

Two of the uniforms from the next car went over to the brewery to shut it down and secure any members of the public already in the shop.

Good luck with that...

Marshall got out into the thin rain himself. The lower of the two buildings looked ready for demolition. A quiet place where Robinson could come and go as he pleased. Unlike others, the brewery didn't have a tap room, though, so Robinson didn't have to worry about people leaving after eight schooners of ten percent liquorice-raspberry stout.

Bruce was out too, gesturing at the faded signage. 'Well, would you look at that...'

Elliot was with him. 'Vickers Haulage? As in—'

'Aye.' Bruce winced. 'He's the pal. Alexander Vickers is the pal.'

Elliot shifted her scowl to focus on Bruce. 'He met Robinson when he was interviewed?'

Bruce shrugged. 'We'll find out. Don't you worry. He's in custody, talking to my lads. We'll get a result. Maybe they knew each other beforehand.'

'Aye, but this goes a lot deeper than interviewing someone about red squirrels.'

Marshall walked over to the building. Two massive roller doors, each big enough to drive a lorry through – easy to bring his victims here undetected. Roll up, drive in and nobody would be any the wiser. Marshall walked up the steps to a side door straight out of a late Eighties double-glazing catalogue, bare aluminium. He tried it. Locked.

He looked around the industrial courtyard, the old, faded parking bays splashed with paint. Twenty officers there. And the ambulance.

Ready.

The door didn't put up much resistance from his right foot and tumbled in, hauling the screws right out of the wall.

Marshall motioned for two of the uniforms to secure it – last thing he needed was someone losing an eye on the rusty old screws sticking out of the wall.

The lights worked. Robinson must've been stealing power from the brewery over the courtyard. The room was huge, with the far end dominated by a giant machine.

Marshall hadn't really considered how big a device you'd need to entirely wrap someone in industrial cling film, but it was colossal. Big as a bin lorry and as grimy. Feed in a pallet loaded with something heavy and cover it in layers of strong film, ready for transporting.

Or wrap a human being wearing an oxygen mask.

Marshall peered inside the jaws of the machine, but there was no sign of Grace in there. He ran his hand through the mechanism and it was empty inside. 'Clear!'

'Over here!' Bruce was at the back of the room, next to an office. Wire glass windows. Desk. Chair. Ancient computer. Filing cabinet, but paperwork everywhere. He opened a double door to reveal a ramp leading down to another pair of doors. 'Perfect place to store a body, right?'

Marshall didn't want to think about it. He set off down. 'A storage room?'

'Right. Most distribution firms need a lot of storage. Perfect place for it, eh?' Bruce seemed to shiver as he twisted a handle, then opened the doors wide and stepped through.

A loud rattle.

Something launched down from the ceiling.

Marshall pushed Bruce out of the way, into the darkness. There was a wet sound, like chopping meat. Dull clanging. A thud.

'Help!' Marshall flicked on his phone torch and shone it into the gloom. Bruce should've been just in front of him, but he was gone. Jesus Christ. What happened?

He swung his torch around and found the swaying remains of Robinson's trap. Like an industrial version of something from Indiana Jones. Not sharp spikes, but pipes with filed-off ends. Hung from the ceiling, ropes connected to the door – there must've been a safe way through for Robinson.

Robinson had set this up.

Robinson hadn't told them about this.

Robinson knew this would take one of them out.

Marshall couldn't see any more triggers, so he crept through the darkness past the trap to where he thought Bruce was.

There – a bloody mess lying on the floor. Deadly still. A massive gouge was taken out of his shoulder. Jesus Christ.

Marshall felt his neck. Still alive, just. 'I need help!' He swung the torch again. A long corridor, leading deep into the bowels of the building.

Footsteps behind him – two uniformed officers with the paramedics, their torchlight bouncing off the walls in the darkness. 'We've got him.'

'Get a light down here and watch for other traps.' Marshall would have stayed to help, but he needed to push on. He managed to squeeze his way through into the vault beyond. Another long corridor with subdivided rooms partitioned off.

The place smelled of oil and the bitter fug of diesel. Each one he tried was locked.

Shite, had they been played? Had Robinson done this to get one final murder? Were there other traps?

'Mmmf!'

What was that?

Marshall walked along the corridor, heading deeper into the gloom and towards the sound.

'Mmmf!'

It came from a door at the end.

He raced towards it.

Unlike the others, this one opened.

A ten-foot metal shipping container filled most of the room.

Marshall scoured the room for— There, a crowbar. He gouged it into the door catch and flipped it open.

A young woman lay inside. Naked, wrapped in cling film, sliced in a few places where her skin was a riot of reds of all shades.

But those eyes were alive. 'Mmmf!'

Grace!

CHAPTER SEVENTY-TWO
SIYAL

S iyal opened the door and there it was – the hallowed St Leonards observation suite. So many times he'd been on the other side of the video feed, helping his clients, while two senior cops sat in this room and watched, occasionally feeding information to the interviewers in the room, some little nugget that would undermine his clients' cases and destroy their worlds.

Now, though, Jason Craigen and Michael St John were in there, talking to another two cops.

The smaller of the two wore a sharp suit, his moustache and soul patch didn't look as cool as he thought in that shade of red. Pretty guy and he acted like he knew it. Siyal took him to be a DI.

His mate was taller, built like a bear. The kind of guy who needed to shave again at lunchtime.

Siyal didn't want to ask their names. In a room like that, you acted like you owned it. That you didn't need to know people's names. Or you already did.

Moustache grinned at him. 'Ah, the famous Shunty, isn't

it?' He had the slowest accent Siyal had ever heard, like he was half asleep.

'Infamous, more like...' Siyal smiled at him. He didn't know where to put his paperwork so just kept it in his hands. 'Bit early for Movember, isn't it?'

The man smoothed down the tache. 'Cheeky bugger.'

St John looked up at Siyal. 'Alright, Rakesh? Good work on identifying Davidson.'

Siyal shrugged. 'I'm only interested in his mate on that video.'

'Objective number one in there.' Moustache clapped Craigen and St John on the backs. 'Okay, lads, get in there and see what's what.'

They left the room.

Siyal blocked the entrance. 'I want in on this.'

That got a stern look from Bear Man. 'I like the cut of your jib.' He was from the Borders, or his accent was. 'This is a Professional Standards job. I'm taking it.'

'This case has significance for me. And after all, I unearthed the evidence.'

Moustache laughed. 'Okay, then. That's got me persuaded. The best interviews have people running vendettas against the suspect.'

'I'm...'

'The big man's leading, Sergeant.' So Moustache *was* a DI. 'Who do you want? St John or Craigen?'

Bear Man looked down his nose at Siyal. 'What do you recommend?'

Not really a choice. That saying – keep your friends close and your enemies closer.

Siyal stood up tall. 'I'd take Craigen.'

'Why him?'

'Because I think Craigen is the man with Davidson.'

Bear Man's eyebrows shot up. 'You got any evidence?'

'Not really. But I'm pretty sure it is. The video evidence disappearing from the evidence store was the clincher – Davidson needed help on the inside. Stands to reason it's Craigen. I want to see how they interact.'

'Thanks.' Bear Man opened the door, walked over to the interview room and wrapped his giant paws around Craigen's shoulders. 'I'm leading in here, Constable. Mike, go make yourself scarce.'

'Fill your boots, mate.' St John made a cup of tea motion with his hands.

'I'm fine.'

'Up to my eyes in the stuff.' Craigen knocked and entered.

'Suit yourselves.' St John strolled off along the corridor.

Siyal shut the obs suite door and watched the screen. He hadn't been in that interview room for such a long time. And back then, he'd been a lawyer on the other side of the table.

Now, Mark Davidson was there, waiting in contemptuous silence for them to sit. He didn't have his own lawyer with him. 'This is absolutely ridiculous.' He glared at Craigen, then Bear Man. 'Not only did your boss interrupt an interview to spread scurrilous allegations against me, I've been driven up from County sodding Durham to bloody Edinburgh to—'

'You don't want any legal advice, right?' Craigen arched an eyebrow.

'I'm one of the foremost legal minds in Scotland. Of course I don't need any legal advice.'

'Cool.' Craigen leaned back. 'Sarge?'

Bear Man reached into his wallet and placed a piece of paper on the table. Face up. 'This is a CCTV still from outside the Debonair pub on the night of the fifteenth of August 2021. This is you, Mr Davidson. So please don't give us any more denials.'

Davidson inspected them with a sarcastic sigh. 'So I went to a bar. Who cares?'

'A woman was abducted outside and taken down to the basement where she was raped by two men.' Bear Man tapped the still. 'This is you entering the building prior to the assault.'

'Look.' Davidson smiled, his thin tongue running along his thin lips. 'This is unfortunate, isn't it? But it's a mere coincidence.'

'A coincidence?'

'I happened to be there at the time that poor woman was being sexually assaulted. But it is a coincidence. I'm sure you can both see that.'

'Sure.' Craigen kept his poker face up. If he was in league with Davidson, he was a great actor... But then he'd have to be to do what he'd done.

'My colleagues have been through everyone who was in the bar at that time.' Bear Man tapped the page. 'You and your companion here are the only ones unaccounted for.'

'In the whole bar?'

'Quiet night. Aside from the victim, we've identified seven people in there. Two bar staff. A chef. Two other punters. And you and your friend here. As it stands, we don't have an account of your movements. Obviously, we'll check that against the other patrons of the bar.'

'And you think that'll stand up in court?'

Bear Man shrugged. 'I do, aye.'

'Two drunks and two knuckle-draggers who can only get bar jobs?' Davidson grinned. 'Do me a favour.'

'You don't appear on any CCTV after you arrived until this.' Bear Man put another page down on the table, showing Davidson leaving. 'Again, your friend was unable to be identified. Had a hat on. Collar pulled up. Walked alongside you. Several hours later, *after* the assault had occurred.'

'This...' Davidson swallowed hard. 'This... I... This is preposterous.'

'One word for it.' Bear Man grinned but it turned to a snarl. Even through a TV screen, it terrified Siyal. 'Rape would be another. The fact you then made sure the victim was reported for illegal entry to the country and fast-tracked for deportation... I'm not sure there's a word for *that*.'

'I've no idea what's going on here. This is... You think *I* raped her?'

'We pretty much know you did, Mark. Now. I'm giving you a choice. Unfortunately for you, it comes with a time limit. The victim is on her way up from Dungavel House just now. Our colleagues are going to interview her about this. She'll identify you. That leaves you an opportunity. When it comes to charging you, you're screwed. But when it comes to sentencing, if you identify your co-conspirator, then the judge will look favourably on that.'

Siyal kept his focus on Craigen, watching for any tells. Any sign he was stressed. Any sign he was communicating with Davidson, forcing him to keep quiet.

A bead of sweat ran down his forehead.

Bear Man was getting the result.

Siyal let out a deep breath.

Davidson's lips were twitching. 'You honestly think I'm involved in this?'

'We know you are, Mark. Your only saving grace will be giving up your conspirator. After all, someone's messed about with our CCTV evidence.'

'That wasn't me! How could I have done that?'

'Didn't say it was.'

Davidson got to his feet. 'I know the way out, gents. I'll see you—'

'Stop.' Craigen stood, towering over him. 'We're not finished here.'

'Oh, we are.' Davidson made to move past him.

Craigen blocked him. 'No.' He pointed at the seat. 'Sit. I'll let you know when we're done.'

Davidson laughed, then took his seat again. 'Very well.'

Craigen sat down again.

Bear Man took a long look at Davidson. 'As you were being driven up, I paid the Debonair a visit. The two bar staff still work there. The chef's moved on. Managed to have a nice wee chat with your client. Mr Darroch was most accommodating. Showed me the CCTV camera in the kitchen.'

News to Siyal. He tried to hide his frown from Moustache but it came out anyway.

'He's a bit of a naughty boy for holding that back from the investigation. But he showed me what happened that night. The bar might've been busy, but the chef wasn't. They started doing Travis Food, or whatever it's called, during lockdown and still do it. He was flat out all night. So that clears the chef. Leaving the bar area. Where you were. Good thing there's a sneaky camera behind the optics to keep an eye on the staff. Good news is it covers the staff plus the two lads propping up the bar. They were all in there at the time of the incident. All there after too.'

Davidson adjusted his cufflinks. Trying to appear unruffled, but there was a bead of sweat sliding down his forehead. In a cold room. Cool, at best.

Bear Man raised a hand. 'The good news is we managed to clear your client's name. Mr Darroch wasn't there that day.' He placed two more pages down. 'You'll have to extend our apologies to Mr Darroch, but when evidence goes missing, these things happen and innocent people like him suffer tarnishing to their reputation. Still, he could've come forward with that footage and saved us a lot of time and himself a lot of grief.' He left a long pause. 'Do you want the bad news?'

Davidson was staring at the sheets, fixated by them. 'Do I get a choice in the matter?'

'While we've cleared your client, we can't clear you. Or your mate.'

Davidson wiped the sweat away from his forehead.

'We've got you on video outside and now in.' Bear Man put another sheet down. 'Here you are, buying a round of drinks. One. That lasted you over five hours. Now, I can nurse a pint with the best of them, but that's going some.'

Davidson swallowed hard. 'What do you want from me?'

Bear Man narrowed his eyes. 'The way through this is a proffered statement. The PF is already on board, has already signed off on it and has agreed to it. You confess and name your co-conspirator. You participate in the trial as required. You serve five years and are disbarred. You keep shtum, then you take your chances with the justice system.'

Davidson tapped the desk. 'Five years. I'll take that.'

'Good.' Bear Man grinned. 'We need a lot from you now. So come on, Mark, tell us who it was.'

'I need serious protection. He'll kill me.'

'We can talk about that, but we need to know who it is.'

Davidson stared hard at Craigen. Something passed between them, some spark of something. Then he looked back at Bear Man. 'It's a cop. He... He was with me. He deleted the evidence from your servers. The video. The witness information. I...' He tapped the page showing them entering. 'This is him.'

Funny how the biggest talkers crumpled under pressure.

Bear man laughed. 'I know that, but we can't see his face. If you want five years, Mark, you need to give us his name.'

Davidson stared hard at Craigen, eyes narrowed. 'Michael St John.'

Bear Man's eyes bulged. 'What?'

'He told me we'd get away with this. He'd fix it, but... Those fucking cameras inside.'

Moustache was on his feet, racing over to the door.

Siyal followed him out into the corridor.

Craigen and Bear Man were in the interview room doorway.

'Stay with him!' Moustache jabbed a finger at the door. He stopped. 'Where is St John?'

Siyal pointed along the corridor. 'He went to the canteen.'

Moustache ran off, fumbling his phone onto the floor. He bent over and picked it up. 'Jim, is Mike St John still in the station?' He held the door for Siyal, phone to his ear. 'Okay, hold him there. Cheers.' He put his phone away and bombed it along the corridor. 'He's just leaving now.'

Siyal was struggling to keep up with his pace. 'He was... So he...'

'He knew it was coming and he scarpered.' Moustache charged through the door and hurtled along the corridor, then hammered the door release button and tore it open.

The security guard lay on the floor, his face a wash of red.

Siyal charged through after Moustache into the cold afternoon.

St John was over by his car, tugging at the handle.

Their feet slapped off the wet tarmac.

Moustache leapt through the air and crashed his shoulder into St John's side. St John tumbled over but landed on Moustache. He clawed at his face.

Siyal snapped out his baton and lashed at St John's thigh. He screamed and rolled over onto the tarmac.

Siyal braced the baton between St John's bicep and forearm, leveraging it upwards.

St John squealed. 'Stop!'

'Mike St John, I'm arresting you for the rape of Afri Shamsuddin.'

A hand gripped him. 'We'll take him.' Bear Man, flanked by two uniforms.

Siyal let him go and stood up. Dropped the baton at his feet. Sucked in a deep breath. His pulse thudded in his ears. Everything was super-sharp.

Moustache was on his feet. 'Cheers, Shunty.'

'Well done. Pair of you.' Bear Man smiled at them, then led St John back towards the station.

Siyal tried to get his breathing back under control but was struggling.

Moustache was fine. Cool. Calm. Not like someone who'd just leapt through the air and rolled across a car park. And ripped his suit's knees. 'Pretty impressed by your work there, Shunty.'

'Thanks.' Siyal leaned back against the car. He was sweating in the freezing air. 'Didn't think it was St John who...'

'I did. He's a sleazy bastard.' Craigen was shaking his head. Siyal hadn't seen him come outside. 'Sleazy, sleazy bastard.'

Siyal held his gaze and something passed between them. Some understanding. Some shared disgust of St John and of Mark Davidson. 'To be honest, Jason, the reason I wanted you in there was I suspected you.'

'I don't hold it against you.'

'Really?'

'Rather everyone was suspected than nobody was.'

A car pulled up and a tall man got out the driver's side. Owen Greening, his thinning hair all slicked back. He waved at Siyal. 'Long time no see, Rakesh. Can't seem to escape you.'

'No, sir.' Old habits died hard. 'Why are you—'

Afri got out of the back seat and looked around like she was in the most wondrous place in the world rather than in a police station car park in the cold. Her eyes bulged when she saw Siyal coming towards her. 'Rakesh.' She wrapped him in a big hug. 'Thank you.'

'What for?'

She broke away from the hug. 'For catching the man who did this to me.'

'Men.' Craigen joined them. 'We've caught both of them.'

Afri's hand went to her mouth.

Greening joined them. 'I've taken up her case. She's been released into my custody, on condition of employment.'

'Employment?'

'I've given her a job, Rakesh. Most migrants aren't as fortunate, but she'll get trained in British law and help others less fortunate.'

She smiled at Siyal. 'Thank you, Rakesh. For all you've done for me.'

'I just wish it'd been a year ago. And you hadn't had to go through all of that.'

'I'm glad to be away from that place now. Thank you.'

CHAPTER SEVENTY-THREE
MARSHALL

Sitting here, Marshall could see his sister working away around the corner. He didn't want to bother her. Didn't want to bother anyone.

Least of all Elliot. Standing out in the corridor, glued to her phone, face like she'd murdered twenty people and been caught red-handed. Kept looking over at Marshall, scowling, then looking away.

The squelch of feet came from the ward. Liana stood there, hands on hips, scanning the faces in the waiting area.

Elliot looked her up and down, then buggered off.

Liana came over and sat next to Marshall. 'I just spoke with the nurse. Jen. She seems to know you?'

'She's my twin sister.'

'Oh, right.' She put a hand to his arm. 'Bruce didn't make it. You pushed him out of the way but the blades caught his throat. Nicked the carotid and ripped open the jugular vein... he'd bled out before the paramedics got to him. Didn't stand a chance.'

Marshall nodded slowly. He'd expected as much. Poor guy deserved more. Deserved better.

'Are you okay, Rob?'

'I'm fine. Not injured.'

'But?'

'It's a lot to process. Could've been either of us. Bruce was... Jesus.'

'I don't understand why he gave himself up like that. On the promise of a deal.'

'He was searching for resolution to what happened to his brother. Subconsciously, he knew he'd never find it. Also, he was probably tired of the hunt. He knew it was over and he couldn't face a life on the run.'

'I guess. Still, Elliot managed to persuade him.'

'Right. Sometimes you don't need a scalpel, you need a blunderbuss.'

More squelching and Pringle came out of the ward. 'Gather round, ye merry gentlemen. And ladies. Just one gentleman, actually, and you're not so gentle, are you?'

Liana gave him a glare that could've sliced steel. 'How is she?'

'Good news is Grace is alive. She'll be in here for a while, will suffer a lot of trauma, but she's alive.'

'And the bad?'

'I've got to make some calls to add the death of DI Bruce to the prosecution of Adrian Robinson.' Pringle stormed off, clutching his phone.

Liana followed him. 'Jim!'

Marshall could get up and follow.

Should do.

But he had no energy left.

'You okay there?' Elliot was standing over him.

Marshall looked up at her then away. 'I will be.'

'Liar.'

'I mean eventually.'

'Okay, Marshall.' She handed him a plastic bag. 'Here.'

He took it from her. The bag rattled. 'What's this?'

'Doesn't take a genius to figure it out...'

Marshall reached in and took out a bottle of Bordeaux. The same one Dean Taylor had given him a few months ago. There was another in there. 'Andrea, this is a very expensive bottle. I can't just accept that.'

'Aye, you can. I've been a right bitch to you and Shunty over the last few days.' She let out a deep breath. 'Truth is, I've not handled coming back to work after my injury so well. You're right – me calling Robinson up was risky. I'm lucky it paid off and I could persuade him to come in, but...' She swallowed something down. Might be pride. 'You and me have got a lot of shite to sort out between us. But we'll do that as adults. Sit down over a couple of coffees from Dean Taylor's place. Chat it all through. Agree where you start and I begin.' She scowled. 'Or something like that.' She laughed. 'You know what I mean.'

'I do.' Marshall smiled at her. 'There's a lot to go over, but we'll get there.'

'It's good to work a case with you where I *don't* get my guts sliced open.'

'Thank you for the wine. It's very kind.'

'I was going to bake you a cake, seeing as how I missed your birthday.' She patted his arm. 'I'm going back to base to sort out the children. See you around.'

'Thanks, Andrea. I mean it.'

'Thank you.' She walked off, tapping away at her phone.

Marshall sat there, shaking his head. She had been a nightmare, but there was a nugget of a good person underneath that. She'd had to endure a lot as a cop and developed a steel shell to cope.

The enormity of it all hit him, but there were no tears. He felt—

He felt nothing. Too many competing emotions – relief, sadness, regret... Even hope?

Grief came out in strange ways and he'd do some thinking about it all on another day. He'd figure out how he felt and why, shove it in a box with a label on the front, then store it at the back of a cupboard. A mental cupboard. In his mental garage.

No wonder most psychologists were head cases themselves.

But he was a cop and cops were even worse.

Those unresolved deaths had lingered for over ten years. Ten tumultuous years. Now the families had closure to them, but so did he. That time with Goldberg and Liana held no part of him now. He could close off the chapter Martin Keane had opened. That Adrian Robinson had been the narrator of.

'Hey, hey.' Someone grabbed him in a hug. Kirsten's sweet perfume enveloped him. She clung on for dear life, hugging him tightly. 'Hey.' She broke off and dabbed at her cheeks. 'Sorry, just... This whole thing... It's... Bruce... I was scared. It could just as easily have been you.' She stared at him, eyes twinkling. 'Listen, I'm sorry I was a bit weird last night. I... I was jealous of Professor Pert.'

'What, Liana?'

'Right. Saw her and Pringle arguing about something in the corridor on the way in. I'm nothing compared to her. I don't have your history. Rob, I'm jealous of her. And I've never been jealous of anyone...'

'Hey, that's... Kirsten. I'm not interested in her.'

'But she offers you that white picket fence life. I could never do that.'

'Why not?'

'So you do want it?'

'No.' He snorted. 'But I don't know what I want. I just want to take things with you one step at a time. See what we are.'

'Okay.' She was nodding but it was like it was to herself as much as to him. 'Listen, I've made that decision.' She locked eyes with him. 'I'm going to take that job in Edinburgh.'

'Oh.'

'It's not just you who needs to process stuff, Rob. I need to sort out how I feel about this too. About you and I.'

Marshall thought he'd have more time to influence her decision. But it was hers. He gave her a smile. 'Congratulations on the promotion.'

'Not quite a promotion.' She smacked him on the arm. 'And if you're ever up in the big city, let's meet up. Aye?'

'I'll be there, Kirsten.'

CHAPTER SEVENTY-FOUR
ADRIAN ROBINSON

Three weeks later

Adrian Robinson slipped his towel off and hung it up, then stepped into the cubicle and hit the silver button. Like at the swimming baths, but this water was glorious – fizzing down onto his scalp. Hot. So hot. He grabbed the soap bar and started building up a lather on his skin.

One Mississippi.

Two Mississippi.

Three Mississippi.

He hated this place.

He was used to wide open vistas or the solitude of a forest that went on for miles. Not a prison shower. Where he had to go in alone and sneak a minute of blissful hot water.

Nine Mississippi.

Ten Mississippi.

Remanded in HMP Frankland. He needed to decide on his plea. He'd killed them all without a thought. He should just say he was guilty and take what was coming. That was the right thing to do.

Eighteen Mississippi.

Nineteen Mississippi.

Then again, at a trial he'd get to see the families of his victims. He'd get to see Grace again.

He'd be able to torment them all.

Twenty-nine Mississippi.

Thirty Mississippi.

Halfway. He hit the button again and washed the lather off his body, then picked up the bar of soap again.

Yes. Stand in court and stare at Grace. Make her experience it all over again.

Forty Mississippi.

Forty-one Mississippi.

Almost done. He'd remember the cascading water and cling to it when he went to sleep at night.

Thump.

What was that?

Was someone there?

Robinson stepped out of the water and grabbed his towel, giving himself a loose dry before wrapping it around his waist.

Heart pounding, he peered out into the corridor.

Nobody.

Just his imagination stealing a few seconds of hot water from—

Something bit into his calf and he went down, sprawling onto the matting.

A sock swung through the air and landed on his arm, pounding like a fist.

Another and another.

He balled himself up as the violence rained down on him. Hard and sharp.

Then it stopped. Just the sound of his shower still going.

Three men stood over him, faces hidden by rags. They each held a pair of socks containing soap bars. They walked off without a word.

He lay there. His whole body ached. Blood seeped out of his wounds. He couldn't get up. Couldn't crawl much less stand.

'There you are.' Martin Keane walked towards him, hands in pockets. 'Sorry I haven't come to see you before now.'

'You little shit!' Robinson gripped the front edge of the shower cubicle and tried to use that as support. He collapsed back down.

Keane crouched next to him. 'That looks like it hurts.'

'I know you blabbed. You got me arrested.'

'I did. And I told all the inmates. You're not just a murderer. You're a serial rapist.'

'What's your goal here? To get me to kill myself?'

'That, or just torment you.'

'Never. I'll never top myself. I'll survive this and get stronger every day. You should enjoy this moment while you can.'

Keane grabbed his hair and hauled him up to standing. Took everything Robinson had not to go down again.

'Adrian, you know how I never enjoyed the long game.' Keane reached into his pocket and pulled out a sharpened toothbrush. 'My speciality was overkill. Still is.'

AFTERWORD

A huge thank you to you for reading this book.

This is my tenth year of being able to write full-time for a living and it's thanks to people like you who buy and read my books, then spread the word to friends and family. I am and will be eternally grateful to you all.

Like most people I guess, I had a particularly challenging 2020-22, suffering from two bouts of heart arrhythmia, which I'm on a waiting list to get a permanent preventative fix done in the next couple of months. Writing in that period (and *about* that period) was a difficult time, although a productive one where I produced a lot of books.

And one thing that helped me through lockdown was walking in the woods at Elibank every day – one of those places where you start wondering not so much where you could dump a body there, but how many. I highly recommend a visit, it's on the south bank of the Tweed between Caddon-foot and Walkerburn and has two distinct paths, one which has the ruins of Elibank castle and the other which is where the bodies lay.

The big lesson I learned from that time was I had spent a lot of time topping up existing series, when what I should've done was focus on something brand new. Well, I did that last year and I've been extremely pleased, not to mention surprised, at how well THE TURNING OF OUR BONES did at launch and continues to do. I'd set my self an aggressive target of sales for the first year – it was exceeded after seven weeks. And the sales haven't slowed. This is territory I haven't had to navigate for a number of years.

And here we are on the eve of the publication of Marshall's second outing, WHERE THE BODIES LIE, which followed a lot of similar pathways to the first one, but had its own meandering route too. I've finished the first cut of the third book, A LONELY PLACE OF DYING, which will be a much more domesticated affair – I think there's only one chapter that has anything but a TDx postcode, so it's all set in the Borders, and has not a single serial killer in it. I'm about to start work on the fourth book, A SHADOW ON THE DOOR, which will culminate the first year of Marshall's story.

And I plan to do a second year of another four books. I've got an initial set of story ideas to flesh out in my "series bible", which lets me track the plots and the character arcs of the main lot. If I've got time this year, I'll probably do another spin-off book in this world, but watch this space for news of that!

As ever, huge thanks to James Mackay for the editing work at outline stage and after the first draft, which fixed the story and really nailed the character motivations. As usual, a massive thank you to John Rickards for his copy editing and to Mare Bate for proofing it. If you notice any errors, which are all my fault, then please email ed@edjames.co.uk and I'll fix them.

And if you could leave a review on Amazon, that'd be a huge help, cheers.

Finally, if you want to keep up to date with my news, sign up my mailing list (link at the end of the book) and you'll get access to some free ebooks, including a prequel starring Shunty.

Cheers,

Ed James

Scottish Borders, April 2023

ABOUT THE AUTHOR

Ed James writes crime-fiction novels, primarily the DI Simon Fenchurch series, set on the gritty streets of East London featuring a detective with little to lose. His Scott Cullen series features a young Edinburgh detective constable investigating crimes from the bottom rung of the career ladder he's desperate to climb.

Formerly an IT project manager, Ed began writing on planes, trains and automobiles to fill his weekly commute to London. He now writes full-time and lives in the Scottish Borders, with his girlfriend and a menagerie of rescued animals.

If you would like to be kept up to date with new releases from Ed James, please join the Ed James Readers Club.

Connect with Ed online:

Amazon Author page

Website

facebook.com/edjamesauthor

twitter.com/edjamesauthor

instagram.com/edjamesauthor

MARSHALL WILL RETURN IN

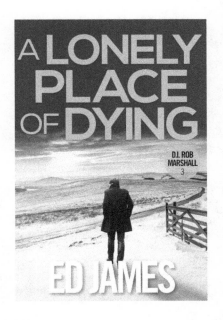

A Lonely Place of Dying
31st July 2023